TRIXY

Elizabeth Stuart Phelps with her dogs, ca. 1907.

TRIXY

—m—

Elizabeth Stuart Phelps

Edited and with an introduction by
Emily E. VanDette

CURBSTONE BOOKS / NORTHWESTERN UNIVERSITY PRESS

EVANSTON, ILLINOIS

Curbstone Books
Northwestern University Press
www.nupress.northwestern.edu

Originally published in 1904 by Houghton, Mifflin, and Company, Boston and
New York.

Frontispiece: "Mrs. Ward on Her Porch," photograph by Notman, in *Suburban
Life* (February 1907), 62. The Miriam and Ira D. Wallach Division of Art,
Prints, and Photographs: Print Collection, The New York Public Library.
"Mrs. Elizabeth Stuart Phelps Ward on the porch of her suburban home . . ."
New York Public Library Digital Collections. Accessed May 9, 2019. http://
digitalcollections.nypl.org/items/42d16c10-e6dd-0132-5b81-58d385a7b928.

Printed in the United States of America

10 9 8 7 6 5 4 3 2 1

Library of Congress Cataloging-in-Publication Data

Names: Phelps, Elizabeth Stuart, 1844–1911, author. | VanDette, Emily E.,
    editor, writer of introduction.
Title: Trixy / Elizabeth Stuart Phelps ; edited and with an introduction by
    Emily E. VanDette.
Description: Evanston, Illinois : Curbstone Books / Northwestern University
    Press, 2019. | "Originally published in 1904 by Houghton, Mifflin, and
    Company, Boston and New York." | Includes bibliographical references.
Identifiers: LCCN 2019018575 | ISBN 9780810140431 (trade paper : alk.
    paper) | ISBN 9780810140448 (e-book)
Subjects: LCSH: Dogs—Fiction. | Animal experimentation—Fiction. |
    Human-animal relationships—Fiction.
Classification: LCC PS3142 .T75 2019 | DDC 813.4—dc23
LC record available at https://lccn.loc.gov/2019018575

Contents

—⟋m⟍—

Acknowledgments   vii

Introduction   ix

Trixy   1

Appendix A: "Eulogy of the Dog" Speech (1855),
by George Graham Vest   173

Appendix B: "A Dog's Tale" (1903),
by Mark Twain   175

Appendix C: Elizabeth Stuart Phelps's Address to
the Massachusetts Legislature (1902)   187

Appendix D: "Tammyshanty" (1908),
by Elizabeth Stuart Phelps   211

Notes   233

ACKNOWLEDGMENTS

—ᴍ—

First and foremost, I would like to thank the team at Northwestern University Press for helping me bring *Trixy* back into the world, especially Jill L. Petty, for her generous support and assistance. Also, I appreciate the valuable suggestions made by the anonymous reviewer who read an earlier draft of this book. For allowing me to quote from their collections in my introduction, I am grateful to the Bancroft Library at the University of California, Berkeley, Harvard University's Houghton Library, the Massachusetts Society for the Prevention of Cruelty to Animals (MSPCA)–Angell Archives, and the New York Public Library, and I thank all of the librarians and archivists at those libraries, as well as my colleagues at Reed Library, who assisted with my research. I would like to offer special thanks to Jan Holmquist, director of the archives of the MSPCA–Angell Archives in Boston, who generously helped me on several occasions. I wish to thank the Elmira College Center for Mark Twain Studies for my Quarry Farm Fellowship, which gave me invaluable research and writing time and reinforced my interest in including Mark Twain's antivivisection short story "A Dog's Tale" in Appendix B of this book.

I appreciate my colleagues in the Society for the Study of American Women Writers (SSAWW), especially Deborah Gussman, who encouraged my work on this project. I am grateful to the friends, colleagues, and mentors who have supported me in various ways throughout my development of *Trixy*, including Ray Belliotti,

Dawn Eckenrode, Susan K. Harris, Christina Jarvis, David Kinkela, Christine Davis Mantai, Jessica Hillman McCord, Aimee Nezhukumatathil, Sandra Stelts, Birger Vanwesenbeeck, and Ici Vanwesenbeeck. I am thankful to my Fredonia students who read Phelps's animal writing with me, especially Stephine Hunt, who helped me with an early round of formatting and editing *Trixy*. I appreciate the support of my siblings, especially my brother Brendan Murphy and sister-in-law Zoya Tsvetkova (and bunnies and Bernie), my wonderfully fun and gracious hosts during my research trips to Boston. I am also thankful to Dennis and Judy VanDette for providing loving care for my children and pets while I was traveling.

My family is my constant reminder that the human-animal connections I study in literature exist in complex and beautiful ways in real life. For all of the ways they helped me complete this book without even knowing it, I am thankful to my supportive husband Scott, our compassionate children Joseph and Elspeth, and the wonderful nonhuman animals we are lucky to share our home with, Charlie, Daisy, and Mo. Finally, my work on this book has been inspired by the many activists today who continue to tell the stories of animal lives and to believe in the power of compassion.

I offer my heartfelt thanks to all of the above-mentioned for their help and their faith in my ability to do this work. Any errors remaining are my own.

INTRODUCTION

—ᴍ—

No one who knows what goes on in our medical schools,
our physiological laboratories, our schools of technology
and some of our public schools can pass certain buildings in
our large towns without a shudder. No prison, no hospital,
no criminal court can cause the counterpart of that sick
horror.

—ELIZABETH STUART PHELPS, "SPIRITS IN PRISON" (1900)

By the final decade of a prolific and socially engaged literary career
that would eventually include fifty-seven volumes of fiction, poetry, and essays and many more uncollected works, Elizabeth Stuart
Phelps (1844–1911) had begun to channel her reform energy into
a single issue: scientific experimentation on living animals. While
Phelps's passionate fight against vivisection emerged late in her career, she pursued it with the characteristic sense of compassion and
justice, literary innovation, and tireless zeal that marked her entire
output as an author. From the earliest milestone in her literary
career, in 1868, Phelps set the tone for her literary social activism
with her first published story, a fictionalized account of the tragic
Pemberton Mills fire in Lawrence, Massachusetts, "The Tenth of
January," which was critically acclaimed as one of the first realistic
portraits of working-class industrial strife in America. The following year she published the novel that would make her famous, *The*

Gates Ajar, in which she represented heaven as a site of reunion among loved ones, offering a timely source of comfort for American readers mourning loved ones lost in the Civil War. She continued to enjoy a prolific and celebrated career for the remainder of her life, with her writing appearing in every major American periodical. In terms of activism, Phelps is best known for challenging traditional gender roles, particularly her advocacy for women's professional roles and clothing reform (famously urging women to "burn the corset!"), and her writing consistently reveals her concern over women's social, political, legal, and economic status. While Phelps's contributions to labor reform and women's social roles have been restored in recent decades, biographers and critics have, until very recently, glossed over the most passionate cause of the author's late career and life—her campaign against vivisection.

From the 1890s until her death in 1911, Phelps took up the fight against laboratory experimentation on living, nonhuman animals as her chief cause, contributing pamphlets, speeches, fiction, and correspondence to protest the practice, which had been steadily growing in American medical schools. In shifting her reform energy to vivisection at the turn of the century, Phelps didn't abandon her advocacy for exploited and oppressed humans; rather, she regarded vivisection as a crisis for animals as well as for humanity, especially given the desensitizing effect the practice had on elite-class men of medicine and science. Among several works of anti-vivisection fiction, the 1904 novel *Trixy* most vividly reveals the author's intersecting concerns for the welfare of human and nonhuman animals, as well as her vision of compassionate social progress, which demanded legislative reform as well as individual morality and benevolence. Through her depiction of human and animal characters in *Trixy*, Phelps engages the nuances of animal welfare campaigns during her own time, while presciently envisioning affiliation across the species divide as the basis for human compassion for animals. In doing so, she bridged some of the more conservative ideas about morality, family, gender roles, and social class hierarchies that were at the center of many nineteenth-century social reform campaigns, with a more modern emphasis on the individual identities of animals and the kinship between humans and animals.

The Emergence of the Antivivisection Reform Movement

The movement to abolish or restrict vivisection emerged in response to the rise in the number of experiments on animals in Europe and the United States after 1870. With the professionalizing of medicine in the 1860s, medical colleges began to introduce physiology labs that used live animals for experiments and classroom demonstrations. In the following decades, vivisection became a standard part of medical training in the United States, required for medical students. "By the 1880s," historian Diane Beers notes, "one physician pronounced vivisection 'in vogue in our medical schools,' and by the turn of the century, Yale, Princeton, Amherst, Cornell, and Stanford wooed prospective students with lavish descriptions of their modern physiology laboratories."[1] Opposition to the practice arose as the public became aware of the painful surgeries researchers performed on animals, often without anesthesia. Animal welfarists especially objected to experiments that were clearly superfluous, such as those performed for classroom and public demonstrations even after a scientific discovery was well established, as well as repeated experiments upon the same laboratory animals.

The rise of vivisection coincided with the rise of the animal welfare movement, which officially landed in the United States in 1866, with Henry Bergh's founding of the American Society for the Prevention of Cruelty to Animals (ASPCA). The animal welfare and "humane education" movements sought to protect animals, particularly domestic animals, from inhumane treatment by humans and to inculcate in people a moral obligation to treat animals kindly. When Boston lawyer George T. Angell founded the Massachusetts Society for the Prevention of Cruelty to Animals (MSPCA) in 1868, he also launched the first monthly magazine devoted to animal welfare, *Our Dumb Animals*, whose motto, "We

Speak for Those Who Cannot Speak for Themselves," was emblazoned on the masthead of every issue. According to historian Katherine C. Grier, "By the 1860s, the domestic ethic of kindness to animals was widely accepted by American families who embraced Victorian culture's ideals of gentility, liberal evangelical theology, and domesticity, and their attendant beliefs in social progress and moral uplift."[2] The "domestic ethic of kindness" campaign extended a sense of benevolent protection to include human and nonhuman members of the domestic sphere. To that end, the American Humane Society, formed in 1877, included animals and children in the purview of its anticruelty mission, significantly bringing together the most vulnerable human and nonhuman victims of human violence and exploitation.[3]

Because of the momentum already achieved in humane education and animal welfare, as vivisection became common in medical schools and physiology labs, an organized effort quickly emerged to protest it. A notable paradox brought the vivisection controversy to the attention of American animal advocacy leaders. With a sudden demand for animals to fill their new laboratories, researchers turned to the newly formed animal shelters for dogs, thus putting their scientific practice on the radar of animal welfarists, who immediately organized to protest the use of live animals in scientific research. Philadelphian Caroline Earle White, who founded the Women's Branch of the Pennsylvania Society for the Prevention of Cruelty to Animals (PSPCA) as well as the nation's first animal shelter, received such a request from the physician famous for promoting the "rest cure," S. Weir Mitchell. She vehemently objected, not only to the proposition of handing shelter dogs over to laboratories, but to the practice of vivisection in general. White later founded the American Anti-Vivisection Society (AAVS), a largely female-dominated organization that sought to eradicate, or at least restrict, the use of animals in laboratory experiments.[4]

Given the large number of women activists in the animal welfare movement in general, it is not surprising that women outnumbered men in the campaign against vivisection. Historians have noted the predominance of women antivivisectionists on both sides of the Atlantic, as well as significant philosophical connections between the antivivisection and women's rights movements, where objectification, bodily control, and domination without consent were targets of resistance and reform.[5] The most prominent women's reform organization in the nineteenth-century United States, the Woman's Christian Temperance Union (WCTU), added animal welfare to its ever-expanding purview of reform initiatives through its collaboration with humane education leader George T. Angell, and in the formation of a Department of Mercy. The WCTU played a significant role in expanding the transatlantic network and shaping the culture of the antivivisection movement, especially with the appointment of antivivisection activist Mary Frances Lovell as the first national superintendent of the Department of Mercy. Lovell, who helped White create the AAVS and edit its monthly magazine the *Journal of Zoophily*, merged the conservative culture of the WCTU, with its emphasis on Christian benevolence steered by the moral authority ascribed to genteel women, with the more radically progressive politics of antivivisectionists who sought to abolish vivisection on the basis of animal rights and the kinship between animals and humans. When couched in the rhetorical framework of what Janet M. Davis calls the "gospel of kindness" movement, the antivivisection campaign took on an anthropocentric stance, emphasizing the negative effects of vivisection on people's morality, and it embraced a philosophy of individual moral action as the basis for a kind culture. The case for the negative effects of vivisection on humanity, though, was often dismissed as sentimental and rapidly lost ground as the science community touted the advances to medical science that resulted from vivisection. By the time Phelps wrote *Trixy*, tensions within the animal welfare movement mounted over the vivisection debate, especially as the AAVS targeted vivisecting scientists and doctors as perpetrators of animal cruelty, whereas "mainstream groups became progressively conciliatory toward the medical community to avoid alienation."[6] The WCTU, in particular, counted on the support of the medical science community for the educational mission of its Department of Scientific Temperance Instruction.

In addition to the general political clashes within the animal welfare movement, the women of the movement faced conflicting criticism for being at once too conservative and too subversive. On one hand, they perpetuated old-fashioned notions of an evangelical benevolence rooted in individual education and action and led by woman in her role as moral guardian; on the other hand, they stepped outside of their proper sphere by advocating social change in the public realm. Elizabeth Stuart Phelps, who stood at the intersection of these debates around social reform, animal welfare, and women's roles, reinforced both the traditional idea of women's moral authority and the responsibility of women to intervene in matters of public interest. Within the WCTU community, Phelps was recognized as an authority on the balancing act between conservative femininity and public activism; in her book about the organization's legacy, long-term WCTU president Frances Elizabeth Willard invokes Phelps in a chapter devoted to "disposing of moral problems." The chapter includes an entire letter in which Phelps pays homage to the WCTU women and asserts the value of women's philanthropic work: "The work of saving tempted men and women from this one form of ruin *can* be made the source of the deepest growth in womanly character, and the sweetest blessedness of womanly content."[7] While such statements on behalf of traditional femininity may be surprising from an author who otherwise advocated for more progressive social roles for women, Phelps frequently balanced her radicalism with rhetorical concessions to conservatism, and she sought to protect women reformers from the common criticism that they "unsexed" themselves by their association with the unseemly sites of their activism, whether the pub or the polls. She would later adopt this strategy in *Trixy*, representing the novel's morally superior heroine, Miriam, in exaggerated terms of Victorian womanhood (the narrator even states flatly that she was "not a new woman"), while leveling a radical attack on the science community and presenting a revolutionary vision of the identities and status of animals.

Despite misogynistic hostility toward their work, and despite divisions within the broader animal welfare movement, women activists persisted in their efforts. Transatlantic networks among women philanthropists were particularly vital to the momentum of antivivisection reform. Most notably, White's activism in the United States was shaped by a visit to England, where she met Frances Power Cobbe, the famous Irish reformer who formed the National Anti-Vivisection Society in Britain in 1875.[8] Cobbe turned to American sympathizers to bolster the effort to eradicate animal testing, especially after Parliament passed the Cruelty to Animals Act of 1876, a law that required researchers to use anesthesia and to limit experiments on animals to "necessary" research. The act represented a landmark in the vivisection debate, as it divided antivivisectionists between "regulationists" and "abolitionists," Cobbe belonging firmly to the latter camp. The 1876 act frustrated abolitionists like Cobbe, who considered it dangerous for facilitating, rather than eradicating, the practice of vivisection. As she explained to a new generation of antivivisection lobbyists in her pamphlet *The Fallacy of Restriction Applied to Vivisection*, such legislation actually legalized and sanctioned the use of nonconsenting animals for scientific research, and she held it "to be a grievous mistake to demand anything short of the total prohibition of Vivisection."[9] Even before the act passed, Catharine Smithies, founder of the British "Bands of Mercy" that George T. Angell later imported into the US humane education movement, initiated a transatlantic appeal on behalf of the abolitionist camp. In a letter to Angell, Smithies reported that the "subject of vivisection is troubling me very much as I fear thousands will believe those horrid Doctors that they are doing it all for the benefit of mankind which is denied by authorities. I am superior to those cruel fellows." Criticizing both the doctors as well as the men of the RSPCA, Smithies implicitly challenged the American humane education leader to rise above his British male counterparts, appealing to a shared sense of cultural values defined by gender, class, and Christianity: "There is a Society for the abolition of the disgraceful practice but Doctors can make their patients believe anything. Don't you think it a disgrace to the Gentlemen's Committee that they do not vote for the abolition but the restriction, which would really be legalizing it. I am happy to say The Baroness is decided for the abolition. I cannot think how any Christian can be silent on such an abomination."[10]

Frances Power Cobbe continued her active campaign against animal experimentation, especially working to expose the practice in American laboratories and recruiting animal welfare leaders like White to lead antivivisection reform in the United States. In her pamphlet *Vivisection in America*, Cobbe described graphic scenes of animal testing in American laboratories, quoting extensively from methods and findings published in medical science journals. She especially targeted the trend of duplicating experiments to affirm or demonstrate established facts, exposing the superfluity of much animal testing done in American labs. After cataloging the painful manners in which dozens of dogs died as a result of his experiments, one of the medical science journal authors Cobbe quoted concludes, "I shall not record the rest of my experiments on circular suture of the intestine, because most of them *seem now rather absurd to me*, and none of them admit of classification." Cobbe appealed to the growing cohort of American animal advocates to intervene: "Men and Women of America! Suffer us who are laboring to stop vivisection in our own country, to plead with you for its suppression in your younger land, where as yet the new vice of scientific cruelty cannot be deeply rooted."[11]

On both sides of the Atlantic, the movement against vivisection emphasized animal sentience as a rebuttal to the assumption that animals were less sensitive than humans. The question of animals' capacity to feel pain and trauma appeared to have been settled by the end of the nineteenth century, but it resurfaced as vivisection became widely accepted. Before the rise of animal welfare consciousness, seventeenth-century philosopher René Descartes and his followers infamously posited a mechanistic theory of animal bodies as machines incapable of feeling. During his gruesome demonstrations of experiments upon animals, Descartes "assur[ed] his squeamish students that the shrieks they heard were merely the sound of the springs that operate the machinery of the animals."[12] But the understanding of animals as mechanistic was mostly outdated by the middle of the nineteenth century, largely thanks to animal welfarists who popularized utilitarian philosopher Jeremy Bentham's ethical position: "The question is not Can they reason, nor Can they talk, but Can they suffer?"[13] The rise in vivisection in medical science in the last few decades of the nineteenth century reignited the debate, as scientists of the era often claimed hierarchies of sensitivity that downplayed the pain animals felt in laboratory experiments.

The premise of animal sentience was central to the debates over the use of the drug curare, which vivisectors used to paralyze and silence animals in order to facilitate experiments on their bodies. While not providing any anesthetic relief from pain, curare suppressed an animal's ability to express suffering through cries and physical struggle. Given the pro-vivisection claim for the diminished capacity of animals to feel pain, the use of curare to stifle animal pain presented a paradox or hypocrisy that outraged animal welfarists. In his first public statement denouncing vivisection, Mark Twain deplored the use of curare for facilitating painful experiments on "unconsenting animals" and suppressing animals' ability to respond to their pain and fear. He also criticized scientists who ignore the pain expressions of uncurarized animals, as in the example he quotes of a scientist who paradoxically notes an animal's shriek while denying its suffering: "Rabbits, we know, are not sensitive, but in this operation they invariably send forth a prolonged shriek."[14] Twain thus exposes the scientist's failure to recognize a "shriek" as a legitimate expression of pain, thereby suppressing the animal's voice and exacerbating the violence of the experiment.

Twain, Phelps, and other activists objected to the practice of vivisection not only for the wanton suffering it inflicted upon sentient beings, but also because of the elitist scope of its intentions and its deteriorating effect on the morality of doctors. The vivisection controversy shifted the attention of animal advocates from working-class animal abusers to a more elite, and therefore more accountable, sector of society: educated gentlemen of science and medicine. This represented a significant shift from the rhetorical scope of the broader humane education movement, in which elite-class activists sought to regulate the working class's treatment of animals.[15] "The perpetrators of vivisection were from those layers of society from whom moral guidance was traditionally sought: educated, often wealthy middle or upper class men."[16] The anti-vivisectionists' departure from the humane education movement in terms of class consciousness is reflected in popular dog fiction of the two campaigns: whereas the villain of Margaret Saunders's *Beautiful Joe*, winner of the American Humane Education Society prize in 1892, is an uncouth dairy farmer, the violent characters in Twain's "A Dog's Tale" and Phelps's *Trixy* are elite-class, educated scientists. The elevated status of scientists made their cruelty to animals especially reprehensible, as they were expected to embody a higher moral standard. Also, antivivisectionists were suspicious of the elitist scope of the new medical advances that were touted as the rationale for animal experimentation, as the wealthy and privileged members of society stood to profit the most from such medical progress.[17]

Exacerbating concerns that the medical science field was increasingly elitist and insensitive to suffering, pro-vivisection discourse often asserted a hierarchy of pain sensitivity, claiming, for instance, that "lower" animals were less sensitive to pain than higher-ranking animals. Arguing that pain capacity can be ranked even within a given species, University of Glasgow anatomy professor John Cleland stated, "I do not suppose that there can be any serious doubt that the pain occasioned by a given amount of lesion varies according to the fineness of the impressibility of the nervous system, and that civilisation and education, as well as certain alterations of nutrition in disease, do greatly enlarge the capacity for feeling pain."[18] Indeed, the pro-vivisection position relied heavily upon a nuanced understanding of sensitivity to make distinctions between species and within a species, thereby justifying the selection of some animals for protection and love and others as the subjects of painful and invasive experiments. "I do not doubt," Cleland maintained, "that a high bred horse or a high bred dog has a greater capacity for pain than the horse or dog of low degree."[19] Such bias was not limited to pro-vivisection philosophy. Municipal dog policies regarding how and which stray dogs were captured, and whether or not they were euthanized, were often shaped by what Janet Davis calls the "racial and class hierarchies of canine purebreds and mixed breeds." The fact that the same women who would eventually establish the AAVS, Caroline Earle White and Mary Frances Lovell, had earlier launched the nation's first animal shelters to provide humane alternatives to city pounds and violent dog-catching practices that discriminated against mongrels, is no coincidence, given the antivivisection activists' apparent class consciousness compared to the broader humane education movement.[20]

Antivivisectionists sought to debunk the class-based biases of pro-vivisection discourse, especially by insisting upon the sentience of animals and, most subversively, by turning the tables on the social hierarchy theory to condemn the insensitivity of supposedly elevated members of the human species. Twain made both of those points, for instance, when he highlighted a vivisector's refusal to acknowledge a rabbit's shriek as an expression of pain: he implicitly recognized the suffering of a rabbit, a low-ranking species, and exposed the callous insensitivity of the educated gentleman who could be thus oblivious to the suffering of another being.[21] Antivivisection arguments emphasized the desensitizing effect of modern medical training, which required students to perform painful experiments on sentient beings and to emotionally detach from their research subject's trauma and suffering. "No one who has studied the writings of physiologists," asserted antivivisectionist Mona Caird in her 1908 pamphlet *The Inquisition of Science*, "can possibly doubt that the practice is hardening and blunting to the sensibilities, or can regard without distress and foreboding, the mania that now prevails for vivisectional methods of all sorts."[22] On one hand, the objection to vivisection for its coarsening effect on doctors seems to be in line with the conservative culture of the humane education movement, as it reinforces both social class hierarchy (i.e., elite-class doctors should have a refined sense of morality) as well as the human benefits of animal protection. But on the other hand, in exposing the desensitization of doctors, as Phelps does in *Trixy* and other writings on the subject, radical antivivisectionists were not simply motivated by an anthropocentric impulse; rather, they sought to subvert the hierarchies that informed which species and classes were thought to be capable of, or devoid of, feeling. Moreover, in case the general public took any comfort in believing that vivisectors only experimented upon low-ranking species and unwanted mutts in their laboratories, antivivisectionists, including Phelps in her fiction, typically portrayed purebred dogs and cats, usually stolen pets, as the victims of vivisection.

The event that drew the most public attention to the vivisection debate, and which likely prompted both Twain and Phelps to contribute their important antivivisection dog stories within a year of its occurrence, was a sensationalized trial known as the Brown Dog Affair. The trial involved a book that lifted the veil from the practice of vivisection in a university laboratory: *The Shambles of Science*, written by two students at the University College of London, Louise Lind-af-Hageby and Liese Schartau. One of the most inhumane examples described in the book was the experience of a small brown dog who was subjected to repeated superfluous experiments, and the scientist who performed the experiments sued for damages to his reputation. Although the court ordered that the passage in question be removed from future printings, the graphic description of the dog's suffering received substantial public attention on both sides of the Atlantic.[23] A month after the sensational trial concluded, Twain published his sentimental short story "A Dog's Tale," in which a mother dog recounts her heartrending experience in the household of a cold-hearted vivisector, who callously kills her beloved puppy in a superfluous demonstration to prove to his pandering colleagues that a certain brain injury will cause blindness.[24] Within a year, Phelps, who was already deeply involved with the antivivisection movement, published her novel about Trixy, a beloved canine abducted from her human companion for the purpose of vivisection in a university laboratory.

Whether in exposés like *The Shambles of Science*, philosophical essays such as Cobbe's "The Consciousness of Dogs," or imaginative literary contributions like Twain's and Phelps's fiction, dogs were the most common animal subject in antivivisection discourse. At the time of the vivisection debate in the latter part of the nineteenth century, the status of dogs on both sides of the Atlantic was elevated as a result of the "Victorian cult of pets," which regarded domestic animals as cherished objects of love and familial attachment and invested them with traits that humans related to and admired, such as loyalty, love, and wisdom.[25] Ubiquitous images of the loving, protective, and intelligent family dog in literature and art both instilled and reflected the notion that dogs were an essential part of families. Recognizing the cultural power of sentimental dog representations, antivivisectionists adopted iconic images such as Edwin Henry Landseer's paintings of friendly and protective Newfoundland dogs, still familiar to dog lovers today, in their organizational branding and publications. Popular tributes to dogs, such as Scottish doctor-author John Brown's 1853 short story "Rab and His Friends," a heartbreaking story of a dog who witnesses his human companion's breast surgery in the days before anesthesia, and Senator George Graham Vest's frequently reprinted "Eulogy of a Dog" speech, took on new significance when reprinted or cited in the context of the antivivisection campaign.[26] Through visual and literary representations, the "cult of pets" put dogs on a special pedestal for their capacity to be a part of the venerated domestic circle, and that affiliation was a crucial basis for antivivisection activists to evoke people's sympathy with dogs as the victims of invasive scientific experiments.

Keenly aware of the cultural power of the sentimentalized domestic sphere, Elizabeth Stuart Phelps capitalized on the dog's special familial status in her antivivisection fiction. In *Trixy*, Phelps addressed social concerns that she recognized as intricately connected—the exploitation of nonhuman animals, the declining role of compassion in modern medicine, and class-based social inequities among humans. With a lovable title dog character and relatable dog-human dynamics, *Trixy* rejects the notion that animals are expendable, and it promotes interspecies compassion and mutuality. Even more radically for the time, *Trixy* exposes the desensitizing effect of vivisection on doctors. The growing acceptance of vivisection signaled, for Phelps, not the "progress" promised by the scientific community but rather a decline in civilization, and she turned to fiction as her usual outlet for bringing that possibility to light.

Elizabeth Stuart Phelps and the Antivivisection Movement

Like many antivivisection activists, Phelps was committed to a range of reform efforts. But her special devotion to the cause of ending or restricting animal testing likely stems from the same reason the British Union for the Abolition of Vivisection prioritized this issue over other social reform goals: they recognized vivisection as the site in which the "'forces of egoism' were gaining grounds against the 'forces of humane progress,'" and they believed that "a victory against vivisection would mean a general advance for all humane causes."[27] The intersections of Phelps's concerns about women's roles in society, the patriarchal and often misogynistic medical profession, and the practice of vivisection aptly reflect the feminist tradition of the antivivisection movement. Phelps's commitment to reforming women's roles within and beyond the domestic realm is by now an established facet of her legacy, most famously captured in her progressive novels *The Story of Avis* (1877), a novel centered on the trials of a woman artist, and

Doctor Zay (1882), which explores the challenges a woman doctor faces in a male-dominated profession.[28] In envisioning a place for women doctors, she also advocated for a compassionate, patient-centered approach to medicine, feminist ideals reflected in much of her fiction, as well as, interestingly, her fascinating correspondence with "rest-cure" physician (and proponent of vivisection) S. Weir Mitchell.[29] Given the rising institutional presence of physiology labs in medical colleges, and given Phelps's compassion and love for animals, it makes perfect sense that Phelps's interest in reforming women's roles and promoting compassionate medicine would eventually lead to activism against vivisection.

In her lifetime, Phelps witnessed and participated in a phenomenally successful model of social reform, popularized by her mentor Harriet Beecher Stowe, which centered on Christian benevolence and women's moral authority within the domestic sphere as the basis for social change. But she also witnessed and participated in progressive reforms surrounding women's roles, social class structure, labor systems, and civil rights. In addition to those broader societal shifts, Phelps witnessed the changing status of animals, as the cries echoing from physiology laboratories and the apparent complacency of people toward animal suffering in the name of scientific progress were rapidly normalized in her society.[30] In her antivivisection writing, Phelps negotiates the tensions between the humane education movement's focus on the human-centered consequences of vivisection and belief in individual benevolence as a path to social reform, and the more radical branch of activism that promoted the rights of animals through emphasizing kinship across the species divide and demanded institutional and legislative reform.[31] In *Trixy* in particular, Phelps depicts what she saw as the deterioration of compassion in the medical profession and the profound impact that would have across differences of species, class, and gender.

Like her contemporary Mark Twain, Phelps put her literary fame to the service of the antivivisection movement, producing literary as well as polemical writing on the subject. But Phelps was far more prolific for the cause than Twain or any other American author at the time, contributing consistently to the antivivisection campaign from the 1890s until her death in 1911. Phelps's literary fame provided her unique opportunities to champion her favorite cause for wide-ranging audiences. In a 1896 piece about her literary craft for *McClure's Magazine,* in which she defended the artistic merit of morality during an era when moralizing literature was falling out of favor, she listed vivisection reform among the top "creeds" that inspire her fiction: "I believe that the urgent protest against vivisection which marks our immediate day, and the whole plea for lessening the miseries of animals as endured at the hands of men, constitute the 'next' great moral question which is to be put to the intelligent conscience, and that only the educated conscience can properly reply to it."[32] Given her celebrity status, Phelps was included in a *Ladies Home Journal* piece that featured the responses of "nine famous women" to the quintessential American question of what they would do "if they had a million dollars."[33] Phelps, whose response appeared first in the feature, did not waste an opportunity to rebuke the "multi-millionaires" of her era, who "give a million dollars to sustain in a single institution what is called scientific research—that is, in point of fact, to endow the vivisection of dumb animals." Phelps states unequivocally that she would "give twenty millions if [she] had them to condemn vivisectors before the law and restrain the whole inhuman practice" and that she would use the hypothetical million dollars specifically to "endow the movement to the restriction or abolition of vivisection."

In addition to exposing the ethical implications of vivisection in her fiction, Phelps lobbied for legislation to restrict the practice. Rounding up support for a law to regulate vivisection in 1902, she reached out directly to Theodore Roosevelt. In her letter, she appealed to the rugged individualism the president was known for; as antivivisection reform went against the medical establishment, she argued, "more than any progressive movement which I have ever studied in my life this needs the independent . . . mind."[34]

While Roosevelt initially declined to offer his support, because he worried about setting a precedent to those lobbying for other endorsements, in a letter to Phelps later that year, he explained why he had finally come around to it: "At this moment, my daughter being out, I am acting as nurse to two wee guinea pigs, which she feels would not be safe save in the room with me—and if I can prevent it I don't intend to have wanton suffering inflicted on any creature."[35]

As a self-described invalid whose declining health kept her frequently housebound during most of this period, Phelps's public participation in the antivivisection campaign is especially significant. As Carol Farley Kessler notes in her biography of Phelps, "Only on this issue could she muster the physical strength to make public speeches."[36] Phelps's speeches to the Massachusetts legislature in support of a bill to regulate vivisection were quoted in newspapers and published as pamphlets for distribution by animal welfare and antivivisection societies on both sides of the Atlantic. The American Anti-Vivisection Society reported that "because of much admiration expressed by readers of the 'Journal of Zoophily' for Mrs. Elizabeth Stuart Phelps Ward's address on the Bill 'Further to Prevent Cruelty to Animals in Massachusetts,' it was decided that our Society republish the same in pamphlet form. . . . 200 being sent to Miss [Frances Power] Cobbe, of England, by request."[37] The arguments Phelps made in her speeches and pamphlets largely parallel the claims she highlighted in her fiction: namely, she exposed the devastating effect of vivisection on animals (especially stolen pets), the humans who love them, and the humans who experiment upon them and are desensitized as a result. In a 1901 speech to the Massachusetts legislature, she shared an anecdote that closely mirrors the plots of her antivivisection novella *Loveliness* and, later, *Trixy*:

A small dog—a great pet—disappeared from the rectory, which was situated not far from a medical college. At once apprehensions were entertained lest this dear member of their household had met a cruel fate. Through a medical friend search was made, and the dog was found within the laboratory, emaciated, mangled, in a distressing condition. He was taken home and the family physician summoned, but the cruel thrust of scientific inquiry had done its fatal work.[38]

While she wrote happier endings when she adapted that story in the plots of *Loveliness* and *Trixy*, the parallels between the anecdote from her polemical speech and the plots of her fiction are significant: the beloved pet's identity as a family member; the looming proximity of a medical college whose inhumane laboratories are starkly at odds with the genteel community around it; the scientists who transgress social affiliation by experimenting on the family pets of neighbors and community members.[39] In *Loveliness*, Phelps draws on professional relationships to make that last point. Loveliness's owner, a psychology professor, is shocked to find his stolen dog strapped to a science colleague's laboratory table: "His own university! His own university!"[40] Phelps depicts the betrayal with even greater effect in the figure of a wooed woman in *Trixy*; the discovery that her fiancé is a vivisector who had been experimenting on her own dog leads the novel's heroine to break off their engagement. Although Miriam finds out about her lover's professional work in time to avoid a union with him, that near miss echoes the claims made by many antivivisectionists about the insidious effect of a vivisector's degraded sense of morality, which could infiltrate and pervade the sanctity of genteel domestic spaces.

As a further indication of Phelps's stature in the vivisection controversy, her writing was perceived as a threat to the medical establishment. A writer for the *Cleveland Medical Journal* specifically targeted and refuted the arguments of her pamphlets. "It is but natural," the editorial states, "that the question of vivisection should appeal so forcibly to such sympathetic and imaginative minds as Mrs. [Phelps] Ward's." The editorial complains that Phelps exaggerates and envisions worst-case scenarios to depict the cruelties of vivisection (a similar rebuttal, it is worth noting,

to what antislavery activists faced).[41] The other side of the debate also recognized her influence. Albert Leffingwell, an American doctor famous for his antivivisection activism, acknowledged
Phelps's literary reputation and activism when he appealed to her
in October 1904 to lead a campaign in her professional network.
He proposed to Phelps that she use her influence in the literary
world to circulate pamphlets and a petition among other prominent authors. "It has seemed to me and to others," he told Phelps,
"that if you would consent—as the most widely known of romance
writers in this country,—to have put forth a letter of this sort
printed, perhaps, but with your signature in fac-simile,—it might
induce attention where without it, literature would be absolutely
disregarded." Leffingwell included a sample solicitation letter that
he asked Phelps to distribute to other authors, by which she would
recruit their support for "what seems to me the greatest ethical
question of the present day,—the unrestricted vivisection of dumb
animals." Phelps forwarded the request to Mark Twain, whom she
hoped would take the lead instead, and she enclosed a copy of
Trixy to induce his further sympathy and activism for the cause.
Although Twain declined, the exchange reveals their comparable
legacies as major American authors navigating their power to sway
the public's opinion about a practice that was increasingly normalized in medical science and in society.[42]

By 1908, Phelps's voice in protesting vivisection was so famous
that the *New York Times* could pit her opinion against that of
the medical science establishment's most powerful benefactor at
the time, John D. Rockefeller. Under the headline "Differs with
Rockefeller, Mrs. Ward Says There Is No Justification for Vivisection Torture," the article highlights the key point of disagreement
between the two—that is, whether medical advances that benefit humanity may justify the sacrifice of animals. Firmly opposing Rockefeller's view that vivisection is vital to the progress of
medical science, Phelps (who was then using her married name,
Ward), argues, "Ten thousand things learned, if this were possible,
from vivisection, would not justify the intolerable and unpardon-

able torture to which animals have been subjected by this brutal practice."[43] The feature is significant not only for affirming Phelps's prominent status in the movement against vivisection, but also for casting Phelps in opposition to Rockefeller, the most famous patron of the modern medical science movement and the embodiment of the sort of materialistic progress that animal rights advocates protested.[44] Phelps feared that the new direction of medical science research signaled, not the advance of civilization, but rather the deterioration of moral standards in society, and she promoted a social progress based on compassion and mutuality across hierarchical differences.

Phelps's Antivivisection Fiction

In her imaginative literature Phelps made her best case for the type of compassion that bridged species difference and signaled true progress in society or, conversely, the absence of which signaled social decline. In fictional works that aim to expose the evils of animal testing, Phelps portrays character dynamics across the species divide, remarkably anticipating modern-day posthumanism. *Loveliness*, a novella that appeared in *Atlantic Monthly* and was reprinted by Houghton Mifflin in 1899, highlights the bond between an invalid child and her dog, who is stolen to be used in a university laboratory. As a testament to the fame of *Loveliness*, the *New York Times* printed an elegiac announcement on February 6, 1904, upon the death of the title character's real-life namesake, the author's own Yorkshire terrier.

Indeed, the real Loveliness was a meaningful basis for the fictional character, as Phelps's correspondence with her publisher reveals. In several letters to Houghton Mifflin, Phelps requested that the frontispiece and cover of the book feature a photograph of her dog Loveliness, of which she says, "Though it *is* my own dog, I find [it is] generally considered a most beautiful and appealing likeness."[45] With persistence, Phelps argued that the cover of the

Frontispiece to Loveliness, 1899.

book must feature the photograph, "an exact copy of [her] dog," as she doubted that "any artist's illustration can ever give the peculiar sweetness of expression belonging to that photograph." While she also weighed in on potential illustrations for the interior of the book throughout this month-long correspondence, Phelps maintained that a photograph on the cover would enhance her depiction of the title character's authentic identity, a gesture she saw as crucial to evoking human empathy with nonhuman animals. "I think there's much in the sense of one 'portrait from life' to carry on the purpose of the book," she argued, citing an example of a British antivivisection pamphlet "which sold 300,000 or thereabouts" and included "a life-portrait of the dog who really suffered the unspeakable tragedy set forth in the lines." The choice of Loveliness's likeness for the frontispiece was apparently effective, as one reviewer, otherwise offering lukewarm sympathy with the book's cause, acknowledges that the press has "outdone themselves in the picture of the beautiful terrier with which they have decorated the cover."[46] Phelps's wish to use a photograph on her book cover to convey the title character's authenticity reveals a consciousness about animal representation that was, in many ways, ahead of her time.

In the final decade of her career, Phelps continually returned to the theme of vivisection in her fiction. In 1901, she published the short story "Fée," in which the title character narrowly avoids vivisection and reunites a pair of estranged lovers who both claim him as a companion.[47] Her 1908 novel *Though Life Us Do Part*, which was published as a book after being serialized in *Woman's Home Companion*, featured another vivisector-suitor comparable to Olin Steele of *Trixy*. Perhaps most intriguing is "Tammyshanty," published in *Woman's Home Companion* in 1908. "Tammyshanty," which is included in Appendix D, tells the harrowing tale of an Irish setter who is stolen from his companion, a poor Irish immigrant newsboy. After a heart-wrenching scene of the boy's desperate search for his dog, the story climaxes with his transformation into a canine-like character; crouched on all fours and howling his dog's name, he leads a mob of sympathetic newsies and other outraged community members, who confront the vivisector in front of his home to demand the release of the laboratory dogs. A rare example of Phelps's experimentation with literary naturalism, "Tammyshanty" compares the experiences of immigrant children and stray dogs and showcases their bond as the basis for their survival in a hostile world that sought to exploit them.[48]

As Phelps's most expansive work to protest vivisection, *Trixy* presents a progressive model of compassion that crossed boundaries of species and social position, while exposing what Phelps saw as the insidious effect of vivisection on society. It maps out these concerns throughout two plots: the first is a conventional love triangle between an elite-class woman, Miriam Lauriat, and two suitors with sharply contrasted moral characters, her sensitive family attorney,

Philip Surbridge, and a vivisecting physiologist, Dr. Olin Steele. Intersecting with that romantic plot is the story of the title character, a dog abducted from her loyal human companion, Dan, a poor and disabled youth who is Miriam's tenant as well as the object of her philanthropic care. Dr. Steele, Miriam's more aggressive suitor, loses his capacity for compassion as a result of his years performing experiments on live and unanesthetized animals. Upon the discovery that Trixy was stolen to be used as a laboratory subject in Dr. Steele's lab, two crises are averted: Trixy escapes the scalpel and reunites with Dan, and Miriam realizes that her suitor had been experimenting on her own lost dog in time to avoid a marriage to him.

In *Trixy*, Phelps places species, along with gender and class, on a spectrum of social inequality, and she portrays the elite-class, educated man of science as a threat to all those with less privilege. Characterizing the vivisecting doctor as a suitor who strategically ensnares the object of his ambition, Phelps links the wooed woman and the trapped and vivisected animal. For Phelps, a man who causes suffering to animals has no place in genteel society, and Miriam's strict morality functions both as self-preservation and a form of social regulation. She rejects Olin Steele and all of his colleagues on behalf of genteel womanhood when she states in her letter to him, "I cannot see how any true woman can take a vivisector's hand" (159). Miriam's feminine repulsion toward her vivisecting suitor mirrors the moralistic position Phelps conveyed in her account of a debate over a proposed antivivisection bill: "I have always said that I would never take the hand of a vivisector, if I knew it. When one, with a face in whose every line his cruel life had carved its repellent mark, passed near the chair in which I sat, his very proximity was so repulsive that I found it hard to keep back the 'God forgive him!' which came surging to my lips."[49] By giving Miriam the opportunity to escape a marriage to a vivisector, Phelps also offered a democratic alternative to the story of Marie-Françoise ("Fanny") Martin, a French animal welfare and antivivisection activist who was married off to the one of the most notorious vivisectors of the nineteenth century, Claude Bernard.

Whereas the dowry paid by Fanny Martin's father funded her physiologist husband's experiments on animals, Miriam's financial independence and freedom to choose her spouse empowered her to avoid a match with a vivisector, even if the highly moralistic tone of her decision reflected old-fashioned codes of "true womanhood."[50]

Depicting Miriam as "not a new woman," Phelps negotiated between the conservative world of the humane education movement and the more progressive world of radical antivivisection activism. Miriam's philanthropic work with her working-class tenants, which her aunt frowns upon as not befitting a genteel woman, is carefully couched within the codes of traditional femininity, and reflects the WCTU and humane education movement's culture of individual acts of benevolence, rather than institutional or structural social reform. In addition to her moral authority in her relationships with humans, especially men, and her patronizing benevolence toward her social inferiors, Miriam's relationship with her dog, Caro, is characterized by maternal devotion and care, which Alyssa Chen Walker considers to be a strategic gesture to legitimize and codify the status and proper treatment of dogs. Walker notes that "Phelps presents sharply gendered portrayals of human-canine interactions, such that appropriate treatment of dogs is necessarily appropriately 'feminine' or 'masculine.' . . . In *Trixy*, the filching of the family pet disrupts the maternal imperative of woman and violates the property rights of man."[51] By gendering and sentimentalizing the character dynamics, Phelps saves her radical politics for her antivivisection messages, and she exploits the gendered codes of traditional domesticity as a premise for asserting the value of dogs and as a basis for collapsing species boundaries.

The novel's most radical claim is that the practice of testing on sentient beings has a desensitizing effect on medical students and doctors. In her portrayal of Dr. Steele and Dr. Bernard as cold and unfeeling, Phelps severely criticizes the science community and thus aligns herself with the most radical faction of antivivisectionists. The novel opens with Olin Steele as a sensitive young medical student running away from a lecture hall in horror as his professor is about to experiment on a kitten and tearfully vowing to abandon the profession; but the next chapter reveals his maturation, a decade later, into a hardened doctor who lacks sympathy for the lower-class characters he has quarantined because of his (incorrect) diagnosis of diphtheria. While the mere prospect of watching a vivisection traumatized him as a young medical student, as a distinguished researcher he performs repeated experiments on the same animals in pursuit of professional glory. Lori Duin Kelly notes that the novel's "exploration of the impact that repeated exposure to vivisection had on physicians—is truly innovative" in the context of the vivisection debate at the time. "With Steele, Phelps explores the impact that long hours spent vivisecting animals have on a young medical student's 'moral nature' . . . with Bernard, she unleashes a nightmare vision of the kind of physician who is the end product of this kind of training."[52]

Opposition to vivisection on the basis of its coarsening effect on humans seems to be in line with the conservative stance that posits human benefit at the center of animal rights ethics. But in the context of the debates of her day, Phelps's depiction of inhumane physicians and scientists places her in a more progressive position than the WCTU and humane education leaders who were more reluctant to alienate the science community. *Trixy's* radical abolitionism was not lost on Phelps's readers; one reviewer complained, "That vivisection should be limited and controlled by law we do not doubt, but Mrs. Ward's book seems to deny it any rightful place."[53] Despite her otherwise strict adherence to the conservative social culture of the broader animal welfare movement, Phelps pointedly exposes the limitations of humane education reform, and even the potential hypocrisy of animal welfare societies, by making Dr. Steele the president of the "Society for the Prevention of the Docking and Cropping of Tails and Ears."[54] By portraying the vivisecting doctor as an advocate of animal welfare reform, Phelps engaged a growing conflict between the humane movement and antivivisectionists. Anxious to avoid alienating the science community, humane movement leaders increasingly began to take their organizations out of the vivisection debate altogether, and proponents of vivisection sometimes joined humane organizations to reinforce their public image as compassionate doctors. While the American Humane Association advocated for the regulation of vivisection under Albert Leffingwell's leadership, when William O. Stillman took over as its president in 1904, he specifically distanced the organization from the antivivisection campaign. Stillman let the AHA's pamphlets for the cause go out of print and kept the topic out of the organization's major conferences, and he invited key proponents of vivisection to become members of the AHA.[55] By aligning the fictional "docking and cropping" animal welfare society of *Trixy* with the heroine's vivisector suitor, Phelps significantly calls out the animal welfare movement's growing neutrality toward and even, to some extent, complicity with vivisection.

In addition to criticizing the medical profession for shaping scientists and doctors who are unfit for genteel society, Phelps is ahead of her time in her portrayal of human-animal bonds. If the proponents of vivisection drew upon species hierarchies to justify sacrificing animal bodies to advance scientific knowledge, then Phelps wielded narrative and character techniques to blur species distinctions and challenge assumptions of human superiority. In a compelling example, she defers revealing the title character's species until well after introducing the dog's relationship to Dan. In the following dialogue, Dan responds to Miriam's concerned inquiry about his inability to pay his rent:

> "So Mr. Smithers was going to turn you out, was he? Why did n't you pay your rent?"
>
> "Couldn't," said Dan patiently. "Trixy's been sick with a cough."
>
> "Where is Trixy now?"
>
> "Gone to market for supper—acrosst the alley. I'm a watchin'."

In this exchange, Dan could be referring to a wife, sister, or daughter. Miriam's response—to invite them both to stay with her—further validates the egalitarian human-dog bond, the priority Dan placed on Trixy's health, and Trixy's socioeconomic position in relation to her human partner. The resulting confusion about Trixy's species has a disruptive effect, as it is only after the narrator relays the attachment and interdependence of the pair that her identity as a dog is revealed, thus overthrowing the reader's likely assumption that Trixy is a human counterpart to Dan's character. Phelps further disrupts linguistic signifiers of species ranking in Dan's exchange with Miriam's elitist Aunt Cornelia after Dan invites the aristocratic lady to shake "hands" with Trixy: "'You mean paws,' corrected Aunt Cornelia. 'No I don't, marm,' persisted Dan. 'Trixy don't know she's got paws.'" Aunt Cornelia, representing an antiquated social order, reveals the hierarchy-shaping function of language, particularly in her annoyed reply, "You can't make the higher races out of the lower races. I maintain that the Creator knew what he was about. When He made paws, He did n't mean hands." If Olin Steele represents the science community's Darwinian rationale for species hierarchies that justify using animal bodies for human benefit, Aunt Cornelia asserts the divine authority behind human dominance over other animals. Also, as the "Docking and Cropping" society is her favorite philanthropy, Aunt Cornelia's unconscious snobbery reflects Phelps's characterization of the broader animal protection movement, especially in contrast to the more progressive antivivisectionists: generally benevolent and well meaning, but nevertheless elitist.

With such narrative and linguistic gestures, Phelps disrupts conventional rules for the ordering and dynamics between the species. Effectively assigning primacy to nonhuman characters, she anticipates modern-day philosophies of animal ethics and posthumanism. In the novel's canine-human character dynamics, Phelps challenges the anthropocentric conditions of identity, subjectivity, and worth, a gesture she considered essential to convince her audience of the moral status of laboratory animals. In doing so, she performs what Carol J. Adams and Josephine Donovan have termed the "ethics of care" and what Donovan has further theorized as the "aesthetics of care," which "*enables* ethical concern for the subject matter, which is seen not as dead material available for aesthetic manipulation and framing but as a living presence, one located in a particular, knowable environment, who has a history and is capable of dialogical communication."[56]

In her analysis of Phelps's prescient treatment of the nonhuman animal, Roxanne Harde points out that Phelps "prefigures posthumanism as she works to remove humanity from the pedestal on which humanism had placed it and return it to its place as one of many animal species."[57] What makes Phelps's portrayal of dog-human relationships especially progressive for her era is the interdependence of the dynamics, the mutual shaping that posthumanists deem integral to compassionate interspecies dynamics.[58] Reinforcing this prescient theory through significant repetition, *Trixy* envisions the capacity for such mutual impact and fluidity between the species in three dog-human character pairs in the novel: Miriam and Caro; Dan and Trixy; and even the vivisector, Olin, and his Saint Bernard companion, Barry. In each pair, the human and the canine are both significantly altered by their relationship and by the events of their shared encounters. Introduced as the purebred Trixy's inferior, the humble Dan is elevated and enriched through his affiliation with his companion, and Trixy, in turn, bonds more closely to Dan after her harrowing ordeal as a laboratory prisoner. Miriam's Caro makes the ultimate sacrifice, as the victim of brain experiments for two years in Dr. Steele's laboratory, and his reunion with Miriam is mutually fulfilling for both of them. During his absence, Miriam remains loyal to Caro's memory, refusing to adopt another pet and welcoming him back with maternal love and protection upon his escape from the laboratory. In turn, Caro's reunion with Miriam leads her to recognize her fiancé's occupation in time to avoid marrying him. Even the desensitized Dr. Steele retains his attachment to his beloved dog, Barry, whose unwavering devotion leads to the doctor's death-bed remorse for the many dogs he sacrificed to advance his career. In thus exploring affiliation as the basis for eradicating vivisection, Phelps signals her alliance with the more radical antivivisectionists of her day, who "charted a more comprehensive consideration of rights by collapsing the species divide."[59]

Reception and Legacy of Trixy

Upon its initial publication, the critical reception of *Trixy* was largely favorable. In a literary notice published on September 4, 1905, the *New York Daily Tribune* reported that Phelps's novel "has, it appears, appealed to royalty," as a private secretary to Queen Alexandra "has written to Houghton, Mifflin & Co. to say that her majesty has been greatly interested in this 'charming story,' and to inquire concerning the author's present address and 'her other books.'" The *New York Times* review, published on November 5, 1904, acknowledged that the author skillfully depicted "the effect of vivisection upon the operator as well as upon his victim," cautiously concluding that "whether one agrees with her or not in her final judgments, one must concede that Mrs. Phelps has the gift of an eloquence that at least sets her readers thinking." Later in the year, the *Tribune* also recommended the novel among a short list of "Best Xmas Books" (December 10, 1904), and the *New York Times* included it on the same day in its list of "Books That Sell Well." Not surprisingly, *Trixy* was also well received by the animal advocacy community, particularly the remaining leaders who still publicly supported the antivivisection cause. After a second edition of the novel came out in 1905, Angell, the MSPCA founder and long-serving president, reviewed it favorably in the April 1905 issue of the organization's monthly magazine, *Our Dumb Animals*, and he especially recommended it "to the careful consideration of medical students and medical men."[60]

But that critical acclaim did not translate to market success; sales were so low that Houghton Mifflin sold off five thousand copies to the New York firm Grosset and Dunlap.[61] Phelps seemed less interested in the financial prospects of the book, though, than in its capacity to reach readers. She told her publisher, "I should not like to surrender the royalties on the original edition, but I should gladly surrender them for the cheaper edition for the sake of the Cause."[62] Partly, the declining market reception of *Trixy* may have been the result of an overall decline in sympathy with the novel's reform purpose. By the time *Trixy* was published, the movement to abolish vivisection had proved to be a losing battle, especially because of advances in medical science that were held up as proof that experimenting on animals was justified and necessary.[63] Indeed, that powerful rebuttal is captured in a medical journal's especially vitriolic review of *Loveliness*; to counter the novella's emotional appeal, which it sums up as a "rich man's pet 'stretched, bound, gagged, gasping. . . . kissing his vivisector's hand,'" the review asserts the benefits of antitoxins with the image of a dying human baby, "burning with fever, gasping, choking, tearing at its throat in the struggle for life."[64]

Proponents of vivisection were not the only readers to object to what they saw as Phelps's sentimentalizing of the issue. While animal rights advocates generally appreciated Phelps's antivivisection fiction for raising awareness and support for the cause, some readers within the movement criticized Phelps for glossing over the realities of the laboratory—the actual experiments on animals. A review of *Trixy* in a London-based antivivisection magazine complains that "the authoress has attempted to hide the horrors of vivisection by the thinnest of artistic veils." Objecting to Phelps's choice of romantic fiction for her antivivisection message in *Trixy*, the review argues that "what is wanted in this war [against vivisection] is the skillful use of weapons of precision, cold and calm and rigidly correct statements of the awful facts of the thing . . . without any attempt to array the frightful truth of the matter in the garb of an artistic setting."[65] While she included graphic examples of experiments in her polemical speeches on the subject, Phelps strategically avoided doing so in *Trixy*, focusing instead on the status and lives of dog and human characters and on the pervasive personal impact of vivisection. In the preface to the novel, Phelps rationalizes her strategy of avoiding graphic descriptions of experiments: "If TRIXY were a polemic, there might be presented a variety of authentic physiological diversions as sad as they would seem to be incredible. Such being the material of the apostle rather than of the artist, these pages have been closed to scenes too painful for admission to them." The criticism of that choice from within the animal rights movement resonates with contemporary debates over whether graphic representations of animal abuse and exploitation actually help or hurt campaigns for animal rights. Many activists today believe in a middle-ground approach that includes depicting both the realities of animal suffering and the possibilities for animals' peaceful lives (indeed, just as Phelps arguably did if we take into consideration her antivivisection writing as a whole). Activist Karen Davis notes that "images of animals suffering and abject need to be in contrast to images of these same animals living in happiness—images that are not just 'postcard' pretty, but expressive, evocative, and moving." Also, activist Jasmin Singer emphasizes the positive aspects of an animal's unmolested life, commenting that "sometimes, it's the happy stuff that packs more of a punch, because—as in my case—the viewer says, 'LOOK WHAT WE ARE TAKING AWAY FROM THEM!'"[66] The "happy stuff" is precisely what Phelps captured in her depictions of the loving bonds between dog characters and the humans around them, and the heartrending narratives of their captivity in laboratories function to remind people of what is taken away from them, as well as the impact that has on the humans who love them. The strategic choices behind Phelps's fictional depictions of suffering animals make her antivivisection writing especially timely and relevant today, given the continued conversations in activist movements about representing animals.

A related factor could also explain *Trixy*'s low sales in its own time: in addition to the novel's ideological opposition to vivisection, its literary representations of nonhuman animals were sometimes off-putting to readers of Phelps's era. With a novel that challenges species-based hierarchies of consciousness and sensitivity, Phelps anticipates the posthumanist concept of interspecies interdependence as a basis for compassion. In doing so, she imaginatively intervenes in her era's materialistic definitions of "progress" with innovative visions of cross-species unity that were ahead of her time, inconvenient notions for a world complacent with the campaigns of imperialism and scientific progress at the expense of human and nonhuman suffering. Indeed, the playful narrative confusion over Trixy's species, Trixy's individuality and distinct character, and Dan's insistence that she shake hands with even the most elite human characters were narrative devices calculated to elevate the status of nonhuman animals. Phelps's decision to invest the title character with agency and identity was not lost upon readers of her own day, who sometimes deemed those gestures absurd, such as a reviewer who marveled that "Mrs. Ward speaks of a 'poodle *who* sat like a statuette'; or talks of 'the God of little lost dogs.'"[67]

Whereas readers in her own era scoffed at Phelps's human pronoun usage for dog characters, her linguistic choices in *Trixy* were powerful and strategic interventions. Contemporary animal rights theorist Joan Dunayer analyzes the role of language in perpetuating humans' dominance over other animals, and she challenges animal rights advocates to make exactly the sort of linguistic changes that Phelps was experimenting with over a century earlier. In an argument that Phelps herself implicitly makes throughout *Trixy*, Dunayer asserts that "because nonhuman animals are conscious beings, it is misleading and speciesist to refer to them as 'that' or 'which' rather than 'who.'" Indeed, Phelps would have especially agreed with Dunayer's statement that "designating any non-human an 'it' . . . classifies them with insentient things."[68]

In Phelps's era, though, her elevated treatment of nonhuman animals was likely to be met with skepticism. Even reviews that applauded the literary merit of *Trixy* often qualified their praise with criticism about the novelist's personal investment in the rights of animals. While granting that "Mrs. Ward is so admirable a literary artist, such a master of form," a reviewer for the *Independent* challenges the author's commitment to humanity, asking "whether the charity which she gives to beasts does not make her forget the charity which is due to human beings."[69] Such questioning of the author's loyalty to her own species reflected a typical criticism leveled at animal welfarists of Phelps's era, particularly women, whose advocacy for another species often led to harsh judgments of their sense of humanity or even their mental health.[70]

Phelps was a consistently successful and popular author throughout a career that spanned five decades and included fifty-seven books and numerous uncollected essays, poems, pamphlets, and short stories. If her most elaborate fictional response to vivisection did not fare well in the literary market of her day, it is partly because *Trixy*'s elevation of animal characters belongs less to Phelps's era of strenuous speciesism than it does, perhaps, today, with shifting cultural attitudes about the roles and rights of nonhuman animals in society. When she portrays the dog characters of *Trixy* as distinct individuals, Phelps defies their generic classification as "laboratory subjects" and acknowledges the importance of individuality as a basis for compassion. In doing so she anticipates Carol J. Adams's analysis of how "massification" causes people to ignore social injustices: "False mass terms function as short hand. *They* are not like *us*. Our compassion need not go there, to their situation, their experience, or if it does it may be diluted. Their 'massification' means our release from empathy."[71] Phelps highlights dog individuality by making her dog characters relatable, lovable, and nuanced, and giving them backstories and dynamics with other dogs and humans, a strategy that resonates with the narrative trend in antivivisection campaigns today. The impressive mainstream popularity of the California-based rescue organization Beagle Freedom Project, for instance, is largely the result of its effective use of social media as a platform to tell rescued dogs' stories. The organization, which rescues laboratory animals and promotes legislation to mandate the release and adoption of healthy animals who survive experiments, focuses less on exposing the graphic realities of the laboratory than on the dogs' rehabilitation experiences and lives post-laboratory. In addition to web articles that tell the story of successful rescue missions and describe each rescued dog's personality and circumstances in detail, many of the rescued dogs are featured in their own Twitter profiles, where their human companions post daily updates about the dogs' home life, adventures out in the world, and positive interactions with humans and other animals.

Beagle Freedom Project considers the dogs' power to affect others, the potential for mutual impact that contemporary animal rights theorists maintain is at the heart of compassion, as the key to their success: "Whether in groups of 2 or 200 Beagle Freedom Project exists to save these 'research' animals and to tell their stories. These little dogs can do more with a wag of their tales to convince people to go cruelty-free than people can with their best words."[72] Riley, one of the beagles rescued from a laboratory in San Francisco in July 2014, "is not only surviving and thriving—he is inspiring. His presence in his new home sent the family's incredible daughter to go throughout the house and mark with a big X every product that was tested on animals—so they knew to avoid those in the future." Riley's ability to inspire such change in his human family signals his personal agency, his subjective existence, which was denied within the walls of the laboratory. Throughout the dozens of web articles, and especially through social media profiles that daily insert the dogs' identities into the public sphere, the Beagle Freedom Project highlights the rescued dogs' personalities and relationships. In doing so, the dog rescue stories make a powerful case for the subjective experience of the dogs, in stark contrast to their status as laboratory animals.

In seizing upon the power of character-based narratives to assert the subjectivity and identities of nonhuman animals as a method of campaigning against the exploitation of animal bodies, the Beagle Freedom Project and the many other activists who focus on nonhuman animals' stories pick up where Phelps left off over a century ago. *Trixy* transports us to a time when the use of animals for the sake of modern medical science had just become normative in American universities, and it gives us a glimpse into the feminist consciousness that railed against that new norm. Perhaps *Trixy* was ahead of its time in 1904, but it speaks to readers today of a compassion capacious enough to transcend differences, and it represents a well known author's tireless dedication to the rights of nonhuman animals.

Notes

1. Diane Beers, *For the Prevention of Cruelty: The History and Legacy of Animal Rights Activism in the United States* (Athens: Ohio University Press, 2006), 122.

2. Katherine C. Grier, *Pets in America: A History* (Chapel Hill: University of North Carolina Press, 2006), 182.

3. For that history, see Susan J. Pearson, *The Rights of the Defenseless: Protecting Animals and Children in Gilded Age America* (Chicago: University of Chicago Press, 2011), 21–56.

4. Beers, *For the Prevention of Cruelty*, 123.

5. See especially, Craig Buettinger, "Women and Antivivisection in Late Nineteenth Century America," *Journal of Social History* (Summer 1997): 857–72; and Hilda Kean, "The 'Smooth Cool Men of Science': The Feminist and Socialist Response to Vivisection," *History Workshop Journal* 40 (1995): 16–38. Also, as Beers (*For the Prevention of Cruelty*, 124) notes, "For some Victorian women, images of the vivisected animal strapped to a table bore an uncanny and frightening resemblance to the gynecologically vivisected woman. As women agitated for greater rights, this analogy of shared oppression linking themselves and animals provided a powerful motivation for their critique of the dark side of a decidedly patriarchal profession."

6. Janet M. Davis, *The Gospel of Kindness: Animal Welfare and the Making of Modern America* (New York: Oxford University Press, 2016), 83.

7. Frances Elizabeth Willard, *Woman and Temperance: Or, the Work and Workers of the Woman's Christian Temperance Union* (Hartford, Conn.: James Betts, 1883), 434.

8. For the history of Cobbe's influence on White, see Janet M. Davis, *The Gospel of Kindness*, 55.

9. Frances Power Cobbe, *The Fallacy of Restriction Applied to Vivisection* (London: Victoria Street Society,1886), 2.

10. Catherine Smithies to George T. Angell, September 8, 1875, MSPCA-Angell Archives. The "society" to which Smithies refers was likely the National Anti-Vivisection Society, also known as the Victoria Street Society, founded by Frances Power Cobbe in 1875, and the "Baroness" was likely Baroness Angela Burdett-Couts, known for her involvement in the Royal SPCA.

11. Frances Power Cobbe, *Vivisection in America* (London: Victoria Street Society, 1889), 29, 30.

12. Stephen T. Newmyer, *Animals, Rights, and Reason in Plutarch and Modern Ethics* (New York: Routledge, 2006), 67.

13. Jeremy Bentham, *An Introduction to the Principles of Morals and Legislation* (1789; repr. Oxford: Clarendon Press, 1907), ch. 17, note 122.

14. Twain's letter to Sidney G. Trist (May 1899) was printed in several different formats; the example of the scientist's disregard for animals' shrieks is not included in the original letter but was added to some later versions, including a pamphlet titled *The Pains of Lowly Life*, published by the London Anti-Vivisection Society in 1900, and another titled *Mark Twain on Vivisection*, published by the New York Anti-Vivisection Society, circa 1903.

15. According to Pearson (*The Rights of the Defenseless*, 5), animal welfare groups typically "used 'cruelty' as a trope to stand in for other anxieties—about the unruly and indecorous behavior of the working class, about immigrants, about industrialization."

16. Kean, "The 'Smooth Cool Men of Science,'" 21.

17. Kean (ibid.) remarks that "some campaigners went so far as to accuse physiologists of seeking to arrogantly usurp the powers of God and nature by prolonging the life of the privileged few."

18. "Experiments on Brute Animals" (London, 1883), in Susan Hamilton, ed., *Animal Welfare and Anti-Vivisection 1870–1910: Nineteenth-Century Woman's Mission* (New York: Routledge, 2004), 3:261.

19. Ibid.

20. The sheltering initiative emerged as a distinct effort and wasn't initially supported by some of the larger animal protection organizations. According to Janet M. Davis (*The Gospel of Kindness*, 95), the early advocates of animal shelter reform, mostly women, "wanted to focus exclusively on sheltering and care for strays rather than prosecution—a policy that complemented traditional notions of separate spheres for women and men." Davis points to additional evidence of the class-consciousness of this branch of the movement, in that they strategically "responded to

public criticism regarding the [broader animal protection] movement's alleged indifference to poor pet owners by offering to subsidize the cost of licensing and veterinary care."

21. Jed Mayer notes how antivivisectionists subverted the logic of species-based hierarchy: "The abdication of responsibility toward our nonhuman dependents could place the human operator in a lower position than the dog under his knife." "The Expression of the Emotions in Man and Laboratory Animals," *Victorian Studies* 50, no. 3 (Spring 2008): 412.

22. In Hamilton, *Animal Welfare and Anti-Vivisection 1870–1910*, 2:10.

23. Coral Lansbury, *The Old Brown Dog: Women, Workers and Vivisection in Edwardian England* (Madison: University of Wisconsin Press, 1985), 8–12. After the sensational trial, antivivisectionists erected a statue in London in memory of the brown dog, which eventually provoked protests and riots from large groups of medical students; for that history, see Peter Mason, *The Brown Dog Affair: The Story of a Monument That Divided a Nation* (London: Two Sevens Publishing, 1997).

24. Shelley Fisher Fishkin explains the connections between Twain's "A Dog's Tale" and the "brown dog affair," including a letter exchange between Twain and *The Shambles of Science* author Lind-af-Hageby. Fishkin, ed., *Mark Twain's Book of Animals* (Berkeley: University of California Press, 2010), 276–77.

25. Harriet Ritvo, *The Animal Estate: The English and Other Creatures in Victorian England* (Cambridge, Mass.: Harvard University Press, 1989), 86–87.

26. Brown's "Rab and His Friends" was frequently cited in antivivisection literature (also, Brown was a friend and correspondent of Twain's). Vest's "Eulogy of a Dog" was also reprinted frequently, including in a pamphlet that also featured Mark Twain's famous antivivisection letter: *Mark Twain on Vivisection/Eulogy on the Dog by Senator George G. Vest* (New York: New York Anti-Vivisection Society, ca. 1903). Phelps specifically refers to Vest's speech in the courtroom scene in *Trixy*), and for that reason, the speech is included in Appendix A.

27. Kean, "The 'Smooth Cool Men of Science,'" 19.

28. See Frederick Wegener, "Few Things More Womanly and Noble: Elizabeth Stuart Phelps and the Advent of the Woman Doctor in America," *Legacy* 22, no. 1 (2005): 1–17.

29. See Jennifer S. Tuttle, "Letters from Elizabeth Stuart Phelps (Ward) to S. Weir Mitchell, M.D., 1884–1897," *Legacy* 17, no. 1 (2000): 83–94.

30. In a 1907 letter, Phelps expressed her exhaustion after her losing battle to end vivisection, and she comments upon the "dogs' cries in the beautiful, merciless Harvard buildings—the new ones now so near us. I can't pass there in the car without choking bitter prayers and curses." Elizabeth Stuart Phelps to Richard Watson Gilder, January 30, 1907, Richard Watson Gilder Papers, Manuscripts and Archives Division, New York Public Library, Astor, Lenox, and Tilden Foundations.

31. Davis (*The Gospel of Kindness*, 77) notes the WCTU and humane education movement's conservative belief in the power of individual benevolence as a foundation for social justice; she points out that "their emphasis on individual initiative, rather than collective action, limited their reach."

32. Phelps, "A Novelist's Views of Novel Writing," *McClure's*, November 1896, 78. The editors of the American Anti-Vivisection Society's monthly magazine, the *Journal of Zoophily*, promptly recognized Phelps's statement and appreciatively claimed her as their newest recruit to the cause (February 1, 1897).

33. "If They Had a Million Dollars," *Ladies Home Journal*, September 1903, 10.

34. Elizabeth Stuart Phelps Ward to Theodore Roosevelt, February 28, 1902, Theodore Roosevelt Papers, Library of Congress Manuscript Division, http://www.theodorerooseveltcenter.org/Research/Digital-Library/Record/?libID=037137. Theodore Roosevelt Digital Library, Dickinson State University.

35. Theodore Roosevelt to Elizabeth Stuart Phelps Ward, October 20, 1902, Theodore Roosevelt Papers, Library of Congress Manuscript Division, http://www.theodorerooseveltcenter.org/Research/Digital-Library/Record/?libID=0183335. Theodore Roosevelt Digital Library, Dickinson State University.

36. Carol Farley Kessler, *Elizabeth Stuart Phelps* (Boston: Twayne, 1982), 112.

37. "The Twenty-First Annual Report of the American Anti-Vivisection Society, for the Total Abolition of All Vivisection Experiments on Animals and Other Experiments of a Painful Character, for the Year 1903" (1904), 4.

38. Elizabeth Stuart Phelps Ward, "A Voice from Massachusetts. Being an Address to the Legislative Committee at the Anti-Vivisection Hearings, in 1901," *Report of the Proceedings of the Twenty-Fifth Annual Convention of the American Humane Association* (Chicago: Stromberg

Allen, 1901): 55–56. Versions of Phelps's remarks to the Massachusetts Legislature in favor of House Bill 856 in March 1901 (which included, apparently, two separate speeches) were reprinted in several publications on both sides of the Atlantic, including, in addition to the American Humane Association report cited above, the British Anti-Vivisection magazine the *Zoophilist and Animals' Defender*, May 1901, 13–16; *Boston Herald*, March 27, 1901; as well as in part in the pamphlet "Plea for the Helpless," published by the American Humane Association (New York, 1901).

39. Alice Chen Walker uses the term "stolen pet plot" to describe Phelps's antivivisection stories. "Bringing the Laboratory Dog Home," *Humanimalia* 4, no. 2 (Spring 2013): 104.

40. Phelps's characterization of Loveliness's owner as a psychology professor may be a tribute to the Harvard psychologist and philosopher, and antivivisectionist, William James. For the evolution of James's opposition to vivisection, see James Campbell, "Pragmatism and Moral Growth: William James and the Question of Vivisection," *Pragmatism Today* 6, no. 1 (2015): 61–66.

41. "Anti-Vivisection Again," *Cleveland Medical Journal* 4 (January 1905): 233.

42. Phelps's description of Leffingwell, whose name was practically synonymous with the regulationist position in vivisection reform, would not have been persuasive to abolitionists like Twain: "[Leffingwell's] opinion carries weight everywhere, even among vivisectors. His position is a very conservative one, since he believes in restricted vivisection, and the society which he represents seeks to reform rather than to abolish it. This gives him an influence in places where we abolitionists would be more cautiously welcomed." Elizabeth Stuart Phelps Ward to Richard W. Gilder, October 13, 1904, Mark Twain Papers, Bancroft Library at University of California Berkeley.

43. "Differs with Rockefeller. Mrs. Ward Says There Is No Justification for Vivisection Torture," *New York Times*, November 29, 1908, 1.

44. John D. Rockefeller founded the Rockefeller Institute for Medical Research (in 1901), which Bernard Unti calls a "lightning rod for the controversy over vivisection." Unti explains the Rockefeller Institute's powerful role in suppressing efforts to regulate vivisection in New York. Bernard Unti, "'The Doctors Are So Sure That They Only Are Right': The Rockefeller Institute and the Defeat of Vivisection Reform in New York, 1908–1914," in *Creating a Tradition of Biomedical Research: Contri-*

butions to the History of the Rockefeller University, ed. Darwin H. Stapleton (New York: Rockefeller University Press, 2004), 175.

45. Elizabeth Stuart Phelps Ward to George H. Mifflin, August 18, 1899, Houghton Library, Series A, 2233. All quotations here are from this letter; Phelps appealed to Mifflin to use her dog's photograph in the book in at least four letters in July and August 1899.

46. The Cincinnati Lancet-Clinic 82 (December 23, 1899): 637.

47. "Fée" was published in Century 39 (March 1901): 671–780; and reprinted in her short story collection The Oath of Allegiance and Other Stories (Boston: Houghton, Mifflin, 1909). Phelps may have named one of her companion dogs after the title character of this story. In the article that announces the death of Phelps's dog Loveliness, the New York Times reports that the author's "new dog is called Fay." "Boston Notes," New York Times, February 6, 1904, 91.

48. Two relevant contexts for the bond between an Irish setter and an Irish newsboy in "Tammyshanty" are the newsboys' strike of 1899, led by Irish immigrant youths, and the notoriously brutal treatment of poor immigrant families, particularly Irish families, by dogcatchers. A harrowing example of the latter was a dogcatcher's murder of a fourteen-year-old Harlem boy, James Doyle, during a violent raid on his shanty home. Davis, The Gospel of Kindness, 93.

49. Phelps, "The New Inquisition," The Independent, April 5, 1900, 811.

50. Keri Cronin, "Fanny Martin," Unbound Project, September 8, 2016, https://unboundproject.org/fanny-martin/. Since the character of Olin Steele's laboratory assistant, Dr. Bernard, is clearly based on Claude Bernard, it is likely that Phelps was aware of the history of the famous vivisector's marriage to an animal rights activist.

51. Walker, "Bringing the Laboratory Dog Home," 104.

52. Lori Duin Kelly, "Elizabeth Stuart Phelps, Trixy, and the Vivisection Question," Legacy 27, no. 1 (2010): 65, 66.

53. The Independent, January 12, 1905, 100.

54. Such a criticism likely reflects a tension between the vivisection and animal welfare movements. Davis (The Gospel of Kindness, 80–81) notes that the radical antivivisectionist Frances Lovell "loathed how the medical community deftly appropriated the humane movement's language of civilization and humanitarianism to serve its own pro-vivisection agenda."

55. Unti, "The Doctors Are So Sure That They Only Are Right," 180. Phelps would likely have been aware of this change in the leadership of the

AHA, as she is listed as one of the organization's vice presidents in 1901–2 in the *Report of the Proceedings of the 25th Annual Convention* (1901).

56. Josephine Donovan, *The Aesthetics of Care: On the Literary Treatment of Animals* (New York: Bloomsbury Academic, 2016), 11. Also see Carol J. Adams and Josephine Donovan, eds., *The Feminist Care Tradition in Animal Ethics* (New York: Columbia University Press, 2007).

57. Roxanne Harde, "'Doncher Be Too Sure of That!': Children, Dogs, and Elizabeth Stuart Phelps's Early Posthumanism," *Bookbird: A Journal of International Children's Literature* 53, no. 1 (2015): 15.

58. For example, Elisabeth Arnould-Bloomfield reinforces animal ethics philosopher Donna Haraway's theory of cross-species relatability characterized by "intra-action," a "process of internal mutual shaping," in which individual beings across species are changed as a result of their interactions. Elisabeth Arnould-Bloomfield, "Posthuman Compassions," *PMLA* 130, no. 5 (October 2015): 1472.

59. Davis, *The Gospel of Kindness*, 82.

60. George T. Angell, "Trixy," *Our Dumb Animals* (April 1905), 148.

61. Kelly, "Elizabeth Stuart Phelps, *Trixy*, and the Vivisection Question," 79n8.

62. Elizabeth Stuart Phelps Ward to George H. Mifflin, February 2, 1906, Houghton Library.

63. Lori Duin Kelly points to the vivisectionists' campaign, which "contributed to a growing acceptance of research conducted on live animals as essential to medical progress," as a likely reason that *Trixy* did not sell well. Kelly, "Elizabeth Stuart Phelps, *Trixy*, and the Vivisection Question," 73.

64. "Book Notices," *The Corpuscle* 9 (July 1899): 272.

65. *The Zoophilist and Animals' Defender* 24, no. 10 (February 1, 1905): 192. The British magazine quotes a review from the American magazine *Our Animal Friends*.

66. Mark Hawthorne, "How Do Graphic Images Affect Animal Advocacy?," *Striking at the Roots: Animal Activism around the World*, November 1, 2012, https://strikingattheroots.wordpress.com/2012/11/01/how-do-graphic-images-affect-animal-advocacy/. Karen Davis is the founder of the nonprofit organization United Poultry Concerns, and Jasmin Singer is cofounder with Mariann Sullivan of the advocacy website *Our Hen House*, which describes its style as "*indefatigably* positive" (http://www.ourhenhouse.org/about/).

67. *Catholic World*, March 1905, 833.

68. Joan Dunayer, "Mixed Messages: Opinion Pieces by Representatives of US Nonhuman Animal-Advocacy Organizations," in *Critical Animal and Media Studies: Communication for Nonhuman Animal Advocacy*, ed. Núria Almiran, Matthew Cole, and Carrie P. Freeman (New York: Routledge, 2016), 93.

69. *The Independent*, January 12, 1905, 99.

70. The diagnosis of "zoophil-psychosis," for example, was promoted as a way to pathologize animal advocacy. Diane L. Beers (*For the Prevention of Cruelty*, 129–31) criticizes the gendered bias of this pseudo-pathology, explaining that "women, because of their weaker constitution, disproportionally fell victim to the malady, and radical female antivivisectionists nearly always suffered from it" (129).

71. Carol J. Adams, "The War on Compassion," *Antennae* 14 (Autumn 2010): 6.

72. Kevin Chase, "Our San Francisco Treats!," Beagle Freedom Project, July 2, 2014, https://web.archive.org/web/20151001084810/http://www.beaglefreedomproject.org/our_san_francisco_treats (accessed on March 13, 2018).

Works Cited

Adams, Carol J. "The War on Compassion." *Antennae* 14 (Autumn 2010): 6.

Adams, Carol J., and Josephine Donovan, eds., *The Feminist Care Tradition in Animal Ethics*. New York: Columbia University Press, 2007.

Angell, George T. "Trixy." *Our Dumb Animals* (April 1905): 148.

"Anti-Vivisection Again." *Cleveland Medical Journal* 4 (January 1905): 233.

Arnould-Bloomfield, Elisabeth. "Posthuman Compassions." *PMLA* 130, no. 5 (October 2015): 1467–75.

Beers, Diane. *For the Prevention of Cruelty: The History and Legacy of Animal Rights Activism in the United States*. Athens: Ohio University Press, 2006.

Bentham, Jeremy. *An Introduction to the Principles of Morals and Legislation* (1789). Oxford: Clarendon Press, 1907.

"Book Notices." *The Corpuscle* 9 (July 1899): 272.

"Books That Sell Well." *New York Times Saturday Review of Books*, December 10, 1904, 881.

"Boston Notes." *New York Times*, February 6, 1904, 91.

Buettinger, Craig. "Women and Antivivisection in Late Nineteenth Century America." *Journal of Social History* (Summer 1997): 857–72.

Campbell, James. "Pragmatism and Moral Growth: William James and the Question of Vivisection." *Pragmatism Today* 6, no. 1 (2015): 61–66.

Chase, Kevin. "Our San Francisco Treats!" Beagle Freedom Project, July 2, 2014, http://www.beaglefreedomproject.org/our_san_francisco_treats.

Cobbe, Frances Power. *The Fallacy of Restriction Applied to Vivisection.* London: Victoria Street Society, 1886.

———. *Vivisection in America.* London: Victoria Street Society, 1889.

Cronin, Keri. "Fanny Martin." *Unbound Project*, September 8, 2016, http://unboundproject.org/historical-stories/fanny-martin/.

Davis, Janet M. *The Gospel of Kindness: Animal Welfare and the Making of Modern America.* New York: Oxford University Press, 2016.

"Differs with Rockefeller: Mrs. Ward Says There Is No Justification for Vivisection Torture." *New York Times*, November 29, 1908, 1.

Donovan, Josephine. *The Aesthetics of Care: On the Literary Treatment of Animals.* New York: Bloomsbury Academic, 2016.

Dunayer, Joan. "Mixed Messages: Opinion Pieces by Representatives of US Nonhuman Animal-Advocacy Organizations." In *Critical Animal and Media Studies: Communication for Nonhuman Animal Advocacy,* edited by Núria Almiran, Matthew Cole, and Carrie P. Freeman, 91–105. New York: Routledge, 2016.

Fishkin, Shelley Fisher, ed. *Mark Twain's Book of Animals.* Berkeley: University of California Press, 2010.

Grier, Katherine C. *Pets in America: A History.* Chapel Hill: University of North Carolina Press, 2006.

Hamilton, Susan, ed. *Animal Welfare and Anti-Vivisection 1870–1910: Nineteenth-Century Woman's Mission.* 3 vols. New York: Routledge, 2004.

Haraway, Donna. *The Companion Species Manifesto.* Chicago: Prickly Paradigm Press, 2003.

Harde, Roxanne. "'Doncher Be Too Sure of That!': Children, Dogs, and Elizabeth Stuart Phelps's Early Posthumanism." *Bookbird: A Journal of International Children's Literature* 53, no. 1 (2015): 10–23.

Hawthorne, Mark. "How Do Graphic Images Affect Animal Advocacy?" *Striking at the Roots: Animal Activism around the World*, November 1, 2012, https://strikingattheroots.wordpress.com/2012/11/01/how-do-graphic-images-affect-animal-advocacy/ (accessed March 12, 2018).

"If They Had a Million Dollars." *Ladies Home Journal*, September 1903, 10.

Kean, Hilda. "The 'Smooth Cool Men of Science': The Feminist and Socialist Response to Vivisection." *History Workshop Journal* 40 (1995): 16–38.

Keen, William. "Our Recent Debts to Vivisection." *Popular Science Monthly* 26 (1885): 1–15.

Kelly, Lori Duin. "Elizabeth Stuart Phelps, *Trixy*, and the Vivisection Question." *Legacy* 27, no. 1 (2010): 61–82.

Kessler, Carol Farley. *Elizabeth Stuart Phelps*. Boston: Twayne, 1982.

Lansbury, Coral. *The Old Brown Dog: Women, Workers and Vivisection in Edwardian England*. Madison: University of Wisconsin Press, 1985.

"Literary Notes." *New York Daily Tribune*, September 4, 1905, 8.

Mark Twain on Vivisection/Eulogy on the Dog by Senator George G. Vest. New York: New York Anti-Vivisection Society, [1903].

Mason, Jennifer. *Civilized Creatures: Urban Animals, Sentimental Culture, and American Literature, 1850–1900*. Baltimore: Johns Hopkins University Press, 2005.

Mason, Peter. *The Brown Dog Affair: The Story of a Monument That Divided a Nation*. London: Two Sevens Publishing, 1997.

Mayer, Jed. "The Expression of the Emotions in Man and Laboratory Animals." *Victorian Studies* 50, no. 3 (Spring 2008): 399–417.

Newmyer, Stephen T. *Animals, Rights, and Reason in Plutarch and Modern Ethics*. New York: Routledge, 2006.

Pearson, Susan J. *The Rights of the Defenseless: Protecting Animals and Children in Gilded Age America*. Chicago: University of Chicago Press, 2011.

Phelps (Ward), Elizabeth Stuart. "Address of Mrs. Elizabeth Stuart Phelps Ward before the committee on Probate and Chancery, in favor of House Bill 856 for the Regulation of Vivisection in Massachusetts." *Boston Herald*, March 27, 1901.

———. Letter to Richard W. Gilder, October 13, 1904. Mark Twain Papers, Bancroft Library, University of California, Berkeley.

———. Letter to Richard Watson Gilder, January 30, 1907. Richard Watson Gilder Papers, New York Public Library.

———. Letter to George H. Mifflin, August 18, 1899. Houghton Library.

———. Letter to George H. Mifflin, February 2, 1906. Houghton Library.

———. Letter to Theodore Roosevelt, February 28, 1902. Theodore Roosevelt Papers, Library of Congress Manuscript Division, http://

www.theodorerooseveltcenter.org/Research/Digital-Library/Record/
?libID=037137. Theodore Roosevelt Digital Library, Dickinson State
University.

———. *Loveliness*. Boston: Houghton, Mifflin, 1899.

———. "The New Inquisition." *The Independent*, April 5, 1900, 811–13.

———. "A Novelist's Views of Novel Writing." *McClure's*, November
1896, 78.

———. *A Plea for the Helpless: An Address before a committee of the Massachusetts Legislature*. New York: American Humane Association,
1901.

———. "Spirits in Prison." *Independent* 52 (March 22, 1900): 695–97.

———. "Tammyshanty." In *The Oath of Allegiance and Other Stories*. Boston: Houghton, Mifflin, 1909.

———. "A Voice from Massachusetts. Being an Address to the Legis-
lative Committee at the Anti-Vivisection Hearings, in 1901." In
*Report of the Proceedings of the Twenty-Fifth Annual Convention of the
American Humane Association*. Chicago: Stromberg Allen, 1901.

Ritvo, Harriet. *The Animal Estate: The English and Other Creatures in Victorian England*. Cambridge, Mass.: Harvard University Press, 1989.

Roosevelt, Theodore. Letter to Elizabeth Stuart Phelps Ward, October
20, 1902. Theodore Roosevelt Papers, Library of Congress Manuscript Division, http://www.theodorerooseveltcenter.org/Research/
Digital-Library/Record/?libID=0183335. Theodore Roosevelt Digital Library, Dickinson State University.

"Trixy." *Catholic World*, March 1905, 833.

"Trixy." *The Cincinnati Lancet-Clinic* 82 (December 23, 1899): 637.

"Trixy." *The Independent*, January 12, 1905, 99–100.

"The Twenty-First Annual Report of the American Anti-Vivisection
Society, for the Total Abolition of All Vivisection Experiments on
Animals and Other Experiments of a Painful Character, for the Year
1903" (1904).

Tuttle, Jennifer S. "Letters from Elizabeth Stuart Phelps (Ward) to S.
Weir Mitchell, M.D., 1884–1897." *Legacy* 17, no. 1 (2000): 83–94.

Twain, Mark. *Mark Twain on Vivisection*. New York: New York Anti-
Vivisection Society, [1903?].

Unti, Bernard. "'The Doctors Are so Sure That They Only Are Right':
The Rockefeller Institute and the Defeat of Vivisection Reform in
New York, 1908–1914." In *Creating a Tradition of Biomedical Re-
search: Contributions to the History of the Rockefeller University*, edited

by Darwin H. Stapleton, 175–89. New York: Rockefeller University Press, 2004.

Walker, Alice Chen. "Bringing the Laboratory Dog Home." *Humanimalia* 4, no. 2 (Spring 2013): 101–29.

Wegener, Frederick. "Few Things More Womanly and Noble: Elizabeth Stuart Phelps and the Advent of the Woman Doctor in America." *Legacy* 22, no. 1 (2005): 1–17.

Willard, Frances Elizabeth. *Woman and Temperance: Or, the Work and Workers of the Woman's Christian Temperance Union.* Hartford, Conn.: James Betts, 1883.

Trixy

Elizabeth Stuart Phelps

"Cruel is the world.
Then be thou kind."

Note

This book is a story. Although it verges towards one of the great tragedies of the day, the facts with which the tale is intervolved have been used in subordination so severe that it is due the truth to say: the scientific incidents herein related have their counter-parts in history. To each one could be added its superlative, in some cases often repeated. If TRIXY were a polemic, there might be presented a variety of authentic physiological diversions as sad as they would seem to be incredible. Such being the material of the apostle rather than of the artist, these pages have been closed to scenes too painful for admission to them.

Yet a novel, which cannot be a homily, may be an illumination. This one approaches regions whose very existence is unknown to the majority of readers, and doubted by many intelligent and kind-hearted people. I take this opportunity of saying that I am familiar with the map of these dark sections of life and know whereof I write.

E.S.P.W.

"Mercy and truth are met together."

Chapter I

—⁂—

The sun struggled to enter the windows of the lecture-room. The tall adjoining building prevented this. The shaft of light stopped on the window sill, and wavered with an uncertain and troubled air.

It was November, and one bare bough from a neighboring tree pointed straight at the glass. Beyond, the sky was blue and beneficent. The wind was quietly rising, and the bough moved like a finger extended in silent admonition.

Some such thought as this occurred to the second student in the tenth row. The lecture-room was in the form of an amphitheatre, the seats rising in tiers. Young Steele could see the professor's desk and table quite distinctly, as, in fact, could every man in the room. Our student was twenty-one. He was rather a handsome fellow in his way, with a good head, and forehead well developed over the eyes. These were gray and kindly, but set a little near together. His face was more finished than the faces of the students about him. His mouth was not coarse, and his features were agreeable. He had the bearing of good birth and breeding. At this time he was not destitute of imagination, and his heart surged with the fervors of youth and of science. He was at the beginning of his professional career. He had graduated at a neighboring college with honors, not five months ago. He had been but a few weeks a member of the medical school. His studies up to this time had been of a rather pleasant, preliminary nature. He had made as yet no friends in the upper classes, and few in his own, so that he knew little of what was going on in other parts of the building.

Olin Steele had not chosen his profession lightly. He was capable of ideals, and at this period of his life he cherished them. Nor had he abandoned what is known as religious aspiration. By healing men's bodies, he meant to heal their souls. How could human utility rise to finer heights? By nature gentle and tender, he felt that he loved science for her nobler possibilities, and would rejoice in all those investigations in which he elected to be led. To this lad, life was not only sacred, it was adorable. The vital spark was the bond between God and man. To preserve this bond he believed to be a holy privilege. Steele considered himself fortunately fitted for the profession which he had chosen. He was like a worshiper between whom and his idol a faint cloud floats. His attitude towards his calling was at once aesthetic and devout. His professor was his high priest.

The lecture-room was filling rapidly. The boys came in laughing and talking. Some had their cigarettes in their mouths, for the professor had not yet arrived. There was a certain tension in the air that would have been noticeable to a fine observer. Some of the students had a constrained look, and others exhibited a species of nervousness.

Olin Steele sat very quietly. Now and then he glanced at the door by which the lecturer would enter. Some of the fellows chaffed him for his silence, but he scarcely replied. He was absorbed in the subject of the morning's lecture.

He was aroused from his reverie by a small, sharp pain in his neck. A broadside of laughter from the students brought him to his full senses. He then became aware that he was at once scratched and caressed. A little claw clung to his collar, and something fuzzy and soft nestled under his ear. Putting up his hand with the instinct to protect the small, he clutched a puff of warm life, and was greeted in return by a little purr.

"What the—" began Steele. "Who's putting kittens down my back?"

He turned completely around, and his eyes met those of a classmate who regarded him mockingly. The newcomer was short, ill-favored, and muscular. His hair was red and coarse, and stood up like a broom from his forehead. His eyebrows and lashes were too pale to be visible. His complexion was muddy, his ears prominent, and his mouth low.

"Oh, it's you, is it, Bernard? I might have known it," said Steele without cordiality. At the same moment he drew the kitten from his neck to his lap, and began to stroke it. He was rather fond of cats, and the kitten knew it. It began to purr loudly. It was a beautiful maltese kitten, clean and well-brushed; a broad pink ribbon was tied around its gray neck.

"What's this?" demanded Steele, "a class mascot? Where shall we keep it? Where did you get it, Bernard?"

"Oh," said Bernard, "I—it—I picked it up; that is, it followed me."

"Couldn't keep away from you?" suggested one of the fellows.

"Where did it matriculate?" asked another.

"Never you mind," retorted Bernard, with an unpleasant wink. "It will matriculater."

The kitten was now quite at home with Steele, who began to analyze his classmate's pun with vague apprehension. Olin's hand closed over the little creature protectingly. With a sinuous motion it turned on its back, and daintily began to claw. It exhibited all the graceful and exasperating coquetry of its race. It withdrew, it challenged, it kissed, it purred, it scratched, with that bewildering inconsistency which makes a kitten the most fascinating and inconsequent creature in the animal kingdom.

"What are you going to do with it?" asked Steele abruptly.

The students had now formed a circle about him, and the kitten looked confidingly from face to face.

"Oh, I don't know," replied Bernard. "I haven't made up my mind."

"I understand we're short of material," observed a man carelessly. "The frogs have struck."

"What!" cried Steele.

Several hands had stretched out to caress the kitten, who, pleased with the hospitality of the lecture-room, was now playing from shoulder to shoulder, like a squirrel from bough to bough.

"Let me have it." Steele got to his feet.

"No, you don't!" replied Bernard. "Whose cat is it, anyhow?"

"Not yours!" said Steele quickly. "Tell me where you got it. I'll take it back. It must live right around here. It is a lady's pet. Look at the ribbon!—Let me have it!" urged Steele, appealing from Bernard to the students.

These glanced from the happy kitten to their red-headed classmate doubtfully. Over their faces warring expressions chased. Most of them looked troubled and sorry.

"Oh, come off, Bernard," said one of the fellows. "Let him have the cat!"

The speaker held the kitten towards Steele's outstretched hands; but Bernard's cold fingers, interrupting, closed upon the little shrinking creature.

"I'll take care of it," he said sullenly.

The kitten hesitated a moment, and then looked into the young man's mutinous face, and purred insinuatingly.

"There!" cried Steele, dropping to his seat. "It trusts you. Now take it back."

His clouded face cleared as Bernard turned away. When the kitten was taken from the room, some of the students applauded slightly; others exchanged significant looks, and were silent.

The room was now full. The lecturer was already overdue. He appeared suddenly in a fresh, white blouse. He began to talk at once, without any preliminaries, upon the subject of the day.

It was the first time that the class had met the professor of physiology in the amphitheatre, and they were singularly attentive. The subject of the lecture was elementary, and one which text-books have always amply illustrated.

Steele listened conscientiously. He had been a high-honor man, and his industrious pencil flew over his note-book. He did not find the topic abstruse, and he was rather disappointed at its simplicity. He glanced at some of the nearest students to see if the subject seemed as clear to them. Meanwhile Bernard had returned to the room, and had resumed his seat, which was directly behind Steele. The kitten was gone, and Steele drew a breath of relief. His eyes sought the window, and he noticed that the November sun had clouded. The wind had now risen, and the bare bough knocked on the glass. A pair of white pigeons flew across, and one of them, pausing, dropped to the sill of the window, and seemed to peer for a moment into the room.

"Look at the dove!" whispered one of the boys.

"That's no dove. That's a pigeon," sneered Bernard, from behind.

The professor, annoyed by the whisperings paused and shot a reproving glance at the class. The white bird flew away.

"And now, gentlemen," continued the professor, "we have reached a point in our studies where experimental illustration becomes a clear necessity. I have endeavored up to this time to impress upon your minds the fundamental nature of the great discovery with which we deal. I have tried to show you how"—he proceeded to explain learnedly what he had tried to do. "But," he pursued, "in our profession, gentlemen, unsupported theory—I might add, unsupported fact—may confuse the mind of the student more than it enlightens. I have now been lecturing to you for half an hour upon this basic principle, yet probably many of you, possibly most of you, have received but an obscure impression of the beautiful workings of this great law. Gentlemen, am I right? Is this not so?"

"Yes, sir!" came from various parts of the room.

Steele looked about him with a touch of intellectual scorn on his parted lips.

"Why, no, sir," he said respectfully. "If you will excuse me for saying so, I have found your explanation of the subject remarkably clear. I think I understand it."

"I should like to see it demonstrated," interpolated Bernard, in a strident voice.

The professor smiled blandly. He paused, laid aside his notes, and beckoned to his assistant. This person left the room, and passed into the adjoining laboratory. The professor examined his instruments and apparatus. He touched them with deft and craving fingers.

"Ah, gentlemen," he announced with an expression of something like pleasure, "here is our subject."

The laboratory door opened silently. The returning assistant, who held something before him in his outstretched hands, reached the professor's table before young Steele had seen what the man carried. Half a hundred students caught their breaths. It was their first experience of this sort, and most of them were still soft, kindhearted lads, fresh from their homes, where dogs sprang down the doorsteps to meet them, and kittens played with skeins of yarn held on mother's or on sisters' hands.

But Steele, unconscious that he did so, got to his feet. His face had blanched. His lips, drawn over his teeth, quivered. A vein in his temple throbbed.

Before him, on the operating board, strapped down, lay a little downy form. Seeing it in its unnatural position, one's sense of its beauty gave way to a sense of its color and size. The kitten was gray and small. It seemed to Steele's horrified eyes the smallest kitten he had ever seen. By some mistake on the part of the assistant, a ribbon, caught under the body of the animal, hung over the edge of the board. This ribbon was pink.

"No! No!" gasped Steele. "Not that one!"

"Oh, shut up, and sit down!" growled Bernard from behind.

But Steele did not sit down. He swayed slightly on his feet. A sick faintness surged upon him. Every fibre of his body and soul protested. For the medical student had a soul, and it was young and sensitive.

The professor, who had been regarding his subject critically, now took up his instruments. Steele stood staring. The kitten swam before his gaze. It seemed to him to turn its eyes (for it could not turn its head) towards him. He felt that it sought protection of him. He wheeled, and scorched Bernard with a look. The room grew dark about him, and he made for the door.

"Damn you!" he said.

Swaying and groping, he tried the handle. The door was locked. The professor laid down his instruments. In taking up this department with his junior classes he was not without experience in the reflex action of unsullied natures. He was always considerate of this juvenile weakness which he knew that time and himself would train away.

"Go for the janitor," he whispered to his assistant. "The boy is ill. Let him out."

When Steele found himself in the outer air, he sat down on the granite steps of the college. He was still faint and giddy. He was so ashamed of himself for his weakness that he could have cried. He put his face in his hands, and ground his teeth. He fancied himself the jest of every student in the amphitheatre. This intolerable thought drove the blood to his head; and his physical weakness, which otherwise might have lasted longer, fled before his keen emotion. He started to his feet, and stood hesitating. Should he return to the lecture-room?

Swiftly there seemed to sweep before him that pretty fluff of maltese down—the broad, pink ribbon—the little gymnast, leaping like a squirrel from shoulder to shoulder—its cuddling touch beneath his ear—its happy and confiding purr; he thought of its pulsating vitality, its spark of divinity. As swiftly, there smote upon his consciousness a vision of that warm, live, small creature—as it was, now.

"I can't go back!" he cried; then in a different tone, "I won't go back!"

He ran down the long gray steps and into the street. This he crossed quickly, but with an aimless movement. His mind was in a whirlpool of indecision. He seemed to be swirling nearer and nearer—to what? A gulf? or a rescue? The familiar blue cars of his suburban street passed him without appealing to his attention. He walked because he must walk, and he walked a long time. It occurred to him at last that he was headed towards home, and, with a clutch at the heart, he felt that it was the only place where he could go. By this time the pallid sun had been gulped by massing clouds, and a dark storm was imminent. Olin bent his head, and pushed his way into it. The surcharged air, like his surcharged emotion, lashed him on. He felt that no tempest could be fierce enough to flush the imagination that tormented him. It seemed to him that he would have offered up his soul if he could have been born without sensitiveness—like that big-eared fellow for instance. He was lacerated, and he must be healed. He pushed on mechanically. The blue cars passed him. Before he was aware of it, he had reached the group of stately elms at the corner of his father's street. He had tramped six miles. As he turned in at the long avenue, his dog—a fine St. Bernard—leaped upon him with boisterous caresses. He was so absorbed that he did not return them, and the dog, drooping, followed him wistfully.

Olin fitted his latch-key with trembling hand, and went into his father's house. The dog remained on the porch. Afterwards he remembered that he must have shut the door in Barry's face.

"Why, my son!" his mother called from somewhere, "I didn't expect you until night."

Olin murmured something unintelligibly, tossed off his dripping hat, and went upstairs to his own room. Then he locked the door, and there he remained until night. His mother came up and knocked gently.

"I am sorry, mother," he pleaded, "I can't see you now. Please let me alone."

His sister, who was a very modern girl, came and whistled like a boy through the keyhole.

"Go away, Jess," he said, "don't bother me."

These were women, and easy to manage. The boy reflected that his father and brother were yet to come home, and that with them he must absolutely reckon.

At dinner time nothing had been heard from him. His troubled mother, with the pathetic patience of her sex, had watched for the light in his windows, but these were still dark. She could contain her anxiety no longer, and he heard the rustle of her skirts at his door. She knocked timidly.

"Dear Olin," she said, "let me come in."

He rose at once and admitted her. The room was dark, except for the glow of the open fire. She saw his wet coat sprawled on a chair before him. He had returned to the lounge on which he had evidently been lying all the afternoon. His bright-colored bath-blanket was drawn over him.

His mother sat down on the edge of the couch, and took one of his hands in both of hers.

"You're feverish," she said. "You have taken cold. What is the matter, Olin? Tell me all about it."

"Mother!" cried the young man, sitting up sharply against the pillows of the couch, "I can't go back to that medical school. I never can. I am going into business. I hate them both!"

His mother was silent for so long that he repeated his phrase mechanically: "I never can!"

"I am sure, my son, that you must have a good reason for this unexpected decision," replied Mrs. Steele, with an agitation of which she gave no evidence whatever. She had an unobtrusive, well-bred voice, but it was as monotonous as a metronome.

"Reason!" Olin exploded, "I should think I had!"

He was about to tell the whole story, when there was a tramping in the hall outside his door. His father and brother came into the room, led by the sister to whom he had denied entrance. With a twist of his fingers, Mr. Steele turned up a light.

"What's the matter here?" he cried. "Are you sick, Olin? I thought this was your night for being in?"

"I am not going back, sir," replied Olin manfully. He got to his feet and faced the most formidable obstacle that a young man can meet or conquer—the opposition of his entire family. In a few blazing words he told his story.

His sister interrupted it now and then with girlish outcries (these were ejaculations rather of incredulity than of sympathy) and his mother visibly winced. But the two men exchanged glances, and it was Olin's elder brother who spoke first:

"I assure you, Olly," he said, "you'll get over that, very soon. You must have been a little out of order. I felt so, once."

"You felt so once, and you don't feel so any longer," persisted Olin, "and that's my very point. I don't mean to get where you are. Since you've been teaching biology you're not the same fellow you used to be, Dick. You can do anything and not turn a hair."

"I am sure," said the girl, with a hard lifting of the eyelids that was quite natural to her, "that it can't be as bad as you think."

"Oh, do be still, Jess," said Olin testily.

"You can be squeamish in any business you undertake, you know, Olin," observed his father. Mr. Steele spoke gravely and not unkindly. "I understand," he proceeded, "that the medical profession is the noblest in the world. I should be disappointed if you abandoned it. How is it, Dick?" He turned to his oldest son. "Are these things really as bad as Olin thinks? I don't remember that you ever mentioned it?"

"Science today is based upon such experiments," replied the young professor of biology firmly. "Modern medical science is founded upon the rock of comparative physiology, and it's no use Olin's beating his head against it."

"Are you sure, my dear," asked Mrs. Steele feebly, "that Olin is entirely wrong?"

The young professor flushed. "I should think I ought to know," he said.

Richard Steele, senior, stood thoughtfully silent. His commercial importance was enviable, and his social position was that which his wife, whose family was as influential as his fortune, had brought him. But it must be admitted that he felt himself at a loss in a biological or pathological direction. If it had been Assam Pekoe, or Young Hyson—but bacteria and antisepsis were out of his line. The tea merchant looked from one of his highly educated sons to

12

the other in a perplexity which he would on no account have acknowledged. When he spoke, he did so slowly and seriously.

"I have told you what I think, now, Olin. But you are old enough to judge for yourself. Take what time you need to decide this matter to your satisfaction. Isn't dinner ready, my dear?" He turned to his wife with a courtly smile.

Olin stood at bay before the four people whom he loved best in the world. The two gentlemen and the ladies were in dinner dress. Standing there in his shirt-sleeves, with that ridiculous bathrobe over his shoulders, he felt himself at the distinct disadvantage which external trifles may create. His purpose had not wavered, but the power to express it had weakened.

"I've told you how I feel," he said desperately. Instinctively his eyes sought his mother's. Hers answered him with an ineffectual sympathy.

"Don't you want me to send Tibbs up with your dinner?" she asked affectionately.

"Thank you, Mummy, dear, I am not dry yet. You see it will take so long to dress."

The girl had already gone downstairs. The two gentlemen followed. The lad's mother lingered for a moment. She put her arm around his neck, and laid her cheek to his.

"Was it a very pretty kitty, dear?" she whispered.

The boy put his head upon her shoulder and began to sob.

"Oh, mother—it was so small. Oh, mother, mother! It was damnable!"

Now they had all gone away—except Tibbs, who brought up the dinner and set the tray down on the little table by the lounge, as if he were serving a sick person.

Olin tried to eat, but could not. At every effort some disturbing memory of the morning's experience or the afternoon's emotion prevented his healthy young appetite. He flung himself back upon the lounge, and lay there, face down, in the pillows. He was torn by the first great moral conflict of his life. It seemed to him almost like a living thing, some savage thing that had been endowed with intelligence, but not with mercy. It was to this excited and exhausted lad as if he could feel its claws upon his heart. In the actual sense of the word he writhed beneath it.

"I won't!" he cried. "I will not go back to that—I never can. I never will!"

While he lay there wrestling with his angels, something tried the closed door. A slight push, a bumping scratch, and a long whine pleaded for admission. Olin opened the door at once, and the St. Bernard came panting in.

"Why, Barry," he said, "I'm glad to see you. I'm afraid I was rather uncivil to you, too, when I came home—out there . . . How it did storm, Barry!—And how it storms now!"

The dog lifted serious ears towards the window, which shook beneath the malignant rain.

Downstairs Olin's sister was singing at the piano—some foolish thing. The smoke of his father's cigar and his brother's came up through the closed door.

"We've got to have it out alone, Barry," said Olin aloud. "They can't understand, Barry, can they?"

Olin put his arms about the big dog, and looked rather piteously into his eyes. Barry kissed his master, but with dignity. In the drawing-room the girl had left the piano, but while Olin sat with his arms about Barry's neck another hand brushed the keys, and the low strains of a fine rendering of Tennyson's great prelude breathed through the house.

"That's mother, Barry," said Olin. "Jess never plays anything sacred."

His mother did not sing; she was not young enough; but she played delicately and well. The young man's memory fitted the words to the chords by which, he thought she seemed to be trying to speak to him.

"Strong Son of God, immortal Love!"

Olin respected the religion of his mother, and he listened, not without reverence.

"There's something in it, Barry," he said. "Some time I'll make up my mind how much. Come, Barry! Say, Barry, what shall we do?"

Barry observed him solemnly.

CHAPTER II

—⚍—

If there were one thing more than any other to which Miss Lauriat cultivated a robust objection, it was colored teas; and this one was yellow.

"Orange corset covers on the electric bulbs, and lemon petticoats on the lamps," she thought. "Ochre bonnets on the candles, and corn-satin sashes on the tables! This is no place for me—I am going."

She had already sacrificed to this occasion an hour of her impatient young life; she felt that she had better uses for it. So far, she had seen only the too familiar faces of her social system. The astronomy was old, and it had become wearisome. She sought her hostess to take her leave. A gentleman, evidently bent on the same errand, retreated a step or two, to give her precedence.

"Wait a minute, Miriam," said the lady, "before you go I must present—" She turned to the hesitating man, and introduced him with that indifference to the personal cognomen which is characteristic of social elocution.

The two accepted their fate resignedly.

"Do you like these colored things, Dr. Reel?" began Miss Lauriat promptly.

"Candidly," replied the young man, "I don't think pink teas are the final expression of existence."

"But this one is yellow."

"Is it?" He looked at the decorations with the unseeing gaze of a man whose color-blindness is not that of the optic nerve. "I thought they were always pink."

Miss Lauriat laughed merrily.

"Is the palette of your life couleur de rose? Fortunate man!"

A scarcely perceptible change of expression replied to her.

"Do you know," she said promptly, "I was just going."

"So was I," he returned, looking straight at her, "but even a man may change his mind."

Miss Lauriat was a tall girl, so that her eyes were quite on a level with those of the young man. She answered his look with the amused indifference with which she was accustomed to receive admiration. Her air of distinction was enhanced by her clinging black dress (according to the code, she should have ceased to "mourn" for her father some time ago), through whose sleeves and high yoke of lace her throat and arms gleamed faintly. Her hair was black, but her eyes, though dark, were blue. Her expression was at once earnest and playful. She was a woman of twenty-seven; but she had kept a certain girlish look of which she herself was unconscious.

The two talked for a little, as people do at such functions, drifting as they did so leisurely towards the door. Beneath the inevitable persiflage each discerned a certain seriousness in the other.

"Now, Dr. Peel," she said at last, "I really must go. I have an important engagement."

"A blue tea, I suppose, this time?" His eyes mocked while his mouth smiled.

"They make it in an earthen teapot where I am going, and steep it all day, and drink it out of a bowl—with condensed milk."

"That seems somehow familiar," said the doctor. "Perhaps we are going to the same place."

"Who are you?" asked the young lady outright, "and what do you do?"

"For one thing," replied the physician lightly, "I am a member of the Board of Health. This is my last day in that illustrious position—which I have resigned. I go out of office tomorrow. By the way," he added, with the air of a man who wanted to escape the topic, "I think my father used to know yours."

"Oh, we're all in the same set, I suppose," replied the young lady indifferently. She did not ask any questions. He flushed slightly at this obvious omission, bowed, and left her.

Her carriage was waiting, and she made her way to it as quickly as she could. As she gathered up her short train and stepped in, she hesitated.

"I'll tell you in a minute, Matthew; I haven't quite made up my mind. How late is it?" She glanced at the carriage clock. "I think there's time. I must see Dan. How is it about taking the horses down that alley? Do you think they're equal to it?"

"They was snowballed into highsterics last time," replied the coachman cautiously.

"But I don't suppose you're dressed for walkin', Miss?"

Miss Lauriat glanced at her thin, long dress, over which she had closely folded her carriage cloak.

"I'm afraid I'm not," she said. "If you think you can manage— No! Drive home first. I can get ready while you're turning around. It is not dark yet, you see. We can't have Dan evicted for a few dollars' rent—can we, Matthew?"

"You're the only friend the gossoon's got," said Matthew, with his forefinger at his hat. He drove rapidly; Miss Lauriat's house was but two blocks removed, in fact, from the yellow tea; and within five minutes she was running up her own steps with the girlish energy of her perfect health and absorption in subjects outside of herself. In the vestibule the parlor-maid offered information: Mr. Surbridge was in the library—him and Mrs. Jeffries.

"Don't tell them I've been in, Maggie," said the young lady hurriedly. "It's a business call, and they won't need me till I get back. If they ask—say I've had to go right out again, and Auntie will please invite Mr. Surbridge to stay to dinner. I'll be back in twenty—no, in twenty-five minutes."

She changed her dress with the deft swiftness of a young lady who is independent of her maid,—making a pretty transformation from chiffon and lace to broadcloth and furs,—ran downstairs quietly, and Matthew whirled her away.

It was the middle of March, and still light. One of the heavy snowstorms characteristic of the month—swiftly coming and as swiftly flowing—had exasperated the city with a foot of now grimy slush. Miss Lauriat, with the sense of color which was strong in her, thought of country fields and lawns where the deep blue light, never seen on sea or land, answered to the eye that loved it, and knew when to seek it. It could be found only in late snow-falls, or after sundown. In the east side of the town, whither Matthew was driving, the streets were not cleared, and the horses soon began to put their noses down and drag. The man stopped them at the head of a black alley. Driving the wheels upon the sidewalk, he let the young lady out. Matthew had the resigned expression of a coachman whose mistress is hopelessly given over to philanthropy. He was quite used to this sort of thing.

"I shall be gone fifteen minutes," said the young lady. "Wait for me just here."

She picked her way more quickly than daintily down the filthy street. (It went by the name of Blind Alley.) She did so with the ease of one who was quite accustomed to it. Here and there she was recognized with the sullen respect or the servile flattery of people who have to be benefited against their wills. She stopped before a large wooden building, recently painted, well-ordered, and conspicuous among its neighbors for a front door that shut, light in the entries, unbroken windows, and fire-escapes. As she put her foot upon the lowest step the door opened, there was a penetrating hospital whiff, and a gentleman followed.

"You can't come in here," said a deep voice gruffly. "Nobody can. I'm going to station a policeman at the door to keep every one in—and every one out."

As the speaker stood with his back against the closed door, he suddenly lifted his hat.

"You! I beg your pardon; I did not recognize you."

"What are you doing in my house, Dr. Beal?" Miss Lauriat let the words out slowly and haughtily. She ascended the steps, and would have brushed by him. But he faced her with his hand upon the latch.

"There is a case of diphtheria here. I'm going to have the card up immediately."

"I can't believe it!" cried Miss Lauriat hotly. "I know every family in the building. I keep them very clean. The sanitary conditions are excellent. It is impossible. I've got to see one of my tenants immediately. My agent was going to evict him—Please stand aside, sir. I am going in."

"The Board of Health has taken possession of your tenement, madam, and I am very sorry, but I must insist."

"So must I," she retorted. "The house is mine."

"But the responsibility is mine," he flashed, reddening. "You cannot come in."

It was now a duel between the citizen and the state, and the girl yielded perforce.

"I am sorry to have to use my authority," continued the physician in a different tone. "The laws, you know, are strict; and life," he hesitated, "is precious."

"Oh, I suppose you can't help yourself," replied Miss Lauriat, not very graciously. She took a sudden step or two backwards and lifted her face towards the windows, most of which were crowded with weeping women and angry men.

"You poor people!" she cried, "I can't help it, and you know I can't. I would if I could. I would do anything. Who is it that's sick? Where is Dan Badger? I must speak with Dan."

Her upturned throat, showing white through the hurrying twilight, rose from her furs like a carving by Canova set upon velvet. Her impassioned face, fired by the beauty of selflessness and pity, swam before the doctor's eyes. It puzzled him as much as it thrilled him.

A woman's voice, shrill and sobbing, came down from above. "It's Cady's Molly—Dan's right behind you, Miss. He's lucky. He's outside. I wish't we was!"

"I won't forget you," Miss Lauriat called up in her rich, generous voice. "I'll see the doctors. I'll send a nurse. I'll do all I can. Perhaps there isn't anything in it after all. It may not be diphtheria at all! Perhaps it's only a sore throat."

The doctor smiled at this unconscious insult to his profession and his office; but the tenants were comforted.

"Here I be, Miss," said a plaintive voice behind her.

"Oh, Dan!" The young lady turned quickly. An undersized, crippled lad, leaning on one crutch, stood in the muddy snow, watching her like a dog. "So Mr. Smithers was going to turn you out, was he? Why didn't you pay your rent?"

"Couldn't," said Dan patiently. "Trixy's been sick with a cough."

"Where is Trixy now?"

"Gone to market for supper—acrosst the alley. I'm a watchin'."

Still with his back to the door, the doctor silently observed the scene. He was waiting for his assistant to come back with an officer.

"You can't go back there, Dan," said the lady ruefully. "This gentleman won't let you. Somebody's sick inside. What will you do?"

"We'll get in somewheres," said Dan sweetly; "there's places. Don't you fret, Miss Laurie."

"Oh, I can't have that sort of thing," said Miss Lauriat decidedly. "You and Trixy come to the coach house this evening. We'll put you up, somehow."

The officer arrived at this moment, and the physician gave way, escaping from his uncomfortable position with evident embarrassment. As Miss Lauriat turned to go back through the darkening alley, he joined her timidly. She noticed that he kept as wide a space between them as the narrow and now freezing sidewalk permitted.

"I am really very sorry," he observed with a touch of something like humility which sat awkwardly upon his dogmatic manner, "that I was forced to annoy you so."

"It does not signify," answered Miss Lauriat, without cordiality. He did not reply, and they had walked in silence and constraint for some twenty paces, when something whirred through the air, and the young lady stopped and staggered. A big chunk of half-frozen slush, shot from an angry hand in the quarantined building, and aimed at the retreating Board of Health, had missed, and hit the girl. A tiny trickle of blood stirred over her soft cheek.

"Oh, damn them!" cried the doctor between his ground teeth,— "I beg your pardon!—Where are you hurt?"

"Nowhere, I think," replied Miss Lauriat quickly. "Really, it is nothing—just a scratch. It's only my ear—a little. They didn't mean to. You know they didn't. Oh, how sorry they will be!"

She put up her soft handkerchief, and brushed away the warm stain on her face.

"Get out of this as fast as you can!" commanded the doctor savagely. He hurried her along. "It's no place for you, anyhow," he persisted. "Why do you come here? what do you do it for?"

They had now come in sight of the carriage, where Matthew, in his robes, cape, and cap, sat like an Esquimau in a fur bag. Something in this little touch of ease and luxury caused the doctor to draw his breath with quick relief. At least she was now quite safe,—and really not hurt; no, plainly not hurt, as she said. Meant to hurl an ugly blow upon the Board of Health, the missile had cost the lady but a scratch.

"What do I do it for?" repeated Miss Lauriat, without looking at him. "I doubt if I could make you understand why, Dr. Reel."

She put her gray-gloved hand upon the open carriage door. His eyes, which were not of a warm tint, scrutinized her in chill perplexity.

"Pardon me, Miss Lauriat," observed the young man, "since you are not hurt—are you quite sure?"

"Perfectly."

"And you do not need any help, professional or any kind? And you do not wish me to accompany you home?—I can ride outside—I would not expose you to the least risk, of course."

"It is quite unnecessary, thank you, Dr. Deal."

"Then allow me to say," protested the young man, "that my name is not Deal. Neither is it Beal, nor was it ever Peel. And

I particularly object to being called Dr. Reel. My name, at your service, is Steele."

"Thank you, Dr. Steele," repeated Miss Lauriat, laughing heartily. "I will try to remember."

Laughing too, he bowed and left her. As he turned, standing bareheaded before her, she began at once talking to Matthew.

"Oh, Matthew, before I forget! I've invited Dan and Trixy to come and stay till we can find a place for them. You can put them up somehow, in the coach house—can't you?"

Matthew assented to this astounding proposition with the puzzled patience of a man whom no sociological caprice could stagger. Miss Miriam was capable of so much worse than this, that Matthew counted himself lucky to escape with entertaining Dan and Trixy for a few days. He remembered the fall when she brought home from the shore an old woman who had never seen the city, or been on a railroad before; installed her in the big guest room that had (Maggie to witness) the best lace spread; brought the old lady to the table with the family, and required the servants to wait on her for a week; which, it must be admitted, they did with attention and amusement, as if they had been participating in a pretty play.

It was quite dusk when Miriam got home. She lingered only to give a few orders about the comfort of the crippled lad, and went at once to the library, where her aunt and her lawyer were still deeply engaged.

Surbridge, at the herald of her first footfall, had risen, and stood awaiting her with that perfect command of expression for which his calling equipped him. Yet one could suppose that he was by nature spontaneous and candid, and that, like most men, he had been modeled by his avocation quite as much as he had moulded it. His warm, dark eyes warred with his firm lip, and his quietness of manner was of the sort which may reveal the presence or conceal the absence of ordered strength.

At this moment, for example, Miriam knew—she had known him all her life—that he was nagged to exasperation by his professional call upon Mrs. Percy B. Jeffries, who was the fussiest investor, and the most unmanageable client on the young attorney's list.

Miss Lauriat extended her hand with an unconscious expression of condolence.

"Auntie, I hope you've cultivated the sweet quality of mercy for Mr. Surbridge? Between the two of us I should think he would regret that he was ever admitted to the bar. Last time we kept him an hour drawing up a lease that could have been written in five minutes. And now—Has she decided yet how to place that two hundred and fifty dollars, Phil?"

"It is one thousand," replied Mrs. Jeffries severely, pushing her papers about the library table; she stirred them as if she were making a pudding.

"Pardon me," suggested Surbridge gently. "You will lose those X. and R.A. coupons. Allow me—" He secured the X. and R.A.'s (these were wafting towards the fireplace) with a motion that seemed in itself a tribute to the business qualities or the personal quality of his client. He had the deference of manner which, while it may be a stimulant to young women, is a cordial to an old one.

"One would suppose," complained Mrs. Jeffries, "that I was ever inconsiderate of Mr. Surbridge!"

Miriam's eyes waltzed. But those of the young lawyer met hers sedately; neither the music nor the merriment in him responded. She experienced something like a sense of being rebuked. She thought: "Phil is a loyal fellow. Poor Phil!"

Miriam stood between firelight and gaslight, still in her furs and her small black hat. Her long cloak had fallen from her shoulders. Her color was warm and fine. Her young face and high head, touched with a swift humility which sometimes beatified as much as it beautified her, drooped a little, and the flare of the fire revealed, when she turned her soft throat, a small crimson stain below the right ear.

Surbridge uttered an inarticulate exclamation.

"You're hurt!" he added audibly.

But Mrs. Percy B. Jeffries snapped a rubber strap around her X. and R.A. bonds before she put on her glasses to examine her niece's cheek.

"It is no more than we can expect," she said without agitation. "I live in constant fear, Philip, of that child's life. Such places—such people—such risks! If she's gone two hours beyond her time, I telephone to the hospitals. I am always conscious that I may find her there in some mangled condition. Turn more to the light, Miriam—so."

"I'm not hurt in the least!" cried Miriam angrily. "I told you so!"

"Excuse me," said Surbridge, "you did not tell us anything about it."

"Well, I will," replied Miriam, in a tired voice. "It's all the same."

"Maggie will get the Pond's Extract," decidedly said Mrs. Jeffries, with her hand on the bell.

"Oh, Aunt Cornelia!" pleaded Miriam rather crossly. "I'm going right upstairs. I'll take care of myself. All I want is a drop of water. If you don't let me alone, I won't tell you how it happened. I'm not hurt in the least. Why don't you believe me, when I say so?"

She threw off her furs, and, standing with one hand on the knob of the dark door, began, rather reluctantly, to give the story of the afternoon. Surbridge heard it without a word. But Mrs. Jeffries mused:

"Steele? Steele? I wonder which Steeles—the Theodores or the Richards?"

"This must be one of Richard Steele's sons," suggested Surbridge thoughtfully. "He has two. I know them both. One of them is rather a brilliant fellow—the other is slower. Can you describe the man you met?" He addressed Miriam with more abruptness than was natural to him.

"No," replied Miriam, after an almost imperceptible pause. "I don't know why I can't describe him, but I can't. I think he was rather pale—and tall, and stern. It seems to me his eyes were gray, and cold, and perhaps set a little near together. He said he was a member of the Board of Health."

"That," answered Philip Surbridge, "is the new professor of physiology at Galen. He has held the assistant chair for a year, and now he takes the place left vacant by the old professor's death. He is considered one of the most brilliant young men who ever came back from Berlin and Vienna."

The lawyer gathered three more X. and R.A. coupons which Mrs. Jeffries had contrived to whisk into the waste basket, and filed them neatly in a small envelope, carefully inscribed with his client's name.

"That," he added gravely, "is Olin. It is Olin Steele."

CHAPTER III

—⚹—

When Miss Lauriat's carriage stumbled through the freezing slush and staggered away from him, Dr. Steele stood for a moment with his lifted hat in his hand. He could not have told why he did so, and recalling himself with a slight change of color, walked rapidly away. He did not go home, but with the impulse which leads a man to delay impending thought or feeling by distraction, turned in the direction of his club. There he dressed and dined. He sat at what was known as the doctors' table, by courtesy and custom relegated to members who represented his profession. The usual crowd was there, and fell into the usual talk; that evening it was something about the new bacillus. Steele took but little part in it; he was taciturn to a marked degree. When a rising young specialist commented on his silence he retorted: "I don't feel like talking shop tonight," and changed the subject to the art school that had been opened near the medical building.

The specialist stared a little; he retreated before the topic, with which he was unfamiliar; he regarded art somewhat as he did Christianity, homeopathy, or psychical research; one of the inevitable delusions of an uninstructed class of minds.

Dr. Steele left the club as soon as he had smoked, and went directly home. A storm of wind and sleet had come up, and when he plunged into it from his blue street-car, some gad-fly of association stung into his brain the acute remembrance of another evening, ten years ago, when he had come home in a storm,—it seemed to him a storm which had lasted ever since.

The tense experience at the amphitheatre, the disturbed scenery, the agitated actors at home, returned to him like the impression of an old play, a good deal set with mock thunder and mechanical weather. He recalled it with a smile as small and as sharp as a scalpel. A something between disdain and incredulity cut into his face. He thought of that young being, afire with aspiration, molten with sympathy, to whom his profession was a veiled god, and its worship a beautiful cult—that rather noble, altogether pitiable boy.

"Poor fellow!" he said; as one says it of a cripple or any defective who is worsted in the scheme of things. And yet so unmanageable are the immaterial laws, he had this perfectly unreasonable and unwelcome idea about the storm, as if, as we say, the tempest that had set in that night, ten years ago, had never been laid.

To family preference, to professional influence, to the accepted view of things, he had succumbed. The powers and principalities of the reigning science had arrayed themselves against the student's passionate protest,—and what was the outcry of one lad? He had "no language but the cry"; and that had been stifled almost in the utterance. From the hour when he had said, "Yes, Father, I will go back," he had never lifted his young voice again. Yet in brain and heart the winds had gone warring on. In every cavern of his being turmoil had raved. For now a comfortable time, as a man estimates time and comfort, he believed himself to have escaped the whirlwind. Was there an undertow in the air, as in the sea? What was this suction which dragged him back?

In the course of Olin Steele's career he had experienced not a few things which it was more agreeable to forget than to remember.

One of these was his flight from the lecture-room to his father's home—he reeling under the first great shock, and hitting out blindly anyhow in the first great moral battle of his life.

"Then," he said aloud, as he splashed through the stiffened snow of his own avenue, "why, then I was a sensitive and devout boy!"

He spoke as if that boy had died. Besides that lad, his father too was gone—which of them had met the kinder fate? Fate hits one man by way of a faulty mitral valve, and another through an enfeebled aspiration. Heart failure counts its thousand victims, but conscience failure its tens of thousands.

Olin had returned from Germany to a changed and colorless home. Since the day when her dead husband was brought to her from the Chamber of Commerce, where he had fallen in the middle of a speech on reciprocity, Mrs. Steele had lapsed into an uncomplaining and incurable invalidism. Her mind, always more gentle than strong, had partaken to some extent of her bodily weakness. She had become a sweet dependant, to be spared everything. It was a long time since Olin had shared anything with her. His sister had left home some years ago; it was his forever unuttered conviction that the girl married to avoid the care of her invalid mother; it was difficult to postulate Jess as in love, under any social syllogism; it amused him that she had married a retired Arctic explorer. His elder brother was still a member of the household. But Dick was considering a call to the presidency of a technical institution in California. The house, now silent and dull, would grow, as Olin reflected when he had time to think of it, stiller and duller; yet he found it difficult to cultivate any acute emotion at the prospect of Dick's leaving him; it did not seem to matter profoundly. What did?

Barry did not come out into the snow to meet his master that March night; for Barry had the reserve of age and rheumatism. But the old dog was waiting in the vestibule. Old dogs, like old men, acquire a patience unnatural to the species, and Barry, probably because he had suffered some physical pain and learned how to bear it, had a pathetic gentleness and reluctance to give trouble. He got up stiffly, and tried to embrace his master, but failing in the power to do so, lapped the bare hand from which Dr. Steele had removed the glove. It was the right hand. Barry sniffed at it critically, seemed to examine it from some point of view not in his power to elucidate, and turned thoughtfully away.

Olin went up at once to his mother's room, kissed her, and talked a little, kindly, as he always did.

"All right, Mummy dear?" he said, as he used to say when he was a boy. But these filial duties were soon fulfilled, and he went down to his own room.

He found Barry there upon the tiger skin before the fire. The grate was bright, and the light in the room was soothing and soft. Olin got into his smoking-jacket and flung himself upon his lounge. After a while he rose and turned the key in the door.

"I may as well have it settled," he thought, "once for all." He did not smoke again, but lay staring at the fire. "Inexplicable, these phenomena," he mused. "As if I hadn't known women enough! Why one specimen should so differentiate—It's inconvenient, look at it anyhow."

Olin Steele was proceeding to apply the scientific method to the state of mental ferment in which he unexpectedly found himself, when he was annoyed by a knock upon his door.

"Well—what is it, Tibbs?"

"It's Dr. Bernard, sir. He wants to know if he can come up."

"No, he can't—that is—yes, he can," replied Olin. "I suppose he must. Show him up, Tibbs."

After all, Olin was not sorry to have his reverie interrupted. It was beginning to be a little too muscular for a reverie, and his second thought welcomed a talk with his assistant.

There was a time in the plastic period when he did not like Bernard, but now that expert young man, by the imperious process of stratification, had become a necessary part of Dr. Steele's official life. Bernard, too, looked older. Ten years had fulfilled the threat of his physiognomy. It was red clay then; it was brick now. His face was coarser than Steele's, as it always had been, and—as it always had been—brutal. He had the eyes of an inquisitor, lowering and shifty. To an ordinary citizen his was a face to be dreaded. It was the type that was common in the sixteenth century. It was broad, flat, and surmounted by a rebellious, fiery mane. But, if his face would inspire dread, his hands gave the layman a nameless apprehension. These were stocky as a blacksmith's and yet the fingers were long and sinuous. The backs of the hands were all muscle, and the palms all grip. These extraordinary hands betrayed enormous power, and suggested an ability to clutch and hold. They looked like a marvelously developed vise.

Dr. Steele rose to meet his visitor. They did not shake hands. As they stood opposite to each other, a close observer who had known them ten years ago would have noticed that a curious, indefinable likeness existed between the two. Bernard had developed into what he was foreordained to be, while Steele had become fitted to a mould that was made for another soul.

"Well, Bernard, what's up now?" Steele asked, with the genial air of a superior. "Barry! Keep still, sir. Go back and lie down."

For Barry had limped up and stood midway of the room, growling. The dog obeyed his master, but sullenly, and returned to the tiger skin. From this vantage he scrutinized the visitor with marked disapproval.

"Frogs!" said Bernard shortly. "Let's have a cigar."

"Anybody else would have waited until it was offered to him," thought Steele as he proffered the Havana. Bernard accepted it without remark. After a few luxurious puffs he observed:

"We're short of them again. A student must have hooked a lot."

"I have my doubts about this private experimentation," said Steele.

"Yes, it's awkward to run out so," admitted the instructor. "You see the frog-man fails to appreciate his opportunity to serve science. He had an order for ten thousand, you remember, from the medical schools of this region. He writes that he never has been able to fill it, and now the damn things are all frozen up. What are the boys going to do? We need fifty on nerve experiments right away."

"Oh, well," said Steele wearily, "it's always something. One can fall back on guinea pigs or rabbits."

He made a visible effort to change the subject, but Bernard did not quickly perceive this; he did so after a while, and rose to go. With his hand on the door he turned his ill-favored smile:

"Say, Professor," he began, showing his teeth, "do you remember that—"

"Oh, drop that!" cried Steele.

The young men parted without further ceremony, and Olin started to lock his door again. But Barry stood in the way. The dog pushed out and stiffly followed the departing guest. Suddenly Barry's growl grew into a roar. Bernard raised his powerful hand.

"Be still, both of you!" cried Steele, greatly annoyed. "Barry, that's my guest; Bernard, that's my dog."

"Your dog!" repeated Bernard, as Barry slunk away.

Steele locked his door again,—this time in good earnest. The interruption had disturbed him. He felt as if he could have locked out his life; but it came in through the barred door as apparitions are said to come in haunted homes. He flung his hands behind him, fingers shut together, and paced the room. Questions, like arrows, each sharper than the last, shot him through.

How came he where he was? How came he what he was? Is the fate of the soul a matter of choice? If so, what dark election had he made of his? For ten years he had carved the living animal in the interests of physiology; he was accustomed to say to ladies and clergymen that he pursued scientific research for the sake of suffering humanity. The tissue, the muscle, the nerve, the vital spark, tortured to a flicker, and resuscitated to a spasm—these had darkened the divine in him, and illumined the material. One of the problems that had been given him was to locate the brain-cells wherein dwelt the sense of maternal affection in the higher animals, and to see whether the mother's instinct could be destroyed or not. This interesting series of experiments in Berlin led the young doctor, who, as we have said, was not without imagination, to extend the investigation, and he spent two months in trying to demonstrate the source of love. Half a hundred living brains he opened. Half a hundred dogs looked up into his face pathetically questioning what darkened their irritated thoughts. But love was too evasive. It was not to be cut out by a scalpel or grasped by pincers; and Dr. Steele therefore read a paper, learnedly contending that love was only a Greek hypothesis, a psychic disease, the dream of the past, the illusion of the present, and did not exist. For this invaluable contribution to science he received his degree of Doctor of Philosophy.

It occurred to Steele, as if he had originated the metaphor, that life is a long stairway. Where upon it did he stand? And which way was he turned? It was of no use to try to bewilder himself. He had begun at the top of the broad white marble flight, and the descent had been easy, imperceptible; and as he descended, the stone changed from carrara to sienna. Was the bottom still below, or had he reached it?

Abruptly he stopped pacing the room, and dropped into the easy-chair. His fingers, where he had clenched them, were purple from the knuckles to the tips. The circulation returned slowly; with it flowed a series of reminiscences. He could no more repel them than he could stop at will the current in his aorta.

He had witnessed many sad sights in the course of his professional life, but the saddest sight he had ever seen was the expression of the dogs as they were brought to the laboratory from the cellar for sacrifice.

One of these stood out apart from the rest. Dr. Steele was working out the last of a series of experiments performed by him in Vienna; this was the brilliant achievement that had given him his professorship. The experiments concerned themselves with the ligation of coronary arteries. The series was made on twenty-eight dogs. This one, whose ghost pursued him now, was a beautiful greyhound. He had given it a little morphia. He had carved about its heart for one hundred minutes.

He thought of this without self-accusation. It was scarcely in justification of the deed that he said, half aloud, "But my results were opposed to the conclusions of Gültz and Magendie—and here I am."

His thoughts reverted swiftly to that essay of his on the seat of the affections. His mind was vibrant and clear; it swung like a pendulum between the laboratory and love.

"I have demonstrated," he thought coldly, "that there is no such thing. If I am going on like this, I might as well surrender my Ph.D."

Now, abruptly, the red scenery of the scientific shambles shifted before him. In its stead a gentle stage gave up a woman's figure—stirring as he looked. She moved in a glimmering, yellow light. Her distinction of form and manner, her filmy black robe, her delicately mocking smile, blurred before him and blended with a setting of snow and blue twilight. Against this she stood, fair and indignant as a priestess disturbed at some altar whose worship was inexplicable to himself—her cheeks aflame, her lifted head expressing against her dark fur the turn of her throat, her whole beautiful being on fire with a divine self-oblivion,—she, pity personified, mercy made magic.

Oh, well,—admit it!—magic.

"The world is compact of illusions," thought Olin Steele. "Life is a hallucination. And so is love. I am at present confused by a lantern slide. Will it dissolve or hold?"

But now his thoughts paused through the haze, and he began to analyze his sensations just as he would differentiate lines in a spectroscope. For an element as new, as startling as radium had suddenly entered his life. Ignore it he could not; welcome it he did not.

What was he that he should absorb this wondrous thing? At one moment coldly critical of himself, at the next maddened by his consciousness of her, he paced the room blindly. He had known many women, as he said: the frivolous, the weak, the severe, the patrician, the subject. Beyond the moment few of these had touched him; none had inspired. He had always been sufficient to himself, and he had a certain pride in the fact that kept him apart from experiences which deflect a man from his capacity for the noblest feeling.

On a little hanging shelf across the room were a few books that he had collected when he was a boy—Byron, Moore, and Shakespeare, and the modem classics. It was years since he had handled any of them. Moved by some impulse that he did not understand, and but half respected, he went over to the bookcase, and with an embarrassed air took down the third volume of the dark blue set of Tennyson that his mother had given him in his sophomore year.

"Seems to me they've said a good deal on the subject—these makers of verse," he thought. But he could not have told what or where.

Quite by accident he opened the book at the prelude to "In Memoriam," and perplexedly read aloud:

Strong Son of God, immortal Love,
Whom we, that have not seen thy face.
By faith, and faith alone, embrace,
Believing where we cannot prove.

He closed the book, and turned away with a gesture such as a man makes when he stands midway between incredulity and conviction.

"It strikes me," he thought, "that I am reversing the process. I am in danger of proving what I do not believe." With a sudden change of manner, he repeated solemnly:

"'Strong Son of God!'—Why, that's what Mother used to sing!"

"Immortal love," he reiterated. All the militant forces of his training contended with the phrase. He did not believe in immortality. He did not believe in love.

On the other hand, there was the girl.

He had not known her a day, but she had invaded his nature. He had not exchanged two hundred words with her, but she had undermined his creed. He saw her—he saw her and could not help it. He was enchanted by her; he knew it; and the knowledge wrought in him a bitter contempt for his own weakness. But what could he do?

He had been told in romance and song—in the days when they told him anything at all—of a mysterious and beautiful force. It seized the soul and body; it bewildered the reason; it transformed the character; it transfigured life; it irradiated death; it promised immortality. This miracle was love at the first sight of the beloved.

At this, as at other miracles, he had sneered for years. Now what was he doing? Worshiping? He? His stern lips yielded, his hands relaxed, his face fell upon them.

"I shall love her," he said. "I shall love her!"

Then he lifted his head, and his fingers locked again. "She is a woman. I am a man. Since I determine, she shall conform."

More gently then, he spoke aloud:

"I will win her—anyhow. What the price is, who can say?"

It occurred to him suddenly that he was thinking in a quotation—he who had read no poetry for a dozen years. He could not even have told who said it. How had he happened to slip into clouds and ether? As well be a woman—a Diana—and blunder headlong into fate.

"I will win her," he repeated, "so help me God."

How was a physiologist who in one day had begun with poetry, fallen upon love, and ended with God, to reckon with himself?

The young professor perceived that the time would come when he must do so. But he did not care.

CHAPTER IV

—꧁—

"Here, you gossoon, how the devil can I groom that horse with Trixy on her back?"

Matthew stepped into the box-stall, while Dan held up his finger with that admonitory gesture which is better obeyed than a whip by an intelligent dog. But the chestnut mare turned her head, neighing gently at a little white poodle who sat like a statuette upon her shoulders.

"They like each other," said Dan. "Trixy's saying good-by. We're going right away."

"Are ye out o' quirintine?" asked Matthew.

"There wan't no quirintine," replied Dan. "Them city doctors don't know much. Cady's Molly,—she's all right. 'T wan't no kind of dipfever, nohow. Come along, Trixy."

Trixy confidingly walked the length of the chestnut mare's spinal column, and flew like an acrobat to Dan's crooked shoulder.

"I suppose," Dan added, casting a regretful look around the warm, exquisitely clean stable, "we must go up and see Her. She's sent fur us."

"You 're in luck, gossoon," said Matthew gravely; "there's them I know would give their Derby hats to say as much, or do it, either."

"They ain't crooked, be they?" asked Dan thoughtfully.

"No," said Matthew promptly. "They're straight—and pretty tall, as a general thing. There's quite a number of 'em."

"I reckon that's so," retorted Dan proudly.

The boy and the poodle made their way quietly up the padded stairs to the library (Trixy was as silent as Dan) where Miriam and her aunt, having never been able to agree upon the same morning paper, sat reading two rival sheets.

Dan stood, cap in hand. His eyes sought Miss Lauriat's with more of the absolute canine than looked from Trixy's when she glanced at him. For Trixy was something of an elf, and loved moodily, and at times, the lad thought, mockingly. She had feminine caprices, and little pets and pouts. Dan was not always sure of her; hence he adored her.

For instance, at this moment Trixy hesitated a little whether to salute her hostess, then unexpectedly walked over to Mrs. Percy B. Jeffries, and solemnly sat up before her.

"Shake hands like a lady," said Dan, in an undertone.

"You mean paws," corrected Aunt Cornelia.

"No, I don't, marm," persisted Dan. "Trixy don't know she's got paws."

"Now that," complained Mrs. Jeffries, "is just an illustration of what I was saying, Miriam, when the boy came in. You can't make the higher races out of the lower races. I maintain that the Creator knew what He was about. When He made paws, He didn't mean hands."

"Oh, Auntie, don't be so literal!" said Miriam, laughing. "Shake hands with Trixy, and defer the argument."

"But I can't see," urged Mrs. Jeffries, "how such a high class of physicians—men of position, I'm sure, Miriam—Galen men, too— how they could make a mistake. I always thought—"

"Don't think, Auntie dear. I never do. Cady's Molly had a simple case of pharyngitis."

"That sounds bad enough!" Mrs. Jeffries dropped the dog's paw quickly. "I am sure I should have quarantined it. How do you know we haven't got it—all of us?"

Miriam's eyes laughed.

"Oh, Auntie dear! Don't you see? A sore throat unadorned is adorned the most."

The crippled boy stood looking from one lady to the other; his silent face made the comments that ignorance and obscurity pass upon intelligence and position—that steady, ominous undertone of criticism to which we seldom pay attention.

"Now, Dan," said Miriam, turning brightly to the boy, "we've enjoyed your visit very much. You've made no sort of trouble. And everybody in the house loves Trixy. Mr. Surbridge thinks she is the most remarkable dog he ever knew. When do you give your next entertainment—I mean your next important entertainment?"

"Four weeks come next Tuesday"—Dan blushed with gratification—"at half-past seven sharp. No postpayment on account of no weather."

"Oh, yes, I see. And where?"

"At the Grand Mooses' Retreat, Miss Laurie." Dan raised his bent shoulders.

"In Heaven's name, who are the Grand Gooses?" demanded Mrs. Jeffries, pushing Trixy off her lap. Trixy, with a hurt expression, ran to Miriam, who cuddled her heartily.

"I said Mooses," replied Dan with dignity.

"Mooses, then," said Aunt Cornelia, "though I can't see what possible difference it can make."

"Mebbe you would if you was us, marm," replied Dan, without smiling.

"Oh, I dare say I should," admitted Aunt Cornelia more kindly.

"Hain't you never heard of the Grand Mooses?" asked Dan in a tone of gentle patronage, not unmixed with pity. "That's our Lodge. I'm a charter member. None of us don't drink. But they pay tickets to see Trixy. It costs ten cents to get in."

"Who gets the money?" asked Aunt Cornelia severely.

"Why, I do," said Dan slowly. "You see I'm crooked—and lame— and I ain't very strong. I can't do a great many things for a living. That's the way me and Trixy make ours."

"I'll take ten tickets," said Miss Lauriat quickly.

"I'll take five myself," observed Mrs. Jeffries.

"I'd rather shove ye in dead-heads," said Dan pathetically, "an' have ye come."

"No," said Miriam, "we'll take the tickets, and come too. We'll bring a party, Dan."

"You're in for it now, Miriam," groaned her Aunt Cornelia, when the boy and the dog had left the library.

"I hope so, Auntie dear," replied Miriam, with that exasperating cheerfulness which is one of the fine arts of domestic life.

"I suppose you know this is the morning for your pastel lesson?" continued Mrs. Jeffries plaintively. "Now that, my dear, is quite clearly a proper occupation for a young lady—sheltered and aesthetic. Your mother would have felt just as I do about all this philanthropic fad."

"My father wouldn't!" flashed Miriam.

"You never appreciated your mother," retorted Mrs. Jeffries.

Miriam started to return irreverently: "She never gave me a chance"; for her mother had died when the child was three years old. In fact, she said no such thing. Yet she was so constructed that she felt as if she had, and repented accordingly.

She went out of the room dry-eyed, for she was not a crying woman; but once alone, the tears smarted to her lashes. She and Aunt Cornelia had never "got on" together. Miriam, who knew that this was partly her fault, sometimes blamed herself for it, disproportionately. She dreaded becoming one of those people who are happy with their inferiors, but not with their relatives.

She was about going back with a sweet magnanimity quite natural to her, to say, "Forgive me. Auntie," when a maltese kitten that had been hiding somewhere from Trixy scudded across the hall, and into the library—immediately running back, however, to Miriam, who received it with a dutiful air, plainly lacking in enthusiasm.

"You don't love cats. I don't see why you don't get a dog, Miriam," said Mrs. Jeffries, folding her newspaper with a neat and irritat-

42

ing motion. The penitent words fainted on Miriam's lips. Her face stiffened instantly, and became cast into an expression that no one in the world, least of all her mother's sister, knew her well enough to have understood. She dropped the kitten from her arm, and turned away without a word.

The Grand Mooses' Retreat was opened and lighted. The kerosene lamps were smoking placidly. The men of the audience were not, and seemed to miss their accustomed privilege; but the word had gone around that swells were coming—and real ladies—to Dan's show.

Most of the spectators were Miss Lauriat's friends. These were of two kinds: the party she brought with her, and the people to whom she brought it. Her tenants were there in large numbers; Cady's Molly, in a red dress, pink hair-ribbon, and purple tam-o'-shanter, being conspicuous among them.

Molly had become somewhat of a heroine since the incident of the quarantine, and Dan, who cherished a camaraderie for her, had provided her with a prominent place. A big, boisterous mason, who was now known to history by the ambiguous title of Cady's Molly's father, sat beside her.

The front seats were reserved for Miss Lauriat and her invited guests. Among them Dan claimed a personal acquaintance only with Mrs. Jeffries, Mr. Surbridge, Matthew, and Maggie. The lad was not on speaking terms with Professor Steele, who came in late, and sat by the door, but Dan identified him at once as the "dip-fever" doctor. At sight of Dr. Steele, Cady's Molly's father swelled proudly, and remarked audibly to Molly:

"We fired him, Molly—didn't we?"

But the doctor, quite unconscious of his personal unpopularity, changed his seat for one where he could watch Miss Lauriat's warm and beautiful profile.

The stage was small and murky. It contained a table, two chairs, a clothes-horse with a narrow, light board resting upon it, and a waste-paper basket without a bottom; several rubber balls, a squeak-chicken, a feather duster, and a little costume.

Dan and Trixy appeared quietly upon the platform. The boy limped slowly, holding Trixy's right paw with great gallantry, and both bowed to the audience at the same moment, and with solemnity.

The crippled lad was undersized and pale. He could not have been over sixteen, and he looked less or more according to the light that was rude to his drawn features, or the shadow that was kind to them. Though he was not strictly a hunch-back, his shoulders were bent, and one leg was so much shorter than the other that he had to walk with a crutch.

His manner was gentle, and so was his face. He had that refinement which suffering only confers, and that air of cheerfulness and good humor which sometimes springs from a desperate lot bravely borne. Dan was of the uncomplaining type that would have made him a favorite in any society. At the applause which greeted his appearance, he smiled down at his goddess on the front settee. Miss Lauriat radiantly smiled back. She was as pleased as he.

Trixy was a French poodle, white and fine. More strictly, one might classify her as a Spanish poodle; but she was of the variety well known in France, where she would be called a lou lou. Although Dan had found the puppy freezing in an ash barrel, she was of high descent. Her hair was tightly curled; her nose was black. Her black eyes blazed from her white face with a startling intelligence that, though other, was never less, and often more than human. She was sinuous, coquettish, cuddling; then defiant and dignified. She was born to be loved; but she was born to be admired. She could never be long happy off the stage. Indeed, she would have played to empty benches rather than not to play at all. Her ears lifted at the applause which greeted her. She critically measured her audience; then she curtsied to her master, and, still standing on her hind feet, awaited his orders.

Many of Trixy's performances were elementary; but some were worthy of a larger stage. Trixy was better educated than her master, and experienced the disadvantage of the more alert intelligence leashed into a subject condition. She tripped with enthusiasm through her little repertoire. She was a dead dog; she rolled over; she said her prayers; she played leap-frog; she teetered on a board across the clothes-horse; she was blindfolded and found the squeak-chicken in Mr. Surbridge's coat pocket. She dove through the waste-paper basket like a ballet dancer through a paper hoop. She did a dozen clever things with the rubber balls; she turned a back somer-sault on her master's hand; she took the feather duster in her arms, walked jauntily down the aisle, and deposited it in Mrs. Percy B. Jeffries's horrified lap. Perceiving that lady's discomfiture, Trixy proceeded by way of consolation to dust her off.

After this episode, which was received by the audience with marked applause, Dan dressed Trixy up in a little white tulle-covered dress, with a shirt waist and hat.

"Now, ladies and gentlemen," said Dan, "you will be treated to the only performance of the kind in the world. This alone is worth your money. Miss Trixy is the only trained dog in the United States who can sing soprano to a gent's tenor."

Trixy stood on the table in her fluffy dress, one paw lightly resting on Dan's shoulder. Her eyes sought his eagerly for orders, but they began to have their elfish expression, and Dan felt a little uneasy. He never was sure of her—never, and he hurried the performance along.

The lad now began to sing. He had a sweet voice, untaught and immature, and sang not without real effect, something in this manner:

> In kind or cruel weather,
> We have traveled on together;
> She and I.
> Whate'er the skies above her.
> She's my lady, and I love her.
> Who knows why?
> She's my lady,
> And I'll love her
> Till I die.

As Dan sang this ditty to a pretty tune, Trixy, with a sentimental manner, lifted up her voice and joined in the strain, singing from beginning to end. There was a curious concord between the voices of the boy and the dog. It was that of love rather than that of music; one hardly knew whether to laugh or to cry.

After this Dan put Trixy through a little skirt dance, which he prefaced in the following manner:

"Ladies and gentlemen, you've all heard of Adeline Patty. It costs a thousand dollars to see her dance. None of us have, unless the front row. But Trixy, she'll dance anywheres, any time, for ten cents a head. You see her now, ladies and gentlemen, a little dog in child's clothes; but you wouldn't understand mebbe as well as I do—that really, Trixy is a child in dog's clothes. She will now proceed to give the last performance of the evening."

When the little dance was over Dan added an impromptu feature of the entertainment.

"Trixy," he said, "go down into the audience and find the lady you love the best."

Trixy obeyed with alacrity, but the elf look had come into her eyes again. She tripped down the aisle on her hind feet. Mockingly she paused before Cady's Molly, flinging as she did so a roguish glance at her master. The audience had grown very still. Dan did not interfere. After a moment's hesitation Trixy turned her back on Molly, walked to Miss Lauriat, sprang into her lap, and put both paws around the young lady's neck. Tumultuous applause attested the popularity of the dog's choice.

Cries came from different parts of the room:

"Speech! Speech! The Lady! The Lady!"

Mrs. Percy B. Jeffries bit her lips; but Miss Lauriat graciously responded. It was not the first time she had been on the platform of that hall, and had helped the people's entertainments. They all loved her, and she knew it. She was quite at home with them. With the little dog clinging to her neck, white against her black dress, Miriam went up and stood beside the crippled lad. In that dull place she was a radiant being. She illumined the dark background of that paltry stage as she had illumined the dark lives which found their best—perhaps their purest—pleasures in amusements such as this.

For a moment she stood there smiling, the little creature cuddling in her neck—both silent. The face of the dog could not be seen, and its child's dress and infantile attitude gave a strange impression, as if some new Madonna, gently owning her kinship to the subject races, had arisen to protect them.

At first, Miriam thought she would have said a few words, but the cold eyes of Olin Steele were fixed upon her. Something in their expression deterred her; she could not have said why. She felt a little chilled, as if he did not approve of her position. She bowed, and gave the dog back to Dan.

But the audience, finding that there was to be no speech from Miss Lauriat, and unwilling to be cheated out of their rights and privileges in the lady, thronged towards the platform.

Philip Surbridge, however, was there first. His face was warm with sympathy. The finer meaning of that evening's scene appealed to every fibre in his being. He felt it all with her. He felt it all for her. He grasped her hand with the enthusiasm of a boy and the reverence of a man.

"You have done a beautiful thing," he said, "and I honor you for it!"

He stood beside her for a moment, in a protecting attitude, like a brother's, between her and the people who were hurrying up the steps.

"Thank you, Phil," she said in a low voice. "But I've got to shake hands with them. It would break their hearts if I didn't. Speak to Dan, please, and then we'll go."

"Dan," said Surbridge, "if ever you and Trixy want a friend, count on me."

He held out his hand heartily, first to Dan, and then to the pretty dog. Then Dan put on Trixy's blue coat (it was embroidered with her name) lest she should take cold after the excitement of the performance, and led the little actress away.

Professor Steele did not come up with the remainder of Miss Lauriat's party. He stood for a moment watching her, while fifty people grasped her delicate hand. Cady's Molly's father was one of them. The scene was foreign to Olin's experience. He had experimented upon the poor; he had meant to be kind to them; sometimes he had cured them; but he had not been their friend. He was by no means sure that he wanted to be, or wanted her to be. He envied the look of genuine appreciation on Surbridge's face—that spontaneous sympathy with this extraordinary situation. Deterred by a discomfort in himself which he did not understand, the doctor took his hat and left the hall.

As he went downstairs, he heard some young people moving out behind him, humming:

She's my lady, and I love her.

Who knows why?

He waited outside, pacing up and down Blind Alley, till the rest of the party should come out. Most of Miriam's guests returned as they had come, by carriage or by trolley. But a few preferred to walk, and among these, Steele, who had rather obviously offered his escort to Mrs. Jeffries, noticed Miss Lauriat and her lawyer.

Surbridge and Miriam walked on for a few moments without talking. Then Miriam said carelessly:

"It was nice of Dr. Steele to look after Auntie. She appreciates that kind of thing."

"Perhaps I ought to have—" Philip spoke in a nettled tone.

"She would have preferred you, of course," interrupted Miriam. "She reveres Dr. Steele, but she loves you."

"Reveres Olin Steele?"

"That was her word," said Miriam, with mischief in her eyes.

"But I thought you wanted to walk home," protested Surbridge.

"I did," returned Miriam quietly. "It was so stuffy in there. I wanted the air."

"Well, then!" cried Surbridge.

"Don't be cross, Phil!" said Miriam.

Philip received this little sisterly speech as a matter of course. He and Miriam had been on quite comfortable terms since they went to dancing school together. He smothered his flitting pique, and began to talk about Dan and Trixy. "I'd rather have seen that than grand opera," he said heartily.

"You do care, don't you?" said Miriam. "So few people do."

"He's a poor little chap," continued Philip, "and he's got a remarkable dog. And as for you—" He broke off.

"Yes, I know," said Miriam contentedly. "We are apt to like the same things. How's your practice, Phil?"

"Oh, I've just been retained by the News-boys' Association."

"You take too many charity cases. You are quixotic and—and—splendid, Phil. You'll never get rich that way."

"I never expect to get rich." The young lawyer spoke quickly, and a little defiantly.

"Oh, well, that's quite immaterial," returned Miriam, with the indifference to an income felt by a girl who had never experienced the want of one. "Nobody likes you the less for it."

"You are very good to say so," replied Surbridge; he took the tone of a man who does not propose to dip below the surface. "By the way, I wonder why Steele didn't speak to you tonight?"

"I didn't feel like it, and I presume he didn't," answered Miriam. "I think he disapproved of what I did."

"What business is it of his?" flashed Surbridge.

"Not any," returned Miriam very slowly. "That is—well, no—not any. All the same, he's the kind of man who makes you feel as if he thought it were his business."

"That doesn't lessen the cheek," persisted Philip.

"He's always very courteous," observed Miriam coldly. "He is a perfect gentleman. I'm sure you'll admit that he's eminent in his profession. Auntie has taken a fancy to him."

"And you?" asked Surbridge.

In the darkness he could see her lift her chin with a little haughty motion that she rarely made.

"I have seen something of him," she replied evasively. "Auntie invites him a good deal. He is president of one of those animal things that she's director of. It's the S. P. D. & C. T. & E."

"What in the name of—mercy—is the S. P. D. & C. T. & E.?"

"The Society for the Prevention of Docking and Cropping Tails and Ears," said Miriam demurely.

"Olin Steele president of a society for—Oh, Lord! Oh, Lord!" Surbridge groaned with half-choked laughter.

"I cannot imagine why you find it so funny," answered Miriam severely.

Philip sobered instantly. "Shall I beg your pardon?"

"Not for the world!" cried Miriam, regaining her good nature. "I suppose they'll be waiting for us," she added in a different tone. Surbridge made no reply, but he quickened his pace.

When they came into the brightly lighted, laughing house most of Miriam's guests had preceded them. Dr. Steele, without manifest intrusion, seemed subtly to claim her, and Philip quickly gave way to an indefinable something—whether an acquaintance or a friendship he could not determine—which he felt existed between the two.

They did not seem to talk much; which to the lawyer's mind was the gravest symptom. Miriam had an absorbed and sweet expression; this deepened slowly into an exhilarated beauty. As for the man's face, Surbridge could not watch it, and turned away.

"Tell me what you are thinking," demanded Olin Steele, in the commanding tone which it was his private belief that women liked; for her happy face had suddenly fallen.

"I am repenting," replied Miss Lauriat, without a smile.

"Be all my sins remembered!" exclaimed the doctor in a deep voice. Miriam glanced up gravely. Half attracted, half repelled, she seemed to stir and sway upon her steady feet.

"I am thinking," she sighed, "that I forgot to invite Dan and Trixy to come and get some ice cream."

But Dan and Trixy were blessedly beyond the need of ice cream, viewed either as a conscious loss or as a possible possession. In the lad's closet bedroom, across the entry from Cady's Molly's father's, the two were drowned in the blissful sleep of the tired and successful wage-earner. They had reached the deeps below the waves. Memory and forecast had passed them by; trouble was not, nor hunger, nor cold; homelessness and orphanage, deformity and helplessness, had overlooked these waifs of fortune. Trixy dreamed of her audience; but Dan did not dream at all. He was too tired. Trixy lay on the foot of his cot, covered with a ragged coat of her master's—for the little actress was of a delicate race. Twenty times a night Dan's thin hand stole down and covered Trixy up. Dan knew that he loved Trixy better than she loved him, but he loved none the less for that.

❖

Miriam Lauriat was not a new woman. She had no career, and she had never wanted one. By birth and training she inclined to accept the existing, and clung to the traditions of her class. But with these she often found her nature contending. On the map of her being were large, unexplored spaces, arctic and torrid. She did not know whether she were more afraid of or more unable to traverse these.

Most of the affections of life had reached her only by induction. She had felt deeply, but not often, and her tenderness had been touched through her sympathies. She had loved but two beings: her father, and one other.

She had experienced society. But now she remained on the bank, and the rapids flowed by her. The torrent had really never interested her, and she turned from it to philanthropy as women of noble and unoccupied hearts are apt to do.

Miriam had highly developed in herself the passion for humanity. The wants, the woes, the joys of denied and overlooked people, had become the important events in her life. The human element, which demanded everything and could give nothing, absorbed her leisure vitality. She had given much happiness and had received some. Incidentally she was beloved by the objects of her bounty, but this fact, which is so often an end in itself to a lonely and tender-hearted woman, had received from her no concentrated attention.

Indeed, there were times when she was forced to admit to herself that Blind Alley did not satisfy the heights and depths of her nature. This was a confusing admission to a woman who, believing herself a primary color, was in fact a prism. Miriam had that versatility of temperament that is so bewildering in youth, and so satisfying in later life. She found in herself a capacity for doing or being a variety of things, which presented itself to her sometimes as a misfortune or even a fault, and at others as a source of strength.

She vibrated between the extremes of her nature, and wondered that she had neither content nor rest. She allowed herself forays into untried powers. Now and then she wrote verses. Under pen-names, which she changed often for fear of identification, she occasionally contributed little stories or essays to a newspaper or magazine. She had the love of color and form which may make an artist or an amateur. At present she was experimenting to learn which of these she was. When the new art school was opened within a few blocks of her house, Miss Lauriat joined a private class. For some months she had been working in pastel.

It was perhaps a week after the little performance which Dan and Trixy gave at the Mooses' Retreat, that Miriam found herself hurrying up the broad steps of the art school, for her morning lesson. She was late, and her master was not a man to accept excuses from the rich. He received her with a frown, and indicated her subject curtly. It was a nocturne by Whistler.

"I can do nothing with it, Signor," she said. "The sails look like crucified angels. Please give me something suited to my ignorance."

"I forgot," retorted the teacher, "the color scheme is above you. Try this, then."

Smiling sarcastically he flung on the easel before her a large Arundel print of Fra Angelico's Christ Transfigured.

Miriam flushed, but went to work silently and solemnly. There were but few pupils in the large room, and the spot was still and inspiring. Near her stood a cast of Rodin's Pity. Beyond were the antiques, powerful and calm. Their strong influence pulsated through the place. But the Christ before her seemed to fill it.

With a sense of awe, Miriam sketched in the sacred figure. The atmosphere of the room was almost religious. She felt herself possessed by peace, and upheld by aspiration.

While she sat, her head bent over her sketch, something flitted past the window and cast a light reflection upon her bowed face. Glancing up quickly she saw a white pigeon—to her sensitive imagination it looked like a dove. The bird fluttered from window to window, and then drifted away. At this moment there came from the adjoining building a sound which startled Miriam to her feet. It was a long, piercing, piteous cry. It was the cry of a sentient being in mortal agony. It rose and fell, and rose again.

Miriam dropped her crayon, and stood quivering; something in that agonized voice drove the blood from her heart. She went as white as the frightened pigeon. She stood as still as the statue of Pity beside her. Her eyes sought the face of the Christ blindly. The heart-rending sound increased, and died away. What wound did it open in the girl's heart? She looked smitten and ashen. Her sketch fell to the floor. Panting and faint, she fled from the room.

CHAPTER V

Miriam ran out from the art school and went straight to the neighboring building. Through the inattention with which one treats familiar points of interest, she had forgotten that this was the Galen Medical School. The fact occurred to her now with no special significance. She listened for a few moments for the piercing sounds that she had heard, but there was no repetition of them. With the assurance of position, and the impulsiveness of her agitation, she went up the steps and spoke to a man (presumably the janitor) who was sweeping the vestibule.

"I heard a dog's cries in here," she began hotly; "he is in suffering somewhere. Go and find him!"

The man leaned with his chin on the broom, and regarded the lady with a blank, impassive face.

"I don't understand you," he replied frostily.

"I am sure of it," insisted Miss Lauriat. "It was a dog's cry of agony—I thought—the voice—" She broke off.

"Probably, Miss, it was an accident in the street. Those blue cars often run over them."

The sweeper leisurely resumed his occupation as if he had no interest in a subject so remote from his experience. "Excuse me; it ain't very clean here for you, and the young gentlemen are just coming out."

A cloud of dust puffed around Miriam as she turned. She felt as if she were being swept down the steps. At the bottom she stopped again, and looked up at the building irresolutely. Hovering high in the air she thought she saw the white pigeon that had tapped on the window of the art school. A very young student came out of the door at this moment, and ran whistling down.

"Pardon me," said Miriam, with the tone and manner which instantly brought the hat from the young man's head, and the cigarette from his mouth. "Won't you tell me before the rest come out—I came here—I'm so disturbed—I heard distressing cries! I came here to find out what they mean."

The janitor—if he it was—had stopped sweeping and was closely watching the two. But the very young student, who stood with his back to this sub-official, frankly answered the lady's question.

"Oh, it's nothing of any consequence, madam. Do not disturb yourself."

"But it was a dog!" cried Miriam. "It sounded as if it were a little dog."

"I know what that was," answered the boy candidly. "We are having some very pretty psychological experiments."

"Oh," said Miriam, a little relieved, "that means mental experiments, doesn't it?"

"Certainly," replied the student pompously. "It means experimentation on the intelligence, the affections, and the will. One subject is all we need for the purpose, and I assure you, madam, it never suffers."

"Then I"—began Miriam with her charming manner—"must have been mistaken—but—" At this moment a torrent of students poured from the door. Baffled and perplexed, Miss Lauriat turned away.

She could not forget the incident, however. It pursued her painfully. She did not return to finish her pastel lesson, but went directly home, and shut herself up alone for the rest of the day. She was glad to have the house to herself, and once a year this privilege fell to her.

Mrs. Percy B. Jeffries, who, in common with many of her neighbors, found it convenient to change her legal residence on the first of May, had already been some ten days at the shore in Miss Lauriat's summer home. She was accustomed to say that she went in advance to open the house for Miriam, and sustained the little pose even with her lawyer, to whom she had said plaintively, when Surbridge accompanied her to the safety vaults to cut her May coupons: "That child can't do such things for herself. She is absorbed. She is unpractical. Those people down there are monopolizing all her youth. I wish you had never allowed her to invest a dollar in the slums."

"Pardon me," the young attorney had explained, "you forget this was an inherited investment. My father was responsible for that, and I assure you," he added loyally, "it has proved an excellent one. She has nothing better; and consider the usefulness of it. She makes a lot of people happy, and clean. Permit me, Mrs. Jeffries—these P. and Q. coupons are worth thirty dollars apiece. I wouldn't put them in the ink bottle, if I were you."

"You have your father's manner, Philip," said Mrs. Jeffries sentimentally. "It is always a comfort to have you around. There! I'll mind my P's and Q's to please you. Be sure and run down this summer as usual. We expect a good many pleasant people. Dr. Steele is coming out every Saturday. The S. P. D. & C. T. & E. is an important society, and we have to confer. I wish Miriam took more interest in it; but she doesn't care about the animal philanthropies. She says the human race is enough for her."

It so happened that on the evening of the day when the episode at the art school occurred, a matter of business took Philip Surbridge to Miriam's house. She received him in the drawing-room. The windows were open; the gas was low. The large room, which had gone into its linen shrouding for the summer, had a dismal, unfamiliar air. When Miriam paused before the gauze-covered mirror, it reflected her mistily, as if she had been a ghost. She seemed somehow unreal to Philip; her body looked uninhabited like the house. When he explained his errand—it was some mechanic's contract—he saw that she was giving no attention to it. She assented indifferently to his suggestions, and sat with listless hands crossed over her black skirt. The evening was warm, and she wore a white silk waist, which Philip noticed because it was so long since he had seen her in anything but mourning. She had an unusual pallor—perhaps a reflection from the ivory-tinted stuff into which her face seemed to melt, or out of which it seemed to grow. She was so unlike herself that Philip refrained from any unnecessary conversation, and with his natural delicacy quickly terminated the interview, and arose to go.

"So soon?" asked Miriam languidly.

"You seem tired; I think it's better."

"Wait a minute." Miriam uncrossed her hands slowly, and, rising, stood tall and still in the dim room beside him. He could feel how constrained she was.

"Such a strange thing happened today," she began. She had not meant to tell him, nor to tell any one; in fact, though she could hardly have explained why, she felt a poignant reluctance to repeating the experience of the morning. But she was used to telling things to Philip. She always had; sometimes she suspected that most people did. He was that kind of a man. His presence in the lonely house (deserted now of the whole family excepting the old seamstress and Maggie) indefinably soothed her. Suddenly it seemed to her necessary to speak, and she told him the story.

Surbridge listened in silence. As she talked, he crossed to the open window and stood with his hands in his pockets.

"Go on," he said when she paused.

"That is all," said Miriam with a sigh of relief.

Philip turned away from the window and asked a few quiet questions, naturally enough; but Miriam quickly detected the professional instinct beneath the personal sympathy.

"You cross-examine!" she cried.

So Philip laughed and left her. Now, as he passed up the street, he came face to face with Dr. Steele.

"By the way," said the lawyer carelessly, "may I walk a few steps with you? I want to ask you about a certain matter."

Philip retraced his way, and the two gentlemen walked back towards the house. Surbridge spoke in a low voice, and could not

58

have been overheard by passers, but as the physiologist listened an expression of cold annoyance stiffened his face. Before they came to Miss Lauriat's door he halted.

"Why should I answer these questions?" His lips sharpened. "I am not on the witness stand. You will excuse me, Surbridge."

Surbridge laughed again—he had a singularly quiet, pleasant laugh—and walked back. He had not gone a block when he admitted to himself an unpardonable curiosity. He glanced around, and saw Dr. Steele coming away from Miss Lauriat's house. Plainly he had not been admitted.

"Now," thought Philip, "what's the meaning of that?"

This question Miriam herself could not have answered.

Dr. Steele plunged his hands deep into the water. He bathed them with something more than his usual scrupulousness, repeating the act a good many times. As he held his long and slender but strong fingers to the light, a slight shadow fell upon them from the window near which he stood—there was a coo, a whir—and some pigeons flew from the sill; one, it seemed, was white. He glanced at it idly. The principal thought that it suggested to him couched itself in some such words as these:

"Those Germans have done remarkably interesting work with the brains of doves."

"Down!" A raucous voice jarred from the adjoining room. "Down, I say!"

There was no mistaking the tone or the accent of his assistant. Somehow, it always grated on Steele, even now, and after all. He turned impatiently, and looked into the laboratory. There, a picture, something new even to his wide experience, presented itself.

A black spaniel of the cocker breed stood upon the table before which Bernard was stationed. It must have been originally a very beautiful spaniel; its scarred forehead was parted with white, and a white ruff like a shirt-frill stood out thickly from its breast. It had large hazel eyes, perhaps also once beautiful, but now, for reasons and by processes known only to these two men, the spaniel's expression had become mysteriously dulled. Yet a flicker of terror lighted it at the touch of Bernard's significant hands. At this moment, when Dr. Steele looked up, the little creature had raised itself with difficulty, and, reaching up, put both arms around the experimenter's neck. Bernard unclasped them roughly. The dog repeated the piteous gesture; he did not cry nor whine, but with the inextinguishable trust and tenderness of his race entreated the man. But Bernard pushed the spaniel off. As he did so he fingered the dog-board greedily.

Steele stood hesitating. The scene annoyed him—who should say why? He had witnessed a thousand worse. It occurred to him that he had never seen that particular pose before. Perhaps another thought—but again, who could say why there should be any such thought?—at that hour, and in that place?

"Let the dog be for today, if you please," he said with authoritative courtesy. "Give it a rest—for a while."

"What's the matter with you?" demanded Bernard roughly. He dropped the spaniel (who, cowering from him, leaped from the table), and turned his sullen face towards his superior.

"I'm going out of town," replied Dr. Steele. "I can't go on with these experiments today."

"But I can," urged Bernard, with an evil expression. "Vacation's the time for it—no students around."

"Oblige me by regarding my wishes," persisted the professor. "I prefer to be present when these researches are continued. Send the dog back to its cage."

"All right," answered Bernard, with his unpleasant smile. "I understand."

The released spaniel, moved by God knew what impulse, stopped as it passed by the young professor of physiology, and tried to kiss his hand. An expression which could not be interpreted as one of pity, and which was far from indicating a sense of regret, but which might have been called a consciousness of discomfort, brushed the face of Olin Steele.

He went directly out from the medical school, and hurried to the wharf; whence he took the boat for the familiar shore where Miss Lauriat spent her summers.

The day was hot,—it was July,—and Steele, as the little steamer tossed along the coast, luxuriously turned his face towards the salt wind. He had spent all the morning in his laboratory, and felt that he had earned his holiday. A faint memory that he had seen it spelled another way tapped with muffled fingers at his barred imagination. The word had some time since gone out of evidence in the physiologist's vocabulary; yet he might have said that this, if any, if ever, was a holy day to him.

White of soul and fair of body, the woman seemed to float through the summer air before him, and without a glance, without a gesture, silent and maidenly, she drew him on. From sounds and sights which would have rent her with recoil had she dreamed of them in her darkest dream, he turned his hurrying feet to her, complacently. Red-handed he sought her; iron-willed he hunted her.

Yet a man who has ever known and cherished the nobler ideals is haunted by their shadows when he has foresworn their substance; that which was left of the high and the fine in Olin Steele was concentrated with a dedication in which there was something to be respected, upon his passion. On all the altars of his soul the sacrifices were consumed—only on this one, only for her, the fire burned.

Halfway up the avenue to her summer home he met her slowly walking down. She was in white from head to foot—a foamy white, with ivory laces that stirred in the strong wind. He had not seen her dressed like this before, and marveled at the sublimation.

Suddenly contrasting with her mourning black, there was a subtle suggestion in the happy dress at which his head whirled giddily. He did not, could not, would not help it.

"There is something almost bridal about these beautiful white costumes," he said, without preface or apology, as he held out his hand.

"Forgive me!" he cried, when he saw the expression of her lifted face. It seemed in a moment to have fallen away from him, and the hand which she had extended heartily dropped from his.

A dozen years ago Steele would not have said a thing like that; it occurred to him as soon as he had spoken that there was a different way in which he used to dream that he should woo a woman. His face flushed with mortification at his faux pas; Miss Lauriat had never seen the doctor blush before, and she who winced from every evidence of pain in other organisms as if it had been her own, melted instantly into a sweet pardon of this man to whom she felt imperiously drawn, or by whom she was mysteriously disenchanted a score of times in every hour that they passed together.

These, that summer, had been already many. She had treated him graciously, indeed, with such cordiality that Olin's spirits had risen, and his courage with them. He needed both for a wooing in which the man found himself more at a loss than in any undertaking on which he had ever deliberately entered. Deliberate he was, and determined. He meant to win this woman; and he had always done what he had meant to do. But she daunted him and taunted him. When he advanced, she retreated. When he retraced a step, she seemed to stand still. She was as elusive as fortune, and as alluring as mystery. When he loved her most, he admitted to himself that he understood her least.

"I thank you for forgiving me," he said in a tone so gentle that in another man it might have been called humble. This gave him an advantage which he was not slow to perceive; adroitly he changed the subject at once, and they passed up the wooded avenue, chatting of little things.

As they came in sight of the piazza where Mrs. Jeffries, with the expression and manner that she reserved for Docking and Cropping Tails and Ears, was waiting for them, a kitten blew around the corner of the house, head and tail slantwise, steering its way in the brisk sea wind. So running, it dashed against Miriam, and climbed up the lace of her dress. It was a maltese kitten, and around its gray neck was tied a broad pink ribbon.

"Professor Steele!" cried Mrs. Jeffries, getting heavily to her feet, "you are faint—you are ill! What ails you, my dear friend? What can we do for you? What can I—"

On the palette of her sentence the words ran together like gamboge and Prussian blue, and became a puzzled silence, which was a new color.

For, at sight of the kitten, Olin Steele had blanched as a man does who is smitten with ill tidings. He stood staring, as if he saw some little animal ghost. When Miss Lauriat caressed the kitten and dropped it gently though not affectionately to the ground, it began to purr loudly. The sound reverberated in Steele's ears. It seemed to him to come from a great distance.

He recovered himself quickly, made some sort of apology for a passing indisposition, and threw the matter off as lightly as it was now possible to do.

"You are over-worked!" said Mrs. Jeffries tenderly. "I revere the consecration of your profession, Dr. Steele. You shall not go back to town tonight. You are not in a fit condition to discuss the painful objects of our society. The S. P. D. & C. T. & E. can wait till you are in a less sensitive state. You shall stay and rest until tomorrow."

With outward languor (as that of the consecrated who is exhausted by devotion to sacred duties) but with an inward ecstasy so powerful that he dared allow no sign of its whirlwind to escape his dizzy heart, Dr. Steele accepted the invitation. He had now resumed himself completely. After dinner he hovered over Mrs. Jeffries and the affairs of the S. P. D. & C. T. & E. for a conscientious hour. Mrs. Jeffries was making the usual pudding of her papers, and Miriam occupied herself in suggesting that Mr. Surbridge ought to be made counsel for the society.

"Nobody else can handle Aunt Cornelia when it comes to papers," she said, looking over her shoulder with that mocking smile which was the more enchanting because it was always unexpected, and clearly at a certain variance with her gentleness and sincerity of manner.

Dr. Steele studiously concerned himself with what Mrs. Jeffries called "the literature" of the society. He separated the circulars on Docking from the pamphlets on Cropping with a slow and conscientious hand before he observed quietly:

"I have the highest regard for Mr. Surbridge's professional abilities—there can be no two opinions on that. He is a growing man, and has a future beyond doubt. But I confess I have sometimes wondered how so young a lawyer came to be in the position he occupies in this family; not that it is in the least any business of mine."

"His father was Mr. Lauriat's counsel," explained Mrs. Jeffries, warming promptly to the subject of her favorite. "He has inherited the position, and I assure you, Professor Steele, we count it as one of our best and dearest legacies. Mr. Surbridge is a lovely fellow.— Miriam! there's that kitten again. Do send it away. I am sure that cats are unpleasant to our guest. There are people, you know, so constituted. Aren't there, Doctor?"

Mrs. Jeffries rose, and herself went out of the room with the maltese. Miriam and Steele could hear her in the hall politely adjuring the kitten:

"Scat! scat! scat! Why don't you scat?"

"You don't like cats," began Steele in his authoritative tone, "any better than I do. Why don't you have a dog? You need something of that kind. You need something to love. You are so constituted."

Miriam walked over to the long, low window, and stood looking out to sea. Her white dress blew straight back around her in the rising wind.

"I lost one," she said in a very low voice. "It was a good while ago. I don't want another."

"I have sometimes thought," ventured Steele, "if you would allow me—"

"Scat! scat!" plaintively entreated Aunt Cornelia on the piazza. "Oh, you have scatted!"

"On no account, whatever." Miriam quickly turned around.

"I beg your pardon," said Olin Steele.

64

"I am going out on the piazza," observed Miss Lauriat coldly. "You can come if you like."

He followed her, distanced and dejected. Mysteriously, in the lifting of an eyelid, she seemed to have evaded him. Yet in a moment, as mysteriously, she seemed to pause and retrace a step or two in his direction. When he sat down beside her, silently and unobtrusively, she gave him her sweet and natural smile. He began anyhow, hardly knowing what he said:

"I have such a fine old dog of my own. He's a St. Bernard—a dear fellow. I should like to have you see him."

"And I should like to," replied Miriam heartily.

"And my mother," ventured Steele, "she is an invalid. My sister is not at home; she married. Mother is a lonely woman; a very sweet one. I wish you knew my mother."

"I don't know much about mothers," said Miriam in an odd tone. "Mine died. I was three years old—

"I am sorry for yours," she added gently. "It is hard—to die while you are alive like that."

Her low, vibrant voice, her gentle attitude, all the womanliness of her, and the magic of her, went to Olin Steele's head like a fine, celestial wine—sometime, somehow, to be quaffed, but now for the first time tasted at the brim.

"Come down to the shore with me," he said suddenly; "I wish it very much."

She might have defied, but she yielded. She might have daunted him—he never knew what she would do—but she graciously deferred. She might have taunted and tantalized, but she melted and bent.

The moon was at the full, and so was the tide. The two walked down the road and over the beach silently. Miriam had the strong step of a healthy, happy woman; he could not remember that any woman had ever kept pace with him before. He looked at her with half-blind eyes. In her white laces, with the thrilling light on her face, she looked remote from him—he could not have explained why—and yet how near!

"She shall be nearer," thought the man.

He brought his lips together; they made a mouth of iron. The woman's had a gentle, almost a helpless look in contrast.

The beach, by chance, was quite deserted; it was not a rowing beach,—there was the wharf for the boats; and the summer people were floating dimly on the water, or clustered darkly on the rocks.

The wind was going down, and the surf with it. The long throb of the third roller pulsated regularly, with little agitation and less foam, but with a steady and advancing force which Miriam sensitively felt.

At once she loved the sea and hated it. Sometimes she wished never to look upon its face again; yet it drew her back as the ebb-tide sucked the seaweed. The complexity in her nature vibrated before inevitable power, whose deficiency of mercy repelled and estranged her, even while she yielded to it.

Oppressed by the silence that had subtly settled down between herself and the man, she broke it, half audibly:

"It will carry you safely anywhere—and drown you cordially any time—that's the sea."

Lifted swiftly, her candid eyes snared him unawares, and for one troubled moment it seemed to her that she saw the ocean in his face.

Most illusions have their spiritual sentries whose subtle guardianship may be felt long before it is perceived by the soul. There is a prefiguration granted to a woman on the approach of fate; in this solemn prescience she elects or escapes her lot, with a perfect intelligence which she can never forget, but which she will ignore to her last hour. After such a moment she has no accusations to hurl in the face of life. As Lucifer of hell, so she of experience is compelled to answer: "Myself am destiny."

Miriam stood looking quite steadily into the eyes of Olin Steele. The man was nothing less than formidable. His passion swept around her as the sea heaved about the little boat,—it seemed to be leagues away at that moment,—crossing the splendor of the dazzling path set from eternity between the moon and the sea. The sigh of the surf, the calm of the shore, the separateness in which they two stood, rose around her solemnly like a tide in which she must drown.

Nothing seemed to her quite real—nothing except that she was loved; she was loved as she had dreamed of being loved, as she had not hoped to be or even always wished to be,—by a man who would scorn denial, and laugh at reluctance; who would hurl her feminine subterfuges into star-dust, and create the planet on which she should be his. Yes, and a man who had loved her without waiting to find out that or why he did, and who would love her, whether she yielded or defied, as long as he lived, or she.

Before he had spoken a word Miriam knew what he would say. She made no effort to deter him, but listened gently, when, with a quietness that subdued her and astonished himself, Steele said:

"Ever since I saw your face—that first day—you have been the only woman in the world for me."

Miriam, casting about blindly for words, found none. She turned her agitated face to the sea. The surf was rising, and began to rage upon the cliff. In the unreal light the unreal boat had floated on and away. Nothing now obstructed the path between the sea and the moon.

"I have never seen any other woman whom I wished to make my wife," said Olin Steele. "I did not know that a man could feel like this to any woman. I love you . . . Do you understand? . . . I love you."

"How much do you love me?" asked Miriam in an unsteady voice. She was conscious of the weakness of her words as soon as she had uttered them. She did not look at him any longer. Steele wished that he could have seen her head droop, or her color change.

"Give me the right to show you!" he cried. But Miriam shrank.

"I cannot—I do not like to—talk about it. I do not wish to be what you say. I like it better—the way we are."

Steele laughed.

"Do you think you can escape me? . . . Try!"

67

Her beautiful color came now, wave upon wave, till her face was lost in the flood of it. It was as if she hesitated and swayed towards him.

"Miriam!"

A voice that seemed to come from a great height, and to be freighted with supernal solemnity, dropped like a boulder upon the two. Steele wheeled as if he had been struck and mangled; but Miriam—she could not help it—laughed.

"Is it Azrael? Or Gabriel?"

"Atropos, it seems"; Steele ground his teeth. "And you can laugh." He turned upon her with a certain brutality; she had never seen anything of the kind in him before.

"Mir-i-um?—Look up here. See who has come to spend Sunday."

Miriam lifted her beautiful chin. Mrs. Percy B. Jeffries, affectionately attached to the arm of Philip Surbridge, solidly ornamented the cliff-top.

"Let us go back," Surbridge was heard to urge his clinging client.

"No," said Miriam distinctly. "Do not go away. Come—and bring Atropos with you."

She dashed at a tear which was creeping into her not very happy smile. How should a man know that a woman laughs lest she should cry, and cries because she has laughed?

At that moment Dr. Steele could have cheerfully chloroformed Mrs. Jeffries, or experimented (without anæsthesia) upon Surbridge.

But Olin's face was the finely finished mask of a man who has for years had more in his life to conceal than to reveal.

He made no effort to address Miriam again that evening, and in the morning took so early a train that she was not down. But he wrote to her as soon as he reached town—madly and powerfully. It was a letter which would have brought almost any other woman whom he knew to his arms. He wrote without rereading, without pausing, without reflecting. He wrote as rivers rush, as fire burns, as torrents fall, as nature would and willed—yet reverently and even delicately; almost as that sensitive boy might have written, who died that a physiologist should live.

Chapter VI

—ınnı—

Miriam was moved by Steele's letter. She answered it gently, but, for so young a woman, guardedly. She wrote with a fine, old-fashioned courtesy, and thanked him for the honor that he did her; begged his tolerance for a state of feeling which made it difficult for her to reply with the finality that he had a right to expect; expressed her preference for the relation of friendship as opposed to that which he sought, with the naïveté given to woman only at such stages of experience, admitted that she should be sorry to lose this friendship out of her life; distinctly granted nothing more, yet refrained from insisting that nothing more could ever be possible.

Olin Steele carried the letter against his heart like a boy. When he was alone with it, he scorched it with kisses. His step rang, his eyes assumed the look that a man wears but once in life, and many never. He was like one who is climbing into a high altitude slowly, but of his power to reach the summit has no troublesome doubt.

To power, indeed, as a factor in life, he was inclined to give its foil mathematical value. Sheer strength, ample advantage, seemed to him the basis of calculation. The solution of most problems he had found to lie in superiority, mental or even physical. His professional existence depended upon the doctrine that dominion argued rights rather than obligations. Almost every day of the last decade of his life he had sacrificed the weak to the strong, the small to the great. He had become so accustomed to such a transposition of the moral claims, and to such disarrangement of spiritual values, that he had lost the delicate micrometer by which he was used to measure the meaning of things.

Perhaps he had never distinctly reduced his views of the great relation of life to words; but, if he had, they would have been something like these: The world is divided into the reigning and the subject races; man, clearly, belongs to one of these; woman, plainly, to the other. A man who loves a woman not easily to be won must gain her by some species of force—what, will depend upon the specimen of her race with whom he has to deal. The chief element in the struggle will be his personal determination.

Into this determination Steele now hurled his being, as a child drops the boat he has carved into Niagara. Miriam Lauriat was a woman of intellect; she deferred to the supremacy of his. She was capable of a profound and passionate love; she would yield to the torrent of his. She was in so far attracted to him that it rested with himself—he now believed—to beleaguer her thoroughly, to over-come her absolutely. He perceived, indeed, that he had forced his opportunity; that he had spoken too soon. He passed the summer in a confident attempt to retrieve the mistake; for this delay he was conscious of purposing that she should sometime atone to him.

Their relation had now become an absorbing one. They had entered upon the ancient warfare for which history has never yet recorded the protocols of peace—that between the loving and pur-suing man and the attracted but reluctant woman. Steele seemed to himself to be steadily gaining upon her resistance. With hope in his heart and light in his eyes he went to her one August afternoon.

He was intending to take the boat, as usual, but when he reached the wharf he found it crowded with a class of passengers who were not agreeable to him. He had no mind to join an excursion from the slums, and, suddenly changing his purpose, went out by train. When he left it at the seaside station he was pleased and surprised to see Miss Lauriat's black pair, with Matthew on the box; in the carriage, however, there seemed to be other guests. Matthew did not stop at the station, and as the carriage whirled by, Steele had a good opportunity to see that it was filled, and filled to overflowing, with women and children of the social species that he had left behind him on the wharf in town.

When he arrived at the house, tired and dusty from his walk, an unexpected pastel greeted him. Framed by the tall trees of the avenue where the vistas were cut out, a perspective of sea met a foreground of lawn party. Rugs were spread, a tent, and tables. The shrill crackle of uneducated voices came to his ear before he had come near enough clearly to see Miss Lauriat's guests. These were twenty or thirty in number, and plainly they represented her tenants and protégés in Blind Alley. Ecstasy was in their voices, and adoration in their eyes. Old women were there, and children of assorted sizes. Cady's Molly was there in her red shirt waist and pink hair ribbons, tastefully relieved by a yellow hat. Cady's Molly's father was there, and Dan Badger—in fact, the leading social circles of Blind Alley were represented.

Miss Lauriat, in a plain white linen dress, moved merrily about among this pathetic group. Dr. Steele stood under the trees for a moment before he made his presence known. A consumptive woman, with a baby in her arms, and three little girls rolling over her, was sitting on the grass quite near him. Attached to this family was a dingy white mongrel of a melancholy disposition, who regarded Dr. Steele in cynical silence. But the woman looked up with the cheerful smile of her disorder.

"Nice!" she said, "ain't it? Say, did yer ever see anything like it, anywheres else?"

Dr. Steele's eyes sought Miss Lauriat's exalted face. "No," he said heartily, "no, I never did."

"Say," repeated the woman, "d'you s'pose heaven's anything like this here?"

"It is very possible," replied Steele fervently.

"Because," said the woman, "if I thought it was—"

"What would you do?" asked Steele indifferently, "if you thought it were?"

The woman had caught the indefinable accent of patronage in his tone, or perhaps she perceived that her grammar was corrected.

71

(We remember that Patrick Henry talked to the backwoodsmen in their own dialect.) She glanced at Steele sharply, and did not finish her sentence. In fact, she took her children and moved away.

Now Dr. Steele was more astonished than gratified to see Philip Surbridge, who had been teaching a little boy to ride a bicycle, catch up the three little girls and put them, with his ringing, boyish laugh, in three little swings which he personally conducted. Perceiving the doctor, he called out:

"Ah, Steele! We are having a beautiful time. You are just in season to enjoy yourself!"

Miriam turned to the doctor with a sweet shyness.

"I never was so happy in my life!" she said. "Most of these people haven't got into the country all summer; some of them have never seen it. I cannot explain to you how it makes me feel. Everybody is here—everybody I asked!" She spoke with the flattered gratification of a hostess whose salon is filled. "And Dan—and Dan, too," she added, "and Trixy!"

The crippled lad was lying in a hammock luxuriously reading a book on trained dogs. His crutch fell to the grass, and Miriam impulsively sprang and picked it up for him. Dan's eyes leaped to hers with the worship that deformity gives to beauty, and weakness to sympathetic strength. Dr. Steele watched this little episode with a puzzled expression.

"I don't see Trixy." His gaze wandered about the lawn. "But then, I shouldn't know if I did see her. Is that she?" He pointed to the melancholy mongrel who was regarding the scene without enthusiasm.

"I am ashamed of you!" cried Miss Lauriat, laughing, "not to recognize so famous an actress! Trixy is in the coach house with Matthew. That poor, old, plebeian thing is not very clean, and Dan wouldn't let her associate with him. Trixy, you know, is an aristocrat. The ice cream will be sent in to her on a cut-glass plate."

"Is that gray dog one of the invited guests?"

"Why, of course. He came out on the steamer with the rest. He has a cough—that poor woman's dogs always do—and it was expected to do him good. He belongs to the little girls Mr. Surbridge

72

is swinging. Come, Dr. Steele! There are two boys who don't seem to be having a very good time. Would you mind playing Bear with them? Or perhaps Puss in the Corner. Or Wolf and Red Riding Hood ; or—something!"

"I can try," said Steele grimly. "But I am not sure how far I am to be flattered by your choice of roles."

"You don't care for it," said Miriam under her breath. "You don't care for it at all. And it makes me so happy!"

"I care for anything that makes you happy; you know I do."

"Go, then," commanded Miriam, "and discuss the tariff with Cady's Molly's father. It needs a man to entertain him. He has views about protection and free trade. The subject is beyond my depth, and I have never been able to keep up with it. It requires a masculine intellect."

Steele laughed and obeyed her, awkwardly enough. His personal comfort was not enhanced, nor the subject of the tariff advanced, by the reception which he met.

"Oh, it's you!" said Cady's Molly's father. "You are the fellow that quarantined us, ain't you? We fired you once. I never expected to see you again."

Thus forced to feel his lack of position in slum society, conscious that he was unjustly made to suffer for a plain performance of duty, and therefore not in the best of humors, Dr. Steele retreated from the lawn party and made his way to the piazza, where for an hour to come he solemnly discussed with Mrs. Jeffries the first arrest made by the Society for the Prevention of Docking and Cropping. The tail of a two weeks' puppy had been cut off, and the society had appealed to the humane sentiments of the state, and the majesty of the law. Dr. Steele did not return to the lawn party, which broke up directly after supper.

In the little stir consequent on the departure of Miss Lauriat's guests, he stood embarrassed and apart. None of the people addressed him, and he was glad of it. Philip Surbridge went down the avenue with the consumptive woman on his arm; in his other he carried the baby, and the three little girls clung to his coat-tails.

"You're coming back, aren't you?" pleaded Mrs. Jeffries. "If you don't, there won't be anybody to talk to me."

"I'll come out to see you next week," answered Surbridge, with his tender smile. He did not meet Miriam's eye. "I will say good-night now. I think I'll see them all safely back to town. They are a pretty helpless lot."

This was in an undertone, but Miriam heard it, and warmly held out her hand. Dr. Steele watched her with compressed lips. She went part way down the avenue with Surbridge and the children. Dan Badger limped beside her with Trixy on his neck. The sea wind was shrewish, and Trixy wore her little overcoat with its hood. Miss Lauriat's poor people clung to her wistfully; some of them kissed her, all blessed her, and then the turn in the avenue hid them.

She came back walking rather fast, breathless and beautiful. Steele went down to meet her. He had a paper in his hand; it was a printer's proof-sheet.

"It fell from your pocket," he began, "as you went down the steps. Will you pardon me? It was print, and I did look at it. I didn't read it, though. I didn't know that you wrote."

Miriam flushed and held out her hand for the proof-sheet.

"Let me read it, won't you?" he entreated.

"As long as you have seen it—well—yes. I do not know that I mind—that is—not very much."

"I did not know that you were an authoress," observed Steele.

"I am not an authoress," flashed Miriam, "and no reading man ever uses that word, Dr. Steele. Let me have my proof-sheet, if you please."

"Oh, forgive me!" cried Steele. "I am always saying or doing the wrong thing."

"And I am always forgiving you," she answered in an unsteady voice.

Steele read the verses. There were but two, and they ran like this:

SONG

To the spaces between the stars
We went, my love and I,
Among the uttermost things.
For my love hath wings;
With twain he covers his face,
With twain his feet,
With twain he doth fly.

To the earth and our rose-red door,
We came, my love and I.
Among the dear, daily things,
He folded his wings.
But the wingèd watch their time.
And when he starts,
Ah, how shall I fly?

He returned the proof-sheet to her. "I don't understand it," he said perplexedly. "It is graceful, but I don't think I know what you mean."

Miriam put the verses back in her pocket.

"Now your taste for painting," began Dr. Steele, "that appeals to me. I have never lost my interest in art. There are so many things that a man does lose, you know. I hope you have not given up whatever you were doing at the school? I like to think of you in that peaceful and aesthetic place."

"I have not been there this summer," said Miriam, in a constrained tone.

"Why not?"

Miriam made no reply. Her attraction for Dr. Steele had now reached a stage where she was conscious of wishing to harmonize with him in everything, and uncomfortable when she might not. She could not have explained to herself why it was that she often found it impossible to give him a confidence which she longed to offer. His presence brought her pleasure, but not peace. He came often; the summer passed dreamily; and she slowly began to admit to herself—but not as yet to him—that he was becoming necessary to her. As the doctor's visits increased in frequency, those of the lawyer diminished. Miriam, who had been often beloved, had never counted Philip Surbridge among her suitors, and when she found that she missed him, felt quite at liberty to tell him so.

DEAR PHILIP [she wrote one day]: Aunt Cornelia is playing Mariana in the Moated Grange for your sweet sake. I mind it a little myself, that you stay away.

Yours faithfully,

MIRIAM LAURIAT.

Surbridge responded to this recall, but leisurely, and it was the second week in September before he came out to dine and spend the evening. Miriam was unaffectedly and heartily glad to see him. He took her out to row, for there was a rowing moon, and she sat in the stern, in her white boating dress, with her hands clasped behind her head, and looked at him affectionately.

He rowed well, and she thought how square his shoulders were, and how sturdy his arm—for so studious a man. The values of his face in the strong, soft light were like those of a Reynolds portrait, which had the repose of an earlier, calmer age than ours. His very presence quieted her; it always had. Did he soothe most people in the same way? She sometimes asked herself the question. She was conscious of that old impulse to tell things to Philip Surbridge. It was not only that he belonged to one of the confessional professions; but he had the confessor's temperament.

As he rowed her out from the shore she regarded him wistfully. There were no other boats about them, and they seemed to be quite alone with the sea and the sky. She thought of that other moon-bright night when she and Steele had stood upon the shore. But she and Surbridge were going straight out to sea.

"It is the same sea, the same sky, the same moon," thought Miriam, "but it's not the same woman."

They talked little and lightly, with long silences between their quiet words. She felt a distinct relief from the mental turmoil of the summer. For this one hour it was not peremptory to decide anything, and she was conscious of a sense of reprieve.

Philip's boyish smile in itself was a comfort to her, as it always was, and his dark, mute eyes seemed to protect her from herself. He did not urge her confidence; indeed, she was half aware that he fended it off.

To Miriam, as to all high-minded girls, love had always seemed to be a demonstrable thing; it never occurred to her that she could have any doubts about it when she should experience it, or that she could cast up the divine sum of her happiness in more than one inevitable way. Love was inexorable, in a sense mathematical; it was of the celestial sciences; it would be eternal, like the ordering of the stars, and she should follow its commands—brain and heart, soul and body, will and imagination—as the sea follows the moon. She was bewildered by the perturbation in which she had passed the last six months. If she had obeyed her maddest impulse, she would have cried out like a distressed girl to her elder brother:

"Philip! Philip! What shall I do?" But in point of fact she said no such thing.

"You are looking tired," Surbridge observed quietly; but that was all.

"I am tired," Miriam passionately exclaimed—as if he could help it; as if she expected him to.

She held out her hands to him girlishly.

"If I thought I could really do anything—" began Surbridge, laying down his oars. His manner had changed, and his tone, which at first was but gently troubled, rose into the ring of acute feeling. "But you must see—you cannot help understanding. It's—hard!"

"Look out there!" interrupted Miriam. "The steamer! You are getting into her wake!"

Surbridge, veering sharply, skillfully escaped the serpent of foam which had begun to coil about their little rocking boat, as the steamer from the city passed them on her last trip out. Both looked up at the crowded deck. An undersized lad, who was leaning over the rail, seemed to be making an effort to attract their attention.

"Why, there's Dan Badger!" cried Miriam quickly. "Look—look at his face. Row me ashore, please. Quick! As fast as you can!"

Surbridge rowed rapidly and powerfully; he beached the boat on a little cove below the wharf at which the steamer was somewhat slowly and clumsily making a landing. She was late, and would put about immediately on her return trip. Miriam jumped from the dory and ran up the bank without waiting for Surbridge. As soon as he could secure his boat he hurried after her.

The crippled lad stood leaning on his crutch. He was trying to speak, but his words came thickly. His face was gray and pinched, like that of a little old man, and he shook from head to foot. Dan had neither eaten nor slept for twenty-four hours.

"Where's Trixy? Where's Trixy?" Miriam was saying over and over.

Dan stared at her stupidly as if he did not understand what she said.

"Come, Dan," urged Surbridge very gently, "tell us all about it."

With a gesture never to be forgotten by those who witnessed it, the cripple dropped his crutch and threw both hands above his head, as one does in unendurable physical pain.

"Trixy's lost!"

"No! No! No!" cried Miriam.

"Not stolen?" exclaimed Surbridge.

But Dan repeated dully: "Trixy's lost. I tell you Trixy's lost. I've hunted for her everywheres. Everybody's hunted. Nobody can't find her."

"Give me the circumstances," urged Surbridge, "if you can. Tell me when it happened, and where. Try, Dan. Think how it was."

"I can't," muttered Dan, "my—my head won't let me. It was last night—she had on her little coat you made her, Miss Laurie—it

78

was sort of cold—and we'd been playing at one of them beaches—I can't think the name—my head is bad. We was jest goin' home—you never see her play so pretty—I put her down—I—think I put her down, and when I looked she wasn't there. I tried to hurry, but I'm lame, you know. She wasn't there.—Sir?"

For the first time since he had known her, Dan, disregarding his goddess, turned elsewhere for divine interference; it was as if he felt that his extremity was a matter between men.

"Mr. Surbridge, sir," said Dan, "you told me once if ever me and Trixy needed a friend, to count on you. So here I be."

"Come with me, Dan." Surbridge caught the boy quickly, for Dan swayed and tottered. "Come! The boat starts right away. I will go back to town with you."

"And, Dan!" cried Miriam, "listen to me. I'm sure Mr. Surbridge will find her. Do you hear me? Sure. Mr. Surbridge always finds everything that he tries to."

She put her arm around the lad's neck, and kissed him and patted him, thinking no more of the people on the wharf than if they had been starfish on the rocks.

She and Philip grasped hands. He did not even ask how she was going to find her way home without him, nor did she like him the less for that.

She stood on the wharf watching the steamer till it reeled out of sight. Once Philip lifted his hat. He was tenderly enfolding the boy, whose face was hidden against the young man's heart.

"Dan is crying in his arms," thought Miriam.

CHAPTER VII

—ⱳ—

Among the worlds of woe allotted to sentient life, there is one which hangs quite apart from the rest of the system, and holds a place unique in the astronomy of pain; this may be called the world of the lost dog. In this alone the human and the animal can strictly be said to suffer together. In other catastrophes shared by the higher and the lower races, each endures or perishes thinking of his own pang. When fate separate master and dog, each undergoes the pang of the other. It has been well written that the dog is the only animal who has elected to give himself utterly to the worship of man; and man, to a certain extent, has returned this profound and pathetic attachment. It cannot be claimed that he has done this on even terms. "Dogs," said a student of the species, "have the grandest of created qualities: love, gratitude, and fidelity." But the man, though he may never love as nobly as his dog, has requited the touching devotion that he receives with an affection which cannot be duplicated in the range of human feeling.

Dan haunted the streets, the wharves, the steamers, the stations, the beaches, the kennels, the saloons, as a little crippled ghost might shadow the scenes of his former life. His face and figure had acquired such a look that happy people shrank from him, and the careless of heart avoided him. He had grown as silent as an insomniac; he slept little, and ate less. The grasp of Mr. Surbridge's hand, the tears on Miss Lauriat's cheeks were more than he could bear; the lad crawled away into his anguish as some little blind mole, mortally hurt, crawls into a hole where it cannot be found. All day he searched—and searched. All night he lay pondering where he should search tomorrow.

More than once Cady's Molly's father tiptoed in and found him with wide eyes, staring at the ceiling of his narrow bedroom. The lad lay far over at one side of the cot, with his feet drawn up, as he was accustomed to do to give the little dog room. His ragged coat with which he used to cover Trixy was folded in its place. Sometimes he dreamed that she was there, and his thin hand stole down to pat her. Cady's Molly's father happened once to see this touching action, and the big fellow came away blubbering like a boy.

Trixy had whirled out of sight as utterly as a feather caught by a cyclone; and into the fate of this little creature the human lives whose story it is ours to tell were inextricably drawn. Only this could be said in palliation of Dan's misery, that he was not left to bear it alone. The bereaved lad was carried through it with a tenderness and a fidelity finer than that which most men and women offer their own flesh and blood. Nothing that wisdom or power, sweetness or light, could do for him was denied to the afflicted lad. Miss Lauriat poured out money upon the search for Trixy as if she had no other earthly uses for it, and Philip Surbridge threw his professional skill and experience at the feet of Dan's extremity with a large, reckless generosity characteristic of the man.

At the outset Miriam had made it plain that she wished to retain her attorney in Dan's behalf. With a naive confidence in the law, born of confidence in the lawyer, she had directed him:

"Spare nothing, and spare nobody, but find that dog."

"I'll find Trixy if she is alive; but I cannot take your money for it," said Surbridge unexpectedly.

Miriam, as unexpectedly, flushed. "I cannot see why. The time—the trouble—the skill, and you—"

But Surbridge took fire.

"Yes, I know I do for other things; but for this I can't, and I won't. Dan retained me before you did."

"Very well," said Miriam, "have it your own way, then. But—Philip—"

"But what?"

"It is not necessary for me to hear everything, is it? I know just how that sounds," she faltered. "I don't expect anybody to understand. But most people don't feel as I do about—you know, since—"

Philip looked at her compassionately.

"I wish you could outlive that!—No, you shall not be worried. Trust me, and leave it all to me."

This was a favorite phrase of Philip's. Miriam had heard it—how many times in how many troubles! "Leave it all to me." She held always found it natural to leave everything to him. Like a sister she had leaned, like a brother he had guarded. She took their unemotional relation as a matter of course.

In the agitation consequent upon the loss of Trixy, Miriam seemed like a person whose emotion is strained with a tension disproportionate to the disturbing cause. The poise of her perfect nerve shook a little, and she became uncertain of movement, and moody of impulse. At the first announcement of Dan's calamity she would have closed her house at the shore and moved back to town. But Mrs. Jeffries, who had no moods, few whims, and inexorable habits, could see no reason why the household should leave the coast four weeks too soon because a boy in the slums had lost his dog. Miriam, therefore, took Maggie and the old seamstress, opened the town house, and vibrated restlessly between the two homes. It seemed to her impossible not to be near the scene of Dan's misery; yet when she was there, it seemed impossible to bear it. For days she would leave the lad's affairs entirely to Surbridge, herself falling into a silence that was not broken by a question. At other times she brooded over the boy more tenderly than his mother would have done, if Dan had known one, and dwelt upon his bereavement as if it had been her own. From this too sensitive sympathy she would wince away like a wounded nerve, and occupy herself with anything and everything except the disappearance of Trixy. She was, in fact, overwrought, and not altogether reasonable. Afterwards—long afterwards—she perceived what at the time she was quite unconscious of, that this unnatural condition gave a subtle deflection to her own lot. It threw her more than usual into the society of Olin Steele; and the young professor did not talk about lost dogs. He had expressed his regret for Dan's affliction in language that he felt would appeal to the excessive sympathy which he perceived Miss Lauriat to be cherishing. It was a relief to him that she evidently preferred not to discuss the matter, and thereafter he tactfully avoided it. One day he happened to say:

"I lost Barry once. He was gone a week. I had the whole state looking for him."

Miss Lauriat received this remark in silence so unlike herself that he looked at her shrewdly. He was not naturally patient with inattention to what he chose to say. Some day, he thought, he would ask her what she meant by it.

Some day—ah, that day! As God lived, he swore, its sun should rise and set. In the magic of its haze, in the marvel of its splendor, she should be his. Oh, and willingly! Yes, and joyfully. For his love had grown fastidious, epicurean. At the first, as he had told himself, he meant to win her "anyhow." Now, this would not content him. She—no subject that he should seize her against her own heart's will—she, the strongest and tenderest woman whom he had ever known—she, out of whose strength came her sweetness, and whose capacity for love he knew that no heart had measured—she should come to him like any lesser woman, yielding, and glad to yield. Oh, she should crave him—as he, her. She should hunger and thirst for his love as he had hungered and thirsted—and maddened and waited—for hers.

He pursued his suit with the ardor of an oriental despot, and the tactics of an occidental diplomat. He knew he was gaining upon her defenses; he made havoc with her reluctance; he antedated his triumphs in a delirium of victory the mightier because it was controlled and unexpressed, and already he flaunted banners in his own heart.

Miriam treated him with a guarded sweetness which at times took on the tint of tenderness, and at others deepened into reserve amounting almost to rebuff. Then she would pause again, and seem to wait and look at him over her shoulder. It could not be said that as yet she experienced either peace or joy; but she was now conscious of living in a world apart with Olin Steele.

It has long been one of the psychological mysteries that a delicately reared and finely fibred woman may idealize a man of coarser grain and manifestly lower moral nature. Even an infatuation for brute force may possess an otherwise clear-headed and true-hearted woman. Call such emotional defectives; from their lineage Miriam Lauriat's was by the heaven's width removed; yet was she subtly swept within the extended shadow of that unhappy fate? Sheer physical perfection did not interest her. If she had been thrown solitary upon some planet with a low-browed, dull-minded gladiator, he would not have attracted her in any sense of the word. But to intellectual athletics she was very sensitive, and this kind of prowess she felt in Steele. His well-trained mind, his large learning, his professional preeminence, commanded her. In his department he was a scholar; in conversation he was stimulating, in manner finished, in character without reproach; and in the difficult art of courtship he was without fear. In love he would take no denial. He surrounded her with a sense of power more dangerous to her because more fine than the kind of domination to which a weaker woman yields.

Miriam was besieged by his determination. She had begun to feel that she had no escape from the strategy of a love that was all will, and of a will that had become all love.

"I suppose you know," said Philip Surbridge one day, "I suppose you understand—pardon me—what Olin Steele is?"

Surbridge turned very pale as he uttered these words. They seemed to be forced from his lips by a deliberate and solemn purpose, that he would have concealed, if he could, in an incidental manner.

Miriam lifted her chin with that pretty, haughty motion which Philip so seldom saw.

"Why, everybody knows. He is professor at Galen. He is at the head of one of the most important departments in the school."

85

She brought these sentences out with little dents between as if she had bitten them.

"But you know," Philip hesitated, "you know what he teaches? You know what he does?"

"He teaches physiology," said Miriam proudly. "It is the basis of all medical education. I understand he teaches it thoroughly and brilliantly."

Philip looked at her in silence. There was a certain compassion in his eyes which hers instantly resented.

"Is there anything new about Trixy?" she asked abruptly. "Any more clues?"

"Yes, a new one. And there may be something in it. I came to say so, but I see you don't wish to hear about it this morning."

"I will hear it tomorrow," answered Miriam nervously. "Tell me all about it tomorrow."

But tomorrow when he came to tell her, she had gone to the shore; and Steele had followed her. Maggie handed Surbridge a hurried note which had been left at the town house for him.

DEAR PHILIP [it said]: I am tired out and nervous, and I am gone to spend a couple of days with Aunt Cornelia. Telephone if I am needed. It occurs to me that if you have a new clue you may need to increase your detective force. I inclose a signed check, which you will please fill out to any extent that the expenses of the search for Trixy may require. I cannot tell you how I feel about what you are doing, and the way in which you are doing it. All I can say is that it's just like you. I am a good deal worried about some other matters, and I must leave it all to you. How many times in my life I have done that!

I am always your grateful
and faithful
MIRIAM LAURIAT.

❖

There was no moon, and the early September dark had shut in softly. The sky was lightly clouded; with only here and there a star. The black gulf of the sea lay sheer below the piazza, and the rising tide reverberated against the cliff which rose straight as the side of a cañon. In fact, the broad piazza overlapped the water, and one had the sense of hanging in mid-air above the abyss. The night was warm, the wind southerly, and the surf heavy.

Miriam and Steele sat side by side in the screened, half-lighted place. The long, unshaded windows revealed Aunt Cornelia reading by a lamp with a blue globe that lent to her face the ghastly effect which it is given only to this particular species of domestic art to offer. In fact, it seemed to color the shaft of light that lay across the piazza; this had a sickly tint like light blue marble. It made Miriam uncomfortable, and she moved into the shadow. Steele immediately followed, taking a piazza chair directly in front of her. She stirred uneasily, and made as if she would lean over the railing of the piazza, but the galvanized wire netting prevented. She drew back impatiently.

"These screens keep the mosquitoes out—but the comfort, too. What's the use of a piazza that you can't look over? I feel as if I were in a cage."

"And so you are," said Olin Steele.

When Miriam looked up and saw his face, half black in the shadow, half pale in the cold light, every drop of red blood deserted her own.

"Why did you come tonight?" she pleaded. "I did not expect you."

"Why did you try to escape me?" he demanded. "I do not permit you."

Miriam's chin rose instinctively with its haughty motion.

"I have given you no right to speak to me like that!"

"No," he said firmly, "but you are going to give it to me."

He was obliged to speak very distinctly, or the roar of the surf would have quenched his voice. Ten feet away nothing they said could have been heard. They were shut apart in the rage of wind and wave.

87

"I have waited till I can wait no more," he said desperately. "You have played with me as long as I can bear it."

"I have never played with you!" cried Miriam.

"Well, defied me, then; it is the same thing. I have resolved to end it. My misery—"

"Are you miserable?" asked Miriam, with unexpected tenderness. "I don't want to make you—unhappy."

"I know you don't," said Steele, "because you love me."

Miriam flung her hands up against the screen; he thought how well she had spoken when she called it a cage. Her whole being seemed to beat upon it. She looked like a creature entrapped.

"You love me," he insisted, "only you won't own it. You won't own it to yourself—or to me."

Miriam's forehead fell against the metal netting. She felt the spray from the gulf fifty feet below upon her face. "Oh, perhaps I do," she sighed, "perhaps I do."

The noise of the surf was so great that Steele could not be sure he had distinctly understood her. His heart throbbed in his body as the waves throbbed on the rocks; his brain hammered on his temples.

"Let me hear it!" he cried. "Let me hear it again."

Miriam lifted her head and raised her eyes. In them he might have seen the infinite sadness with which a woman yields to a powerful but imperfect love. "Perhaps I do," she repeated. "I am afraid I do."

As the waves to the shore Steele turned towards her. Her soft shoulder quivered beneath his arm. She felt his breath on her cheek. Then Miriam shrank.

"Oh, no! Not now! Not yet! I can't—Not yet—not yet!"

In a moment, without seeming to repel, she had eluded him. So mystery eludes science, so the spirit escapes the body. Trembling and white she leaned against the fine, invisible bars of the narrowing space in which they stood together. She regarded him solemnly. There was that in her eyes before which Steele felt his

88

head grow light; but he could no more have touched her than he could have torn the sphinx from the desert.

"Next time!" she entreated. "Perhaps next time."

Steele's outstretched arms fell.

"I shall reprieve you," he said very slowly, "till next time."

Now, Miriam, wincing from these words, yet leaning to them, hid her face upon her hands, and when she lifted it he had left her.

"That was merciful," she thought, and the tide of her tenderness for the man rose by one of the abrupt and powerful waves below whose high-water line, if the laws of feeling are not intercepted, a woman's love will not ebb. Sensitively craving solitude, she opened the screen door that led from the piazza to the garden, and, hardly knowing what she did, or why she did it, paced to and fro alone with wild feet among the frosted flowers. The nasturtiums and salvia were still alive, and since she brushed and bruised them, they splashed her white woolen dress with red petals that clung to it.

But when, an hour later, she went into the house, she found Aunt Cornelia excited and annoyed. Philip Surbridge had been ringing at the telephone ever since Dr. Steele went away. "And I told him you had probably jumped into the ocean, for I could not find you high or low."

"And what," Miriam inquired absently, "did Philip say?" "He said: 'When she jumps out again tell her I called her up on a matter of some importance, but she's not to mind; she can leave it all to me.' And I must say, Miriam—"

But Miriam did not stay to hear what Aunt Cornelia must say.

In the city the September night was sad and sultry, and Surbridge, who had hurried back to his rooms after his ineffectual effort to consult Miriam by telephone, flung open the window and leaned out a little over the sill for a breath of such air as there was. As he did so he heard the thud, thudding of a rubber-tipped crutch upon the sidewalk, and the uneven sound of a crippled foot trailing with it. Both stopped directly beneath his window.

"Mr. Surbridge, sir?"

"Yes, Dan, yes,—anything more?"

"Oh, sir, I've found—Oh, sir!" Dan stood choking. Terrible sobs tore the words out of the lad's throat. He held up something in his shaking hands.

"I can't see, Dan. Don't try to come up! It's two flights—I will come down."

Surbridge ran down and out upon the sidewalk. Dan stood staring at him.

"I've come—to count on—you," gasped the boy. With a feeble moan as if his own life were gashed out of him from a severed artery, Dan laid across Surbridge's arm a little dog's coat of blue flannel, soiled and stained and torn. Part of the embroidered name on the coat had been worn off or cut off; but some of the stitches were left where the lettering had been, and by the street lamp Surbridge plainly read:

TRIXY

Chapter VIII

—⚡—

The night, which was warm at the shore, and sultry in the city, was stifling in the laboratory. The windows were closed. This was found desirable because complaints had arisen in the neighborhood of occasional strange sounds that seemed to come from the school of science. It was rumored that protests from the art school had taken shape; that the hotheaded old signor had complained of something affecting the nerves of his pupils. In the rear of the medical building was a hospital, and during the hot weather when windows were open, patients had described to their nurses and doctors signs of animal distress which now and then disturbed the human sick.

The medical school of Galen was an ancient and independent institution, not affiliated with a university. All that age, endowment, and intellectual prestige could bestow was at the command of this powerful scientific centre. Its alumni could be found throughout the civilized world, and cherished a remarkably strong attachment to their school. They were ready to defend her as most men defend their country's flag, through evil report and good, were she right or were she wrong. Among the graduates (and especially, let it be noted, among the elder men belonging to an earlier day, before modern physiology had begun to control the curriculum) were to be found many of the noblest representatives of the medical profession—men of aspiration, self-denial, and consecration; men on whom the sick leaned, and whom the dying trusted; men whom women honored, and children loved, and the poor blessed; men who hesitated at no sacrifice, halted at no danger, and who would hurl away their own lives without a thought, to save a patient. These men, too busy in healing the sick to inflict the ingenuities of a decadent science upon small, speechless creatures, thought little and knew less about what was going on in the fastnesses of their own medical school. Yet, the moment when her fair fame should be touched, they would spring to her defense like soldiers blindly following the colors through a fight in a fog. So widely scattered and so deeply united were the alumni of this celebrated school that they carried its powerful influence everywhere, and sustained in the public mind a respect for the institution amounting to idealization. Among the first to recognize and respond to this pervasive influence had been the men of fortune. A multi-millionaire, who had devoted his superfluous thousands for some years to the endowment of societies for the prevention of cruelty to animals, one summer day upon a yachting cruise fell under the beguiling influence of the old professor of physiology at Galen—since gathered to his fate in a world where he may look long for a congenial occupation. The result was that Galen, although, as we say, a very ancient school, had a very modern building. This—a gift outright from the philanthropic capitalist who had devoted himself hitherto to the interests of animals—was new from roof to cellar. It was not intended necessarily to be a replica of other buildings of its kind. The old professor had full swing, and had carried into execution some ideas of his own.

The first floor of the school was given up to the lecture-rooms, offices, and so on, and to the physiological laboratory. This was separated from the lecture-room which we shall call the amphitheatre by a short passageway, and by double and deadened walls. Every device that the modern building art could offer for the dulling of sound had been employed. Floors and ceilings were tremendously thick, and heavily lined with mineral wool. In the basement of the building the unhappy creatures who furnished the material for experimental physiology were confined. The room where the dumb prisoners were incarcerated was in a wing; some of its windows looked upon a yard that separated it from the hospital.

This lower room could be reached in several ways; for instance, by two flights of stairs—one running from the physiological laboratory—and by a corridor that led out to the rear of the building. This corridor, which ramified in more than one direction, led to a low door (one of several exits) somewhat hidden from observation by a porch or balcony whose purpose seemed to be ornamental only. This door, which opened upon an alley, was used by the janitor and laboratory assistants. Most of the students knew nothing of its existence, and a casual passer would not have noticed it. The corridor of which mention has been made contained two closets; one was used for the disposal of brooms, mops, snow-shovels, pails, and so on; another for hanging coats and hats. This latter closet was not far from the low door of which we have spoken.

It was now eleven o'clock. In the hospital the sick slept, or prayed that they might do so before dawn. In the school of the arts the silent studio, at night given over to the shades and shapes of beautiful things, aroused slowly to the consciousness of itself. The antiques regarded each other solemnly; the statue of Pity seemed to breathe and turn its face; but the figure of the Christ did not stir; it hung at about the height of a cross, upon the wall. In the medical school a few stray students had finished their work in the dissecting room and had gone for the night. With the exception of the janitor and the engineer, the building was deserted now of human presence, and in its upper stories quiet. In the basement it could seldom be called quiet. In that inferno the circles of misery gave out the inarticulate expression of a doom worse because neither understood, elected, nor deserved. For the most part these signs of anguish were gentle and docile, and at night were much in abeyance. Now and then a dog howled, or, if not badly injured, barked; and broken moans of pain answered from some awakened or some dreaming creature; but most of the victims endured with the silence and patience by which the suffering animal shames the human race.

The room was dark, and the atmosphere heavy, as has been said. Creatures accustomed to freedom and to fresh air gasped the night away. The large place was lined with cages, each occupied by its little prisoner. The inoculated victims were many—rabbits, guinea pigs, and the like—all vicariously, and for the most part uselessly, enduring for the vagaries of science the maladies of man. Sights which the readers of these pages could not bring their delicate sensibilities to witness, facts which you who follow this narrative would not permit its writer to relate, crowded that den of anguish.

Those four walls, packed with suffering, kept their secrets well. Into this tragic place no curious reporter was admitted; from it the omnipotence of the press was excluded; into this pit no sister of mercy stepped; to these wounded no hospital nurse brought the ministrations of her gentle art; into this lair no preacher entered, and, leaving it, challenged Christian civilization with its existence; into this hell no Christ descended.

It was well after midnight when a slight disturbance occurred in the animal room. A newcomer, who had not yet been operated upon, and who was not caged, but tied, awoke whining. Restless calls of response echoed throughout the large room. The little white dog that had caused the trouble pulled frantically at its rope, and in its most pathetic way called for its master. A low reply came from an adjoining cage, and a black muzzle pressed itself against the netting. The white poodle returned a few sympathetic remarks, and the two carried on a short conversation. The debutante in that sad society, who though sometimes leashed, was not, until her recent unhappy experience, accustomed to be tied, resented her captivity with intolerable astonishment. She pulled and pulled again at the stout rope, and then, yielding to the stifling closeness of the room, stopped, panting and exhausted. Low whines from the black spaniel in the nearest cage greeted this failure.

Most dogs, even the most intelligent and the best educated, are numbed by despair when they are lost. Their very powers of thought or recognition are affected by the supreme catastrophe.

For two weeks the French poodle had been bewildered by the agony of homesickness. Torn from its master, from its home, from its occupation, it had fallen into a lethargy that had dispossessed it of its natural reason. Now, after the last desperate and futile attempt to break or gnaw the rope, the baffled creature had cast itself upon the floor. In that moment of exhaustion, memory flooded its brain. With a bound the dog leaped to its feet. It uttered a short, piercing bark of triumph. Suddenly Trixy had found herself.

It now occurred to her for the first time that, no matter what might be the case with more ignorant dogs, it was quite unnecessary for her to remain a prisoner. She could slip her collar, as she had done scores of times before. She bent her head down, put her paws up to her neck, and with a wriggle or two, deftly drew the collar over her ears. Contemptuously she picked it up and tossed it away. Trixy's intellect, although close on the keenest order known to her race, paused on the hither side of the facts that an attempt had been made to remove the plate from her collar, and that, this having failed, the name of her master had been scratched into partial illegibility.

The little actress now had the freedom of the room. The first use that she made of it was to examine its occupants, her companions in misfortune. She addressed herself at the outset to her neighbor, the black spaniel; but he, for some reason which was beyond Trixy's power to fathom, responded only by feeble moans. Hoping to find some more sociable playmate, Trixy made a tour of the room. She was especially interested in a cat, to whom some extraordinary thing had happened, for it neither spit nor scratched, nor, in fact made any reply to Trixy's advances. In point of fact, this was considered upstairs a very interesting case. The cat had been subjected for five hours to a treatment of which it is impossible on a page like this to speak in detail. The downstairs view of the experiment was another matter, and the cat was as much in the dark as Trixy as to the why and wherefore of her suffering.

Discouraged by her reception there, Trixy sought the acquaintance of a few guinea pigs and rabbits, one monkey, and a pigeon or two. These were too ill to respond, and, as Trixy had not learned their language, she passed on.

Dogs, like human beings, make their friends instinctively, and stick to them. In the dark, and in what she half consciously perceived to be danger, Trixy craved companionship. She trotted back to the only place where this could be found. She sat up on her hind legs in front of the spaniel's cage, and prettily begged him to come out. Grieved at his indifference, Trixy began to whine and scratch at the cage door. Her higher intelligence now grasped the fact that the dog was in suffering of some kind, for some reason, and she proceeded to investigate both these mysteries; but it was too dark to make much headway with them, and she lay down in front of the spaniel's cage. Here she remained patiently until the first gray sign of dawn entered the window.

Trixy had been transferred the evening before from another part of the cellar, which, had she but known it, though more dismal, was to be preferred to her present quarters, and for a sinister reason that fortunately was beyond the scope of her power to forecast, because it was outside the range of her experience. In that other prison she had found no opportunity for society; she now stood up, and in the fast-growing light began to inspect her new acquaintance closely.

Through the netting of the cage she saw a cocker spaniel, black, with a white shirt-frill, and what seemed to be a white part in the middle of his forehead, but of this it was difficult to be sure, for the dog's head was bound with a bandage of cloth. This perplexed Trixy, and struck her as a novel circumstance. Indeed, the whole situation of the spaniel mystified and saddened her. One thing only was clear—the dog was in pain, and she, generously sharing his misery, for the moment, as human philanthropists do in similar cases, forgot her own.

Among animals of the higher class feelings are more contagious than with men. Lacking a system of intricate communication, they catch emotion instinctively. The black spaniel now began to respond to Trixy's advances. It arose, wagged its tail feebly, and came to the door of its cage, looking at its new friend with great, mournful, mystified eyes. This attention Trixy received with little yelps of ecstasy.

She stood up again on her hind legs and tried to kiss the spaniel, but could not, for the wire forbade the caress; which, besides, tasted metallic.

Yet Trixy could not be denied. She made a few desperate scratches, but found the cage too strong for penetration. That it must have an opening she did not doubt. Her black eyes began to snap and glisten. Her hot, black nose dilated with eager sniffs as she investigated the front of the cage. Ah! Here the scent of man! Here must be the opening of the door—this wooden, much-worn pin. Trixy began to work furiously on that new thought. She tugged with her teeth, every now and then scratching the side of the cage to see if the entrance yielded.

All the while the spaniel stood patiently. At each of Trixy's efforts his dulled eyes took on a lighter shade of intelligence. For two years he had never known a free hour—a moment of happiness—a sign of tenderness. If he had ever had a home, the memory of its delight was only a clot on the brain. For misery was his life, and torment his pastime. He had been existing in a black cloud, and the interest of this little white poodle was the only thing his incarceration had offered to show that all breathing creatures were not inquisitors or victims.

Suddenly with a jerk Trixy fell back. In her mouth was the wooden pin. This she had pulled out like an under tooth from the top. She regarded the round piece of wood with intense hatred. She bit at it, and then, in a moment of inspiration, ran away with it and hid it—where, no man to this day knows. Then she came back triumphant. Now, her poor friend was free. She pushed at the door, but this diabolical contrivance was made to open out—not in. All the while the black spaniel looked on stolidly. He wanted to respond, to help, but he did not know how.

Then Trixy began a course of instruction. She put her right paw up and patted the door sharply, and looked at the prisoner with a pleading whine. "Do what I do!" she said, as plainly as articulation could have said it. Her imprisoned friend was a stupid fellow in her critical estimation, and responded to her teaching slowly. But at length he learned the lesson, and pushed the cage door open.

With the instinct which might or might not be called forethought, Trixy, with a light bound, closed the door of the cage. She did not wish to lose her playmate, and so made sure that he could not return to his cage. It is not impossible that she desired to conceal the fact of his escape. The freed spaniel was evidently not relieved from his suffering by this release. Puzzled by the fact, Trixy inspected her new friend carefully, uttering, as she did so, low cries of sympathy. To these the spaniel replied with moans. Overwhelmed with pity, Trixy conducted him on a tour of the room, seeking an exit.

She had not yet discovered the door. Her attention, in fact, was diverted from it by the condition of her companion, whose evident pain did not lessen under exercise. Trixy now examined the bandage on the dog's head, and thinking that the trouble must be there, gently tore the cloth off, and licked the wound. This hospital treatment the spaniel received gratefully, but, as he did not recover his health and spirits under it, Trixy now devoted herself once more to her search for a means of escape.

It was now so light that she could see the door plainly, and to this she ran, the spaniel following slowly.

It was one of the boasts of the faculty of Galen that the animals "dedicated" to the rack of science were treated with great consideration during their imprisonment, previous to their sacrifice; and with even more consideration and greater tenderness after their wounds had been inflicted. Incidentally, this was good economy, as well as good surgery.

With a regard for the feelings of the victims in itself worthy of note, Professor Steele had directed that some air should he admitted into the animal room on nights when the windows were closed. The college carpenter had ingeniously devised a strong wire netting about a couple of feet high, which, hasped both to the door and to the jamb, kept the door ajar, and yet allowed no egress for small creatures.

Trixy proceeded to study this invention curiously. She had been educated to hasps, but had never seen a door fastened in this manner. She was quite familiar with the nature of a hook and screw-eye, and had been taught to open them. Indeed, to release herself from a little cage that had been hasped tight had been one of the most dramatic accomplishments of her stage career.

Stimulated rather than discouraged by this obstacle, the trick dog now concentrated her intelligence upon the carpenter's skillful design. It was by this time quite light, and footsteps were heard stirring in the building. Spurred by the consciousness of danger and the necessity of haste, Trixy thrust up the upper hook from its socket; the lower one stuck. She could easily have leaped the whole obstruction, but she knew her friend could not. With a few more tugs, Trixy released the lower hook, and the netting fell back. The performing dog was so pleased with this achievement that she stood up on her hind legs and bowed to the caged audience which the freed prisoners were leaving behind them. Trixy was surprised to notice the absence of applause.

The two now found themselves in the corridor of which we have spoken, Trixy leading with impatient slowness, and the wounded spaniel following painfully. Trixy made at once for the large outer door. This was hitched, locked, and barred. No canine skill could prevail against that inexorable human barrier.

By this time the spaniel was tired out, and lay down. Trixy stood over the poor creature in despair. Was all her super-canine effort to be in vain? At this tragic moment the footfalls of the janitor were heard descending the stairs. Trixy scampered up and down the corridor in desperation. The door of the closet nearest to the outside entrance was slightly ajar. With one of those inspirations which are given only to hunted creatures, Trixy ran back to her companion, and prodded him to his feet. This was done in perfect silence; as silently, the spaniel obeyed her. Trixy led the way to the closet door. The bewildered and wounded dog followed her.

They had scarcely hidden themselves in the darkest corner of the closet behind some rubbish—collars, rubbers, and the like—when the janitor reached the foot of the stairs, and entered the animal room. There he paused with some expression of surprise, and examined the door. Other steps were now heard upon the stairway, and a sleepy and scowling boy appeared in the wake of the janitor, who was plainly an important personage, and carried himself with a lordly air. He gave a few sharp directions, to which the boy responded, grumbling.

Trixy—she who had always loved and trusted man the friend—now with ears erect, breath held, listened with agonizing apprehension to each maneuver of man the foe. She was perfectly self-possessed. But the spaniel, at every thud of the janitor's heavy feet, had a fit of nervous shivering, as if its poor body were being disrupted on an electric rack.

To these two spirits in prison moments became eternity, and ignorant hope wrestled with instinctive despair. The terror of the fugitive, strained through canine sensitiveness, is a doom apart.

Now the shuffling steps of the boy were heard coming from the animal room. Trixy let her whole weight of seven pounds drop protectingly upon the spaniel's shoulder. The boy had a pail and a mop. He slammed the door of the animal room behind him and went to the low door at the end of the corridor. This door he unlocked and left open. The fresh morning air swept in, penetrating even the dark closet. Trixy sniffed joyously, but the black spaniel beneath her feet breathed hard; he still had spasms of violent trembling.

The boy began to mop the floor, morosely whistling as he did so. He left the outside door open to air the corridor, and slammed himself again into the animal room. The corridor was quiet.

Now Trixy allowed herself the luxury of a joyful yelp. She tugged at her friend, leading him by the ear to the closet door. Here, on the threshold, these two prisoners of man's misguided convictions stopped and listened, palpitating.

The white poodle did not hesitate any longer. It was as if she gave the word of command. Beyond that open door were liberty, and the hope of love, and home.

Dazed, the spaniel deferred to her. What was release to that suffering creature? He had been held too long to grasp its meaning. Almost the last instinct for locality and home had been trephined out of him. But Trixy passionately urged him on. Hers was the saving mission, and it had, as all salvation, whether of the higher or the lower being, must have, its element of potential sacrifice. Perhaps—who can say?—she knew that she was risking her own chance. But Trixy waited for the weaker dog. She uttered low sounds of encouragement to which the spaniel replied by feeble wags. Trixy, looking out, could see the sunshine, sky, and liberty. Under the low, projecting balcony, what hiding-places! Beyond was the walled yard, but here was an alley or narrow roadway, lead-ing—oh, joy!—to freedom. Trixy had happened upon the only egress by means of which she could have escaped. She pushed her friend over the sill upon the ground, and herself crouched to spring and follow.

At the very moment when her courage and resource, worthy of a higher organization, had won her liberty, the catastrophe oc-curred. A gust of wind took the door and slammed it with a crash in her white face.

This tragic accident, undreaded because undreamed of, shut out the sun, and shut her in to a nameless fate.

Chapter IX

—∿—

Dr. Bernard approached his private operating table. It was a little after ten o'clock, and he was impatiently awaiting some guests of the medical fraternity whom he had invited to witness a novel and interesting experiment, he was clad in a white blouse, and was puffing stolidly at a black cigar. His face had coarsened visibly in the last six months. Take the man away from the protection of his position, and put him in the slums—how would he have been classified? From his brutal mouth, his muddy complexion, his hard, shifting eyes, his spiny red hair, and his massive, prehensile hands, the average police officer would have picked him out as the type of a defective bent towards crime. As it was, some looked upon him through smoked glasses, as one of the saviors of mankind.

He took up one instrument after another and tested the edge on his broad thumb. By his smile the most careless observer could have seen that he was satisfied. Bernard consulted his watch again and turned to his assistant.

"You might as well bring up the dog. Is it properly shaved? You need not put it on the board. I will attend to that myself."

While he waited, smoking vigorously, his guests—three in number—were ushered in; they fell to talking briskly upon the subject of the experiment. One of the visitors was a middle-aged man; the others were young; and all looked absorbed and eager.

"I suppose we have got to wait for the professor," Bernard explained somewhat ill- naturedly. "I expect him here any minute.

He is a good deal out of sorts today. There's been a mishap in the animal room, and he's lost his favorite material. You know that series of his upon the brain?"

"The basis of that essay he's been at work on for a year?" interrupted one of the younger men. "What a pity!"

"It must overthrow the whole scheme," observed the other.

"Well, yes," admitted Bernard, without heartiness. "I suppose it does. Anyhow he's so put out about it he's gone himself to organize a search, and he's got all his fellows at work. He may not turn up at all. I suppose he thought more of that dog than of anything else in the world. You see the value of the continuity of his experiments lies in their being confined to one subject."

"Such research is as rare as it is priceless," suggested one of the younger men.

"If the dog had held out," said Bernard, "we should have finished the series in two months."

The assistant put Trixy down upon the table, and patted her head as he did so. It would be difficult to say when this servant of science had done such a thing before, at least in the presence of his superior officer.

The four men looked at the little white dog with curiosity. Its smallness, its helplessness, its beauty, its evident intelligence appealed to them in their own despite. The physiologists were attracted towards the pretty sprite who looked from one to the other expectantly. Bernard alone remained unimpressed.

Trixy walked around the edge of the table, and as a preliminary to further acquaintance sat up and solemnly shook hands with the gentlemen, each in succession. She paused at Bernard last, and as she offered him her white paw, she looked up into his sinister eyes with an elfish intuition, and then backed away. She had instinctively discerned the enemy; but she was too much of a lady to snarl at the discovery.

Then the little actress, feeling the dark menace in Dr. Bernard's countenance, turned her back upon the operator, stood up on her hind legs, and began to perform for her life. It was not as large an audience as she was accustomed to, but none had ever watched her with greater interest. Here were minds trained in the exact tenets of science. Here was another illustration of the possibility of brain development. These men cared much for reflex action, little for personality. They had much admiration for the evidence of muscle control, but little mercy for the individual. Modern science deifies the experiment, but ignores the subject.

Trixy was rather spurred than daunted by the terrible circumstances in which she found herself, and went through her little repertoire brilliantly. She turned several somersaults with neatness and dispatch; she picked up a long pair of pincers, held it over her shoulder as if it were a gun, and marched through a few military evolutions with a soldierly bearing. She waltzed with an imaginary partner, and went through her skirt dance gracefully, although pained by the absence of drapery. She did the best she could without any of the stage accessories to which she was used.

The middle-aged doctor had been watching her silently. He did not smile as the others did, and a line between his brows deepened. He thought: "What a pity! My little boy would like that dog." But when he glanced at Bernard's cold, repulsive face, he felt that it would be useless as well as embarrassing to make his wishes known; at any rate, the professional esprit de corps restrained their expression. The physician could not, however, or did not help asking:

"Where did you pick that pretty creature up?"

"Oh, it came in the usual way. We can't keep track of them all," Bernard answered peevishly.

Trixy, with the canine instinct for sympathy which is so much stronger than human reason, had now crossed the table, and approached the middle-aged doctor. She felt that this was the only friend she had in the room. She stood up to her full height, put both her hands on both of his, and looked into his face eloquently. At this moment there was a knock at the door, and the janitor came in.

"Dr. Steele has telephoned that he cannot come, and not to delay the experiment any longer, sir." Bernard, with a relieved expression, turned to his assistant.

"Well, let's got to work, John. It's getting late, and what I pro-pose to demonstrate to you, gentlemen, will take some time."

The assistant took a step forward. Trixy still kept her paws in the gray-haired gentleman's hands. This representative of modern science experienced within himself an unexpected civil war. There was a pang at his heart, and a blush on his face; he did not look at the operator.

"Why not give the little creature five minutes more?" he said. "I don't think she has come to the end of her performance."

Reprieved for the moment, Trixy looked the doctor steadily in the eyes; out of her own the elf-look had gone, never from that moment to return.

She had a strained expression, and her little face seemed to wizen and wrinkle as if she had suddenly aged many years. Now, Trixy lifted her head. There was only one thing left for her to do that she had not done. She was more proud of her musical educa-tion than of any other of her accomplishments, and, rent between hope and despair, she began to sing.

Although her master—the God of little lost dogs knew why—was not there to accompany her, she kept along with her part of the duet that she had sung with him before a hundred houses—

She's my lady,
And I'll love her
Till I die.

By one of those mysterious insights given to all creatures who are doomed to death, did Trixy know that she was singing her swan song? Her little claws grasped at the warm hands that held them. Tears started to the eyes of the gray-haired doctor, and because he could not brush them off, they trembled down his cheeks. As the last notes of Trixy's song died away, a slight sound at the window (which was lowered from the top) attracted the attention of the little actress's small but thoughtful audience. A white pigeon, that had been sitting on the sill, started up and flew in and whirred about the room. Bernard glanced at the winged thing greedily.

"Might as well catch it, John," he said. "It may prove useful."

But the bird, lightly hovering for a moment, swept away, circled about the laboratory two or three times, darted across the lowered window, and cooing softly, melted into the blue. It became a gleam, became a sparkle, became a speck, and was not. The gray-haired doctor, who was still holding Trixy's trembling paws, followed the flight of the bird with a grave glance.

"Come, John! Come!" repeated Bernard impatiently. John, at the word of command, took firm hold of the little dog, and fastened her to the dog-board deftly. When Trixy, struggling and crying like a human baby, lay stretched and helpless in the straps, the middle-aged doctor winced and turned his face. There was some difficulty about adjusting the bit in Trixy's mouth (she was so small), and Bernard himself took hold and completed the task; this he did with skill and ease, and without sign of emotion.

At this moment the door opened without knocking. With an agitated face the janitor hurried in.

"Beg pardon, sir—there is a gentleman out here says he must come in. I've done my best, sir, but he says—"

The janitor whispered a few disturbed words in Bernard's ear.

CHAPTER X

—ɯ—

"Moving," said Mrs. Percy B. Jeffries, "is a phenomenon, but like other phenomena is amenable to the laws of nature." She said this with the gratification of a conventional mind that has chanced to originate an idea. "But I flatter myself that I move my household with system, energy, and good spirits."

It was a part of Aunt Cornelia's system and energy to accomplish her flitting from shore to town by relays, and she began by sending the horses a week ahead.

Miriam, who, under ordinary circumstances, found her aunt's system, energy, and good spirits sufficiently trying, on the late September morning of which we speak woke to a consciousness that these domestic virtues were intolerable. She suddenly announced her intention of driving into town with Matthew and the chestnut pair. She could not have said whether her restlessness arose from a wish to see Steele or to escape him, or whether, indeed, it had any relation to Steele at all.

She had waked, while it was still dark, from a troubled sleep, and had aroused to a sense of oppression amounting almost to superstition. For no reason that she could have explained, it seemed to her that she must start. To no end that she could foresee, she felt herself driven. Emotions long held in abeyance, associations resolutely expelled from her memory crowded upon her. In fact, she had been dreaming half the night—an agitated dream in which pain and joy alternately depressed and elated her. Curiously, in this dream Olin Steele bore no part whatever. It was as if he had never existed, or for her existed no longer. She hurried away, still wearing the white serge dress that she had on the evening before; she covered this with a long Scotch tweed coat, that came to the hem of her gown. She tossed on a straw hat, and veil, ran out to the stables, and jumped into the victoria just as Matthew was starting away. It was scarcely more than seven o'clock, and the cool morning air calmed her mysterious disturbance. The horses were in good spirits, and the drive took scarcely two hours.

As Miriam neared the city her mind rebounded from her perplexities, and, according to her sweet habit, the troubles of others came uppermost. Matthew, who had sat in well-trained silence, now shrewdly perceiving her change of mood, suddenly inquired: "Hain't the gossoon found poor Trixy yet?"

"We'll ask," said Miss Lauriat, arousing herself eagerly. "Drive around to Mr. Surbridge's office, and I'll go in."

But Philip Surbridge was not in his office, and, moreover, had left word that he was not to be expected for some hours. Miriam's face sank a little, and she came down and out to the carriage slowly. She seemed to be hesitating as to her next stop, and somewhat dejectedly gave the order to drive home.

Matthew left her standing upon the sidewalk at her own door; she had a weary and irresolute expression, not at all characteristic of her; she mounted the steps slowly, with eyes cast down. Near the top she paused for a minute to unbutton her long coat and untie her veil. While thus occupied she fancied that she heard a strange low sound—stopped to listen, but decided that she was mistaken; and languidly folding her white veil, came up the remaining steps—these were but two or three.

The outer door was open; the inner one locked. Miriam had forgotten her latch key, and delayed to ring the bell. As she did this, the sound that she heard, or thought she heard, was plainly repeated. It was a sad sound, plaintive and low. She went at once into the vestibule, and at its threshold stood, staring. Every fleck of color left her face. Her heart beat so in her throat that it seemed to her she should never draw breath again.

On the black and white mosaic of the marble floor, crouched in the corner of the vestibule, lay a little huddling dog. It was a black cocker spaniel with a white shirt-frill, and a white part in its wounded head.

"Caro!" cried Miriam, in a piercing voice.

The poor creature tried to crawl towards her, but plainly had lost whatever remnant of strength had brought it there. When she stooped to lift him, the spaniel uttered such a cry as would have rent the heart of any man who had not been born a brute, or become one. Only a lost dog can cry like that; perhaps only one that has been deeply loved, and exquisitely cherished.

"Caro, Caro!" repeated Miriam.

At first, no other word came to her dry lips; she reiterated it wildly; her recognition was hardly less piteous than the dog's. She took the heavy little creature in her arms—its face against her own, its paws around her neck—and, when she saw the dog's condition, she began to cry outright, and aloud like a little girl. She pushed by Maggie at the door, and on into the library, where she sank into the first chair with her sad burden in her lap. There she sat, and stared upon it. The dog continued to wail on in a shrill voice.

The old seamstress came in and said: "Why, it's Caro! It's our Caro!"

And Maggie wept with her mistress, and crossed herself as if she had been in the presence of a miracle.

But Matthew, when he came back, and one of the women called him upstairs, stood still, and said nothing but "The devil!"

Nor did he apologize to Miss Lauriat for the word. It seemed to Matthew a weak word, fit for women; a man should say something adequate to the occasion, but nothing else occurred to Matthew.

Miriam sat among her old servants and sobbed helplessly. It was they who thought and acted; she was bereft of herself. She clung to the dog, caressing it pitiably, and her tears rained on the wounded thing. Her first definite thought was that she wanted Philip, but she remembered that he was not at his office.

Confusedly she heard Matthew say that there'd sure better be a doctor, and that recalled her.

"Why, yes!" she said, "send for Dr. Steele!"

When Matthew reported that the professor was not at the medical school, Miriam, with the short, sharpened voice of unsharable and all but unbearable suffering, directed that a message be sent at once to Dr. Steele's club (where he was likely to lunch), that it be urgently expressed, and given in her own name.

She seemed immediately to forget that she had set this order in motion, and herself began to bathe and bandage the wounded dog. Now the spaniel feebly lifted his poor head and kissed her—it was the first time—and when he did so Miriam began to sob again. She was so shaken that the household was at its wit's end with her. She had eaten little breakfast and that very early, and now would take no food; she was absorbed in a series of efforts to induce the dog to swallow some milk. It was not until she had succeeded in these attempts, and Caro had fallen asleep, that she recovered in some degree her composure.

When Olin Steele, who had passed a disturbed and fretful morning, worse than wasted in the fruitless search for his lost material, at noon received Miss Lauriat's message, his face went white with an emotion so deep that the man found himself astonished before it. He had always thought that joy was an integer, or an element, as simple as it was supreme; this which he experienced was a compound feeling—from very excess of bliss dashed through and through with awe, or with a fear that was almost pain. Now, after all, his victory lay in his iron hand. The battle was to the strong as it always was, and would be, world without end. Ok, now at last, her beautiful reluctance had yielded; right womanly as she was, she had surrendered royally. Crossing the little space between them, she had stepped half of the misty way to meet his outstretched arms.

With ringing feet he hurried to her. With lifted head and shining eyes, he disregarded the shadows of men. But they in the substance looked upon him with the attention that the crowd gives to the superior, to the happy, or to the successful; most people who noticed Steele that day thought him to be all these things.

He ran up the steps like an impatient boy. Already the hunger of his arms was fed, the thirst of his lips was quenched. Already she had lifted her beautiful willing face to his—

As he stepped upon the threshold, the door opened and he dashed in. The library portieres were parted, and he entered ecstatically. There in the middle of the room, in the dark chair, which she had not left since she first sank into it, in her white dress, with her white face—and the wounded dog in her arms—she sat, awaiting her lover. She had covered the spaniel with one end of her tweed coat; her hat and white veil still lay on the floor at her feet. At first, Steele did not see the dog. He strode across the thick carpet and stood over her, bending for his betrothal kiss.

He stopped. Her appearance startled him. She looked like a woman who has been shocked from youth into middle life. She gave him one wan smile. Impetuous inquiries, passionate protestations surged to his lips; but these never crossed them.

For now he looked down. He saw the sleeping dog, whose marred head was not covered. He recognized his own work. Spurred by one of the fatuous impulses which drag out into the open the one thing that above all others a man wishes to conceal, Olin Steele uttered these extraordinary words:

"Why, that's my dog! Where did you get it? I've been all the morning hunting for it."

"I do not understand you," said Miriam, with ominous distinctness. "The dog is mine. This is Caro. I lost him two years ago. I thought he was dead. I never cared for any other dog."

Her eyes widened slowly. She raised them to his face; it was as ashen as her own. She read—what did she not read in his tortured countenance?

Horror and despair confronted each other. The man threw up a hand as if to fend off the shock that paralyzed every thought, every explanation. As he did so, he took a step backwards; he could not speak; his lips refused to open. A power greater than any that he had ever acknowledged compelled him. Her stricken eyes pursued him—nay, they forced him out of the room. She had not spoken another word; but he went. He had come like a god; he went like a cur.

Philip Surbridge approached Miss Lauriat's house, happily humming a tune; he found it was the pretty air that Dan used to sing with Trixy. Miriam heard it before he rang, and her whirling brain seemed to stop spinning. He was shown directly into the room, and found her as Steele had left her. Her white dress, with its black finish of velvet at the throat, had a dark stain over the heart.

One glance at the burden on her lap explained everything to Philip, and it was like him to ask no unnecessary questions. His own color changed, but the man seemed to fortify himself for a position in which his heart and his head must race together.

"Philip," began Miriam brokenly. "Oh, Philip—"

"You need not try to explain anything," said Philip gently. "I understand. I understand it all."

"But Dr. Steele says—what does Dr. Steele mean?"

"So Steele has been here, has he?"

"Yes—he came—yes; he did not—did not stay."

"Then it is all out. I suppose in that case I may as well speak, now. Shall I? Do you wish me to?—Or not? It is for you to say what I shall do in these difficult circumstances."

"You must!" cried Miriam. "I must know the worst." In her vehemence she aroused the dog, who stirred and looked at her drowsily. Philip drew his chair close to hers, and for the first time in his life tenderly patted her hand.

He spoke a few encouraging words; what, he hardly knew; what, she scarcely heard. He tried to convince her that the worst was over; and nothing more to fear. But Miriam interrupted impatiently.

"Nothing but the whole truth will help me now. And there is nobody but you to give it to me."

"Very well," said Philip in a changed tone. "You shall have it then. Here it is." He drew out from his pocket a beautiful silver collar, tarnished and bent. The plate had not been removed, and it bore this inscription:

Caro. Licensed. No. 2001.
Miriam Lauriat.

The town, and the street and number were added, but these were less easy to decipher.

"I was in the Galen Laboratory this morning," said Philip, with cold, legal precision. "I was there upon a professional errand. I will tell you about that, later. In the course of my investigations, I picked up this. It had been pulled out from among some rubbish in a closet—but recently disturbed, I am sure—and fortunately no one had noticed it."

He laid the collar in Miriam's trembling hand. Her fingers closed over it spasmodically. She uttered an inarticulate sound.

"Shall I go on?" asked Philip, choking.

He did so at command of her streaming eyes. His voice had now become stern and solemn; it had something of the note which it struck when he was pleading a grave case.

"Galen College prides itself upon its physiological department. The basis of modern physiology is animal experimentation. This means the dissection of living animals. Caro has been in that"— Philip caught his breath—"in that laboratory. What happened to him the first year, I cannot tell you; there may be some scars that will. He is a special case; he is their most valuable subject. For the last twelve months he has been reserved for a series of experiments upon the brain. These have probably—you must be prepared for that—affected his intelligence. He escaped from there this morning; how I do not know, but I have my guess. The professor who has charge of that department is writing a prize essay along the line of this particular research. The prize was offered by the medical society of which he is an officer. It would have made him famous. He is considered the leading physiologist in the state, if not in the country, and this kind of thing has made him so."

Surbridge paused, and looked at Miriam with a pity which she could not have borne from any other human being.

"His name," concluded her old friend beneath his breath—"I do not think I need to tell you what it is."

Miriam, with the collar in her hand, had laid her head back against the tall chair. She had grown very pale, and gasped. Philip sprang for the bell.

"Don't be afraid," she said feebly. "I shan't faint. You know I never do."

"Now look here." Philip spoke in a comfortable, matter-of-fact tone. "Just listen to me. You've got Caro back, and that's the main thing. Let me look at him." He bent over her and tenderly ex-amined the dog. She heard his cheerful voice go briskly on. "It seems worse than it is because the bandage was evidently torn off. You'll feel better to have him looked after, however. I'll send a nice fellow I know around to fix him up. He has a goody big heart and loves dogs.—Maggie"—he turned with the smile that made servants respect themselves, and affectionately obey him—"Miss Lauriat has had a great shock and strain on account of this poor little fellow."

Miriam's grateful eyes thanked him for the delicate elision by which he ignored the fact that she was doubly smitten. But her lips said nothing. Surbridge did all the talking, and in his quiet way he covered a great deal of ground with a very few words.

"Get her some luncheon at once, Maggie. She is going to eat it—Oh, yes, she is. And then we're going to talk a little more. I've got lots of things to say."

Miriam now looked down, and for the first then perceived the crimson stain across her heart. She shuddered, and muttered some-thing about changing her dress.

"I'll hold Caro," said Philip easily. "He'll remember me, and when you come down I've got some news to tell you. You'd better hurry—or no, I'll run over to my rooms a minute, and be back by the time you've got something to eat."

When Philip returned he found Miriam quiet, but not yet quite self-possessed. The dog, who had been gently and intelligently treated, was sleeping in his own old basket, which she had drawn up close to her feet upon the hem of her dress.

"Why, how happy you look," she began in a hurt tone. Miriam was so used to Philip's perennial sympathy that it struck her as contrary to the laws of their nature that he should be in such good spirits, when she was so miserable.

"Come," demanded Philip. "What are you moping about? You and Dan ought to be the happiest people in the world."

Now Surbridge, whose keen perception had grasped the fact that nothing would lift Miriam from the pit of suffering into which she had been plunged but the joys or the sorrows of another soul, leaped at once into his exciting story.

"Trixy's found!" he exploded. "I can't keep it to myself any longer, no matter what else has happened. I can't and I won't. We've got her."

"Trixy found!" Miriam's tears started again. Philip, who had never seen her thus broken, yearned over her for her very weakness, and turned his head away with a gulp. But the girl's tears ran into a radiant smile—the first that he had seen that day. He had not misread her. She would lose herself at any time to find another's happiness. That was Miriam Lauriat.

"You don't tell me how! You don't say where!" she repeated in a stronger voice.

"In the laboratory of Galen Medical School," answered Surbridge in a reverberating tone.

"Was it like—" Miriam glanced at the dog at her feet.

"No, thank God! Not a devil of them had touched her. I was just in time.—Now look here." Philip fell back upon his favorite phrase. "I've got a good deal to tell, and I'm going to sit down and condense it. Sure you are able to hear it all?"

Miriam's blazing eyes impetuously bade him go on. She had quite done crying. Her name-sake, the prophetess of old, might have had something of the look which now confronted the young lawyer; it was the forecasting, farseeing look—deep at the iris, and mystical in the pupil—the look that overthrows the past, and shapes the future, and obliterates self in both.

Mistily it seemed to Miriam that she and they whose lives had been woven into the fabric of her own—yes, and that other, the "gentle fellow-creature" who lay mangled at her feet—were sweeping into the onward movement of strange forces that she did not understand and could not measure, but against whose mighty action she might not, if she would, contend.

For one exalted moment her individual pang, the disorder of her personal story seemed to go out of consequence, or out of sight. She was like one who, for the first time, setting foot into an unknown world of unimagined woe, finds her whole being uplifted by a passion of sympathy before which all passion less divine retreats.

"Oh, you've got lots of pluck!" said Philip. "You're clear grit. Now let's have it over."

Philip pushed into his story, which he told in his curt, professional tone.

"You see I had my theory from the first, but a lawyer has no case till he gets his evidence. There was a lamentable lack of witnesses, until—guess who supplied the deficiency?—No, I'm sure you never will.—Cady's Molly."

"In that red shirt waist and pink hair-ribbon?" asked Miriam, laughing in spite of herself,—"and yellow hat? Or was it the purple tam-o'-shanter?"

"There you have me. Both, I think,—but the evidence lapses there. With Cady's Molly went Cady's Molly's father. As luck had it, this gallant widower invited your consumptive protégée to accompany him, and with the woman, invited or uninvited, went the melancholy dog who has the cough. That dismal creature was the first to see Trixy. He was after her—the woman after him—the man after the woman—and Cady's Molly, who began in the rear—you know what long legs she has, the grasshopper sort?—Well, Cady's Molly came out ahead of the lot of them, and then they saw this dog-bandit—no, we haven't got him, more's the pity, but that's the minor point—leading Trixy by a string. But, you see, she was so dirty and disreputable they weren't sure enough of her to make the claim till it was too late. She must have had on that coat of hers—there's no other explanation—but they didn't all of them see it; it was growing pretty dark, they say. Anyhow, they shadowed the bandit."

"The whole party?"

"The whole party. That gave me three witnesses—four, if you counted the coughing dog. If dogs could testify and sue—perhaps we may come to that yet. Well, the first they knew, the bandit was dragging Trixy up the alley behind the medical school. They saw her go in—they'll swear they saw her go in—and she never came out until I took her out this morning.

"You know how it is with those people; they can't originate; they don't dare do anything unusual. They waited until they saw Dan; and Dan waited till he saw me. Then, that night—why, it was only last night!—poor Dan came to my room with her little blue coat. He had been prowling around, God knows where! He found it in an ash barrel under that porch—I don't suppose you ever noticed it?—where there is a low door. Anyhow, I've got the coat, and the chain of evidence was completed. There isn't a missing link. I went to the laboratory this morning, and demanded the dog."

"Were they willing to let you in?" asked Miriam uneasily.

"Oh, I didn't raise that question. I didn't think it was necessary. The case was too complete, and I told them so. I took the precaution to swear out a search warrant, but I didn't think it would be necessary to use it; and it wasn't. Well, yes, I think they did their best; they put up a pretty good bluff. I searched that building from attic to cellar. In the basement there was a coat closet, and the door open—the rubbish all topsy-turvy. That was where I found the collar,—it seemed to have been dragged out. The very last thing I struck was Dr. Bernard's private laboratory. I can't say that my welcome was strictly hospitable. But I was there to go in, and in I went. Trixy was—well, anyhow, I was just in time."

"Where," interrupted Miriam, with her old sweet eagerness, "where was Dan?"

"About five feet and a half behind me, I should say," replied Philip, drawling a little, as he did sometimes when he was too much moved to be willing to show it.

"Oh, how did he take it? What did Dan do? How did he look? What did he say? Dear Dan! Poor Dan!"

"I thought we had killed him among us," said Surbridge gravely, "He held out till I put Trixy in his arms. Then he toppled over, crash! All the doctors worked over him. He kept them pretty busy for about half an hour. Trixy kissed him all that while. She kissed him alive, it's my private opinion. I prophesy Trixy won't flirt with her master any more. She's his forever, and altogether, now—or I've missed my guess.—You don't want to hear any more of this, now." Philip interrupted himself abruptly. "It's all over. Do you suppose you'd feel able to see them?"

"Can I go?" cried Miriam, rousing with her own fervid look. "Is it very far?"

"It might be farther," observed Surbridge incidentally. "You see I took them right to my rooms, and kept them there till just a little while ago. They're out in the coach house now with Matthew. We rode over—no, your horses were tired—we came over in a cab. Dan is so used up."

"Philip," said Miriam very slowly, "you are a good man; you are a kind man. I don't know what I should do without you."

"Let's see the pretty drama played out," said Philip. "I'll go and bring them up."

Dan came into the room slowly. His wasted body had shrunken away from his shabby clothes, but upon his face the great angel Joy had cast a blinding look. Trixy, blinking happily, was in his arms.

The lad put her down, went straight up to the lady, and kneeled and laid his head upon her lap.

"Oh, Miss Laurie!" sobbed Dan. "Miss Laurie, dear!"

"Dan," Miss Lauriat choked, "it's all over. Mr. Surbridge says so. And Mr. Surbridge knows."

But Philip strode to the window and looked out with wet and happy eyes.

Now, when the three human souls had somewhat recovered themselves, they perceived that a strange little sub-human by-play had been going on unnoticed at their feet. For Trixy, forgetting Surbridge, ignoring "the lady she loved best," disregarding her master, had bounded to the basket where the wounded dog was lying. She crooned over him; she kissed him; she leaped about him; she yelped at him blissfully; she challenged him with little slaps of her paws to come out and play with her. The spaniel responded with a feeble recognition, and the two nosed each other, conversing mysteriously. What Trixy would have said, who knows? And what the mutilated victim of physiology might have told, we shall never hear. The true interpreter between the higher and the lower races is yet to be; and Trixy and her poor friend were born in advance of that predestined moral linguist.

The lawyer studied the two dogs with close professional scrutiny.

"They are my best witnesses," he said in a disappointed tone, "and there isn't a court in the state where I can subpoena them."

It was still early in the evening when Dr. Steele called again, peremptorily asking for Miss Lauriat; but she had already gone up-stairs for the night. Maggie told him that she was too tired to be disturbed, and he went away without a word. In fact, though this the doctor did not know, the agitated household was on picket duty. Reporters had been ringing for three hours.

Surbridge, whose winning manner made him immediately pop-ular with the newspaper men, had stood between Miriam and these intruders. "Leave them all to me," he said. The next morning's press was busy with the story of Dan and Trixy; but, although there were vague suggestions of an interplay in which actors from high life were involved, the lady's name was quite kept out of the affair. Surbridge's was not. The unusual character of the case, and the implication of a famous institution, gave publicity to the incident. The press assumed the responsibility of suggesting that an import-ant suit might follow the dramatic release of the little dog. The uncompromising attitude of the young attorney in pitting himself against the tremendous influence of the college for the sake of a poor boy's pet concentrated upon him attention and respect.

This brought Aunt Cornelia.

Chapter XI

—ᴔᴥ—

The great crises of a man's life may be of his own making, or may be inflicted upon him by a wayward accident, but the most perplexing are those that combine his fault and his fortune. Olin Steele watched the night out. Raving against fate, he acknowledged that he was the Samson of his destruction. With his own hands he had wrenched the pillars of his life, and had brought the structure crashing on his head.

His first impulse was one of defiance; such was his nature. His feeling that he was an unjust victim of circumstances blazed until midnight. His consciousness that he believed himself to be the high priest of an august science, his subtle delusion that he had been the servant of humanity, bore him through the first skirmishes of the struggle upon which he had entered. His colleagues respected him; his students deified him; the woman he loved spurned him— how was he to coordinate these clashing facts? His character was irreproachable, his position unassailable; he was a good son and a good churchman. The Bishop of his diocese was his personal and admiring friend; society and religion, as he understood religion, upheld him in his life's work. He was fortified at every point. The only weak spot in the ramparts was the nature of the girl he loved. Other women whom he knew would have forgiven him, or so he thought. He ground his teeth and cursed his luck. If he had finished those experiments he would have been famous. His reputation would have leaped beyond the confines of his college—and indeed, of his country. Experimenters and biologists had been expecting brilliant discoveries of him, nor would he have disappointed them.

And it was only a dog!

He paced his room blindly. His heart was hot within him. He resented the infringement of her delicate nature upon his professional rights. Once he had called her mercy made magic. Now, he felt her mercy made tyranny. Her position was sentimental and unscientific; he flung these unsparing words at her; they were the catchwords of his profession, and came easily. How could she measure the value of his great work? How could she presume to set the life of a dog, or the discomfort (that was his word) of a dog, against the vast research which might overthrow the conclusions of continental physiologists?

Warring with the medical oligarchy which he represented, this one girl opposed her womanhood, and her humanity. True, her lips had not uttered a word; but he knew their speech and language. He knew that he was condemned without a hearing; he knew that he was foredoomed at the tribunal of her soul. Under this verdict he raged. Yet, with this fever the other rage of his love beat on.

Strange impulses, born of his arbitrary nature, fostered by his merciless calling, seized him with a force before which he stood aghast. Rather than lose her, he felt as if he could have slain her. If such a thing had been possible, he could have tortured her into loving him. He could have—

Olin Steele paused. This madness, like some other forms of mania, ran its course and struck its revulsion of sanity. In the hours which precede dawn the blood runs slowly, courage faints, and truth stares the soul out of countenance. Exhausted, he sank upon his old lounge. A great reaction of tenderness enveloped him. He thought of her sweet, wan face—the horror in her eyes—her quivering lips towards which he had stooped to take the first kiss. Why, they were his, and she was his,—and what was a dog, or a theory, or an experiment, fame, or the world to come between them? By a thousand fold she outweighed them all.

The subserviency of women had been a matter of course in his philosophy. His ideal woman would have followed a man to hell if he had chosen to lead her there, and would have stood by, adoring, while he did a demon's work. If such indeed had not been the eidolon of his youth, he had forgotten that he had ever admitted any other to the habit of his mind. What was the flaw in the philosophy that it did not hold?

Now, for the first time, Steele perceived that there was a theory above a theory, and a law beyond a law. Now he found himself hurled to the conclusion that a man has his share of the mutual surrender of the loving; that he must yield himself to the angel in the woman whom he loves.

He fought until dawn. The battle was not to the swift; nor was it to the strong. Physically weakened, morally chastened, he would react and recall himself, and strike out powerfully at the invisible forces with which he was contending. He passed the remainder of the night in alternations of triumph and defeat. Once his lips moved. "She was mine," they said, "and mine she shall be."

Everywhere that he turned he came up against finality. To every question that he put he was answered only yea or nay. The conflict took him to the uppermost spaces, and to the nethermost deeps. He swung from star to sod, and back again. The vibrations shook him, soul and body.

As the light looked gravely in at his window, from profound exhaustion he fell asleep, and slept for perhaps an hour. When he awoke, his thoughts had clarified. "It is between the two," he said, "and I must make my choice."

He bathed and dressed scrupulously; it was as if he were some novitiate purifying himself for an unknown life. He breakfasted slowly and rested a while; he did not smoke, and read no papers; he did not visit his laboratory; for the first time he thought of it with a species of repugnance as of the thing that stood between himself and her. Towards the middle of the morning, pale but confident, he sought her.

Miriam received him quietly. He was relieved to find that the dog was not in the room, and opened the interview with the more assurance on this account.

"You seem ill," he began. "You have not slept."

"It was hardly to be expected." Miriam did not look at him. The evasion of her eyes troubled him, and he plunged at once into his exculpation.

"I have come to say—you must understand—it was most unfortunate—I am overwhelmed with the accident. I suffer in consequence of it—believe me—as much as you."

For the first time since he had known her, the swift sympathy on which he had come to count as he counted on her delicacy or her loyalty, failed to respond to his touch. She was like a violin in which one string was broken. He drew his bow over it in vain. Her face, like her nature, hardened before him. He started to make some inquiries about the dog, but saved himself just in time from committing this folly.

"You don't understand the situation," he resumed; "you do me an injustice. You don't appreciate the immense value of my work. These experiments have to go on. We must have subjects—if not animal, then human; it's a clear choice. There wasn't one chance in a million that—I didn't know that it was your dog! You know I didn't!"

"You knew," said Miriam coldly, "that it was somebody's dog—a cherished one. He was gentle. He was high-bred.—And there was this." She drew the tarnished silver collar from her pocket, and with shaking fingers put it into his hand.

Steele's white face turned a ghastly gray. "I give you my word I never saw this before!"

"Are you not the head of your department? Where does the responsibility lie if not on you? This collar came out of your laboratory yesterday morning. How many other lost dogs have the faculty of Galen College unlawfully taken besides mine?"

"Our subordinates have charge of such matters," protested Steele, smarting under her lashing words. "We are busy men. We cannot attend to these details. How should we know where our subjects come from? The experiments must go on. You take a very feminine view of the circumstances."

"I wouldn't be a man—such a man—do such a thing—make such an excuse for a deed like this—not for all that you call fame!"

He reddened painfully under her scorn. "You set the animal above the human race!" he cried.

"What if it had been Barry?" interrupted Miriam quietly.

Steele's eyelids almost imperceptibly drooped, but his dogmatic voice pushed on:

"What is one dog—what are ten thousand dogs compared with the life of one baby?" he demanded fiercely.

Miriam now turned her averted head, and, for the first time that morning looked him straight in the eyes. The misery in them held her rising denunciation back.

"You have tormented many dogs. How many, I do not want to know. Have you ever saved the life of one baby? Oh, I have seen men do that, down among my poor people—good plain doctors— kind men, giving their lives for sick children. How many did you say you have saved?"

"But I might have! I should have. I was on the eve of great discoveries. This unfortunate mishap has overthrown them all."

Miriam's tender lip curled. This was a sight that he had never seen before, and it forced this outcry from him: "Your judgment is distorted! You set that creature above me. You value him more than you value me. You care for him more!"

"Why should I dispute you? It is quite true that I love my dog more than it is possible for any one who could—treat him—as you have done—to understand."

"You never loved me!" Steele vehemently challenged her.

"Oh, I thought I did," she answered drearily. "Don't blame me. I thought I did."

The man arose. The muscles of his face were taut.

"Do you mean to say that you will allow this to come between us?"

"How can I help it?" she cried. "I loved another kind of man."

Steele strode up and down the room. His strong head, his stern chin, his professional bearing seemed to have no part in the turmoil of his passion. They seemed to stand aloof from it, and to criticise it, as if they mocked his plight. Once he heard her say beneath her quickened breath:

"You would have known the voice of your own dog. So did I—that day—at the art school."

Miriam had now arisen. The vivisector and the woman confronted each other. Her agitation was as great as his. The infinite pity of her nature did not desert her even then. He felt himself compassionated while he read his doom in her eyes.

"Why should we talk any longer?" she said with that finality of manner against which a gentleman does not argue. "It only makes it—hard—for both of us."

Before she could measure the effect of her words Steele's towering figure seemed to blur before her like a swaying statue. Before she could prevent him he had dropped to his knees; and this unimagined action had in it a certain dignity, and commanded a kind of respect which the most flippant spirit would not have refused him.

Olin Steele held up his hands, and so grasping both of hers, he entreated her; one would have said not that he poured out his love so much as that he lifted it, a worship ennobled by despair, and offered as much in belated justice to himself as in hope of melting her.

"I'll be whatever you loved!" he pleaded. "I will become the man you can love! Name the price of your forgiveness! I will pay it to the uttermost!"

Miriam, mute and miserable, shook her head.

"I will abandon it—all," cried Steele. "I will give up experimentation. I will resign my professorship. I will fling away my ambition—everything that I hoped to do. I will begin all over again. I will become a plain doctor and heal the sick. All I want is you."

The man stopped. His lips trembled before the miracle of the vows that he had uttered. Reverently he pressed his face into her hands, which he was still holding, and he left upon them the kiss of consecration that a perfect love offers to a woman whether she be won or lost.

But Miriam was silent. Her wide eyes were as wretched as his. With a gentle, maternal movement she drew him to his feet, and released her hands.

"You make it so hard—You make it so hard!" she breathed.

Her fathomless tenderness, her solemn beauty, all the lost preciousness of her, flooded his being with an anguish like a mortal pain.

"You torture me!" he groaned.

"Oh, no! Oh, no!" she gasped. "I do forgive you for this. May God go with you—if you do what you say—what you mean—but I cannot."

Now Dr. Steele uttered these uncontrollable words:

"You are more cruel to me than I was to that dog. You vivisect me."

Miriam caught her breath. It was as if the recording angel had read from the Book of Life a sentence in an unknown tongue, and challenged her soul to translate it. She felt how easy it would be to make an eternal mistake in that sacred language. But she did not flinch. Slowly and kindly she stirred from his side. She was blinded with her tears, and groped for the door. He thought she said, "Oh, good-by—good-by!"

But he was not sure.

Chapter XII

—꧃—

Mrs. Percy B. Jeffries arrived at the town house the next morning, and Miriam found herself denied that luxury of solitude which, to a nature like hers, is the first craving of acute trouble. Perhaps it is one of the values of misfortune that it shall not seem bearable until it has become so; and not the least of its veiled advantages, that the superficial relations of life must go on in the teeth of emergency.

Aunt Cornelia found a disturbed household, nor was she the woman to soothe the nervous tension. She precipitated into the electric atmosphere the cook, the chambermaid, and the laundress. She was surcharged with the achievements of a forced flitting, as well as with the mortification of the necessity for it.

Before Mrs. Jeffries had time, or perhaps before Miriam had given opportunity, for reproaches or inquiries, Maggie brought in a special delivery letter. This ran:

> My Dear Mrs. Jefferies: Under the present painful
> circumstances, of whose nature you will doubtless by
> this time have been informed, I find myself under the
> necessity of resigning the presidency of the Society for
> the Prevention of Docking and Cropping Tails and Ears.
> That this noble and necessary work will find under your
> leadership recognition at the hands of the Legislature, I
> have no doubt. I am forced to feel that my connection with
> the cause would be an injury to it now. With thanks to you

for your generous hospitality, and with deep appreciation of
the many pleasant hours that we have passed together, I am,

Very truly yours,

Olin Steele.

Mrs. Jeffries was about to ring for Miriam to come and explain this
blasting communication when she looked down and perceived a
little white statuette on the carpet at her feet. Trixy sat up in the
begging attitude, but there was no beggar in her eyes. These regarded Mrs. Jeffries complacently, and rather patronizingly; in fact,
Trixy had the air of being the hostess of the occasion. Mrs. Jeffries
put on her eye-glasses and examined this incident. Her courtesy
overcame her perplexity, and she held out her ringed hand to the
little dog. At this moment Dan limped apologetically in.

"She wants to shake hands with you, marm. Trixy's glad to see
you home again."

"You mean paws," corrected Mrs. Jeffries.

"No, I don't," persisted Dan, falling back upon his old phrase.
"Trixy don't know she's got paws."

Dan picked up his dog, perched her on his crooked shoulder,
and left the room. Mrs. Jeffries, going out into the hall to call Miriam, heard the lad's uneven step wearily climbing the back stairs; a
fact which at the time she but half noted.

"Come up, Auntie," answered Miriam. "I've got something to
show you. I can't talk. But if you won't ask any questions, you had
better come up and see."

What new blow awaited? With apprehension, Mrs. Jeffries
mounted the stairs. With weariness in her nerves, and disappro-
bation on her lips, the lady entered her niece's room. In his basket
before the fireplace lay the weak and mangled spaniel. Miriam, in
her white négligée, was kneeling beside him.

"It's Caro, Auntie. Speak kindly to him. Don't ask me a question. Philip will tell you. Don't blame me for anything!"

The painful color burned Aunt Cornelia's cheeks.

"I didn't know I was as bad as that, my dear." Then she stopped and saw.

A colder-hearted woman than Mrs. Jeffries might have melted at the sight before her, and Aunt Cornelia's tears fell fast upon the mutilated dog.

Mrs. Jeffries and her dearest lawyer sat together in the library. It was now mid-afternoon, and Surbridge, cheerfully cutting an hour from the busiest portion of his day, had already surrendered himself to the task of soothing the soul of his most adoring and most difficult client.

"Put yourself in my place," said Aunt Cornelia solemnly.

"That, my dear madam," returned Philip with his perfect manner, "I have often done—with envy."

"There you are—your father all over again. You are very graceful, Philip, but you don't help me out as much as usual. If you were I, what, I should like to know, would you do in this extraordinary situation?"

"Accept it," said Philip quietly, "like the grande dame you are."

"Yes, but not in a minute—not with a gasp. I haven't even had time for a good cry. Here I find the press of the city busied with our affairs—the privacy of this household endangered—that boy and his poodle on everybody's lips—your name in every paper—my niece's ostentatiously suppressed. I suppose we have you to thank for that."

"Well, yes," drawled Philip. "I did my best."

"I find Dr. Steele pilloried—whether justly or not, how do I know? I find my niece's imminent engagement to him indefinitely postponed. I find that he has resigned the presidency of our noble society. I am overwhelmed with the responsibilities this will bring upon my poor head. I find upstairs—mysteriously returned to this family—a mangled dog. I find an evidently greater mystery behind him. Nobody tells me how he came to be as he is. Miriam positively refuses to speak about him. I must say, it would have been a great deal better for that child if he had been dead as she thought he was."

Philip held up his firm and gentle hand, as if he were flagging a train. Mrs. Jeffries slowed up, and in a few quiet words the lawyer told her the whole story.

Aunt Cornelia received this recital as if she had been struck between the eyes. The conventionality of her nature yielded hard, and she was convinced that no lady in her class of society had ever been put in such an embarrassing position. She found it not quite natural to suppose that Miriam was not, somehow, to blame.

"If you had been in her place," urged Philip, "with your youth and beauty, and your warm heart—"

"Well," admitted Aunt Cornelia, "I suppose I should have done the same thing."

"Of course you would!" insisted Philip, in his convincing tone. "Knowing you as I do; I should not even raise the question."

"But, Philip, there is one thing more—and I have left that to the last on purpose. I go up into the attic, and I find that boy from the slums apparently established there with his poodle. I ask him if he is making another visit, and he says, No, he is staying. I have not approached Miriam at all upon this painful subject. I feel it too keenly. I am getting to be an old woman, and I wish I were in my own home. I find this house turned into a dog hospital and an orphan asylum. I was not brought up to such methods of life. Mr. Jeffries liked to live as other people did; our tastes were in perfect accord."

Philip got up and put his hand upon his client's shoulder with that affectionate and protecting sympathy to which age is so much more sensitive than youth.

"Dear Mrs. Jeffries, don't you see? How could she do anything else? How could she send the poor chap away after what has happened? She never would have known an easy hour. It's just like her. She's adopted the lad—and Trixy—into the family."

"Is he going to sit at the table?" demanded Mrs. Jeffries, weeping. "Or perhaps they'll both sit at the table? She might give Trixy a high chair. She's capable of it."

Surbridge laughed outright.

"Oh, Matthew and Maggie have bespoken their company. Now, dear Mrs. Jeffries, there is one queer thing about it nobody can explain. Those two dogs have met before—in fact, they are practically inseparable. Anything that Caro wants in this house the poor fellow's likely to have, I fancy, for the rest of his life. And I'm sure you would be the very last person to wish to have it otherwise."

Aunt Cornelia looked up, smiling. She had that rare expression which blurs the wrinkles out of an elderly face. No one but Philip ever saw it.

"You are a dear boy," she said, "and an irresistible pleader. Like your father, you'll be a distinguished lawyer some day. I never could withstand you."

Philip did not answer, for at that moment Miriam entered the room. She had the injured dog in her arms, and Trixy danced behind her, like a pretty page, holding the train of her gown, and shaking it daintily.

Miriam stopped for a moment, irresolute; then, advancing, she stooped and kissed her Aunt Cornelia, and laid the spaniel in the Lady's lustreless black silk lap. Trixy, jealous of this attention, jumped up and cuddled beside her little friend.

"Oh, well," sighed Mrs. Jeffries, "Mr. Surbridge says we must make the best of it, Trixy. Give me your hand. What are you laughing at, Philip?"

Philip pointed to the door, where Dan, irradiate, stood leaning on his crutch. Dan found it quite beyond the question now to have Trixy out of his sight; for her, his eyes had become clairvoyant, his ears clairaudient. Trixy had always reserved her private doubts about her master's omnipotence; his omnipresence was now a fact established beyond reach of skepticism.

Chapter XIII

—ഡ—

The court-room was stifling, for the unsavory place was full. A strange array packed it to the doors, and beyond. When had the lower courts of the city known such an interplay of human rank? The old images of theology occurred to more than one person that morning—the visions of childhood as they formed fearfully about the Day of the Last Judgment, when "great and small" should stand before the Judge. For, since it had gone abroad that a brilliant and daring young attorney (himself of a social status from which one would have expected other, not to say better things) had proceeded against a great institution in behalf of a boy from the slums whose dog was mysteriously concerned, the extremes of society had thronged to this unprecedented, to this incredible trial.

Gentlemen of the clubs and of the drawing-rooms protected clusters of ladies who had never set their delicate feet in such a spot before. Fans and vinaigrettes agitated and protested against the polluted atmosphere of justice to which judge and lawyers were so used that they were conscious of surprise at the discomfort experienced by the leisure classes.

Early seated, and crowded to the front, was to be noticed a group so unfamiliar to, and so unfamiliar with the criminal courts that it attracted a curious, something like a sympathetic attention. This was an academic group—a few professors, the dean of the involved institution, several men bearing the unmistakable air of trustees, one of the defendants (understood to be an instructor),

137

and, sitting beside him uneasily, the janitor of the medical school. The college counsel, a distinguished lawyer, had an expression of patient ennui, as one who regarded the occasion as small and irritating, and his case, in the nature of things, assured. Physicians and medical students of such types as the modern schools turn out jammed every permissible space. Lawyers were present in considerable numbers.

Uncomfortably aware that they were but coldly welcomed by "the other half of the world" in this extraordinary scene, yet stolidly defiant of the fact, sat the uninfluential, the obscure, the children of the poor—whom we are accustomed to forget until we need them—the plain and powerful people whose voice is apt to be clearer, and sure to be stronger in the moral note than our own.

These had come up to champion one of themselves—an orphan lad, at whose instance the great medical school was placed in a position hitherto unimagined, and embarrassing to an obvious degree.

The day was cold (it was January) and a threatened storm was frowning. The courtroom was not quite dark enough to light artificially, but so dull of tint that, when an arrow of sun ran through the army of clouds charging across the sky, and stabbed a window, the effect was followed by every eye in the room. It so chanced that the poignant ray struck the lame lad's attorney, who had at that moment risen, and stood preeminent in the brilliance—his tall height, his strong head, his direct features expressing a certain straight-forwardness and manly sincerity, a certain fearlessness in moral matters united to a marked intellectual force, which commanded instinctive respect.

His little client, who sat silent and pale below him, stirred sensitively as the sunlight faded slowly from Surbridge's face and figure, and the boy glanced towards the rear of the room where his neighbors and friends from Blind Alley were crowded together. Among them, yet clearly to the most careless eye not of them, a lady, closely veiled, sheltered a small object behind her muff. A tiny white ear, cocked alertly above the dark fur, was followed by a little struggling white face, rebellious and determined. The lame boy held up one finger, and the little face disappeared from sight as the proceedings of the day began.

The preliminaries were disposed of rather quickly, and with that indifference to social claims or intellectual position characteristic of abstract justice, and of the concrete judge presiding—an eccentric man, with an irritable mouth, a kind eye, and an imperious manner. The distinguished scientists (from whose number Professor Steele was conspicuously absent) involved in this extraordinary complication were conscious of a vexed surprise at their position. The academic world is not a wide one, the scientific portion of it least endowed with imagination, and neither experience nor fancy had prepared these gentlemen for a serious legal situation; where the latest bacillus or the new serum was without palpable significance, where the standards of the lecture-room, the achievements of the laboratory, or the reputation of a coterie went for nothing. The fact that they might go for less than nothing occurred slowly to Dr. Bernard (all his mental processes were leisurely) when he found himself, like any common, uninstructed fellow, summoned to the bar.

The complaint was read rather impressively. It was an incredibly vulgar charge—that of receiving stolen property. To this Charles Claudius Bernard, Instructor, and Thomas Sleigh, Janitor of Galen Medical School, severally pleaded not guilty: and the trial progressed as briskly as possible.

Surbridge, who handled the case from the outset in a manner as unconventional as the most conventional of professions allowed him, made a brief and blazing opening of the sort which led lawyers who did not know him to whisper: "Effective. But theatricals won't carry this case. It needs a stone-crusher."

"Wait," answered an elderly member of the bar, "you'll have both before he gets through. I knew his father."

The witnesses for the prosecution were put forward rapidly—it seemed to be Surbridge's purpose to avoid tiring the court—and, delayed only by the inevitable cross-examination, these presented their testimony, on the whole, with a clearness which indicated rather an unusual drill, or unusual harmony between counsel and witness.

Daniel Badger took his oath solemnly, as if he had been undergoing initiation vows at the Lodge of the Grand Mooses. He testified distinctly in his plaintive voice. Now and then he gestured a little with his crutch; he had a pleasing expression of confidence in the judge, not entirely lost upon his Honor, whose sharp lips curved into a withered smile when the lad, suddenly overborne by the pathos of his story, forgetting that he had been directed only to answer questions, leaned heavily upon his crutch, lifted one thin hand high in the air (apparently under the impression that he was taking another oath), and, before Surbridge could stop him, thus personally addressed the Bench:

"Ye see, Judge, Trixy she's all I got. Me 'n' Trixy haven't anybody but her 'n' me. It was turrible to steal Trixy. It ain't so much them shows and her bein' edoocated—you never see a dog know so much as Trixy does—an' folks have to make a livin'—me 'n' Trixy used to make ourn before she was took away from me that time. But that ain't it. I'd 'a' starved, Judge, and welcome, any day, an' I would n't 'a' minded much—I druther most anything than have anything happen to Trixy."

Here Surbridge, inwardly delighted, felt bound to interpose.

"You may go on, my lad," said the judge indulgently. "It may be of help in getting at the facts," he added, leveling a straight glance at the respectful protest in the face of the college counsel. "Let us hear what the boy has to say."

"She played so pretty, too," proceeded Dan with quavering voice. "Didn't ye never see her play, Judge? It warn't only ten cents a head. She ain't like most dogs, Trixy ain't. She's a little girl in dog's close, Trixy is. An' then ye see she's so small, Judge. It warn't as if she was a bull-dog, or something big. Trixy couldn't help herself—she was a little dog. It warn't right of them fellars. They was grown-up men. They stole my little dog. I seen her. I seen her in that college. They was a goin' to cut her up alive. I hearn a fellar say so. They was goin'—to—cut—TRIXY—up—alive. I tell ye, Judge, I seen her in the machine. She had a bit acrosst her mouth—so—she was crying somethin' awful. It was a turrible thing for them fellars to treat Trixy so—now warn't it? You wouldn't ha' treated her that way yourself, Judge, would you?"

Dan sat down trembling. He was very white, and went a trifle faint. He felt that he had disobeyed Mr. Surbridge: he had spoken more than he was spoken to; and he experienced a sick anxiety. From the rear of the room a little squeal, immediately muffled by something soft, greeted the subsidence of the complainant.

Very ably cross-examined, Dan stuck to his story like a drowning excursionist to a sound life preserver. He neither slipped nor sank. In fact, he added so many dangerous touches to the evidence that the eminent college counsel dropped the lad as soon as he decently could.

Before the emotion aroused by Dan's pathetic personality had wasted, Surbridge put in his witnesses briskly.

Thomas Cady related the circumstances of the finding of the dog. He knew the dog well; he was "perpared" to swear that it was the dog; he saw her taken up to the medical school; he did not get near enough to release the dog.

Sarah Jenkinson, plainly a consumptive, coughing heavily, offered similar testimony.

Mary Cady reiterated and added to the same. She had observed the blue blanket on the dog as it was being dragged along. She had lingered behind her party, and had seen the man. When the man "see her watchin'," he ran. Mary Cady had addressed a policeman on the subject of the man and the dog. The policeman had "cussed" at Mary Cady. Mary Cady's testimony was rendered picturesque by her costume. She wore a blue coat, and a green hat surmounted by a blue jay, a cat-bird, and the remains of a cockatoo. Her brown muff hung from her neck by a pink ribbon.

Cady's Molly was immediately followed by a witness whose appearance created evident agitation in the professional part of the audience. Robert Souther, practicing physician and surgeon, being sworn, reluctantly admitted that he was present in the laboratory of Dr. C. C. Bernard at the time when the dog was withdrawn from the experiment in question by the interference of the attorney for the prosecution. Dr. Souther was a middle-aged man with grayish hair and beard. He bore himself with an air of distressed protest throughout the melancholy occasion to which he had been subpoenaed: but, being obviously a man who "honored his word as if it were his God," however unwillingly, he told the truth. Shrewdly cross-examined, he did not retract or confuse it. The dog was prepared for an experiment which he was invited to witness. He had inquired of Dr. Bernard where he had picked that pretty creature up. Dr. Bernard had replied that it came in the usual way. The dog was fastened to the dog-board, and the experiment was about to begin, when the interruption occurred. Closely pressed by the attorney for the prosecution, Dr. Souther admitted that he had regretted the sacrifice of the dog; but, being a guest of the occasion, he had not felt at liberty to say so; equally did he regret being obliged to testify against a colleague in this case. Yes; he was quite sure that he should recognize the dog if he saw it. It was in no sense an ordinary dog. He could not deny that he was gratified that the dog had escaped the experiment.

After the court had returned from luncheon the defense unmasked its batteries. These were of a resounding variety. The college took the position, hardly material to the issue, but intended to overawe, that this slight matter scarcely needed attention. That the institution could err, was plainly a social heresy. Its honor was not to be questioned, its scientific dogma was not to be barked at by the courts, and its methods were above criticism. To bring Galen Medical School before the bar of the state was a species of lèse-majesté.

One of the defendants, taking advantage of his privilege, was silent. The janitor was not going to run the risk of any possible incrimination of his valuable personality. He had been in office a dozen years, and had never been in an unpleasant position before, he held himself to be as unimpeachable and almost as important as the dean. In fact, was he not more necessary? At least the "dog banditti" thought so.

Witnesses were many and fluent. Doctors, laboratory assistants, medical students flocked eagerly to the defense of their school. The college could easily have presented ten witnesses to Surbridge's one. The expression of the distinguished attorney was placid and confident. He put forward the chief defendant without uneasiness. Dr. Bernard's arrogant brutality, which was not always popular in professional or private life, made him an excellent witness in his own behalf. He had for so long a time regarded laymen with contempt that he had no fears about the possible outcome. Indeed, his mind was cloudy as to the value of the legal profession; its skill he did not respect; its force he did not fear. Set against a scientific creed, set against a scientific fact, what were the claims of any other profession? The church he despised, the state he defied with a narrow complacency than which none could be more hopeless.

Charles Claudius Bernard took the stand with insolent ease. His enormous hands played with the rail before him as if he had been stripping it of its muscles. His prominent ears seemed to a girl whose wincing eyes followed him behind her veil, to turn forwards a little like those of a listening animal. He told his story in a loud voice that snapped now and then into the irritability of a red-haired man. He assumed a position which he conjectured to be unassailable. He maintained (and the judge allowed him the same latitude that had been allowed to Dan) that it was not an instance, but a principle which was arraigned; and the principle he defended with a certain brutal belief: in it that was not without force. He applauded the practice that he represented, and the institution which chartered it, and himself. He challenged examination of his methods, inspection of his laboratories. To the animals upon which he experimented, he referred with a cold indifference not skillfully concealed behind a perfunctory show of sympathy. He swore that he did not know the dog was stolen. He swore that he was about to anaesthetize the dog. He swore that none of his subjects suffered. He swore that beyond a passing discomfort animals did not suffer.

143

Philip Surbridge, up to this point, had handled the college witnesses with a courtesy that was almost cordial, cutting swathes in the defense with a nonchalant touch. He had begun pleasantly and lightly as if he were trundling a lawn-mower. Now the stone-crusher began to move. In five minutes Dr. Charles Claudius Bernard was uncomfortable. In ten, his cruel, deeply reddened face had taken on purplish shadows about the mouth and eyes. In fifteen, he had admitted half a dozen things which he had begun by denying, and in twenty, if a stone-crusher had been vivisectible material he could have flayed the brain and heart of the counsel for the prosecution.

The judge, who had been listening to the cross-examination with an absorbed attention not expected of a police-court magistrate, now interrupted the natural order of the proceedings. He expressed a wish to have the plaintiff put upon the stand. Was it a slip of the tongue? or was his Honor pleased to be facetious? Surbridge paused in evident perplexity, and made a motion towards Dan.

"I think I fail to understand your Honor's wish?"

"Produce the real complainant," said the judge peremptorily. "I want to see the dog."

"Go, Dan," said Philip Surbridge in a low voice—"or—no— stay where you are. I'll do it."

He went over himself and took the dog from Miss Lauriat so quietly that only a few persons sitting nearest the young lady knew precisely what had occurred. For the instant Miriam lifted the dark veil that was tied about her hat, and her eyes went to Philip's straight. They had a beautiful look, half of wonder, half of pride, and all of trust. They said: "You are making a grand case of it. And yet you are sparing me."

Trixy obeyed his Honor's summons very prettily. She was of the race and of the sex that offer the trick dogs, and was prepared to regard the occasion as a professional opportunity. Yet she paid no attention at first to anything but her master; to whom she flew— more like a bird than a dog—with little squeals of delight and dainty laps of her rose-pink tongue, cuddling and protesting passionately against the separation of the day; she laid her cheek rapturously to the radiance of Dan's face, and, turning her head and neck gracefully, she brought these close beneath his chin, and from this shelter serenely surveyed the court.

It then occurred to her that she was neglecting one of the dearest of friends, and she sprang from Dan's arms to Surbridge's at a bound. Philip gently put her down upon the table, where the opposing counsel, whether of accident or of intent, stroked Trixy. The court smiled and said:

"A point has been raised about the unusual character or value of the dog. I should like to see one or two of the little creature's accomplishments."

Dan stepped forward proudly, and, being something muddled by excitement, hastily began: "Trixy, where is the lady you love the best?"

"No, no!" whispered Surbridge. "Not that! Not now! Trixy should shake hands with the judge."

So Trixy, being lifted up, shook hands with his Honor—very charmingly indeed. Then she volunteered to kiss Mr. Surbridge, but, being deftly dissuaded, boxed the ears of the opposing counsel instead. Then she danced a two-step on the table, and bowed with dignity to the audience. After that, she leaped the bounds of all legal precedent, and, lightly springing to his Honor's lap, put her paws on the bench, her head on her paws, and said her prayers.

The audience was now laughing heartily, and the judge, finding that Trixy, considered in the form of evidence, was more than he had counted on, handed her back to her counsel, and returned severely to his official duties. Somewhat testily he demanded that the defendant be recalled, and the unexpected question was shot at Bernard:

"Do you recognize this dog?"

So Dr. C. C. Bernard put on his distance glasses, carefully examined the little creature, and slowly said:

"I see so many subjects! There are so many experiments! I could hardly be expected to identify any one of them outside the laboratory."

"Answer Yes or No!" thundered Surbridge. "Do you recognize this dog?"

Then Charles Claudius Bernard answered:

"I do not recognize the dog."

Now as the strident accents of this reply grated upon the silent court-room, a remarkable change fell upon the "real complainant." Trixy, who had run to the end of her leash upon the table, pleasantly regarding the audience which she plainly supposed to have assembled in her honor, turned with a motion of unmistakable fear, and looked up into Dr. Bernard's dark, disturbed face. Over that of the dog crept such an expression of horror that his Honor instinctively uttered a clicking noise, made by hitting the tongue against the roof of the mouth. Several persons sitting near enough to see the dog's eyes gave out low exclamations. Whether Dr. Bernard recognized the subject or not, the subject had recognized Dr. Bernard. Cringing with fright, Trixy fled to her master and buried herself in his arms and in his neck. This shelter not sufficing, she burrowed beneath his coat and hid herself from sight. Dan could hear the terrified beating of her little heart, and the arm with which he clasped her stirred with the violent trembling of the dog's delicate body. This unusual court episode created an obvious impression, and it began to be suspected that Trixy was likely to win her own case.

The stone-crusher ground on, more briskly now, with swifter revolutions.

"Did you ever sec this before?" cried Surbridge, sharply wheeling upon a scowling witness known to the students as "janitor's boy." The attorney held out in both hands a dog's blue blanket, soiled and spoiled and torn, on which the embroidered letters I X Y were still plainly to be seen.

The witness, stammering and trembling, said he had seen the blanket before, at the college—on a dog—on this dog, yes, sir. He had put it in the ash barrel. Yes, sir, it was the janitor told him to.

"You were familiar with the appearance of this blanket, of course? You must have been aware of the existence of the embroidered letters I X Y upon it?"

The witness granted that he was familiar with the appearance of the blanket, and that he had noticed the embroidered letters I X Y.

"And then this," suggested Surbridge carelessly. "You must have observed this writing on the inside of the blanket?"

He turned the little blanket wrong side out, and, held up in full view of the court, it showed the legend printed in indelible ink upon a piece of linen that was sewed underneath Trixy's coat:

This belongs to Trixy Badger. She is a little white dog. She belongs to Daniel E. Badger, 123 Blind Alley. If lost, please return her.

Under a terrible cross-examination the witness, sweating agony and crying mercy from every pore of body and soul, admitted that he had seen the label—thought he had mentioned the label to the janitor—thought that Dr. Bernard knew about the coat, but darsen't tell why he thought so.

The janitor's boy panted and shook so that Surbridge, in scornful mercy, released him before he meant to.

"The case is won," said the elderly lawyer who had known Surbridge's father in his prime. "But they will appeal."

The closing arguments were tense and short; that of the defense being remarkably able, and as impressive as it could well be made in teeth of developments so dramatic and so unexpected. Philip Surbridge occupied less than half an hour. He reviewed the evidence briefly, almost brusquely, as if it were idle to waste the time of the court by dwelling upon such a fortification of facts. His manner was cheerful and assured, and seemed to intrust the case to the legal sense of the judge, as a matter of course. It was without a trace of "lawyer's worry" that he rose into the impassioned and original plea which was long and well remembered by every attorney in the room. Some applauded it, some criticised it, but no man forgot it.

Surbridge, having handled the technicalities of his case with significant thoroughness and with real power, now gave himself over generously to its moral and even its emotional aspects. The manner in which he was pleased to do this, though not without a counterpart in the records of the Bar, was unmatched in the courts of our Eastern coast. Without a word of apology for the innovation, the lame lad's counsel launched upon a eulogy of the nature of the dog.

"A man does not have to live very long," he said, "to discover that in this world friends are hard to gain, and harder to keep. At most they are very few. Not many of them are true. All of them are uncertain. None of them can answer the demands of our clamoring hearts. Who comes so near to meeting the conditions of a real friendship as your dog? His devotion surpasses the devotion of most women. His affection outvies the affection of any man. He gives everything; he asks nothing. He offers all; he receives little. He comforts your loneliness; he assuages your distress; he sacrifices his liberty to watch by you in sickness; when every one else who used to love you has neglected your grave, he will break his heart upon it. Who fails you in faith? Your dog is loyal. Who deserts you? Your dog never. Who gashes you with roughness, or bruises you with unkindness? Your dog offers you the tenderness that time and use cannot destroy. You have from him the expression of the uttermost, the unselfish love. This little citizen of the slums, this wronged and suffering lad possessed a treasure which any one of us might envy—the true friendship of an exquisite canine nature. Without excuse in the nature of the deed, without apology in the laws of the land, science put out her red hand and tore from this afflicted boy his means of livelihood, the joy of his hard life, the comrade of his desolation. His tragic experience is one of hundreds that never reach the knowledge of the public, or the protection of the courts. The merciful dénouement of this dark tale does not often await the bereaved household that has mysteriously lost its dumb and cherished friend. Yours may be such a household. Mine might be such bereavement. We, too, may be elected to share this fate into which the physiology of our day drags the animal and the human too. You have heard the defendant in this case assert that he does not know, that his institution does not know, where the victims of his laboratory come from. Your Honor! I claim that his institution ought to know. I say that her faculty and her employees ought to know. I urge that the defendants should be made to

148

know—by the decision of this court—where this material came from, and that they should never be permitted from this hour to forget. I appeal for this wronged boy against the slaughter-houses of science, to the law which is framed to protect the weak, to punish outrage, and to respect the sacredness of property."

It seemed that Surbridge had intended to say something more, but, checked by his own agitation, and moved by the emotion in the court-room, he ceased abruptly. His pale face turned impulsively towards the girl in the far end of the house. It seemed to him that he could see her wet eyes through her veil.

Quickly and quietly she rose and went out. It was as though she could not trust herself to witness the end of the scene.

This came now, in a whirlwind.

His Honor summed up briefly and sternly.

He referred to the importance of this case to the community—to its unusual character—to the standing of the defendants—to their evident assumption that their influential position would afford them immunity. The court, however, proposed to dispense justice impartially, regardless of the consequences. Science was not of such paramount importance to society as the observance of the laws. It was perfectly clear to the judge upon the evidence that both the defendants knew that the dog was stolen, and there was nothing for him to do in the conscientious and fearless discharge of his duty but to find them both guilty of the offense charged.

His Honor imposed the heaviest fine that the law allowed; treated the appeal with sarcastic contempt; and, when he found a chance, said to the young attorney: "You remind me of your father."

The students and the medical men went out in disturbed and scowling groups. But some of the lawyers lingered to give a hearty hand to Philip Surbridge. Ladies who had dropped their fans to put dainty hankerchiefs to their eyes melted away silently and thoughtfully. And the plain and powerful people rose to their strong feet, and—not knowing and not caring that it was against court rules to do so—cheered and roared like the lion that they are for Dan and Trixy.

Chapter XIV

—ᶆ—

The vivisector turned painfully upon his bed; he had lain there now six weeks. He had always been a well man, and by the mystery of physical suffering and disability he was as much astonished as he was infuriated. For the last twelve mouths he had worked with a concentration never exceeded in his studious life. His laboratory had not listened in vain for his expected feet, and the lights in its windows had often burned late into the night. During the year his colleagues had noted that he had shifted his research away from the surgical direction. Whether he had been moved to do this through one of those delusions by which we excuse to ourselves our forsworn resolves, he himself could not have told. At all events, the work upon which he was now engaged—that of serum inoculation—was alleged to be the more merciful form of experimentation.

He had not spoken to Miriam Lauriat since that morning when he was exiled from the paradise of her presence. He had written to her several times, but had received no replies. Beyond a passing glimpse of her in the street, or in some place of entertainment, he had not seen her face. These instantaneous views, caught on the sensitized plate of his consciousness, had caused him so much misery that he had finally withdrawn himself from all but the necessary attrition of life. The vow he had made to her still reverberated through his being, but he excused himself from its fulfillment with the easy sophistry of his avocation. It was a conditional promise. She had not met the condition; why should he sacrifice himself?

At midsummer, about two months ago, he came home from his laboratory one day with a slight abrasion upon his finger. He thought nothing of it at the time. The guinea pig that he had inoculated sickened and died, as it was intended that it should. On the day when the patient creature drew its last miserable breath, Dr. Steele was appalled to discover in himself the too familiar symptoms of the malady that he had imposed upon his timid and unimportant victim.

His knowledge of the nature and consequences of the disorder constituted its acutest feature. He longed for the happy simplicity of the layman; he prayed that certain cells of his brain might be dispossessed of their technical training; he would have bartered twenty years of education for the dull foresight of a man who would know only what his physician chose to tell; he would have sold his brilliant reputation for a merciful nescience of his advancing fate.

Steele, as we say, had never been really ill before; we might add that he had never truly been alone before. The inevitable solitude of sickness—at its best neither tolerated nor understood by the well and the gregarious—was in his instance rather pitiably uncompanioned. His mother was dead; his brother was in California; and his sister's infrequent visits came like ice in April. The attendance of the staff of Galen College did not mitigate his desolation, any more than it cured his disorder. He was alone with his nurse, his servants, and his old dog. Tibbs and Barry were about the same age, so to speak, and both had well outgrown the impatience that youth feels with the sick.

Olin's sister came in on the day of which we tell, to make a little duty call. It was with evident reluctance that she crossed the sickroom. She sat down on a chair at some distance from the bed, and prattled her perfunctory sympathy.

Did he enjoy the flowers? Should she send another tumbler of that jelly? Could he read some wholesome, cheerful novels? Her husband sent his kindest regards. Any more letters from Dick?

How well he was doing at the head of that institution! All her friends were proud of him. He was a credit to the family, he enjoyed the climate, and said he never was so well in his life.

"I must say, Olin—of course, you know, I am very sorry for you, but I should have thought you had experience enough not to get yourself into such a scrape as this. Still, I suppose, it's very interesting studying your own symptoms, especially when they are so rare. You'll be writing a pamphlet about it some day."

"Oh, do be still, Jess!" groaned Olin. He buried his face in his pillow savagely.

"Well, I'm sure!" exclaimed Jess. "It's no use trying to sympathize with you." She pouted, and he heard her skirts swishing out of the room.

Agitated by the disturbance of his sister's call, Olin flung himself into a rise of temperature, and feverishly rang for water and an open window. The nurse was off duty, being out for her two hours' relief, and Tibbs did not hear the bell. Steele called and called again, but no one answered him. The sudden tears of weakness scalded his eyes. He thought of his mother with a boyish, almost a sentimental longing.

"Nobody cares," he muttered. "I am a sick—I am a desolate man."

His reflections ran a bitter race. He who had achieved almost supremely; he whose value science had rated so highly; he whose name was pushed to the front in medical journals; he whose college honored him above the alumni of his time; he for whose revolutionizing discoveries humanity was said to be waiting—he lay there parched and neglected. He had sown professional fame; he had reaped a poisoned isolation. He flung himself over in a helpless fury, and his clenched hand dropped at the side of the bed. It hit something cold, and he drew back with a shiver.

Slowly and laboriously an old St. Bernard dog raised himself to his feet, and followed his master's witless hand. The huge, stiff creature put his head upon the bed; with dim, faithful eyes begging the caress for which he had waited longer than, it seemed, masters know or care. Feeling rather than perceiving—for Barry was now nearly blind—that the sick man's attention was turned to him at last, the dog struggled up and got one paw, then the other, to the pillow, and so across the dear neck that he pathetically sought to clasp.

"Why, Barry!" said Steele faintly. "Why, Barry!—What do you want, old fellow?"

Barry passionately tried to answer, but he had no vocabulary except that of love; he had only love to render; and only love to ask. Barry concerned himself with no small matters; he dealt with nothing less than the greatest thing in the world. He stood quite still and straight—it must have hurt him, but he said nothing about that—and, getting his head over upon the sick man's shoulder, laid it there with a happy sigh. As long as the rheumatic dog could stand, the two remained so, cheek to cheek.

"You stay by me, Barry—don't you?"

Stimulated, perhaps, by this momentary contact with life and love—it did not matter just then that it was offered by one of the subject races—Steele's thoughts took on a character to which for years his mind had given no hospitality. For, now, there marched before his closed and aching eyes the solemn movement of a long processional. Curiously, it seemed to go in pairs, like the animals that went into the ark in the old Bible myth that he used to believe when he was a child. This mute and sentient panorama was all aware of him. As it passed, each martyred creature turned its eyes and looked at him, and looked away; so he had seen on the stage the murdered man look upon Irving in "The Bells." In this glance was neither threat nor accusation, only an instant's width of awful recognition. It was a gentle company that filed by him: the domestic animals that comfort our homes, soft feline pets, purring as they came, and noble-headed dogs who had kissed the hand that carved them; there followed small despised things, that sing in our swamps on summer nights, and lull us to sleep with their cheerful serenade; then came simple-minded, docile creatures with long, lifted ears—little spirits, born to be playthings for children. There were winged things, too, pigeons and doves, whose brains he had sliced. These all went with their heads on one side or the other.

154

The circumstance that forbade them to hold themselves straight did not seem to be as interesting now as it was when he sacrificed these gentle beings to a physiological caprice.

The vivisector returned the recognition of these solemn ranks. His fevered brain, not altogether able to distinguish between the phantasm and the fact, followed these sad shades eagerly. There was a maledict hypnosis in their mournful gaze. They trooped in companies, mute, gentle, uncomplaining, unaccusing. God! If they had arisen and gnashed at him! If they had torn him muscle by muscle; if they had stripped him nerve from nerve as he had lacerated them—he could have borne it better! But they flayed him with gentle endurance; they tormented him with phantom forgiveness; their bitterest revenge was one reiterated question— "Why?—Why?—Why?" Then, from gulfs of distance the voice of a woman invisible cried out upon him: "Was it worth the cost?— Was it worth the cost?"

Unable to free himself, if he would, from this spectral society, Steele watched its inevitable progression. It was as if he were an officer reviewing the ghosts of a scattered army after a defeat. Silent, drooping, by hundreds they passed him by; they offered him no salute; it was his false tactics that had lost the fight.

Here and there in the feeble ranks he identified a sacrifice to his fame—that dog in Vienna—and now, last of all, hers. This one did not raise its scarred head, but dully followed the rest because it had to.

A throe of physical anguish brought Steele to himself, and dissipated this ghostly army. It now recurred to the physiologist that he was bearing in his own body, nerve by nerve, a reduplication of the sensations which he had inflicted in some of his recent experiments. His educated imagination could easily forecast the climax to the tragedy. He had seen it enacted—how many times!

"This is my punishment," he groaned. "This is my punishment for the torments I have allowed the animals to suffer."

His cry rang through the room, and hurried the nurse whose feet were already on the stairs.

"You've been dreaming!" she exclaimed.

"No," he panted, "it was no dream. I wish it were."

"I'll tell Dr. Bernard downstairs that you can't see him. You're not fit. I can't allow it. It won't do."

"—Oh, but here I am. I guess he'll see me alright."

Bernard pushed into the sick-room obstinately. His patients were not people, and he did not know how to treat the human sick. He came to the bedside, and with the arrogance of health looked down upon his chief. He put a few searching questions, asked the nurse for the chart, and regarded the sufferer critically. Steele had seen the same expression of satisfaction on that coarse face before.

"It's a beautiful case, isn't it?" observed Bernard brutally.

Steele lay watching his visitor through half-closed lashes. To himself he said: "This man would sacrifice me, if he could. He would experiment heartily. He has become like that. Or perhaps he always was." Aloud he said: "You remind me of that story about Passerot—do you remember? Probably not. Hand me that black book under the 'Surgical Record' on the other table—will you? Thanks. Oblige me by reading that."

And Bernard read:

"There is a story told of . . . a French scholar of the last century. Dying, he was brought, unrecognized, into the Charity Hospital of Paris. The attending surgeon looked down upon the misera-ble being, and, speaking to his associates in Latin,—the language used by learned men,—he remarked: '*Fiat experimentum in corpore vili.*' At these words the eyes of the dying man opened, and from one they had taken to be a beggar came a scholar's reply: '*Corpus non vile est, domini doctissimi, pro quo Christus ipse non dedignatus est mori.*'"

Bernard closed the book with ostentatious indifference; his muddy cheek did not clarify into color; but he flung one insolent glance at his professor. "Oh, by the way," he said leisurely, "can't you induce the alleged owner of that spaniel to let us have it back? Otherwise, all that work is thrown away."

The stricken man struggled to raise himself upon his elbow, and struggled again, when he fell back. Panting and paling, he cursed his subordinate out of the room.

Then Barry, limping after, swore hoarsely at the inquisitor; who, as he closed the door, kicked the old dog.

The instructor left the house in a bad humor, and went his way sulkily. He had always dully felt that a separateness existed between himself and Olin Steele, such as people not scientifically educated might call a class distinction of the soul; but this was of the sort which a man does not admit to himself in language.

"He is even dying differently," thought Bernard. He resented this last infringement upon his estimate of himself. Nothing in his nature responded to the evident moral agitation and readjustment with which Steele was fronting death.

"What is there to make a fuss about, anyhow?" he asked savagely.

He walked for a while, looking grimly about. It might almost have been said that he was looking for something on which to wreak his discomfort. He paused before a hospital, where it now occurred to him that a curious operation (which, as the event proved, ended in death) was to take place that very day upon the brain of an underwitted house-maid. He went in.

As he watched with absorption this rare demonstration, he said to himself: "No experiment is absolutely satisfactory unless it has been tried on a human being."

The episode gave him a keen pleasure which forced the unpleasant thought of his professor from his mind.

The nurse hurried in remorsefully, voluble as the best of nurses may be at the unfortunate moment. Steele felt as if he could hurl her after Bernard by an objurgation, and had hard work not to tell her so. But she had a letter in her hand, and when he saw the superscription the patient could have kneeled in his bed and worshiped her.

"I'm afraid I'm doing wrong," she parleyed. "You have been under some severe excitement, and the doctor—"

But the patient, damning the doctor, tore the envelope from the woman's hand, ordered her out of the room, and fell upon the letter like some starved animal on living food. Steele, staring and shaking, read:

I have never answered anything you have written because I felt that it would not be merciful to you, nor best, perhaps, for me. But in these poignant days, which are anniversary of those that I am not yet able to forget, it has seemed to me that, perhaps, I should be truer to myself if I did so, and that it might be the better way to break, once and for all, the silence that I have put between us; it has grown a high and solid wall, and a wall it must remain. You will not for a moment mistake me about that. But it has come to me lately to wish to tell you this: while to you it has seemed a wall of stone or marble, to me it has been a wall of glass. It is thick glass; I cannot break it; but I have always felt that I could look through it, if I chose, and sometimes I have chosen. I have observed you; I have watched your life.

I do not mind telling you that it has added to such sadness as I myself cannot escape, to see that you are—as you were; and that the words which you said to me that day, that last day, have not taken form in deeds. It has disappointed me.

Yesterday I heard that you are ill; how ill I do not know, nor from what cause; there seems to be some mystery or reticence about it on which I have made no effort to intrude. But it came to me plainly last night that I should like to tell you that I am sorry you are sick. I should not like to be as you said. I do not mean to be kind to a dog and cruel to his tormentor, not even that; and so I am writing as I am. . . . If you had been a drunkard I might have tried to save you. If I had married you, and you had done some dreadful thing—some quick, hot-headed thing—I should have forgiven you. I might have stood by you if you had committed some impulsive murder. I do not know, but I think I should. But, as it was, I should always have thought—there would have been times when—

Cruelty may be—how do we know?—the unpardonable sin; it is a sin against the Spirit of Mercy; it is such a sin against my spirit that I had, and I have, no choice. I do not wish to add to your suffering, but it may not really do so if I tell you that I have not seen the moment when I have regretted my decision, or felt that any other was or could be possible. I cannot see how any true woman can take a vivisector's hand.

But something else is possible. I do not want to force my feeling about this upon you, but I should like to respect you again, even to honor you again, before I die.

It seems to me that there may be something more in such interruptions of human fate than we suppose; perhaps no man and woman experience a memorable attraction and go quite freed of it, for this life. "I stand forever in thy shadow"—that is the Portuguese Sonnets, isn't it? It seems to me that we have gained something worth having if the shadow of such an intercepted feeling shall be a noble one. I cannot help wishing—in a word—that mine may be to you a noble shadow.

It seems to me the worst thing about the scientific error that has misled you, that it should delude the moral nature of such a man as I thought you were born to be. I have found myself praying that—not because you cared for me, but because you honored some of the things I care for—you should become the man I thought you were. I have written this because I cannot help it; and I shall not write again.

M.L.

Steele read and reread this letter with solemn, shining eyes. When he heard the footsteps of the nurse and doctor he hid it under his

159

pillow, and kept his hand upon it. The doctor's face assumed a shade of gravity. "Too quiet," he thought; "too docile."

Obedient, amenable, Steele lay perfectly still until the nurse in the adjoining room was asleep. Then his own mind and heart awoke.

It was doubtful if he slept at all. All night his soul arose and looked upon him. In its naked countenance he saw unappeasable regret. Its eyes were like hers; they did not scorn him now; they pitied him. Like hers, they seemed to be dismissing him. Curious old words came to him brokenly: What shall it profit if a man gain professional glory (which might be discredited in the next quarter century) and lose his own soul—for how long?

His great essay on the non-existence of love he had himself disastrously disproved. Who could say which of his conclusions, arrived at by what sacrifice of tormented life, might not meet a similar fate?

His profession had called him great, and he had thought he was, but, in the last analysis, for what would he be longest remembered? For an iron thong which he had invented to pierce the tongue of a vivisected dog, and hold it in place. He had experienced his full share of the arrogance of physiology. He had tolerated the practical physician. He had patronized the healer. Now, he thought of them with an avid envy—men who had extinguished themselves in the relief of human suffering; those lovers of life, those counselors of the home, those assuagers of pain, those idols of the sick! These were the men who counted not their lives their own, who were never sure of their sleep, their rest, their holidays, or the society of their families—they who were the servants of the lowest poor, the slaves of the most disordered whims—men who grew gray before their time, because they carried upon their hearts the suffering of the world; they who were the physical and often the moral saviors of sick and tempted people—men of whom the world was not worthy. What had he in common with these? Who depended upon him? What happiness had he conferred? What suffering had he allevi-ated? Who blessed his coming feet? Who regretted his forced depar-ture? Who remembered him in grateful prayers? Who loved him?

The shrieks of his laboratory re-echoed through his ears. He had entered it to torture; he had left in it inexorable agony. Better to have been one of those plain, overlooked, over-worked men whose epitaph is written in the hearts of his patients. Better to have been the obscurest of them all—some country doctor riding his thirty miles over impossible roads, carrying his snow-shovel in the sleigh to dig the drifts out from under his horse's feet; better to be smitten by sun, or parched by dust, or drenched in storms, or starved for sleep, or flinging one's life into the tentacles of contagion.

If he had been such as this she would have honored, she might have loved him. In trying to gain himself he had lost her. So strange, so subtle is the spiritual law; in losing her had he lost, and thus regained, himself?

It was now dim dawn. He drew her letter out from under the pillow, and pressed it feebly to his lips.

He had directed the nurse to leave paper and pencil within his reach. Those he took, and with shaking fingers traced these words:

> I used to think by what names I should call you when I had
> the right. I shall never have it now, but because I am so
> sick, will you let me this one time say, Miriam, I bless you
> for your letter? It is like yourself. If I were strong enough I
> should say more, but I am saving the little strength I have
> left to write my resignation to the trustees of Galen College.
> If I get well, I shall go out to California and start again. I
> shall be one of those plain men of whom you spoke to me,
> and of whom you may yet be proud. I shall try to live to this
> end; but it is not quite certain that I can do so. If I do, you
> shall respect me; if I do not, I want you to know that you
> have restored me. However it ends,
>
> > I am forever yours,
> > Olin Steele.

The next night he was not as well. Waves of delirium came and went. The physician remained in the house. He was puzzled, became apprehensive, and telephoned for a consultant. The patient paid little attention to any person. He noticed no one but Barry, who had taken an immovable position beside his master's bed. Once they saw the professor take his handkerchief and try to bandage Barry's head. The nurse said that he made as if he were handing bowls of water to thirsty dogs. He was heard to say: "Poor things! Poor things!" The nurse was perplexed; but Barry seemed to understand, for he kissed the transparent hand that hung over in his reach; there were real tears in Barry's eyes.

Towards morning: Steele thought he saw beside him the woman whom a man remembers, when all others are forgotten. His mother took his head upon her breast; she whispered sympathetically: "Was it a very pretty kitty, dear?"

Then her tone changed abruptly, and she sang with the voice of a young woman:

"Strong Son of God, immortal Love!"

It seemed to Steele that he took Miriam's letter out from under his pillow and laid it in his mother's hand. His colleagues, bending over him to listen, thinking possibly to catch from his lips some legacy of professional erudition, distinctly heard him say: "*Domini doctissimi . . . pro quo Christus ipse non dedignatus est mori.*"

These *domini doctissimi* were not religious men, but they bowed, as if they bared their heads; and the gentlest of them noticed with surprise the nature of the expression which had descended upon the professor's face. He looked like a sensitive and devout boy with life before him.

Chapter XV

—⟋ⱴ⟍—

As the little steamer rounded the headland the band, which consisted of a German violin, an Italian flute, and an American harp (the musical product of Blind Alley), struck into one of those popular airs that spur even the saddest child to dance. Cady's Molly was not a sad child, and, laughing, she began to pirouette around the deck. Ripples of applause followed her unpremeditated steps. This was too much for Trixy. With one quick look at her master she hopped from his knee, and danced out into the middle of the party.

Cady's Molly took Trixy by the hands and tried to adapt herself to her tiny partner. Molly was dressed with an unprecedented attempt at what she had heard Miss Lauriat call good taste. Her frock was white and plain, her long stockings black and neat; in her shade hat only had Molly allowed her personal views of taste anything like liberty. Molly wore a soft floppy straw surmounted with a wreath of cranberries and violets, relieved by sweet peas and cherries, and touched off with asparagus.

The girl had grown, and so had Dan, but not in feet and inches. Dan was as tall as he ever would be, and except for the lines between his brows he might have passed for a lad three years younger than he was. He gave Cady's Molly a quiet glance, but his gaze and his soul were for Trixy.

The consumptive woman sat in a steamer chair, smiling cheerfully, and her three little girls, like three little brownies, followed

Mr. Surbridge about the boat. Cady's Molly's father observed this monopoly with some regret. He had anticipated the opportunity of discussing the tariff with an eminent lawyer, but amiably contented himself by offering the children's mother the morning paper. She could not read; hence she was flattered by the attention.

"Nice, ain't it?" said the woman, turning her gaunt face to the sea wind. "Did you ever see anybody like her anywheres else?"

"Well," said Cady's Molly's father, argumentatively, "I am not prepared to say that I never did."

Both watched Miss Lauriat where she stood in the bow, looking gravely out to sea. At her feet, on his silk cushion, lay a feeble dog, with dulled eyes that lighted only for herself and Trixy.

"She ain't thinkin' of us," complained the consumptive. "There is times she don't."

"They're tarnation few in my opinion," replied Cady's Molly's father, chivalrously springing to the lady's defense. "Specially, come to think on't, these two years back. Take this here, now—charterin' steamboats to take a crowd like us down harbor—Lord! How many such trips was you ever aboard?"

"I never was out to sea in my life," admitted the woman slowly, "except along of her. I used to think the ocean was black, same's it is along the wharves. I didn't know it was such a pretty color—and clean. I wisht my dog could have come along o' them others. He can't. He died of his cough. Mine most gen'r'lly do. She didn't forget him. She sent him an invitation along of the children."

"She's a lady," announced Cady's Molly's father solemnly.

"Miss Laurie," said Dan in an undertone, "Trixy's got it in her again. Look at her! It's a good while since she's played for anybody but us at home. What shall I do?"

Miss Lauriat, turning with the swift merriment that Blind Alley knew so well (she never suffered her poor people to find her sad), saw a pretty sight. Everybody on board had seen it by now, and Trixy was the centre of a laughing and applauding crowd. The little actress, too long detained in private life, plunged into this momentary publicity with a mad delight. Who could say what blighted ambition had withered in Trixy's soul? What ennui with obscurity had she experienced? What longing for the exercise of neglected gifts? What histrionic passion thwarted? What innocent vanities denied? How shall the superior race decide? How could any one who had never been a little white trick dog presume to answer?

Trixy, sparkling with joy to find an audience again, spurred herself feverishly to recall her half-forgotten repertoire.

"Run along, Dan," said Miss Lauriat quickly. "Give them all a good time—and Trixy too."

Dan obeyed with summer in his eyes. Trixy, now supremely blest, performed ecstatically. She did everything she knew, and a good deal that she didn't. She waltzed, she begged, she said her prayers, she whirled from somersault to somersault, she found a lemon in Mr. Surbridge's coat pocket, and a pamphlet on the tariff in Cady's Molly's father's hat; modestly draped in Miss Lauriat's liberty silk scarf, she danced her little skirt dance; she flirted with the orchestra, she bridled at applause, and coquetted for encores like any diva.

"She used to sing the song," said Cady's Molly. "Give us the song, Dan."

Dan took Trixy by the right paw gallantly, as he used to do in the Mooses' Retreat, and leading her forward a few steps, began to sing:

Oh, we've traveled on together.
In kind or cruel weather.

But Trixy was suddenly still. Dan began again:

She's my lady and I'll love her
Till I die.

But Trixy stood drooping and silent. Some one said that the dog had forgotten her part. Dan looked into Trixy's face; it had grown pinched; and her eyes fled to her master's for protection.

"No," he said, "she hasn't forgotten. She doesn't want to sing that song."

He caught her and crooned over her; he kissed her and praised her. Trixy cuddled in his neck quietly. She trembled and put both her hands in his. The little actress lived to pass many a merry hour upon many a little stage, but neither then nor thereafter could she be induced to join her master in that duet.

Exhausted by her own accomplishments, or frightened by her darkest memories, Trixy played no more that day. Instead she curled into her master's lap and slept through a thunderstorm.

Surbridge came over when the shower was diminishing, and stood by Miriam, who seemed to him suddenly thoughtful and quiet.

"Well?" he asked.

When he spoke in that tone she always told him what was the matter; she did so quite naturally now.

"Phil, I've blundered. I meant to be kind, but I've blundered with those two. How do I know Dan hasn't minded it as well as Trixy? He would be sawn asunder before he'd let me know."

"If you've got so far as that," suggested Surbridge, "suppose you let me have him for an office boy? Trixy could sit on my table. I've thought for some time that doing errands under Matthew, and running the furnace, did not entirely satisfy the higher nature of the lad."

"Why didn't you say so, Phil? Am I so huffy and stuffy about advice?"

"You take advice like a philosopher—and the dear girl you are. I really can't say why I didn't. A fellow may have lucid intervals of modesty, I suppose—even a lawyer."

"It needs a man," sighed Miriam, "to manage a boy. I've bungled with Dan. I dare say he's missed those performances as much as Trixy. Probably he has mourned for the Grand Mooses' Retreat— and Cady's Molly."

"I doubt it," said Philip, "but we can see. My opinion is, the lad has missed nothing—except the sacred right to be a wage-earner in some obvious, active way—and has gained unspeakably and forever. But, if you choose to turn him over to me—as he grows older—I'll try my hand at him. It's too late, in his case, for what is called an education, but I can manage his grammar, and put a few books in his way."

"Help me, Phil," said Miriam, in a very low voice. "I need it. . . . I need you."

Across Surbridge's strong, controlled face there passed a sensitiveness that seemed to sink into it, and make it plastic for an expression which still lacked a moulding hand.

"I thank you," he said quietly, "for that. You've made a lot of poor wretches happy today, including me."

Miriam turned away. "Perhaps so—I hope so. But, oh, Phil, I'm tired."

She walked away from him, nodding and smiling at her guests, until she came to the stern of the boat, where she stood looking upon the wake. The little steamer was now heading into the harbor and the sun. The band was brightly playing. The deck glittered with drops of rain, and steamed. The chatter that had been subdued by the shower broke forth after it like birds. It had suddenly grown very sultry, and Miriam threw off her long coat, and stood in her white flannel boating dress, tall and aloof, against the sky. The steamer was now leaving the rain and the clouds behind.

Slowly, almost imperceptibly, two vast prismatic pillars arose from the sea. Advancing, receding, pulsating, but ever arising, the columns of color approached each other. It was as if invisible hands were building out of beams of light a bridge for a god to cross. The rainbow, seen the hundredth time, is as much a miracle as it was the first. Miriam's poor people broke into simple cries of wonder and delight; but these hushed into low exclamations, and then into the silence of something that they did not understand well enough to call it awe.

In the centre of the radiant arc, white and rapt, she stood—at her feet the martyred dog—over her head the symbol of everlasting hope, into whose mighty span her youth, her beauty, her pity, and her sadness seemed all alike to melt. He who was gone had called her mercy made magic. Mercy made promise, she seemed to yearn out, now, from the heart of the sky to the need of the earth. More than one of those whom she had made happy saw her through tears at that moment, as if she had been transfigured before them.

It was dusk when the steamer was warped to the wharf. The lungs of the city exhaled fire, and Miriam's tender face saddened as she bade her friends good-night.

"Poor things!" she said—"Poor people! Think of the hot homes they go to!" She stirred towards Philip remorsefully. "Forgive me for forgetting—You too! You have given up so much of your vacation for them, for us; you would have been in the country."

Philip laughed gayly. "If you think for a minute I stayed on your account—I've got a newsboy in the police court tomorrow morning. I've got to look after him."

"Philip," said Miriam timidly, "don't snub me! Come! Is there any real reason why you shouldn't come out with us and stay until tomorrow? Aunt Cornelia—"

"Do you wish it—on the whole? Are you sure?" asked Philip gravely.

Miriam hesitated. "I think I do. I'm sure I do. Yes—I wish it altogether."

"Very well, then. I'll take Caro. He's too heavy for you."

In a moment he had assumed all her cares; and the woman in her was mysteriously glad to cast them upon him.

The shore train was crowded and seething. Surbridge turned the seat, and the lame boy and the two dogs sat before them. Miriam was very tired. She glanced at Philip. It troubled her a little to find that he was such a comfort to her. She was almost startled at the turn her thoughts were taking. Something within her arose and clung to his presence as if she could not spare it. She laid her head against the side of the window, and tried to elude the images that pursued her. But Philip sat comfortably reading an evening paper at her side; as if he belonged there.

"Tired?" he asked. "Try to rest. Leave everything to me. I'll look out for the dogs, and the boy—and you, too."

Once or twice she looked enviously at Dan. The lad, who knew none of the discomforts of unclassified feeling, clasped his idol to his heart, and, worshiping what he protected, entered into peace. Trixy had long since ceased to play with her master's pathetic devotion; the elf-look had never returned to her eyes since she and he were reunited after death and science had given up the secrets which were in them. Trixy loved, at last, as she was beloved; and the lonely lad drank deeper of blessedness than most of us do who quench our thirst at the cup of human loyalty.

Mrs. Percy B. Jeffries had dined. The belated two waited for their broiled chicken and raspberries. Miriam ran upstairs to change her dress, and put Caro to bed. Surbridge strolled in from the piazza, and found Mrs. Jeffries conscientiously reading by an ivory porcelain lamp, softened through a white tulle overskirt. For some unexplained reason Miriam had long ago discarded the blue shade. Aunt Cornelia laid down her book, and regarded the young man with a tender attention. It somehow seemed to Philip an unusual one, but for what reason he could not have explained.

"I have been reading," said Aunt Cornelia, "a most extraordinary scientific work. It treats of the subterranean life of India and Tennessee. I have found it very instructive. I had no idea that caves were so convenient; they would make excellent summer hotels. I am particularly attracted by a certain kind of creature—I think they call it a polyaphron—is that it? Well, it doesn't signify. Did you ever hear about it? It is considered the blindest of created beings. Listen a minute, and I'll read you what the author says about it. The book is written by one of those delightful swamis who visit the drawing-rooms of this country."

Mrs. Jeffries put on her glasses, and slowly and impressively read:

"The polyaphron—"

"The polyaphron!" interrupted Philip, "what a delicious name! I suppose that means all kinds of a fool?"

"Does it?" said Mrs. Jeffries. "Just listen. 'The polyaphron is found only in one cave in the world. It has rudimentary wings, and it is supposed that in prehistoric times it could have flown out if it had desired. It is born nearly blind, and dies wholly so."

Mrs. Jeffries laid down her book and looked over her spectacles at the young attorney—a thing which he had never seen her do before. It made her look suddenly an old woman.

"My dear boy," she observed, with that half-whimsical affectionateness which always commanded the young man's chivalry, "I was born too early, or you too late. If you had been studying law when I was a young lady, I should have taken you myself—that is, if I had never met Mr. Jeffries, and if you had asked me."

"Which," said Philip gallantly, "you may rest assured, madam, that I should have done—or else, despairing, envied Mr. Jeffries."

"Gracefully answered," pursued Mrs. Jeffries placidly, "like yourself—and like your father, too. Here's Miriam! You two run and get your dinner, while I finish my polyaphron."

"Is it possible," thought Philip, "that she extemporized that? I shouldn't have given her credit for it." He put his hand out for the book, but Aunt Cornelia laughed, and turned it face down upon her lap.

She read no more in that remarkable scientific volume which had served perhaps a better purpose than it ever had before, or would again. Her eyes did not follow the young people; but her mouth had the wistfulness that age feels for youth, and loneliness for life.

When Miriam and Philip sat down together opposite each other in the bright dining-room Philip uttered a low exclamation.

In the soft penumbra of the rose-shaded candles she seemed to arise before him as the spectrum had arisen from the sea, in a sudden sheen of color—the first that he had seen her wear since her father died. This miracle was nothing more nor less than a prismatic summer silk, but to the young man she seemed to be clothed in a rainbow.

They talked little and lightly, and by a mutual instinct sought the presence of a third as soon as possible. But when they got back to the lace-covered lamp, Aunt Cornelia was not there. They sat down in the large empty room in something like constraint. Philip found himself monotonously repeating,—"The polyaphron is born nearly blind; and dies wholly so."

Miriam was restless, and shimmered over to the long window, where she stood looking out upon the water.

The dead August night was breathless and soundless. Scarcely a sigh crept up the cliffs. On Miriam's face rested the expression which the man who should win her would never see. Like all women whose thoughts are high, and whose years are young, she had never considered the nature of a second love. It would not be too much to say that she had never thought of it as for her a possible experience. She had reached the inevitable emergency of a fine and ardent soul that has given its first, but not its noblest passion.

She had reversed the great quotation. She had begun by loving Love. If she loved again, she would love the lover. If she did so, if she could do so, where was the dream of herself, which is dearer to such a woman than joy?

A subtle allegiance, though to a misguided feeling, oppressed her. There were times when a sense of something almost mystical disturbed her; winds had speech and tides language; the sea lifted arms as if it would drag her; from the spaces between the stars peremptory tones addressed her inarticulately; the atmosphere inclosed her as if it clasped; she seemed to be hunted by a thwarted, but still relentless will.

"Do you mind my coming, too?" asked Surbridge.

Philip had the personality that will elect to lose rather than to win by intrusion. The heart that would not give itself to him happily he would disdain to capture; he had never spoken a commanding word to Miriam; he had treated her with the quiet strength which has no need to assert itself; he had never lacked in consideration, but he had never urged her will. Sometimes Miriam had thought that the woman to whom Philip should offer his chartered affection "for sun and candlelight" would be exceptionally cherished.

Now, when he spoke, she turned a gentle invitation. Her manner was without animation, as her eyes were without hope. She experienced the profound, unnatural weariness of one who in a baffled struggle for freedom had shattered herself against an imprisoning attraction. To that captivity she had been misdirected by force; now, her sensibility looked everywhere for the trodden roads of tenderness. All she could think of in the world that she wanted was kindness—the daily shelter of a safe character; she craved common comfort, she needed simple rest, as though she had been a much older woman than she was. It seemed to her as if her youth had been stunned; she came back gravely to consciousness of it. She found herself inhaling life slowly, and with a certain reluctance foreign to her healthy, joyous temperament. She knew she must breathe the sympathy that she could trust.

Her old friend's firm but lenient nature seemed to encroach upon hers. Her heart leaned towards his bosom. But was this love? She felt as if only he could answer, or teach her how to do so.

"Do you remember," asked Philip quietly, "telling Dan—that night—that I always found everything I wanted?"

"No," said Miriam, "you haven't got it right. I said you found everything you tried to."

Then the crimson dismay of a woman un-wooed fled across her face. She remembered that Philip had never spoken a word of love to her, not one.

"But, dear, I have loved you all my life," he began.

APPENDIX A

"Eulogy of the Dog" Speech (1855), by George Graham Vest

—ↈ—

The following famous speech was a closing argument made in 1855 by George Graham Vest, U.S. senator from 1879 to 1903. It was repeatedly printed throughout the second half of the nineteenth century under the title "Eulogy of a Dog," often in animal welfare publications. Phelps refers to it in *Trixy*, chapter 13, as a comparison to Philip Surbridge's closing argument against a medical college for its theft of a beloved dog.

Gentlemen of the Jury:

The best friend a man has in the world may turn against him and become his enemy. His son or daughter that he has reared with loving care may prove ungrateful. Those who are nearest and dearest to us, those whom we trust with our happiness and our good name may become traitors to their faith. The money that a man has, he may lose. It flies away from him, perhaps when he needs it most. A man's reputation may be sacrificed in a moment of ill-considered action. The people who are prone to fall on their knees to do us honor when success is with us, may be the first to throw the stone of malice when failure settles its cloud upon our heads.

The one absolutely unselfish friend that man can have in this selfish world, the one that never deserts him, the one that never proves ungrateful or treacherous is his dog. A man's dog stands by him in prosperity and in poverty, in health and in sickness. He will sleep on the cold ground, where the wintry winds blow and the snow drives fiercely, if only he may be near his master's side. He will kiss the hand that has no food to offer. He will lick the wounds and sores that come in encounters with the roughness of the world. He guards the sleep of his pauper master as if he were a prince. When all other friends desert, he remains. When riches take wings, and reputation falls to pieces, he is as constant in his love as the sun in its journey through the heavens.

If fortune drives the master forth, an outcast in the world, friendless and homeless, the faithful dog asks no higher privilege than that of accompanying him, to guard him against danger, to fight against his enemies. And when the last scene of all comes, and death takes his master in its embrace and his body is laid away in the cold ground, no matter if all other friends pursue their way, there by the graveside will the noble dog be found, his head between his paws, his eyes sad, but open in alert watchfulness, faithful and true even in death.

APPENDIX B

"A Dog's Tale" (1903), by Mark Twain

—〰—

Mark Twain announced his objection to vivisection in 1899 in a letter to the London Anti-Vivisection Society, which was reprinted many times on both sides of the Atlantic. In it, he declares: "I am not interested to know whether Vivisection produces results that are profitable to the human race or doesn't. To know that the results are profitable to the race would not remove my hostility to it. The pains which it inflicts upon unconsenting animals is the basis of my enmity toward it, & is to me sufficient justification of the enmity without looking further." Four years later, he penned the short story "A Dog's Tale," in which he envisions the tragic effects of vivisection on a dog's life. The story is included here in its entirety.

I

My father was a St. Bernard, my mother was a collie, but I am a Presbyterian. This is what my mother told me; I do not know these nice distinctions myself. To me they are only fine large words meaning nothing. My mother had a fondness for such; she liked to say them, and see other dogs look surprised and envious, as wondering how she got so much education. But, indeed, it was not real education; it was only show: she got the words by listening in the dining-room and drawing-room when there was company, and by going with the children to Sunday-school and listening there; and whenever she heard a large word she said it over to herself many times, and so was able to keep it until there was a dogmatic gathering in the neighborhood, then she would get it off, and surprise and distress them all, from pocket-pup to mastiff, which rewarded her for all her trouble. If there was a stranger he was nearly sure to be suspicious, and when he got his breath again he would ask her what it meant. And she always told him. He was never expecting this but thought he would catch her; so when she told him, he was the one that looked ashamed, whereas he had thought it was going to be she. The others were always waiting for this, and glad of it and proud of her, for they knew what was going to happen, because they had had experience. When she told the meaning of a big word they were all so taken up with admiration that it never occurred to any dog to doubt if it was the right one; and that was natural, because, for one thing, she answered up so promptly that it seemed like a dictionary speaking, and for another thing, where could they find out whether it was right or not? for she was the only cultivated dog there was. By and by, when I was older, she brought home the word Unintellectual, one time, and worked it pretty hard all the week at different gatherings, making much unhappiness and despondency; and it was at this time that I noticed that during that week she was asked for the meaning at eight different assemblages, and flashed out a fresh definition every time, which showed me that she had more presence of mind than culture, though I said nothing, of course. She had one word which she always kept on hand, and ready, like a life-preserver, a kind of emergency word to strap on when she was likely to get washed overboard in a sudden way—that was the word Synonymous. When she happened to fetch out a long word which had had its day weeks before and its prepared meanings gone to her dump-pile, if there was a stranger there of course it knocked him groggy for a couple of minutes, then he would come to, and by that time she would be away down wind on another tack, and not expecting anything; so when he'd hail and ask her to cash in, I (the only dog on the inside of her game) could see her canvas flicker a moment—but only just a moment— then it would belly out taut and full, and she would say, as calm as a summer's day, "It's synonymous with supererogation," or some godless long reptile of a word like that, and go placidly about and skim away on the next tack, perfectly comfortable, you know, and leave that stranger looking profane and embarrassed, and the initiated slatting the floor with their tails in unison and their faces transfigured with a holy joy.

And it was the same with phrases. She would drag home a whole phrase, if it had a grand sound, and play it six nights and two matinees, and explain it a new way every time—which she had to, for all she cared for was the phrase; she wasn't interested in what it meant, and knew those dogs hadn't wit enough to catch her, anyway. Yes, she was a daisy! She got so she wasn't afraid of anything, she had such confidence in the ignorance of those creatures. She even brought anecdotes that she had heard the family and the dinner-guests laugh and shout over; and as a rule she got the nub of one chestnut hitched onto another chestnut, where, of course, it didn't fit and hadn't any point; and when she delivered the nub she fell over and rolled on the floor and laughed and barked in the most insane way, while I could see that she was wondering to herself why it didn't seem as funny as it did when she first heard it. But no harm was done; the others rolled and barked too, privately ashamed of themselves for not seeing the point, and never suspecting that the fault was not with them and there wasn't any to see.

You can see by these things that she was of a rather vain and frivolous character; still, she had virtues, and enough to make up, I think. She had a kind heart and gentle ways, and never harbored resentments for injuries done her, but put them easily out of her mind and forgot them; and she taught her children her kindly way, and from her we learned also to be brave and prompt in time of danger, and not to run away, but face the peril that threatened friend or stranger, and help him the best we could without stopping to think what the cost might be to us. And she taught us not by words only, but by example, and that is the best way and the surest and the most lasting. Why, the brave things she did, the splendid things! she was just a soldier; and so modest about it— well, you couldn't help admiring her, and you couldn't help imitating her; not even a King Charles spaniel could remain entirely despicable in her society. So, as you see, there was more to her than her education.

II

When I was well grown, at last, I was sold and taken away, and I never saw her again. She was broken-hearted, and so was I, and we cried; but she comforted me as well as she could, and said we were sent into this world for a wise and good purpose, and must do our duties without repining, take our life as we might find it, live it for the best good of others, and never mind about the results; they were not our affair. She said men who did like this would have a noble and beautiful reward by and by in another world, and although we animals would not go there, to do well and right without reward would give to our brief lives a worthiness and dignity which in itself would be a reward. She had gathered these things from time to time when she had gone to the Sunday-school with the children, and had laid them up in her memory more carefully than she had done with those other words and phrases; and she had studied them deeply, for her good and ours. One may see by this that she had a wise and thoughtful head, for all there was so much lightness and vanity in it.

So we said our farewells, and looked our last upon each other through our tears; and the last thing she said—keeping it for the last to make me remember it the better, I think—was, "In memory of me, when there is a time of danger to another do not think of yourself, think of your mother, and do as she would do."

Do you think I could forget that? No.

III

It was such a charming home!—my new one; a fine great house, with pictures, and delicate decorations, and rich furniture, and no gloom anywhere, but all the wilderness of dainty colors lit up with flooding sunshine; and the spacious grounds around it, and the great garden—oh, greensward, and noble trees, and flowers, no end! And I was the same as a member of the family; and they loved me, and petted me, and did not give me a new name, but called me by my old one that was dear to me because my mother had given it me—Aileen Mavourneen. She got it out of a song; and the Grays knew that song, and said it was a beautiful name.

Mrs. Gray was thirty, and so sweet and so lovely, you cannot imagine it; and Sadie was ten, and just like her mother, just a darling slender little copy of her, with auburn tails down her back, and short frocks; and the baby was a year old, and plump and dimpled, and fond of me, and never could get enough of hauling on my tail, and hugging me, and laughing out its innocent happiness; and Mr. Gray was thirty-eight, and tall and slender and handsome, a little bald in front, alert, quick in his movements, business-like, prompt, decided, unsentimental, and with that kind of trim-chiseled face that just seems to glint and sparkle with frosty intellectuality! He was a renowned scientist. I do not know what the word means, but my mother would know how to use it and get effects. She would know how to depress a rat-terrier with it and make a lap-dog look sorry he came. But that is not the best one; the best one was Laboratory. My mother could organize a Trust on that one that would skin the tax-collars off the whole herd. The laboratory was not a book, or a picture, or a place to wash your hands in, as the college president's dog said—no, that is the lavatory; the laboratory is quite different, and is filled with jars, and bottles, and electrics, and wires, and strange machines; and every week other scientists came there and sat in the place, and used the machines, and discussed, and made what they called experiments and discoveries; and often I came, too, and stood around and listened, and tried to learn, for the sake of my mother, and in loving memory of her, although it was a pain to me, as realizing what she was losing out of her life and I gaining nothing at all; for try as I might, I was never able to make anything out of it at all.

Other times I lay on the floor in the mistress's work-room and slept, she gently using me for a foot-stool, knowing it pleased me, for it was a caress; other times I spent an hour in the nursery, and got well tousled and made happy; other times I watched by the crib there, when the baby was asleep and the nurse out for a few minutes on the baby's affairs; other times I romped and raced through the grounds and the garden with Sadie till we were tired out, then slumbered on the grass in the shade of a tree while she read her book; other times I went visiting among the neighbor dogs—for there were some most pleasant ones not far away, and one very handsome and courteous and graceful one, a curly-haired Irish setter by the name of Robin Adair, who was a Presbyterian like me, and belonged to the Scotch minister.

The servants in our house were all kind to me and were fond of me, and so, as you see, mine was a pleasant life. There could not be a happier dog that I was, nor a gratefuller one. I will say this for myself, for it is only the truth: I tried in all ways to do well and right, and honor my mother's memory and her teachings, and earn the happiness that had come to me, as best I could.

By and by came my little puppy, and then my cup was full, my happiness was perfect. It was the dearest little waddling thing, and so smooth and soft and velvety, and had such cunning little awkward paws, and such affectionate eyes, and such a sweet and innocent face; and it made me so proud to see how the children and their mother adored it, and fondled it, and exclaimed over every little wonderful thing it did. It did seem to me that life was just too lovely to—

Then came the winter. One day I was standing a watch in the nursery. That is to say, I was asleep on the bed. The baby was asleep in the crib, which was alongside the bed, on the side next the fireplace. It was the kind of crib that has a lofty tent over it made of gauzy stuff that you can see through. The nurse was out, and we two sleepers were alone. A spark from the wood-fire was shot out, and it lit on the slope of the tent. I suppose a quiet interval followed, then a scream from the baby awoke me, and there was that tent flaming up toward the ceiling! Before I could think, I sprang to the floor in my fright, and in a second was half-way to the door; but in the next half-second my mother's farewell was sounding in my ears, and I was back on the bed again. I reached my head through the flames and dragged the baby out by the waist-band, and tugged it along, and we fell to the floor together in a cloud of smoke; I snatched a new hold, and dragged the screaming little creature along and out at the door and around the bend of the hall, and was still tugging away, all excited and happy and proud, when the master's voice shouted:

"Begone you cursed beast!" and I jumped to save myself; but he was furiously quick, and chased me up, striking furiously at me with his cane, I dodging this way and that, in terror, and at last a strong blow fell upon my left foreleg, which made me shriek and fall, for the moment, helpless; the cane went up for another blow, but never descended, for the nurse's voice rang wildly out, "The nursery's on fire!" and the master rushed away in that direction, and my other bones were saved.

The pain was cruel, but, no matter, I must not lose any time; he might come back at any moment; so I limped on three legs to the other end of the hall, where there was a dark little stairway leading up into a garret where old boxes and such things were kept, as I had heard say, and where people seldom went. I managed to climb up there, then I searched my way through the dark among the piles of things, and hid in the secretest place I could find. It was foolish to be afraid there, yet still I was; so afraid that I held in and hardly even whimpered, though it would have been such a comfort to whimper, because that eases the pain, you know. But I could lick my leg, and that did some good.

For half an hour there was a commotion downstairs, and shoutings, and rushing footsteps, and then there was quiet again. Quiet for some minutes, and that was grateful to my spirit, for then my fears began to go down; and fears are worse than pains—oh, much worse. Then came a sound that froze me. They were calling me—calling me by name—hunting for me!

It was muffled by distance, but that could not take the terror out of it, and it was the most dreadful sound to me that I had ever heard. It went all about, everywhere, down there: along the halls, through all the rooms, in both stories, and in the basement and the cellar; then outside, and farther and farther away—then back, and all about the house again, and I thought it would never, never stop. But at last it did, hours and hours after the vague twilight of the garret had long ago been blotted out by black darkness.

Then in that blessed stillness my terrors fell little by little away, and I was at peace and slept. It was a good rest I had, but I woke before the twilight had come again. I was feeling fairly comfortable, and I could think out a plan now. I made a very good one; which was, to creep down, all the way down the back stairs, and hide behind the cellar door, and slip out and escape when the iceman came at dawn, while he was inside filling the refrigerator; then I would hide all day, and start on my journey when night came; my journey to—well, anywhere where they would not know me and betray me to the master. I was feeling almost cheerful now; then suddenly I thought: Why, what would life be without my puppy!

That was despair. There was no plan for me; I saw that; I must stay where I was; stay, and wait, and take what might come—it was not my affair; that was what life is—my mother had said it. Then—well, then the calling began again! All my sorrows came back. I said to myself, the master will never forgive. I did not know what I had done to make him so bitter and so unforgiving, yet I judged it was something a dog could not understand, but which was clear to a man and dreadful.

They called and called—days and nights, it seemed to me. So long that the hunger and thirst near drove me mad, and I recognized that I was getting very weak. When you are this way you sleep a great deal, and I did. Once I woke in an awful fright—it seemed to me that the calling was right there in the garret! And so it was: it was Sadie's voice, and she was crying; my name was falling from her lips all broken, poor thing, and I could not believe my ears for the joy of it when I heard her say:

"Come back to us—oh, come back to us, and forgive—it is all so sad without our—"

I broke in with SUCH a grateful little yelp, and the next moment Sadie was plunging and stumbling through the darkness and the lumber and shouting for the family to hear, "She's found, she's found!"

The days that followed—well, they were wonderful. The mother and Sadie and the servants—why, they just seemed to worship me. They couldn't seem to make me a bed that was fine enough; and as for food, they couldn't be satisfied with anything but game and delicacies that were out of season; and every day the friends and neighbors flocked in to hear about my heroism—that was the name they called it by, and it means agriculture. I remember my mother pulling it on a kennel once, and explaining it in that way, but didn't say what agriculture was, except that it was synonymous with intramural incandescence; and a dozen times a day Mrs. Gray and Sadie would tell the tale to new-comers, and say I risked my life to save the baby's, and both of us had burns to prove it, and then the company would pass me around and pet me and exclaim about me, and you could see the pride in the eyes of Sadie and her mother; and when the people wanted to know what made me limp, they looked ashamed and changed the subject, and sometimes when people hunted them this way and that way with questions about it, it looked to me as if they were going to cry.

And this was not all the glory; no, the master's friends came, a whole twenty of the most distinguished people, and had me in the laboratory, and discussed me as if I was a kind of discovery; and some of them said it was wonderful in a dumb beast, the finest exhibition of instinct they could call to mind; but the master said, with vehemence, "It's far above instinct; it's REASON, and many a man, privileged to be saved and go with you and me to a better world by right of its possession, has less of it that this poor silly quadruped that's foreordained to perish"; and then he laughed, and said: "Why, look at me—I'm a sarcasm! bless you, with all my grand intelligence, the only thing I inferred was that the dog had gone mad and was destroying the child, whereas but for the beast's intelligence— it's REASON, I tell you!—the child would have perished!"

They disputed and disputed, and I was the very center of subject of it all, and I wished my mother could know that this grand honor had come to me; it would have made her proud.

Then they discussed optics, as they called it, and whether a certain injury to the brain would produce blindness or not, but they could not agree about it, and said they must test it by experiment by and by; and next they discussed plants, and that interested me, because in the summer Sadie and I had planted seeds—I helped her dig the holes, you know—and after days and days a little shrub or a flower came up there, and it was a wonder how that could happen; but it did, and I wished I could talk—I would have told those people about it and shown then how much I knew, and been all alive with the subject; but I didn't care for the optics; it was dull, and when they came back to it again it bored me, and I went to sleep.

Pretty soon it was spring, and sunny and pleasant and lovely, and the sweet mother and the children patted me and the puppy good-by, and went away on a journey and a visit to their kin, and the master wasn't any company for us, but we played together and had good times, and the servants were kind and friendly, so we got along quite happily and counted the days and waited for the family.

And one day those men came again, and said, now for the test, and they took the puppy to the laboratory, and I limped three-leggedly along, too, feeling proud, for any attention shown to the puppy was a pleasure to me, of course. They discussed and experimented, and then suddenly the puppy shrieked, and they set him on the floor, and he went staggering around, with his head all bloody, and the master clapped his hands and shouted:

"There, I've won—confess it! He's as blind as a bat!"

And they all said:

"It's so—you've proved your theory, and suffering humanity owes you a great debt from henceforth," and they crowded around him, and wrung his hand cordially and thankfully, and praised him.

But I hardly saw or heard these things, for I ran at once to my little darling, and snuggled close to it where it lay, and licked the blood, and it put its head against mine, whimpering softly, and I knew in my heart it was a comfort to it in its pain and trouble to feel its mother's touch, though it could not see me. Then it dropped down, presently, and its little velvet nose rested upon the floor, and it was still, and did not move any more.

Soon the master stopped discussing a moment, and rang in the footman, and said, "Bury it in the far corner of the garden," and then went on with the discussion, and I trotted after the footman, very happy and grateful, for I knew the puppy was out of its pain now, because it was asleep. We went far down the garden to the farthest end, where the children and the nurse and the puppy and I used to play in the summer in the shade of a great elm, and there the footman dug a hole, and I saw he was going to plant the puppy, and I was glad, because it would grow and come up a fine handsome dog, like Robin Adair, and be a beautiful surprise for the family when they came home; so I tried to help him dig, but my lame leg was no good, being stiff, you know, and you have to have two, or it is no use. When the footman had finished and covered little Robin up, he patted my head, and there were tears in his eyes, and he said: "Poor little doggie, you saved HIS child!"

I have watched two whole weeks, and he doesn't come up! This last week a fright has been stealing upon me. I think there is something terrible about this. I do not know what it is, but the fear makes me sick, and I cannot eat, though the servants bring me the best of food; and they pet me so, and even come in the night, and cry, and say, "Poor doggie—do give it up and come home; don't break our hearts!" and all this terrifies me the more, and makes me sure something has happened. And I am so weak; since yesterday

I cannot stand on my feet anymore. And within this hour the servants, looking toward the sun where it was sinking out of sight and the night chill coming on, said things I could not understand, but they carried something cold to my heart.

"Those poor creatures! They do not suspect. They will come home in the morning, and eagerly ask for the little doggie that did the brave deed, and who of us will be strong enough to say the truth to them: 'The humble little friend is gone where go the beasts that perish.'"

THE END.

Appendix C

Elizabeth Stuart Phelps's Address to the Massachusetts Legislature
(1902)

—ᘏᗩᘏ—

Elizabeth Stuart Phelps Ward delivered the following speech at a hearing before the Massachusetts Legislature's Committee of Probate and Chancery in favor of the bill "For the Further Prevention of Cruelty to Animals," March 14, 1902. The proposed bill would have restricted vivisection to registered university laboratories, and it would require vivisectors to anaesthetize animals during experiments and immediately euthanize them afterward. Also, it would allow authorized agents of animal welfare societies to enter laboratories without notice. The London-based anti-vivisection magazine *The Zoophilist and Animals' Defender* reported on the hearing, noting that the bill was "under the management of well known authoress and tireless opponent of cruelty, Mrs. Elizabeth Stuart Phelps Ward." Phelps's speech was later reprinted as a pamphlet by the American Anti-Vivisection Society of Philadelphia.

Mr. Chairman, and Gentlemen of the Committee. Two prominent citizens of this State met one day, and one said to the other confidentially,—

"I wish you would tell me—don't say I asked—what is this vivisection?" An equal candor would probably reveal an equal ignorance so frequently that astonishment would stumble over the circumstance. I doubt if there is another subject now urging the conscience of the civilized world upon which intelligent people as a class are so uninstructed or so half-informed as that which these petitioners bring to the attention of the Massachusetts Legislature today.

I crave your patience at the start, for no reply to this terrible question can be put into agreeable words. If you can bear to hear what I can bear to say—if you and I can bear to hear or to say what helpless, sentient life can suffer—permit me to be a voice for the dumb, a nerve for the tormented.

It has been poignantly said—and so well said that I cannot venture to improve upon it by any paraphrase—that if a dog were vivisected for one hour at noon some day in Trafalgar Square, London, in sight of the passing crowds, vivisection would be abolished in England within twenty-four hours. Without hesitation, we may assume that if a dog were vivisected in front of the State House at this hour, and this committee went out to see the process, vivisection would be restricted without any unnecessary delay.

There are no silken phrases for this jagged thing. The subject cannot be embroidered. It is not a matter of rhetoric, or art, or politics; it is not an easy bill to present; it is not a selfish bill; it is not a pleasant bill. I know that I shall not entertain you.

Here is a specimen of vivisection which I select at random to open the list.

A little fox terrier, bright of eye, warm of heart, sensitive of nerve, is bought, strayed, or stolen, and his fate brings him into a physiological laboratory. Here he is bound, gagged, and given over to hands calling themselves human. His intestines are cut open, and boiling water is poured upon them. This experiment was performed by an American surgeon, and described by him in a published essay, for which he received a prize.

Or choose this: An animal is selected for experiments upon the brain; "a part of his skull is sawed away, the surface is extended by pincers, and electric shocks are given through copper wires . . .

concentrated chromic acid is squirted into the brain through a small hole in the skull; the animal is kept alive for subsequent examinations." This experiment is on record, is quoted exactly, and the Royal Commission of England sifted the testimony.

Again: A series of experiments are invented for the avowed purpose of studying the nature of pain (in such experiments, remember, anaesthetics are impossible). To an ingenious machine is given claws. These grip and tear an animal bound within them. The acknowledged object of this machine is to produce the most intense agony that can possibly be contrived. This diabolism is proudly put on record. It happened in Florence. It was inflicted by one of the most notorious vivisectors of the world, I will not tempt my lips with his name—to tell the truth, I dare not, lest I find myself unable to utter it without language which, as a woman and a Christian, I should prefer to avoid. Lead us not into evil. And let us turn to the next.

A professor of physiology, interested in what he would have called psychological experiments, teased and plagued a fine dog until the poor creature hated and feared him. Then he put out its eyes. Still the blind dog fell into a fury at the sound of its tormentor's voice. The vivisector forthwith destroyed the hearing of the dog. The wretched animal now ceased, we are told, "to display animosity" to his tormentor. This beautiful specimen of scientific research occurred in Paris. This, also, was inflicted by a lost soul whose name is quite familiar to any vivisector, and you, gentlemen, can read the records for yourselves. They are open to any student of this heart-vivisecting subject.

A horse is driven into the veterinary department of an American institution. A pupil is told to drive a seton into the shoulders of the horse. Another pupil is asked to perform tracheotomy—to make an opening into the windpipe—and a third drives a seton into the hind flank. By this time the horse has been 'hobbled,'—i.e. tied so that he cannot move—and the next student is ordered to dissect the nerves of the foot. No anaesthetics of any kind are given to the horse, and when the demonstration is over, the eye-witness who published the account of these torments, asks what will be done with the animal. He is told, "We leave it here, and if it is alive in the morning we go on with other experiments."

This specimen of vivisection, unlike others which I shall select, is not on record in a scientific publication, but I have taken pains to inquire into it so far as any such account can be investigated after a lapse of some years. While I cannot offer you documentary evidence of it, I believe it to be true. It occurred in the State of Pennsylvania. The operator in this case was a graduate of Alfort, which has been called the "hell of horses." Notice just here. Foreign vivisectors do not always stay at home; Massachusetts is as liable as Pennsylvania to harbor them.

A being in New Jersey bearing the name of man, and holding the title of one of the most sacred and noble of human professions, bound one hundred and forty-one dogs, raised them to a height of twenty-four feet, and dropped them on iron ridges. Some of the dogs lived a few hours, some lived for days; their agonies being noted by their torturer—and by his God.

One is tempted to pause and comment on this physiological amusement, but refraining, hastens on—for, be assured, gentlemen, that I will not extend this sample list beyond the absolute necessities of the occasion. I could not. Every shrinking ear, every quivering nerve, every lacerated sensibility in this room lags behind my own in the performance of this dolorous duty in whose fulfilment speaker and hearer must share the responsibility and the distress.

Permit me a moment at this point. Do you suggest that I have called your attention to cruelties outside the State? Assuredly. I am not a witness, but a pleader, and a student of the subject which brings me here, and, unhappily, cruelty is not provincial.

But I do not forget that this is a Massachusetts bill, and your Massachusetts petitioner craves your close attention as she draws nearer home.

Do you want Massachusetts vivisections? We can offer them. Massachusetts laboratory sufferings? We can satisfy you. Gentlemen, we could give you enough of them, recorded and published,—

many of them under the acknowledged names of the operators,—to keep this committee here in session for a month. I select only so many as will call upon your sympathy and your candor for a few minutes. References and authorities will be given to this committee if desired.

Begin with this: "Ludwig's gimlet electrodes were screwed into the atlas and occipital bone of a rabbit; for direct irritation" . . . "curare" was administered—not ether, not chloroform, you understand, but that terrible substitute which paralyzes the motor nerves, yet leaves the sensory nerves free to agonize. The greatest vivisector of the modern world has testified that curare permits in its victims "atrocious sufferings." Tennyson calls it "the hellish oorali."

In the case of this curarized rabbit, we are told that the "sciatic nerve was prepared;" the vaso-motor centres were directly irritated for "11 seconds"; the entire experiment lasted for "25 minutes." The operator sums up his experiment by adding that "the sensory nerves and the conductors of their impressions up the cord are not paralyzed." This means, in the vernacular, that the rabbit suffered—how much, we may not be able to conceive; how little, I insist it is for the rabbit, not for the vivisector, to testify. This vivisector confesses also to this method of treating a rabbit. "Into the left jugular had been bound a canula, through which the poison was injected toward the heart. As the injection of the poison caused struggling . . . I used curare to paralyze the motor nerves."

These vivisections were not performed in Europe, or in California, or in Michigan. They were Massachusetts vivisections, and were inflicted in the laboratory of one of the most important medical schools of the State. They stand in the published records of the laboratory.

In a famous Massachusetts laboratory, some years ago, might have been witnessed an experiment which I suggest that you follow in imagination—if you can. The subject is a dog, a small dog presumably, since his next successor in suffering is specified as large; perhaps a pet strayed from some anxious home, but that I cannot assert; the vivisectors are modest, and exhibit a constitutional reserve upon this point. The dog's epiglottis is cut out; "he coughs at almost every attempt to eat or drink"; his sufferings are studied "for six days."

This you may call a mild experiment, but it educates you for the next. Observe that calmly—if you can.

You find now a large dog; his epiglottis is cut out; he "chokes in swallowing liquids and solids at every trial"; his sufferings last "for 21 days." Twenty-one days! Three weeks! This is a long time to live, choking and strangling with the epiglottis cut out; a long time, gentlemen, for you—and for the dog. Lest you complain that we prolong these hearings beyond your leisure, I hasten to conduct you to the next selected and recorded experiment performed by a third vivisector. This subject is a small dog. He "is curarized"—that does not mean anaesthetized, remember; he is sentient, not unconscious; he is fully capable of suffering, but is rendered incapable of saying so; "artificial respiration" is sustained—that means that he is forcibly kept alive by scientific ingenuity when nature would otherwise relieve his miseries by death. The "pharynx" of this dog "is plugged; a cord is tied around the head and jaws in front of the ears to compress the cotton into the passages leading upward." His "trachea is divided: a tubulated cork is secured in the upper end." The experimenter adds that "it may be questioned how far an experiment of this kind can be applied to the living human larynx, or with what logical justice we can draw conclusions from it."

These vivisections were not performed on the continent, or in London, or in Maryland. They were Massachusetts vivisections, and were performed by Massachusetts vivisectors.

Our next Massachusetts vivisector occupies himself with cats, and certain of his experiments are thus described by himself:—

"The animals were kept under the influence of a dose of curare, just strong enough to prevent, muscular contractions." This means, again, remember, a conscious animal, a suffering animal, made rigid by a dose "just strong enough" to prevent the hapless and helpless being from writhing, from moaning, from shrieking or from becoming what is called, in vivisector's parlance, "an inconvenience to the operator." Again, "artificial respiration" was maintained. "The sciatic nerve was constantly subjected to stimulation sufficiently intense to produce in unpoisoned animals a tetanic contraction of the muscles. In this way it was found that stimulation of a nerve lasting from one and one-half to four hours (the muscles being prevented from contracting by curare) did not"—and so forth, and so on—I submit that it does not matter what this experiment did, or did not. It was not a merciful experiment, and it should have been a forbidden experiment. It was not performed in Germany, or in France, or in Ohio. It was performed in Massachusetts. And the vivisector who inflicted it sits among the remonstrants to this bill.

To our next Massachusetts vivisector I now ask you to give candid attention, and with his acknowledged record of his own deeds I will close this specimen list of some of the agonies known and admitted to have been inflicted and borne in the laboratories of this Commonwealth.

In December, 1893, this vivisector took a "large, lightly chloralized rabbit"—that does not mean a rabbit unconscious of pain, gentlemen—and cut to the creature's brain, laying bare the fourth ventricle. The operator cheerfully tells us that he "burned away the floor of the left side of the median line with small, hot glass beads." He adds that "respiration continued on both sides in spite of repeated cauterizations."

On Feb. 27, 1894, this representative of the most merciful of human callings selects for sacrifice a dog. He records that he "narcotized the dog "with morphia"—this does not mean a dog unconscious of suffering. Competent, veterinarians aver that morphia does not affect dogs with any degree of reliability. It is the most uncertain narcotic which can be administered to a dog. Some dogs will yield to a light dose. Some will not succumb to any dose.

A foreign vivisector once pinched his own finger with wooden splints for two minutes. He complained that he "panted with the pain" caused him by this immeasurable sacrifice to science. He induced two young men to undergo the same, and reported that they "bore it heroically." We suggest that our Massachusetts vivisector volunteer to experience in his own person the first three or four incisions of the experiment to which he subjected one of the most highly organized, most sensitive, most trustful of created beings. At all events, he took the dog. According to his own testimony he gave it "morphine"—that does not mean that he anaesthetized it. "The cervical cord"—that is, the upper part of the spine—"was exposed in its entire length;" he "severed the cord at the sixth cervical vertebra," and "cut the roots of the cervical nerves." Every one acquainted with physiology knows that this is a piteously painful operation.

On Nov. 20, 1894, this operator turned his attention to rabbits. He chose one of these patient animals "lightly narcotized with ether"—that does not mean an anaesthetized rabbit, you understand, not an unconscious rabbit; it means a rabbit a little dulled to suffering at the beginning of its miseries. This operator cut to "the left phrenic nerve" of the rabbit, "seized it near the first rib, and tore it out of the chest."

"I have made such experiments," he admits, "on 13 rabbits and one dog, and the result has always been the same."

"Other experiments could be added, but they seem unnecessary," says this professor. This is the only instance that I can recall in the published observations of this operator in which I find myself able to agree with him.

These vivisections were not performed in Alfort, or in the Sorbonne, nor even in Johns Hopkins, or some State university of the vivisecting West. They were performed in Massachusetts. The vivisector who inflicted them is a professor in a Massachusetts medical school—and sits among the remonstrants to this bill.

But yet a moment. I have not quite done with this vivisector. Before taking final leave of him the committee will be interested, I am sure, in a brief allusion to some of his more famous vivisections. Carefully recorded by himself you can find the following tragic story. He says: "Dogs were used in my experiments. The second, third, fourth, and fifth dogs of the series of 32 recorded here were given a small quantity of morphia. Voluntary movements were prevented by curare. The heart was reached . . . the edges of the pericardium were stitched to the edges of the thoracic opening. The length of the operation was noted . . . as a factor of importance. In exp. 10 the pericardium was opened 18 minutes after the first tracheotomy incision." In exp. 9, which is described in technical language of no interest excepting to an experimenter, the operator adds that "the entire experiment occupied one hundred minutes." One hundred minutes carving about the heart of a dog curarized and morphiated—that does not mean anaesthetized—one hundred minutes. This has been called by an authority on the subject "a frightful experiment."

These vivisections, gentlemen, need no pitying amplification from your petitioner. Plus a little imagination and natural human feeling, they speak for themselves. They are described by the operator, over his own name, in the leading paper in a number of the "Journal of Physiology," not always easy, perhaps, of access. A copy is in my possession, and will be offered to the committee if desired.

These vivisections were performed by a Massachusetts experimenter in 1892 in the Physiological Institute of the University of Berlin. But there is nothing in the laws of Massachusetts as they stand today to prevent this Massachusetts vivisector from repeating these experiments in this Commonwealth if he should feel inclined.

The next experiment—but I spare you. Let us turn the leaf upon these sad entries in the scientific history of our Commonwealth. One could arraign the vivisectors of this or any State; of this or any country, agony by agony, man by man, till your patience should be spent. But to what end should I imprint upon your recoiling sensibilities the too prolonged portrayal of this world of woe?

By the great law of reaction—what Herbert Spencer has called the law of rhythm—that rules the human mind, you would first sicken at, and then deaden under the revelations with which any student of this subject could dismay you. There is something very singular about the effect of this thing.

When my attention was first called to the subject of vivisection, six years ago, by one braver and stronger than I, I said,

"No. Take them away. I cannot read those horrors. I cannot look at those illustrations."

Behind the subtle excuses of overwork, and illness, and care, I sheltered a crouching conscience, till God dragged it out into the open, and bade it stand. Now, after long study of the shocking facts with which the annals of animal experimentation are packed, I find myself able to come here and share them, gentlemen, with you. It is easy to understand how vivisectors become dulled and accustomed to the sufferings that they inflict.

These sufferings, understand, are not the creation of an anti-vivisectionist imagination; they are scientific facts, they are facts on record, they are facts published by vivisectors in books and in journals open to you and to us.

Out of their own mouths, and not out of our throbbing hearts do we condemn them.

It is impossible to approach our grim topic without clearly understanding this: Vivisection has conjugated the infinitive verb of suffering in every form—to terrify, to deafen, to blind, to suffocate, to shoot, to stab, to poison, to deform, to bruise, to burn, to freeze, to boil, to bake, to break, to scar, to skin, to crush; thus has the vivisecting mind developed.

A literary man said the other day: "I am supposed to be a person not destitute of imagination, and not wholly devoid of originality, but I swear to you that, if I had been put to it, I could not have conceived of such tortures—I never could have devised then, if I had wanted to."

Do you ask for fresh specimens of vivisection—something not down in the physiological journals, something a little new, for a change?

Here is an incident which came straight to me from an irreproachable source this summer. A distinguished physician, professor on the staff of an important medical school, on the way to her lecture room one day, noticed in the college building a fine mastiff.

She recognized the dog as the property and pet of one of her patients. He was without a collar, and the unmatched pathos of the lost dog was in his eyes. At this moment she heard a vivisector say "Oh, this is *dog* day, isn't it?'" and the meaning of the situation suddenly flooded her consciousness. Watching her opportunity, she quietly said,

"Don; don't you know me, Don?" and whistled under breath to the dog. Recognizing the family doctor, Don followed her readily. She opened the door and bade him go home, which you will be glad to know that he did.

In the course of half an hour there was hue and a cry in the college for that vanished "material." But the professor was in her own lecture room by then, and "dog day" was skipped in that laboratory for that occasion.

Perhaps I might say that this incident occurred in this country, though not in this Commonwealth. To return to our own State:—

To my own knowledge one Massachusetts contractor, within fifteen miles of Boston, received last year orders for ten thousand frogs—"unbruised," live frogs—for laboratory purposes. He found it, happily, impossible to fill the order.

In my possession is a letter from a reliable man, formerly a student in a Massachusetts medical school.

"Few demonstrations," says the writer, "ever show all the points they are expected to show; and I know of no new discoveries, and of few previous discoveries, being entirely proved by the students' efforts."

Gentlemen, we know a great deal about this matter which we do not present in evidence. Why? Ask the tacticians of the scientific boycott. Ask the undergraduate who has yet to obtain his diploma. Ask the young physician, with the displeasure of his older and eminent colleagues frowning across his professional career. Ask the influential petitioner approached at the threshold of the State House. Ask the important petitioner subjected to social pressure because he does not desert his colors. There is an invisible line around this subject as powerful as the instinct of self-protection.

There is a kind of sorcery against which these petitioners do not waste their force. Black magic or white deters a score of voices that would otherwise utter themselves to your persuasion.

But, indeed, careful study of this subject has convinced some of us that such additional evidence, however dramatic it might be, is not necessary to the presentation of this cause. Massachusetts vivisectors have condemned themselves. Their own published records are enough. You do not need a line of trembling medical students or a group of busy physicians dragged here to corroborate what Massachusetts operators have openly said for and of themselves. By and by, when their time comes, these gentlemen are going to tell you that the poor creatures on whom they have experimented did not suffer. How do they know? I submit that the facts are all against them.

"To understand the psychology of a sheep, one must have been a sheep," says George Eliot.

To aver that a curarized, or morphiated, or chloralized rabbit, cat, or dog, does not suffer when it is dissected alive, a man must be or must have been a rabbit, a cat, or a dog; he must give his own nerves to the pincers, his spinal cord to the knife, his heart to the scalpel, his ventricles to be burned by hot glass beads. Now, it is understood among physiologists that the published account of an experiment is expected to contain some allusion to such important details as the presence or absence of an anaesthetic. I submit that no vivisector's after-thought should be permitted by this committee to revise the vivisector's published account of the deeds which he records without mention of surgical anaesthesia. I submit that when he records that he has vivisected with morphia, with curare, with light chloralization, he should be held to his words. I protest that he should not be permitted to recall now the etherization he omitted to note then; he should not find it possible to escape now the conclusion of the syllogism he framed then, never expecting it to come up in this committee room against him, and prudently determining—you may be sure—that no such accident shall befall his scientific career again. I protest that what he admitted that he did in 1893 or in 1894, he should not ask to modify or to ameliorate in 1901 or 1902. On a matter so small to the vivisecting mind as the sufferings of an animal, it is wiser to trust to the records than to trust to the memory.

"There were so many experiments," said a vivisector, wearily, last winter, "I have forgotten!"

In my hearing, a prominent Massachusetts physiologist testified in this room that, if one included the smaller species, the number of animals experimented upon in his laboratory ran up into the thousands each year.

An expert on this subject has published the result of his experiences in visiting laboratories both of this and of other countries:—

"The number of animals used for vivisection must be given," he says, "as hundreds of thousands, or millions, every year. Many years ago one vivisector, Pasteur, confessed that the number of animals he had vivisected was beyond the possibility of computation; to another 70,000, 14,000 being dogs, were ascribed. In a single room, one of many containing animals used or for use in vivisection in a single institution in Paris, I *counted* on each of several occasions about 1000 animals; all these had been vivisected, and many or all were destined for further vivisection.

"For a number of years I have personally witnessed a vast amount of vivisection, having seen almost every kind of animal under the knife, including horses, dogs, rabbits, guinea pigs. Never in my life have I seen any animal under the influence of any anaesthetic so as to prevent suffering; and never, with one single exception, have I seen any animal's sufferings in vivisection at all diminished by means of an anaesthetic. . . . On . . . one occasion I did see a few whiffs of chloroform administered to a dog—more, however, to stop his struggles, which were so violent as to threaten to disarrange the apparatus, than to relieve his pain."

Gentlemen, *this* is vivisection. Such as I have studiously and conscientiously selected for your attention are not unfair illustrations of the custom. I have given you nothing legendary. I have avoided the most shocking instances, the most heartrending episodes in the piteous story. Page upon page in the black books of this unholy art I have turned, unquoted. Many I have been unable to read. The worst I have spared you, and what this means, only a student of this subject can know.

Now, if these are the liabilities of the practice of vivisection, what are the assets? Locked laboratories do not tell. You will never know what goes on in a vivisectorium, when visitors are not expected, until you give yourselves the right to know. A regulating law will not, I am sorry to say, abolish vivisection. It is no miracle whereby the mountains of mercy shall fall and choke the sea of wasted suffering on whose shores Christian civilization stands aghast. A regulating law checks irresponsibility, and reduces anguish, and protects the humane vivisector—granting, for the argument, that such there are. That is the least we can ask. Gentlemen, it is the least you can give.

Remember that vivisection is an arraigned practice. It cannot shelter itself behind the silver shield of good character. Its reputation is gone. It cannot look the world in the eye. The vivisector has been well called the anarchist of science. A practice that may pour boiling lead into the ears of a live animal needs, I submit, the regulation of the law if anything ever needs it. A practice that may tie a little dog down so that it cannot move, and smash its legs with a glass bottle, for no better reason than to show the effects of shock; a practice that may tie the heads of dogs in rubber bags to see how long they can live without air; a practice that may put a dove in a machine, called the *tormentatore* or the "tormentor," and pierce the dove's feet and wings "with nails," torture it for two hours, take it out for a rest, and put it back for another hour and fifty minutes—I urge that a practice of which it is known that such are the liabilities, calls for the regulation of the law if anything calls for it.

We have recently been told by an ear-witness that at a physiological lecture in one of the most highly civilized countries of the world, the professor described some experiments of the terrible Claude Bernard's inflicted on a number of goats, whose flesh was carved by knives heated to a white heat. The lecturer, wishing to be facetious, remarked the effect this incident would have on the anti-vivisectionists. His audience responded to this scientific jest with laughter.

We urge that a practice which is liable to train medical students to scenes like this needs the grip of the law on its arm.

It is on record that a little dog, undergoing a shocking vivisection of the vertebral nerves, twice escaped the knife, and struggling up, put his paws about the neck of his tormentor, and kissed the brute, and prayed for mercy, and prayed in vain. We submit that a practice which is liable to an enormity like that needs the hands of the law at its throat.

Let me be as explicit at this point as language can be made. I do not assert of any Massachusetts laboratory or of any Massachusetts vivisector anything that is not already on evidence from sources outside of this plea or this pleader.

I do not say that Clark University keeps a *tormentatore* for doves, or that Boston University or Tufts throws dogs twenty-five feet to see their bones break. I do not say that Harvard Medical School carves goats with red-hot knives. Nor do I say that this vivisector or that vivisector of our own State has to put to the sacrifice any trustful, helpless animal by any methods but those which have been publicly acknowledged. One may have no doubt that he has, but one does not assert it. I say that the fact that such abuses as we have noted are the liabilities of vivisection anywhere is a reason why the practice should be regulated by law in this Commonwealth. And I submit that to keep an animal alive for twenty-one days with his epiglottis cut out, is enough, if we had no more, for a specimen of Massachusetts vivisection. If these petitioners had not another instance to offer you of what may happen in Massachusetts, we urge that this instance alone, no matter where it occurred, no matter when, no matter why, no matter who did it, no matter what he proffers as the excuse for doing it, is enough to call for the right of inspection, and a regulating law. The more famous the laboratory where this was done, the worse for the laboratory. The more important the man who did it, or the professor who sanctioned it, the worse for the man, the worse for the professor. The laboratory in which such a thing could happen—whether years ago or days makes little difference—this laboratory needs a restraining law. If I am not mistaken, this laboratory is under the same control now that it was then. We suggest, in closing, that a regulating law should not be denied us on the ground that the men who represent vivisection in Massachusetts are themselves of otherwise blameless character. Nobody knows that better than these petitioners, nobody feels it more. When the names of these Massachusetts vivisectors have begged at my lips in the course of this plea for mercy to dumb life, I have not uttered them. There are women who love these men, and children who trust them, and friends who believe in them, and others than this petitioner to identify them. Nor are these physiologists themselves unwilling to admit the deeds they have done in the name of that misled and blinded science which they worship in error, and in whose defence they force the sense of humanity conscript. There came to my knowledge recently this incident:

An American physiologist educated his son in his own faith and practice, and the two vivisectors used to come home and discuss laboratory torments in the presence of the ladies of the family. The wife had long recoiled and abhorred, but being a wife, she endured. Wives do. Wives and mothers must, perhaps, but daughters need not. The daughter of this vivisector bore her fate to her last nerve. One day she quietly announced that she had borne all she could, or should; she left her father's home and sought shelter under some kinder roof.

Let us hasten to say that this is possibly an exceptional case. Your true vivisector, if he be of gentle birth and of humane surroundings—and the miracle of it is, that such there are—would try to atone to society for the unpopularity of his avocation. He would be the exemplary husband, the kind father, the loyal friend, the excellent neighbor, the good citizen. He props up every other side of his character, that it may support the weak masonry of the vivisecting side. Irreproachable of conduct, he cries, why should I be called defective in humanity? Sincere in aim—we do not deny that he may be this; otherwise God have mercy on him!—sincere in aim, he pleads, why are my admirable motives misunderstood? He plays upon the falsest string in the harp of the human heart—selfish fear. I would protect your life, he urges; I would save your child, I would sacrifice "thousands of animals a year" to the bare possibility that I may some time discover something that would in some way enable some surgeon to perform some beautiful operation on you, which might preserve your health. Every calling has its delusions: and the delusion of vivisection is, or may be, that it is humane.

This leads us to say: The worse effects of vivisection are not upon the animal; they are upon the man. Unchecked vivisection tortures and slays the animal; it deadens the man. Proofs of this assertion are the truisms of the history of vivisection. The very nature of his occupation, we may say, corrodes the humanity of the vivisector. He may believe that he is doing science service; he may be learned, influential, and a devotee to the terrible creed that he has adopted, but an expert in humanity he can never be. It is too late for this. He has absorbed, like the rest of us, the atmosphere of an avocation.

A well-known physiologist, who frankly catalogued his experiments as those which gave "little pain," "much pain," "cruel pain," and "atrocious pain," has given us this startling testimony:—

"Blood inebriates, like wine and love." . . . "The ancient cruelty is found still spontaneous and irresistible in our children." . . . "I have observed with much attention physiologists, surgeons, soldiers in war, and other official slaughterers, and I have often observed unconscious contractions of the muscles which expressed the pleasure of killing or of tormenting."

Now and then a vivisector, like other erring souls, repents and reforms—and confesses. The latest of these, an able surgeon, has recently told us:—

"Constant witnessing of pain causes a blunting of the feelings. This, by some vivisectors, has been denied. In one case, I am absolutely certain that it is true. That case is myself. The first occasions on which I saw severe pain, which other persons might not inaccurately call torture, inflicted, I was sickened. Later I was less affected. Still later I could look on almost unmoved. I am further convinced that the experimenter estimates the pain his operation inflicts by the effect it has on himself. He is not affected by the spectacle. Therefore, the animal does not feel much."

Psychologists will tell you that it is a universal law of nature that "every effect endures as long as it is not modified or opposed by any other effect." Sensibility to the sight of suffering endures until it is modified or opposed by that insensibility which frequent repetition of the sight may create. This is the law. The physiologist is subject to it like any other man.

Gentlemen, we bring you a bill to regulate the liabilities of vivisection; a bill which asks so little, and permits so much, that it has been hard for some of us to stand here and plead with you to enact it; a bill which leaves open the whole debatable and repulsive ground of serum therapy; a bill which allows every kind of inoculation, useful or useless, good, bad, or indifferent; a bill which permits every kind of vivisection excepting cruel vivisection. How can any humane and candid vivisector oppose this bill? I do not hesitate to say that the vivisector who opposes it is not a qualified witness in the contention. Any intelligent and warm-hearted layman has a fitter place before this committee in behalf of this bill than has any vivisector in objection to it. This bill calls for experts in humanity, not experts in the dissection of living animals. We ask no stronger argument in favor of our bill than the fact that vivisectors and the friends of vivisectors are here to remonstrate against it.

Permit me a word yet. In the fulfilment of the difficult duty that has brought me here to say these difficult things, I cannot allow myself to be misunderstood on one point.

There is no citizen of this Commonwealth who has more regard than this petitioner for the noble aims and often nobler achievements of the medical profession. I do not believe that for sheer unselfishness and ideal devotion to duty it can be surpassed by any

profession for which Massachusetts educates a merciful, a consecrated man or woman.

In emergencies when no friend can help, in mental and moral
peril which no priest or pastor can reach, in the undertow of physical suffering which sweeps you to the depths, your doctor stands;
blurred before your brightening or your fading eyes, between your
blessing and your tears.

A vivisector who admitted that he "once had no pity for the
sufferings he inflicted on dozens of animals," came to face his own
death fiat. Thus he bewailed his past,—

"Those incidents which weigh especially heavily upon me are
when I tortured animals unnecessarily, out of ignorance, inexperi-
ence, folly, or God only knows why."

A vivisector, dying, cried,—

"Will God ever forgive me for having caused his creatures to
suffer so horribly?"

Another, dying with cancer of the tongue, in agony exclaimed,—

"This is my punishment for the torture I allowed the animals
to suffer!"

Of another vivisector it is related that on his deathbed "he referred repeatedly to the fact that the agony which he endured was
through the same nerves upon which he had made so many experiments on animals. He could not divert his mind of the feeling that
there was a special providence in the way he was afflicted. Even
his medical brethren felt that it was significant that this physiologist was doomed to die by a disease which repeated upon his own
body—not in one, but many ways—the agonies he himself had
inflicted on dumb and defenceless animals."

Between such lurid scenes as these, and the sickrooms where
our highest and best physicians minister, beloved and honored always as much for their gentleness as for their skill—what a step! It
is the longest stride that modern science ever takes.

We say our highest and best, but these are large words. They
may or may not mean the distinguished, the eminent, the affluent,
the influential members of the profession. They may or may not

mean what are called men at the top—the specialists, the metropolitans, the professors, the men whose names are most easily before the public.

In the course of a life not unacquainted with the profession I have not seen more careful healing, finer tenderness, truer honor than among the quiet, studious, sometimes the remote, physicians, little known outside of their own clienteles. When Ian Maclaren in "The Bonny Briar Bush'" made a hero of the old doctor of Drumtochty, he struck a note that rang true to many thousand hearts.

Honor to the country doctor—with his long, frozen rides; with his poor and scattered patients, his hard and thankless service, his too often scanty income, and his modest, unnoted, unwearied consecration to the clamor of the sick! Most of us can recall some such men and women of whom the world is not worthy. In the process of preparing for this bill, it has fallen to my lot to be in communication with the provincial doctors of the State, and I am glad of the opportunity to pay tribute to the courtesy, to the promptness, to the heartiness, with which they have responded to the merciful movement for which we plead. Over eight hundred registered Massachusetts practitioners have signed this petition. Of these, a natural proportion represent the country or the provincial practice, and they, like the brilliant urban physicians whose distinguished names we offer you, are to be respected, and should be heard. These are the men who protest against unregulated vivisection in Massachusetts—your constituents, gentlemen, in every county of the State; not what are called your "sentimental" petitioners, but your scientific petitioners; not your moral, but your medical petitioners. They have got far enough away from the powerful vivisecting schools to think for themselves. They have escaped the glamour. They are outside the magic circle. These men are too busy in healing the sick, to stop and torture animals. They do not keep private physiological laboratories. They are not conscious of any such debts to the practice of vivisection as prevent them from signing this petition. They do not torment; they heal. They do not inflict; they relieve. Their sensibilities have not been blunted by years spent in carving living cell and quivering nerve. The instincts of mercy are still alert in them, because the habits of mercy are confirmed in them. This is the law.

Are we to suppose that the vivisecting schools are educating today a class of men worthy to wear the mantle of the highest and best, of the wisest and the tenderest in the profession? We all know what a doctor may be capable of, if he is set adrift on a false or cruel pathological theory. Among the declinations to sign this petition which have reached us—I am glad to say that these have been a small minority of the replies—I cherish and preserve three letters. These remonstrants favor vivisection. All have the candor to add that they would like to see the practice extended so as to include experimentation upon the bodies of living human criminals. Two of these men are members of the most important medical society of the old school of therapeutics in Massachusetts. The third has (happily) now left the State.

An American medical journal (with several Boston editors on its staff) recently contained these startling words from its leading contributor:—

"It would be better for the profession if we would recognize the fact that it is better to have patients die under scientific treatment than to recover under empirical treatment." He adds, "Accept no dictating by the laity."

Is that what we are coming to? Will it be found pretty soon better for a patient to die under the care of vivisectionists than to live without the assistance of vivisection? Are the healing agencies of the future to be quarried out of the palpitating flesh of tortured animals? Shall physiology be permitted to train a race of "official slaughterers" to assume the sacred responsibilities awaiting them in our homes and in our hospitals? Shall our medical schools become shambles? Shall our honored universities become slaughterhouses—and not a cry protest?

Your life may hang upon your doctor's fine perception, upon his instinct of tenderness, as truly as it does upon his therapeutics, more often than it will upon his surgery.

An American poet was slain a few years ago by the blunder of a hospital surgeon.

"But we did not know he was organized like this!" cried the embarrassed staff. "Other men would have come out of it all right. How should we know he was different?"

Ah, but the physician, if any man, and above all men, should know the difference. His should be

The fine eye that separates
The unseen from the seen.

His must be the educated heart, or his educated head will betray him. His must be the skilled spirit, or his skilled hand will fail him. All that is noble in manhood, all that is ideal in chivalry, all that is refined in sympathy, all that is sensitive in mercy, we demand of him; and it is our right to demand of an erring science that she does not experiment these things out of him.

Gentlemen, we present this bill in the name of dumb, tormented animal life—and in the name of its human tormentors; in behalf of the vivisected—in behalf of the vivisector; for the sake of the dog upon the torture trough—for the sake of the medical student, whose nature is thrown into moral confusion by the piteous spectacle; for the sake of the young physicians to whom Massachusetts gave her diplomas last year, nearly two hundred men and women, trained in the icy doctrines of the vivisecting schools. Nor do we omit to plead for the sake of the helpless sick who are at the mercy of the fashionable physiological errors—young mothers, children, the aged, the ignorant and pauper babies liable to be sacrificed to the mania for experimentation upon living flesh which does not pause at the animal, but silently, subtly, often undetected and always unpunished, slides over to the human subject. Massachusetts has had her experience of human vivisection. She is not proud of it.

Gentlemen, in the name of the very forces which are massed here to contend with us—in the honored name of science, we plead with you for this bill. We plead for an art of healing released from an arrogant error, freed by a divine and humble truth; an art intellectually competent, to frame a materia-medica that shall heal the human sick without the torment of the inferior races, and morally unable to inflict upon any sentient organism an unnecessary pang.

> . . . Cruel is the world. Then be thou kind, even to the
> creeping thing
> That crawls and agonizes in its place,
> As thou in thine.

In taking farewell of your patience, may I say this?—It is only "a weakness for the weaker side" that has dragged one of your petitioners into a contention whose demands upon courage, strength, and power to persuade so far exceed her capabilities. But in the progress of a great moral and scientific movement like this the individual counts for so little that I am sure I speak for many of "the voiceless" in our ranks when I say: If the piteous sum of unnecessary suffering in the laboratories of Massachusetts could be annihilated, or even visibly reduced, we should count the utmost cost a paltry thing. Life—one's own life, not some dumb, tormented "fellow-creature's"—would be a small and happy price to pay.

> Say not the days are evil—who's to blame?
> And fold the hands and acquiesce—oh, shame!
> Stand up, speak out, and bravely, in God's name.

Appendix D

"Tammyshanty" (1908), by Elizabeth Stuart Phelps

The September 1908 issue of *Woman's Home Companion* announced a forthcoming short story: "'Tammyshanty, which will be published in the next number of the COMPANION, is the love story of a boy and a dog—a tale as interesting as 'Black Beauty' and as full of import, written with all the sympathy and power that is characteristic of the author of 'Though Life Us Do Part.'" The October publication of "Tammyshanty" followed the same magazine's serialization, earlier in the year (January through July) of Phelps's *Though Life Us Do Part*, a romantic novel with strong antivivisection themes. "Tammyshanty" was later included in Phelps's critically acclaimed short story collection *"The Oath of Allegiance" and Other Stories*, published by Houghton Mifflin in 1909.

❖

The boy curled astride the bowsprit of the schooner, and looked over into the thick water.

There are certain defects in early education of which one is so poignantly conscious at so tender an age that they might as well be, since they seem, irreparable.

Not to have experienced more than a term or two at night school, not to be able to offer evidential parents to society, not to have any home more concrete than the wharves, the bridges, the railroad yard, or a stray bed at the newsboys' lodge, and not to command an appreciable income—these are inferior circumstances about which one does not concern one's self. Not to know how to swim—that is the irrevocable, that is the fatal thing. There is about this affliction an air of finality against which human hope cannot wrestle. The boy felt that it would be easier to get into prison and out again than it would ever be to get into the lake and out.

Once he had ventured to "do time" like a man, but he had escaped like a monkey. Once he had tried to swim, and it had taken two doctors and two hours to resuscitate his valuable life. He had long since come to look upon criminal careers and nautical sports as equally serious and objectionable. But the rebound of attraction to that which one has renounced is as inevitable as the nature of gutta-percha. The boy hung upon the bowsprit and dared himself to drop.

"I stump yer!" he said.

The schooner was silent, and to all intents empty. The cook who was left in charge of her slept the sleep of too much and too recent shore leave. The wharf, deserted, blistered in the scorching noon. An ore barge that had lain alongside was laboring out in charge of a tug which never washed its face. There had been a couple of men fishing in a boat, but these had rowed away.

A pauper dog sat on a pile of lumber to view the scenery; but he had a misanthropic and preoccupied air; he did not notice the boy. There was not so much as a policeman, to say, "Move on, now!"

The child had taken off his clothes, excepting for a rag of underwear, and looked like a crab, half in, half out of its shell. He clung with a desperate daring, born of his conscious timidity, peeping over into the black-green depths; these seemed as solid as malachite, and as impenetrable. He hung by one dirty hand, then by the other—by two grimy feet, then by one—then by all fours; by his chin, on his stomach, by anything, on anywhere, unable to plunge, unable to refuse to plunge—a grotesque little image of irresolution. No observant deity interfered with it.

Now, the bowsprit was shiny and slippery; and the boy was sprawly and not very strong; he had not had much to eat for a few days—in fact, he seldom did have very much.

It would not have been easy to say which came first, the splash or the cry. Without intention to defy the suicide laws of his paternal state, the lad was in the water, whence a final trapeze performance sustained upon one foot and one finger had hurled him.

He dropped, and sank, and rose, and shrieked. But the cook who had too much shore leave did not turn in his bunk in the hot fo'castle. The boy sank, and rose again, and this time he did not shriek. His hair was red—the red that one might expect of a tiger lily crossed with a dahlia—the live, deep-bodied red, touched with orange and flaming. As he came up his head flared on the black water like a torch sputtering before it should be extinguished. He threw up his little thin, naked arms. As he went down he felt himself gripped, and after a while slapped in the face by something.

The pauper dog, who had been cynically regarding the lake, turned his neck slowly to look at the drowning boy—but after that he did nothing slow. He sprang, he leaped, he plunged, he swam; each impressive motion as swift as a noble feeling. Only a kinetoscope could have followed the movements of the flying, battling creature. He was not a handsome dog, but the beauty of the merciful nature was in him; its grand unconsciousness, its splendid disregard of self. To these things a muscle responds, as well as a mind.

The shore officer who ran down to the wharf felt the moisture start in his experienced eyes as he saw the sight. The two men in the boat rowed back with tremendous strokes, shouting:—

"Good dog! Good fellow! Have him, sir! Get him, sir!"

The cook waked, and staggered up the companionway, and said:—

"Damn!"

But the boy and the dog said nothing at all—the one because he was too weak and the other because he was too busy. The child had resigned himself instinctively to his rescuer, and did not struggle. The pauper dog had seized the drowning lad by his little ragged underwear, and tugged at that stolidly, pulling and treading water with his paws.

A dreadful fact had now forced itself upon the animal's intelligence—either he was too small or the boy was too large. In a general way he had always observed that there were bigger dogs than he, but he had never been convinced that he was not their equal, or superior, when it came to the point. When he found that he could not support the weight of the lad, an intense mortification overcame him. Now mortification, when it does not crush, stimulates, and the dog's body, fighting not to be drawn under by the human body, became brain all over where it was not heart, and heart wherever it was not brain.

The animal perceived a chance—his only one—and took it. A rope's end trailed from the rail of the schooner and writhed like a snake in the water. The dog seized and dragged the snake. No man who saw it could say afterwards how it was done; but every stupid, helpless, laggard human of them agreed that the dog and the rope united before the rope and the boy did. One little purple hand reached, and missed, and rose, and clutched—and clung. The lad sprawled dangling; the cook, swearing, held down his drunken arms.

But the two in the boat rowed up on a spurt, and the Good Angel of the Gamin (if there be such a minister of grace) ordained that they should not be too late. The fishermen jerked the little fellow off the rope and in upon the thwarts, where he lay dripping and lobster red. Then, pausing only to let off a curse or two upon the cook, they started back to the wharf with their passengers.

When they had covered a considerable space of fluent malachite it occurred to them in a leisurely way to look back. A little brown spot undulated through the water at their wake; slowly, as if it found difficulty in moving. One of the rowers asked:—

"Where's the dog, Jim?"

"Great Scott!" said Jim. "That must be him. Looks kinder tired, don't he, Bill?"

"Nigh petered out," admitted Bill contritely. "Put about, an' be quick, you!"

With swift and powerful oars the two men put about, and brought up against the dog, who was swimming feebly, as if exhausted by his late exertion.

So Bill penitently pulled him aboard, and Jim said, "Good fellow!" and the boat resumed her course to the wharf. The boy had crawled from the thwarts to the bottom, and lay sputtering and shivering; he did not say "Good fellow" to anybody, either man or dog. When the men had spilled their passengers upon the wharf they rowed away about their business, nodding, and reprimanding the boy:—

"Don't do it again, you!" The child blinked at them stupidly. His purple lips opened and moved several times, but nothing of value to the world came from them; he did not know how to thank anybody for a kindness; in his whole life he had never received enough to learn the art.

The fishermen rowed off. The cook on the schooner swore at the boy for a few minutes, and went below to finish his nap. The wharf officer came up and patted the dog, and shook the boy, and told him to move on when he got dry. Then he, too, went away.

The boy and the dog remained upon the wharf; dripping and shivering, they eyed each other cautiously. The dog saw a red head and freckles, a purple human crab, and a stealthy human grin to which he felt an inclination to respond. The boy saw an Irish terrier. He was a mongrel, and of a considerable size; his tail was stubbed to a humorous shortness, but his ears were uncut; the shock of hair above his eyes was larger and thicker than usual, and gave to the slow imagination of the lad the impression of a tam-o'-shanter cap. The dog's eyes were fine and sad. At the moment they gleamed with something between pride and fear. The animal seemed to be uncertain whether he should expect to be praised or beaten for the deed that he had done. He regarded the boy with the alert wariness that one sees sometimes in the eyes of an experienced old Irishman who has met a new type of employer. After some silent reflection the boy cautiously observed:—

"Hullo!" He had something of the diffidence that he once felt when he talked with a little deaf mute. It occurred to him that the dumb dog had more ways of speaking than the dumb child. Tail, eyes, ears, tongue, throat, each and all knew how to listen and to answer. The boy felt that he and the dog already experienced conversation. With growing confidence he repeated:

"Hullo!"

"Hullo yourself," barked the dog.

"Hully gee," said the boy.

"Hully gee," returned the dog.

"Cold, ain't it? You bet!"

"You bet," rejoined the dog.

"Deep, warn't it? Darn deep," suggested the boy.

"Darned deep," agreed the dog.

"Say," said the boy slowly, "I hain't never had nobody do nothin' for me like you done." To this the terrier did not reply, but the experienced Celt in his eyes came out and scrutinized the lad, as if he weighed the probable meaning of the words.

"You ain't no relation, nuther," added the boy. A flash in the face of the Irish dog seemed to retort, "Doncher be too sure of that."

Now the boy hesitatingly extended a little dripping hand, and laid it on the terrier's drenched tam-o'-shanter. The child could not remember that he had ever caressed anything, even a dog or a kitten; and he did not know how. The dog recognized the attention by a pleasant wag of his too-short tail.

"Say," said the boy, "you 'n' me might be pals."

The dog assented politely.

"I hain't got no partikkelar place to put up," admitted the boy, by way of apology.

The obvious reply, "I hain't none myself," did not come from the dog. The process of thought was too complicated.

"Was you ever hungry?" asked the boy.

The terrier threw up his dripping head, and laughed.

"I be myself, sometimes," explained the boy. "But somethin' or nothin', half's yourn. See?"

"I see," said the dog.

"Me name," observed the boy incidentally, "is Peter Roosevelt Tammany."

The dog permitted himself a look of pained perplexity. "But they *calls* me Jack the Marineer. That's cos I can't swim. Me common Monday edition name is Jacket. Got any name of yer own?"

The dog hung his wet head with embarrassment.

"How's Tammyshanty?" asked the boy.

The dog uttered a hilarious howl. Jacket hesitated for a reply, instinctively seeking something more serious than profane. Now and then, at Christmas time, he had wandered into Sunday-school, and he raked his memory for a sacred phrase.

"Amen," he said, after some thought.

"Amen," replied the dog. The shivering lad solemnly put his arm about the neck of the drenched and shaking animal, and whistled something haughtily, as if he had been the owner of large private kennels. The terrier leaped and sprang to the sound. The boy hunted up his ragged clothes, and he and the dog passed soberly up the wharf together.

In the prelude to any union of spirits there is a solemn moment; and something of the seriousness of an intimate relation settled upon the gamin and the mongrel, as they trotted into the city and disappeared from the lenient eye of the wharf officer, who smiled, as if he had heard a good story which might bear repeating.

Love is a variety in unity, and we hear much, but not too much, about it. We read forever of the love of man and woman, and the love of a mother for a child; we study love as the chief lesson of life, and the choice material of art. In the great heart of human feeling at whose beats we listen, have we thought it quite worth while to count the love of a boy for a dog? A friendless boy for a homeless dog? One should add: A loveless boy for an unloved dog?

217

Jacket the gamin and Tam o' Shanter the terrier came together in one strong dramatic moment and united like rain-drops, or waves, or flame. What had life been to either without the other? In a week, in a day, it became impossible to imagine. The outcast animal, longing always for an unknown master, accepted the sweet servitude rapturously. The desolate child, knowing neither the name nor the fact of love, he who had no human tie, and knew no human tenderness, received with almost incredible emotion the allegiance of the dog. The swish of a stubby tail, the kiss of a pink tongue, the clasp of scrawny paws, the mute worship of dark, pursuant eyes—these became the events of a day, and mounted to the romance of existence. For such signs that he was dear to something the lad watched with an idealization that was well-nigh poetic; and for such cumulative evidence that anything was dear to him, he lived. A few men, but not many, remember or understand the capacity for affection in the soul of the boy. Behind the rough bark what fine sap flows! Below the blazonry, the bluff, the vulgarity, if you will, of a neglected lad, what gentle, what delicate fibres hide!

The gamin acquired that splendid fortune which may be the supreme ennobler of a human creature—he had experienced a great passion. Prince or poet may live and die and miss it, or even never know that he has missed it. Jacket the newsboy had found it, and recognized the fact. Everything that he felt, everything that he had was the pauper dog's—the child's poor corner in the attic of the tenement where he had become a lodger because he felt that Tam o' Shanter needed a home and shelter; the scantiest meals that ever were earned out of a bad day's business, or the biggest that good luck gave a fellow now and then—half of everything there was went to the patient, snuggling terrier, who never begged, who never grabbed, who ate silently, it seemed under protest, when the larder was low. The first quarter that the lad could save gave the dog a strap collar, laboriously marked in indelible ink with a master's name and street and number. One day a deluded philanthropist who had inquired into the circumstances gave two dollars to license the dog. The philanthropist was an old man, with an old-fashioned gray beard, and a water-proof coat; he did not look like every other man; he was an officer in some society that occupied itself with the reduction of human cruelty; but that the street child could not know, nor would he have understood it if he could.

Among the recorded good deeds of many serious years it may be doubted if the gray man in the water-proof coat had ever done a wilder, kinder act than when he flung two dollars into the bottomless sea of gamin life, and trusted an unwatched boy to spend it for the protection of an unlicensed dog.

When Jacket returned from the city hall he lifted his red head proudly. He had become a property holder; Tammyshanty was a tax-payer; both were citizens; they celebrated the event by an extravagant supper. They bought a big bone with much meat on it, cooked it between two stones and an old piece of funnel in a vacant lot, and divided the consequences. In the development of their mutual affection the two tried to interchange tastes, if not natures. Tammyshanty would have lived on apples and potatoes (to which he cultivated a hopeless objection) for his master's sake. The lad would have eaten bones, if he could, for the dog's.

That night they slept ecstatically, Tammyshanty upon the foot of his master's ragged bed. A dozen times a night, whether asleep or awake, the boy felt about with his foot to make quite sure that the dog was there. In cold weather he covered Tammyshanty with his own ragged coat. With some vague reminiscence of his too-brief Sunday-school existence, he had taught the terrier to say his prayers at night. When one cried "Amen!" in a deep, religious voice, Tammyshanty barked, and jumped into bed. In the morning the two kissed rapturously, but sometimes sadly, for it was not always safe or possible to take Tammyshanty upon a journalistic career in the crowded crossings of Newspaper Row. The dog was in the habit of going to the corner of the alley with the newsboy, and returning home alone. There, on the broken steps of the tenement, he sat, a statue of a dog, whom neither fights nor fires, kicks nor caresses could allure, and waited for the lad. If it were very stormy or cold, Tammyshanty climbed to the attic bedroom, and watched soberly through a broken window, listening for a whistle or a call at which the heart of a dog must leap like climbing foam.

"Peppers! Peppers! Tammyshanty! Oh—oo—ee! Tammyshantee!"

Down the steps or down the stairs, across the alley, up the alley—to run as the heart runs, how short a time it takes! Sometimes twice, never more than that, the lad may cry:—

"Pep—pers! Oh—oo—ee! Tammyshantee!"

Then, with clasping arms and paws, with little laughs of delight and yaps of joy, boy and dog are one.

Now it befell that one day, when business was dull, the two went out for pleasure, and took a walk of considerable length. A brown brick house came in their way, a house with an ell, and a yard; a gloomy house, whose shades were drawn. It had old-fashioned wooden shutters, of a dingy white, and in the ell the lad noticed that the shutters were closed.

A man stood in the vestibule of the house. He was a middle-aged man, dressed as a gentleman dresses. For some reason he did not strike the gamin as being a gentleman. The man's face was heavily lined, like a piece of old leather that has been folded into certain creases so long that it cannot smooth out. His eyes were cold, like Bessemer steel, and might have been as useful, for they were not stupid eyes; but something in their expression was indescribably repulsive. Jacket, who was whistling, glanced and stopped. The street boy was shrewd—as the tribes of the street are in the interpretation of character.

"That's a fine dog of yours," observed the man. "You bet," replied Jacket, proudly; but he walked on, without stopping. Tam o' Shanter followed with a passionate docility.

"I'll give you fifty cents for him," pursued the man in the vestibule. He came down the steps and out upon the sidewalk as he spoke. "Here."

He held out a long, sinuous hand, in which a piece of silver glittered. The boy and the dog stopped. The Irish terrier set his teeth and growled. Jacket threw back his red head.

"Fifty cents! *Me? For my dog?* You must 'a' come from 'way back." The child laughed. "You must be orful green for a fellar of yer size," he added.

"Fifty cents is a good deal of money," returned the man with the Bessemer eyes. "I don't know but I 'll make it sixty; seventy-five if you want to drive a bargain. I 've been wanting a dog."

The boy seemed, on the instant, to grow before the man's eyes—as if he had been another man—and to tower above his elder and by all the standards of the world his superior. A terrible torrent of profanity poured from the gamin's quivering lips:—

"I would n't sell that there dog for—not for seventy-five dollars!" Jacket enunciated the words slowly, striving to express the inconceivable in the way of monetary values. Once or twice he had seen a ten-dollar bill. Once in his life he had handled five dollars. He dwelt upon this computation of human wealth with awe.

Then he turned upon his ragged heel.

"Peppers! Pep—pers! *Wireless* extry! Oh—oo—ee? Tammyshantee!"

The soprano cry whistled down the alley. It was night, and a dark one; a winter night, some five weeks or so after the incident of the brick house. It was snowing, and very cold. The boy's feet were wet, and he shivered as he hurried home. From a business point of view it had not been a bad day, and tucked tight under his ragged elbow the newsboy held his supper—their supper; his and Tammyshanty's; a scrap of cooked beef, cast out from a poor restaurant for a poor but possible price.

"I'll give him the biggest half," thought the child. "He's the littlest. See?"

There had been no answer to his call, and Jacket lurched into a run, repeating shrilly:—

"Oh—oo—ee! Tammyshantee!"

As he ran he listened for the sure, dear bark. The lad's lips moved, muttering:—

"Must be so stormy can't hear him. Oh—oo—ee! Tammyshantee? Must be up attic. That's wot's 'e matter. Must 'a' got shet in somewheres. Oh—oo—ee! Tammyshantee? He'll be settin' in 'e winder a-watchin' an' a-yappin' like to split hisself. Oh—oo—ee!"

He pushed on, sprinting through the piling drifts, jerked the fringe of snow from his forelock and eyebrows, and raked the tenement from roof to cellar in one sharpened glance. The dog was not upon the doorsteps; the broken window was empty of his little watching, anxious, Irish face. Jacket dashed on, and up four flights of broken stairs, burst open the door of his attic, and fell in panting.

A wisp of snow had drifted through the broken pane upon the foot of the cot where the child and the dog slept. There was of course no fire, and the attic was very cold. It occurred to Jacket that it was cold enough to freeze even an Irish terrier, and he gasped and gazed. But the bed was as empty as the window. The dog was not in the room.

At the moment when I pause in the story, as one pauses before the thing from which one shrinks, my eyes chance upon these words chosen from one of the people's philosophies of our epigram-loving day:—

"You don't know all of grief and loneliness unless you are a boy, and have lost a pet dog."

The first of it seemed, at the time, the worst of it; though afterwards the lad came to know that it was not. He spent that night in the storm, baffled and beaten, searching alleys and yards, and tenements, calling upon neighbors, friends and foes, newsboys, messengers, letter-carriers, girls in flaunting hats, all the population that exists by locomotion of the throbbing streets. He went so far—and it is difficult for the sheltered and respectable and mature to estimate the extent of this tremendous step—as to consult the arch enemy of mortal man, the police of his own city. Towards midnight the storm stopped, but the little master's passionate search did not. He crawled about town until the gray of the dawn, then stumbled to his attic, and dropped down exhausted upon the bed where the wisp of snow had driven to a drift. There, curled in his drenched clothes, he sobbed and slept a little, and dreamed that Tammyshanty slept and sobbed beside him. In his dream the lad moved his cold foot, and felt about for the dog upon the bed.

"Say, Mister, hev you seen a lost dog anywheres? A licensed dog? A yaller dog, Mister? A pure mongrel Irish terrier dog? The purtiest t'ing of his kind you ever seen. Had a tammyshanty cap acrosst his eyes. You never seen such harnsome eyes. He warn't no common purp; he ain't no poorhouse dog. He's got his master's name—that's me, Peter Roosevelt Tammany—printed on his collar, sir. But I 'll 'low they calls me Jacket gener'lly. An' my residence, Mister, my street and number in case anything happened to him. My dog's name is Tammyshanty. He's a licensed dog. I t'ought I 'd find him long before now. See? Say, Mister, sure ye hain't seen any sech a dog? Not anywheres?"

This question, repeated a score of times a day, as many more by night, quivered plaintively through the city for a week, for two, for three; for more than the boy had kept the heart to count.

In his emergency he consulted all his old friends, and made some new ones. On the wharf endeared to him as the scene of love at first sight between himself and Tammyshanty, he sought, and as it befell, he found his rescuers, the two fishermen. He who was called Jim said:—

"Sho! Can't cher find him?"

But he who was called Bill said:—

"I 'll have a shy at lookin' for that yaller dog, myself."

The shore policeman strolled up and committed himself to the extent of saying, "That so?" and took the description and address of dog and master. Jacket had the pertinacity of purpose belonging to love and anguish. He went so far as to look for the drunken cook. But the schooner had vanished into the storm-swept, frowning lake.

The newsboys rallied around the bereaved child with the alert instincts of their calling. One passed the event to the other. A subterranean intelligence ran through the gamin world. In particular the afflicted boy was aware of the sympathy—as dumb as a dog's, and almost as helpless—of two lads, officers in the Newsboys' Association, and bearing, in that important organization, their own dignities and titles, but known to an indifferent public as Freckles and Blinders.

"Dis t'ing otter be giv to de press," suggested Freckles.

"I'll speak to me Paper 'bout it," observed Blinders with journalistic assurance. Jacket received this stupendous idea slowly. After giving it some silent consideration, he timidly sought his own favorite reporter upon his own staff and told the story of Tam o' Shanter. The reporter glanced up from his yellow pad.

"Why, that's a pity!" he said kindly, and went on writing.

"Say, Mister, hev yer seen a dog? A yaller dog? A *licensed* dog? Wid his street 'n' number on his collar—'n' his name, Tammyshanty, sir? Hair stood up all 'round his eyes. Master's name, that's me—Peter Roosevelt Tammany—printed plain beside. Hain't seen him anywheres? Hain't ye seen *any* sort of a yaller dog? Hain't ye—"

The plaintive entreaty, now learned by heart, and reiterated by rote, fell from the lips of Peter Roosevelt Tammany as a bag of ballast drops from a balloon in full flight, and sank with a thud into a guttural oath. The boy, blinded by grief, had failed to notice where he was or to whom he spoke. Now, the brick house with the ell and the drawn shades revealed itself like an unwelcome scene shifted suddenly upon a stage in an unpleasant people's play; and in the vestibule the man with the steel in his eyes stood looking down coldly.

"Go to thunder, *you!*" screamed the gamin. "Offerin' me money—*money!*—for me dog. Fifty cents—seventy-five—for a pure mongrel Irish terrier. Fished me outen 'e lake 'n' saved me life, blank yer! Cuddled in me neck an'—an' kissed me. Why, Mister, I 'd—I 'd *give* ye seventy-five dollars for my dog. I 'd git it someways er nuther. Probably I 'd git it from me Pepper. Would n't mind ef I had ter steal it an' do time for it. Say! Look here! You! Come back, Mister! Look 'round here! You hain't—you hain't seen him anywheres, hev yer? Mister! Mister! Ef you did, ef yer ever should, you 'd be

224

kind to him, would n't yer? Cos he's 'e littlest. See? You 'd let me know, would n't yer? He was sech an orful cunnin' dog—knowed so much—an' he wagged his tail so—'t wa' n't a very big one—when I got home—an'—an' *kissed* me, Mister—"

But the door of the brick house was shut. Shrilling and sobbing, the child turned down the street unsteadily; he was seldom so demoralized; for composure and fortitude are newsboy traits. As he reeled along, punching his grimy knuckles into his eyes, he ran against an old man, tall and gray, striding in a water-proof coat. Jacket, sputtering out of his bath of tears, recognized the philanthropist who had lavished the incredible sum of two dollars to license Tammyshanty.

"Oh, sir!" he cried. "Oh, sir!"

Wildly he related the circumstances of his experiences at the brick house.

"Ah?" said the old man, sharply. "Show me the place."

The two retraced their steps, and stood before the house. Most of its shades were closely drawn. In the ell the blinds were closed. It was a gloomy house, destitute, it seemed, of family ties, of the sense of home, of the consciousness of human love. While the old man and the boy stood regarding it, a strange sound escaped from the place; it accelerated, then lapsed; muffled, or perhaps stilled.

The child shivered and gasped:—

"Sounds like—sounds like it was—"

"Come away," said the old gentleman, quickly. He grasped the boy's hand and led him, hurrying down the street.

The reporter looked up from his yellow pad. Jacket stood panting, ragged cap in hand. His teeth chattered in his broad mouth.

"Freckles 'n' Blinders says—" he began. "De fellers says he *cuts 'em up*. Critters—an'—an' *dogs*—livin' ones—they heern 'em."

He babbled forth some one of the tragic tales which are so unwelcome to the sensibilities that it is more comfortable to doubt than to investigate their dark significance. The reporter whirled on the revolving chair of an absent editor—the religious one.

"Must be one of these private experimenters," he said below his breath. The chief was passing by, and stopped. "They 're apt to do pretty rough work," added the subordinate. "Shall we take it up?"

The chief stood with his hands in his pockets, and regarded the boy; who cringed when he saw the great man shake his head. Jacket's faith in his "Pepper" was illimitable. That its strong arms encompassed all human powers, and some divine ones, he pathetically believed. His little body bent together like a shut jack-knife before the indifference of the managing editor.

"If there were any sort of story in it—" observed the chief. "It does n't strike me there is."

The pen that wrote the best "story" in the office sighed for its opportunity. But the young man's heart ached for the lad.

"Tell me," he urged gently. "All there is to tell. There might be *something* I could do."

Jacket did not answer. The reporter went out after him; but the child and the night had blended silently.

It was a wild night, and Jacket pushed weakly against the resistance of the brutal lake wind. He ran upon a little squad of whispering newsboys, but veered past them, volleying incoherent, piteous words. His head hung forward, and his tongue lolled from his mouth. It was as if he scented the brick house as a hound scents prey. He flung himself upon the high steps. Choking between sobs and curses, he demanded entrance by fingers and feet, by voice and fists, by prayers and oaths.

"Gimme my dog, you!—Mister! Dear Mister! *Please* gimme my dog. You got so many dogs an' I ain't got nothin' but him—I'll set the cops on you. I'll set my Pepper on you if you don't gimme my dog. Say, Mister, please, Mister, I'll pay you for my dog. I'll gin you a hundred dollars for Tammyshanty. My Pepper 'll start a public sooperscription for him. Don't you *darst* tech my dog. Tammyshantee? Tammyshantee? Amen!"

The door of the house remained shut, and locked, and barred. Jacket shook it furiously, and fell back. Like a cat he climbed up the iron railing into the area; crawled beneath the blinded windows of the large ell, lay flat upon his stomach, and beat back his sobs to listen. Plucking up his broken voice he softly called:

"Oh—oo—ee! Tammyshantee?"

Was it accident, or answer? Did his brain reel with his misery? Or had the lonely lad recognized in that inaccessible inferno the cry of his own dog?

He dashed over the railing and tottered up the steps. There, a raging little figure, hurling blow after blow upon the unyielding door, his friends found him. It was the old philanthropist in the water-proof coat who took the child to his aged heart. But the reporter was there; and the shore policeman (now promoted to an inland beat) and the newsboys, Freckles and Blinders, cursing behind.

"Tree hunderd more of us is comin'!" screamed the lads. "We'll smash de doors an' winders in! *We'll* get Tammyshanty. You betcher life we will!"

But the policeman put out his awful hand and motioned back the thronging boys—three hundred of them, as their little officers had said.

"Nothing can get out that there yellow dog but just a search warrant," said the officer sadly enough. "And the judge he won't give it. He says the evidence is lackin'."

Chattering like monkeys, the newsboys clamored and pressed up against the officer. The old philanthropist patted the child upon his arm. The reporter stood in the foreground; as if he cast his lot in with the boys.

For a moment law and humanity regarded each other silently. Then the newsboys broke into a yell. It was taken up from the alley, from the sidewalk, from the windows of the neighboring houses, and swelled from the street beyond. Freckles pushed Blinders forward.

"Mr. Cop," said Blinders, "we repersent every paper in dis yer city. We ain't er goin' in for no free fight. We 're law-abidin' citizens, Cop, but we 're er goin' to hev da't dog. You betcher life!"

"I wish to Moses you could," admitted the officer. But he stood stolidly between the house and the muttering crowd.

Apparently baffled, the newsboys consulted in whispers, massed and turned away. The philanthropist and the reporter carried Jacket somewhere, and tried to make him eat or drink, to warm him or to comfort him; but the child, refusing, sat with a sly eye upon the door. While the reporter stirred the sugar in the coffee, and the philanthropist was paying for the beefsteak, the boy slid out of the restaurant like an eel out of a basket. He had not spoken a word. His face was pinched. He had ceased to sob. With the look of a little old man who was weary of life, but with the wings of childhood in his feet, he flew to the brick house. There, crawling flat beneath the windows of the ell, he lay and watched and listened. Once he faintly called:—

"Oh—oo—ee! Tammyshantee?"

Towards morning, when it grew pretty cold, he climbed the iron fence, got back to the steps, and coiled himself against the barred door. His heart went through it like a battering ram. It was as if he could force his way in and draw the dog out.

Forty-eight hours is a long time to experience despair, but it is a short time in which to prepare for retribution. Of this the private experimenter found himself unexpectedly and poignantly aware. He sat alone among his victims, and eyed them with a grudging regret. It was well on towards midnight of the second day since the unpleasant scene which the uninstructed public had made upon his premises. The uninstructed public, as fate would have it, had not gone away appeased.

The brown brick house was in a state of siege. Neighbors hooted at the blinded windows; epithets and missiles assailed the man with the steel in his eyes if he raised a shade. A door he dared not open. He sat and cursed. He listened and quaked.

The street that night had grown impressively, almost unnaturally still. He did not ask himself whether there were any reason for this circumstance. It occurred to him that no time was likely to be better for the execution of the purpose that he had formed, and he proceeded to hasten his preparations furtively.

The man, in a word, had been brought to the pass of contemplating flight. Startled by the popular suspicion under which he had suddenly fallen, the vivisector gave up his dreadful game. He yielded it so far as the protection of his life and limb concerned him; he did not propose to yield his "material." He purposed, as is now well known, to betake himself and the doomed creatures in his power to some other, some safer lair; and to select for such a sally the small, dull hours after midnight, when the streets would be relatively quiet and suitable for his venture. The remarkable stillness in the region of the brick house misled him, and he decided to make the move at midnight.

He stepped stealthily about his laboratory. The place was dim, but it was not still.—This pen refuses to portray the sights which met the cold eyes so familiar with them that the man's nerves did not complain. Such of his subjects as could walk he urged to their feet, and leashed them.

It was perhaps half an hour after midnight when the locked iron gate of the area fence swung open cautiously, and a man peered out. The street was quite deserted. Not so much as a yawning officer was to be seen. The vivisector tiptoed out, and down the sidewalk. Behind him followed a strange and pitiable group. Dogs on leashes, as many as the hand could hold; dogs fastened abreast and tandem to a rope dragged at the heels of their tormentor, followed him with the beautiful docility which only the dog, of all created beings, offers to the master man. It was not an uncommon thing for them to kiss his hand while they lay bound beneath his knife. At first this used to make him uncomfortable; but he had become quite accustomed to it.

Skulking, with darting eyes, he dragged the dogs along. He congratulated himself that he was not disturbed. He was surprised at the freedom of his movements. He anticipated that his troubles were over. The fugitive physiologist had proceeded perhaps sixty feet when there burst upon him a sound before which that which he called his heart stood still. No man city born or bred ever mistakes that sound. It was the roar of an oncoming mob. It seemed to him for the moment as if the whole town had become a throat.

The tramp of feet advanced upon him with an ominous steadiness. Out of the dimly lighted streets the crowd took rapid form—neighbors and strangers, women and men. Sobbing and swearing had become audible and articulate. For the first time in his life the man heard himself hissed. Officers in front threatened and beat back, but could not stay the onset of the people. Beyond, behind, surging and shrilling, pushed the newsboys—almost a thousand strong.

The man stood perfectly still. He cringed, but he did not cry out. He expected to be torn to pieces. He felt as if the heart of humanity leaped upon him. It occurred to him that he had no escape. It occurred to him that his subjects, in all the years of his red life, had no escape. He felt the air split with yells and curses. Instinctively, stupidly, he held fast to his dogs.

Gray-white, silent, with his shock of red hair standing straight up from his head, grimy hands clenched, teeth set, and lips drawn back from them like those of a snarling fox, Jacket had got himself to the front of the throng. The newsboys, Freckles and Blinders, pushed zealously to him and tried to support him on either side, he tottered so; but he did not notice them. His favorite reporter and the gray philanthropist in the waterproof coat said something to him, but he did not hear what it was. His old friend, Bill the fisherman, stood under the electric arc, and pushed his sleeves to the shoulders.

"If yer want anybody to punch him to a jelly, I 'm your man," he said.

The officer who used to be shore policeman turned his back and winked a little, but did not see nor hear the fisherman. Jacket noticed none of these things. To human sympathy he had gone deaf and blind. The reporter, trying to keep close to him, saw that the lad had dropped upon his hands and knees and was crawling on all fours like a small animal with some purpose which it cannot share with the superior race.

Suddenly and silently he pounced.

The dogs were of various breeds and all sizes, and huddled, themselves terrified by the rescuing people, clinging for protection to their tormentor, the only master whom their pitiable fate had left them. But some of them struggled, and one made weak efforts to escape from the rope to which he was attached. Plaintively from somewhere in the turmoil a stealthy call arose:—

"Oh—oo—ee! Oh—oo—ee! Tammyshantee? Amen!"

The weak dog lifted up his wounded head, and feebly barked.

Then, as we say, the lad pounced. With one swift stroke he cut the terrier free, and clasped him; but in the making of the effort fell over on the curbing with Tammyshanty in his nerveless arms.

The act was enough to fire the fury of the crowd. It rolled on and swept under the street light. The lake fisherman who was called Bill made the first stroke, and liberated a beautiful spaniel, who kissed his brown, big hand. Knife after knife flashed in the electric tremor—cry upon cry applauded until every dog in the captive group ran free. It was said afterwards that some people in the mob who had dogless homes adopted these poor creatures, and took them to their roused, indignant hearts.

The police, who had mercifully ignored the descent upon the animals, rallied to the protection of the man. They dragged him off behind their billies—where, or to what future, no one at that time knew or cared. It has since been told of him that this practical physiologist fled the city where his scientific amusements had been so rudely interrupted by ignorant laymen, and that he escaped from the metropolis of the West to the metropolis of the East; wherein it is not the province of this story to pursue his professional career.

But Jacket and Tammyshanty lay clasped and clasping upon the sidewalk, and neither spoke. The reporter lifted them in his strong, young arms; and the gray philanthropist, dashing hot drops from eyes too old to weep at much in a world where sympathy must blunt itself to suffering for its own life's sake, said imperiously:—

"Call a carriage and a doctor, and bring them to my house."

So the boy and the dog were lifted into the carriage silently and gently, and a thousand newsboys followed the cab as if it had been a hearse. Rumor ran riot in the streets—now that the dog was dead, and the boy lived; now that the dog lived, but not the boy; then that both were past recall to a life in which they had fared so hardly.

The morning edition of Jacket's paper ran like a freshet through the town. The pen that wrote the best "story" in the office set forth the fact—which had now become of compelling public interest—that the boy and the dog, though weak, and sore bested, would live; and that "The Wireless" had already instituted a public subscription in their behalf. A portrait of Tammyshanty, taken in his bandages, and sprawled in his little master's feeble arms, adorned an extra of that energetic daily. The Newsboys' Association cut this out and framed it, to hang upon their club-room walls.

Jacket and Tammyshanty lay on a clean bed in the old philanthropist's third-story back room, and regarded each other seriously.

"Hullo," said the boy.

"Hullo yourself," nodded the dog.

"Hully gee," said the boy.

"Hully gee," said the dog.

"Warm here, ain't it? You bet."

"You bet," agreed the dog.

"Hard, warn't it?" sobbed the boy.

"Pretty hard," blinked the dog.

"All over, ain't it? " asked the boy.

"All over," smiled the dog.

"Say your prayers, amen," said the boy.

"Amen," replied the dog.

"An' we ain't no relations, nuther," suggested the boy. Beneath the bandages on his wounded head a spark in the eye of the Irish dog fired as if he said:—

"Doncher be too sure of that!"

NOTES

—〰—

The first edition of *Trixy*, published in 1904 by Houghton Mifflin, served as the copy text. Original spellings and punctuation are preserved, with the following minor emendations: *to-day*, *to-morrow*, *to-night* have been changed to *today*, *tomorrow*, and *tonight*, respectively, and end-of-line hyphens have been omitted when not necessary for the conventional spelling of the word.

In the 1904 edition, Phelps's dedication reads: "To my husband Herbert D. Ward. Whose generous sympathy and faithful assistance have made it possible for me to write this book; who has contributed both to its plan and execution so largely that I cannot claim it as my unshared work; who is, in fact (Though, by his own wish, not in name), my collaborator—I inscribe this story." Phelps's first epigraph, on page 1 ("Cruel is the world. / Then be thou kind."), is from Robert Buchanan, "The New Buddha," *North American Review* 140, no. 342 (May 1885): 445–55. The note on the following page is Phelps's preface to the novel, and the last epigraph, on page 3 ("Mercy and truth are met together"), is Phelps's, from Psalm 85:10.

12 "Assam Pekoe . . . Young Hyson": Varieties of tea. Olin Steele's father is a tea merchant.

14 "Tennyson . . . 'Strong Son of God, immortal Love'": Alfred, Lord Tennyson (1809–1892), Victorian poet laureate. The hymn Mrs. Steele selected to play was an adaptation of Tennyson's prologue to his famous poem "In Memoriam A.H.H." (1849), the poet's requiem to his friend Arthur Henry Hallam (1811–1833). Given Phelps's interest in building human empathy for the cries of otherwise "voiceless" animals, the following lines of Tennyson's poem are especially significant: "So runs my dream, but what am I? / An infant crying in the night / An infant crying for the light / And with no language but

a cry" (Canto 54, lines 17–20). Tennyson was an ardent antivivisectionist, frequently quoted by Phelps and others in the campaign.

18 "according to the code she should have ceased to 'mourn' for her father some time ago": A reference to the Victorian etiquette codes governing the periods and stages of mourning attire. The death of a parent generally warranted one year of mourning.

21 diphtheria: Contagious bacterial infection characterized by sore throat, especially common in children.

25 coupons: In the nineteenth century, a reference to stock certificates.

26 Pond's Extract: Considered to be a cure-all solution, consisting of witch hazel, alcohol, and water.

27 Galen: Phelps names the fictional medical college after Galen of Pergamon, Greek physician and notorious early vivisector.

29 bacillus: A type of bacteria. Bacillus research for the purpose of developing inoculations was at the center of much of the vivisection controversy in the late nineteenth century. At that time, the science community was often embroiled in heated debates about the validity and redundancy of bacillus research methods and findings, which antivivisectionists pointed to in their arguments that animal experimentation was often needless and wasteful.

35 "He had witnessed . . . for sacrifice": This sentence corresponds nearly verbatim to a quotation Phelps cites in her 1901 speech to the Massachusetts legislature, an abridged version of which was reprinted in the pamphlet titled "A Plea for the Helpless" (New York: American Humane Association, 1901).

35 Gültz and Magendie: Friedrich Goltz (1834–1902) was a German physiologist and proponent of vivisection; François Magendie (1783–1855) was a French physiologist, infamous among antivivisectionists for his legacy as a pioneer in experimental physiology.

37 "Strong Son of God, immortal Love": An allusion to the hymn Olin Steele listened to his mother play in chapter 1. The hymn is an adaptation of Tennyson's prologue to his famous poem "In Memoriam A.H.H."

40 pharyngitis: Inflammation of the back of the throat (basically, a sore throat).

43 tam-o'-shanter: A traditional Scottish woolen cap with a flat, circular top and pom-pom in the center.

49 News-boys' Association: After the flourishing of the original chapter in Toledo, Ohio, the National Newsboys Association was founded

in 1904 at the World's Fair in St. Louis, Missouri. The children hired to sell newspapers were usually extremely poor immigrant children, often orphaned and living on the streets, and the Newsboys Association played an important role in advocating for their rights and bringing about child labor reform more broadly. Phelps represents the intersecting exploitation of newsboys and laboratory animals in her final work of antivivisection fiction, "Tammyshanty," which is included in Appendix D.

50 The Society for the Prevention of Docking and Cropping Tails and Ears: Aunt Jeffries belongs to an organization devoted to abolishing the common practice of surgically removing parts of the tails and ears of domestic animals, especially horses and dogs (referred to as "docking" tails and "cropping" ears). Such practices came under scrutiny in the United States after the founding of the American Society for the Prevention of Cruelty to Animals in 1866 and the Massachusetts Society for the Prevention of Cruelty to Animals in 1868. Despite her well-meaning activism in defense of animal bodies, Aunt Jeffries unwittingly recruits the leadership of a vivisector, which highlights the disconnect between the broader animal welfare movement, known for its elitist focus on the working class, and the antivivisection campaign, which targeted elite-class "gentlemen of science" like Olin Steele.

50 "Be all my sins remembered!": Olin Steele quotes Shakespeare's *Hamlet*, act 3, scene 1. In this last line of his famous soliloquy contemplating death and suicide, Hamlet turns to Ophelia and asks her to remember his sins in her prayers.

51 "new woman": A feminist model of womanhood that emerged in the late nineteenth century in opposition to Victorian codes that relegated women to the domestic realm as wife and mother. Women who sought education, professional careers, and voting rights, and who married later or remained single embodied the "new woman" ideal.

52 Whistler: James Abbott McNeill Whistler (1834–1903), American artist.

52 Fra Angelico's Christ Transfigured: Fra Angelico (1395–1455), Italian Renaissance artist. His fresco "Transfiguration" (Florence, ca. 1440–42) is especially noted for its sparsely detailed design, which invites the viewer to speculate upon the suffering and sacrifice of Christ.

52 Rodin's Pity: Auguste Rodin (1840–1917), French sculptor; "Pity" likely refers to the artist's 1894 plaster titled *Christ and the Magdalen*.

55 "blue cars": A reference to horsecars, or horse-drawn trams or streetcars.

68 "Azrael? Or Gabriel?": Archangels, Azrael typically known as the angel of death and Gabriel as the angel of life and hope. Atropos was one of the three Greek goddesses who decided people's fates, Atropos determined how humans would die.

71 "consumptive woman": The woman suffers from "consumption," a generic medical term commonly used in the nineteenth century for diseases characterized by the body's wasting away, especially tuberculosis.

72 Patrick Henry: American Revolutionary and statesman Patrick Henry (1736–1799), legendary for his "Give me liberty, or give me death!" declaration, was especially known for his adaptable and populist oratory style.

76 Mariana in the Moated Grange: From William Shakespeare's *Measure for Measure*, and the basis for Alfred, Lord Tennyson's 1830 poem "Mariana," a lonely and despairing woman character who laments her isolation from society and hopelessly awaits the return of her lover.

110 gossoon: Colloquial term for a boy, commonly used in Irish immigrant communities.

142 *lèse-majesté*: French, crime against a monarch; treason.

147 "not without its counterpart in the records of the Bar": Phelps refers to the famous closing argument made by Missouri lawyer and U.S. senator George Graham Vest (1830–1904). The speech, included in Appendix A, was often reprinted in support of the animal advocacy movement in the United States.

154 "Irving in 'The Bells'": The British actor Henry Irving played the part of Mathias in "The Bells," a play by Leopold Davis Lewis about a murderer who hallucinates that he is haunted by his victim. The play opened in 1871, and Irving played the role throughout the rest of his career until his death in 1905.

156 "There is a story told": Phelps quotes an anecdote included in Albert Leffingwell's book, *The Vivisection Question* (New Haven, Conn.: Tuttle, Moorehouse and Taylor, 1901), 188–89. "*Fiat experimentum in corpore vili*": Let an experiment be done on a worthless body. "*Corpus non vile est, domini doctissimi, pro quo Christus ipse non dedignatus est mori*": That body is not worthless, learned sirs, for which Christ himself disdained not to die.

159 Portuguese Sonnets: A reference to the sixth of the "Sonnets from the Portuguese" (1850) by British poet Elizabeth Barrett Browning (1806–61). The sonnet begins, "Go from me. Yet I feel that I shall stand / Henceforward in thy shadow."

162 "*Domini doctissimi*": Olin Steele quotes the Latin phrase he asked Bernard to read to him earlier. "*Corpus non vile est, domini doctissimi, pro quo Christus ipse non dedignatus est mori*": That body is not worthless, learned sirs, for which Christ himself disdained not to die.

Appendix B

179 Aileen Mavourneen: The title of a popular ballad, with lyrics by the Irish author Mrs. S. C. Hall (Anna Maria Fielding Hall, 1800–1881).

Appendix C

187 *The Zoophilist and Animals' Defender*: According to the magazine's detailed reporting on the hearing (May 1902, 11–13), another woman to speak at it was Lillian Freeman Clarke (1842–1921), a prominent social reform activist who served as president of the New England Anti-Vivisection Society (Clarke was the daughter of Transcendentalist James Freeman Clarke).

188 dumb: speechless; Phelps's usage of the word is in line with the animal welfare movement of the day, as in the title of the MSPCA magazine, *Our Dumb Animals*.

190 Alfort: A reference to the National Veterinary School of Alfort (France), founded in 1765.

191 "Begin with this": Many of Phelps's examples in this passage about Massachusetts vivisection are included in Albert Leffingwell, *Does Science Need Secrecy? A Reply to Prof. Porter and Others of Harvard Medical School* (Providence, 1896).

191 oorali: More commonly referred to as "curare," a neuro-muscular blocking agent that was often administered to laboratory animals to prevent them from struggling or vocalizing during experiments. The expression "hellish oorali" is from a poem by Alfred, Lord Tennyson, "In the Children's Hospital" (1880).

194 "I have not quite done with this vivisector": The vivisector Phelps refers to here is Harvard Medical School researcher William Townsend Porter.

195 Herbert Spencer (1820–1903): Famous British philosopher and biologist, influential proponent of evolutionary theory (coined the expression "survival of the fittest").

198 George Eliot: Pseudonym of Mary Ann Evans (1819–1880), Victorian novelist, correspondent and friend of Elizabeth Stuart Phelps.

199 Louis Pasteur (1822–1895): French biologist known for his discoveries related to the principles of vaccination.

199 "For a number of years": The source of the quotation is an article published in a Baltimore-based antivivisection magazine, written by Philip G. Peabody, Boston social reformer and attorney and the first president of the New England Anti-Vivisection Society. Philip G. Peabody, "The Principal Props of Vivisection," *Dawn* 1, no. 5 (Feb. 1902): 30–31.

200 The device known as the *tormentatore* was invented by the Italian scientist Paolo Mantegazza, whom Phelps quotes later in this speech.

201 Claude Bernard (1813–1878): French physiologist known especially for establishing the practice of experimental medicine, and one of science's most notorious vivisectors. He is the model for the character of Olin Steele's assistant, Dr. Bernard, in *Trixy*.

203 The "well-known physiologist" Phelps refers to in this passage is Paolo Mantegazza, the Italian neurologist and physiologist especially notorious among antivivisectionists as the inventor of a pain-inflicting device known in English as the "tormentor." The quoted passage was reprinted frequently in antivivisection publications.

205 "Those incidents which weigh especially heavily upon me": This quotation appeared frequently in antivivisection articles, attributed to the prominent Russian medical scientist and doctor Nikolai Pirogov. For this and the rest of the examples quoted in this passage, Phelps likely drew upon an article titled "The Remorse of Vivisectors," in *Journal of Zoophily* 9, no. 10 (1900): 115.

206 Ian Maclaren: pseudonym of Rev. John Watson (1850–1907), Scottish minister and author. *Behind the Bonny Brier Bush* (1894) was a popular collection of stories about rural Scottish life.

207 "It would be better for the profession": This statement was quoted frequently in the vivisection debate, the original source often listed as a statement by doctor B. F. Posy in the journal *Medical Times* (October 1900).

208 "The fine eye that separates": This is the final couplet of Phelps's poem, "The Message of the Unseen," published in *The Independent*, June 6, 1878, 1.

209 material medica: Latin, "healing materials"; term used for a body of knowledge about remedies.

209 "Cruel is the world": These lines are from "The New Buddha" by Robert Buchanan, published in *North American Review* 140, no. 342 (May 1885): 445–55. Phelps also quotes these lines in the epigraph of *Trixy*.

209 "Say not the days are evil": The lines are from Maltbie D. Babcock, "Be Strong," in *Thoughts for Every-day Living* (New York: Charles Scribner's Sons, 1901): 168.

Appendix D

211 bowsprit: A spar extending from the stem of a sailing vessel.

212 gutta-percha: A tough plastic substance derived from Malaysian trees, commonly used in the second half of the nineteenth century.

213 fo'castle: Forecastle; upper deck of a sailing ship, typically used as the crew's living quarters.

213 kinetoscope: An early device for exhibiting motion pictures, in which images were viewed through a peephole.

214 Gamin: Street urchin, a neglected child who roams the streets.

215 tam-o'-shanter cap: The hat was named after a poem by Robert Burns, "Tam o' Shanter" (1790), the title character of which was saved from a throng of witches and warlock by his horse, Meg.

217 The name Peter Roosevelt Tammany makes several possible historical allusions: Theodore Roosevelt Jr., the governor of New York during the newsboys strike of 1899 and U.S. president when "Tammyshanty" was published, was an advocate of child labor reform as well as a convert to Phelps's antivivisection stance. The name Tammany recalls the powerful New York-based political organization, Tammany Hall, famous for helping the city's poor immigrants, especially Irish (while equally famous for charges of political corruption). Even the character's nickname given to him by his newsboy comrades may allude to the newsboys strike history, as the name of the strike's leader, Jack Sullivan, was well publicized at the time.

229 "It was perhaps half an hour": At the end of this paragraph, Phelps adds the following note, "This narrative in its main incident is history."